Copyright © 2022 Matt Luttrell All rights reserved

The characters and events portrayed in this book are fictitious. Any similarity to real persons, living or dead, is coincidental and not intended by the author.

No part of this book may be reproduced, or stored in a retrieval system, or transmitted in any form or by any means, electronic, mechanical, photocopying, recording, or otherwise, without express written permission of the publisher and author.

To my parents, Chuck and Marie Luttrell. No matter what random career I found myself in, they never stopped bugging me to keep writing.

RIVER JUMPING

Matt Luttrell

1.

A car turned suddenly into the lane ahead. Jake slammed on the brakes, and the car's anti-lock system juddered its tires across the damp cement. His chest pressed painfully into the seatbelt as his right foot was buried into the brake pedal. He slowed down with plenty of room, even as he was bracing for an impact. Jake was gripping the steering wheel so tightly that his knuckles shone in a pale white. He watched the offending car drive away normally, completely unaware of the near miss.

Moments like this would always shoot his heart rate up and make his chest tighten, nearly to the point where he couldn't breathe. Although there were no consequences, he felt that weight on himself for several minutes afterwards, like a bag of cement was sitting on his rib cage. He got the same feeling when a police car turned on its siren behind him; the lingering tension would last long afterwards, even if the cop was pulling over someone else. He breathed in deeply to try and let the feeling pass and exhaled slowly through his nose. He looked down and realized he had spilt coffee on his clean jeans. "Shit."

Looking up at the car in front, which was now cruising unbeknownst down the street, he shook his head. "Douchebag," he muttered, and reached into the glove compartment to see if there were any leftover napkins to blot the coffee out of his jeans. He chuckled to himself on closer inspection of the offending vehicle - it was a BMW I-Ride. There was no one driving it.

Was the computer that operated a BMW still a jerk, just like a human BMW driver? Was it weird to be pissed off at the person in that car, even though they had nothing to do with the turn? Jake had found that the AI drivers often misjudged spacing in traffic and overestimated human response times. The problem was getting worse now that there were more AI's at the wheel than there were people.

Or maybe it was his fault. Maybe he was just distracted. It was a big night, after all.

How long had it been since he had been on a date? He couldn't remember. At least a year, and he hadn't been on a *good* date in much longer than that. He'd like to say that he had 'buried himself in work', and that he had 'no time for relationships', but he knew that wasn't actually true. He had just become sick of dating, really. Sick of the games, the effort, the hassle. He didn't have the energy for the whole routine. But tonight was different.

'A blind date with a friend's friend? How old fashioned...' Jake thought. But it was so much easier and so much more inviting than the alternatives. Online dating was terrible. The whole ritual was down to a choreographed dance now, no one revealed anything truthful about themselves. They only put the appropriate cards down on the table. It drove Jake crazy, even though he knew that he was doing the same.

VR dating was even worse. You'd still hide all the details of yourself, but could now hide behind an unrealistic avatar. Nothing about it felt authentic. Nothing was spontaneous or genuine. Jake gave up on dating for the same reason he stayed in the same job. He hated being interviewed.

But tonight was different. Shannon had spoken very highly of this girl. Apparently, she was funny, adventurous, beautiful... and somehow also single. Jake wondered what Shannon had told her about him - what had convinced this girl to come to dinner? He had to try and make a good impression, somehow. And... he had just spilt coffee all over his jeans. *'Shake it off, Jake, it doesn't matter'* he thought. It was too late to go home and change. It was too late for coffee, to be honest, but he wanted to be sharp.

Jake saw a parking spot up ahead. It was a block and a half from the restaurant, but it wasn't raining, which was rare for October in Vancouver. He parallel parked, double checked the signs to make sure it was free, and started walking towards the restaurant. He didn't want to be too early, but didn't want her to show up first either. *'Stop overthinking it'* he thought, as he looked at his watch again. His pace quickened.

He saw the ramen shop up ahead. He had chosen to meet her here for a number of reasons. Like everything in his life, Jake analyzed the factors of a first date to an obsessive level. He chose this specific restaurant because the neighborhood was hip, but not pretentious. It was also a "North American" style restaurant, but run by a Japanese family, which meant it would play good music but also have authentic food. He chose ramen because it was a short meal, which meant that they wouldn't be stuck for long if it was going poorly. You could get a beer, but neither person would feel pressure to get a second. It was casual without being trashy. Still, even with all those considerations, he always feared that he had made the wrong choice of restaurant.

Jake was getting close to the doors now, and he started feeling that tension in his chest again, just like when the car cut him off. *'Stop overthinking it, just be yourself'* he thought. He really wanted this to go well.

Jake walked through the door and stood near the reception podium. He quickly scanned the room while waiting for the hostess. The restaurant was lively, but not overly loud. An eclectic mix of people sat at tables throughout the cozy space. A group of five women in the far corner was cackling loudly about something. Two younger men sat on the close wall at a small table, both wearing suits, talking in the kind of numbered code that only coworkers could understand. An elderly couple sat behind them, who must have found the restaurant cold as they were still wearing heavy winter jackets. Near the window, a young woman was sitting by herself.

Jake looked at his watch. *'Damn. If that's her, she's early'* he thought. He had really wanted to be there first. He looked at her, trying not to stare. She was stunning. Her hair was shoulder length and jet black, and she wore it in a way that seemed like it took some effort, but not a ridiculous amount. Her floral blouse looked vintage, but it was cut in a modern way. She was reading a paperback novel at the table. Jake smiled, it was refreshing to see someone not staring at their phone or holo-tab. Who was this girl? She had a pint of beer in front of her already!

He cared so much about first impressions; he would never have thought to do that! Of course, it would be great to steady the nerves before your date got there, but what if they judged you for it? He realized, now, that she probably did not analyze these things to the weird extent that he did. Jake became aware that his glance had melted into a creepy stare, and he shook himself out of it. He took a deep, bracing breath, and walked over to the table.

"Mia?"

She looked up, and smiled very wide, eyes beaming with a simple happiness that didn't come across as fake.

"Jake?" She quickly dog eared her page and tucked her novel away into a terry cloth purse hanging off her chair.

They shook hands, and he sat down. "Ummm...any trouble finding the place?" Jake asked nervously, as he settled into his chair.

"I've been here before, it's fine," she said, somewhat rudely. She paused to take a quick sip of her beer and started speaking again while opening her menu. "I don't know if you thought that I was Japanese from Shannon's photos, Jake, but I'm not. We literally could have gone *anywhere* else." The smile was now clearly gone from her face and had descended into a judgmental frown.

'Shit, I sure read that wrong' Jake thought. He panicked. He had thought so hard about all the angles and the positives of choosing this restaurant. He had pored over

the options - how could he not have thought of this? He was instantly uncomfortable, the joy of 20 seconds ago was gone.

"I...I.." he stammered.

She couldn't hold the stern, judgmental look for long. Her face cracked into a bright giggle. "Sorry, that was kind of fun. You just looked so nervous - it made me want to mess with you."

Jake laughed and felt relieved. It was so natural to put his guard up, but she had instantly disarmed him. He relaxed; he felt his shoulders ease downwards.

"But no, I love this place. And I'm Korean, by the way," she laughed. "So, how do you know Shannon?"

Jake smiled. "We've known each other for years. She used to date one of my roommates in college. I lost touch with him, but Shannon and I stayed friends. We both stayed in Vancouver, while most of our other friends moved away. I go fishing with her and her husband sometimes, really nice guy."

"Oh yeah, Gary's great!" she cut in.

"How do you know them?"

"I used to work with Gary. Shannon and I met at one of the office parties, and we just hit it off immediately. We hang out quite a bit." Mia took a sip of her beer. "She speaks very highly of you, by the way."

"You obviously haven't gotten her drunk enough to hear the real stories then," he half-joked.

"Oh, I've heard one or two" Mia winked at him, more jokingly than anything, but she had such beautiful eyes it was hard not to look at the gesture as seductive.

"Shit" Jake laughed. He ordered a beer, Mia passed as she was only half done her pint. "Have you always lived in Vancouver?"

"Not always, no. I grew up in Alberta, but we moved here when I was a teenager," she replied. "My dad lost his business during the 2020 pandemic, and we moved around the prairies a lot when I was young. I didn't move out to the coast until high school. I like it here, but I do miss

Alberta sometimes. I liked the sunshine and wide-open skies."

"And the frostbite?"

"I don't miss that, for sure. I've gotten B.C. weak," she said. "I was tough as nails growing up in the prairies. Now, I get cold when it's, like, fifteen degrees outside." She took another sip of Sapporo, glanced around the room at the random collection of Vancouverites, and smiled. "How about you?"

"Always B.C. for me. Although I lived up in Smithers until I came down here for university. So, I wasn't always 'Vancouver' weak, we had real winters up there," he smiled. "So, what do you do, Mia?" Jake asked as he glanced down at the menu.

"I work in occupational health and safety" she replied.

"You know what, this has been fun!" With exaggerated seriousness, Jake backed his chair away from the table and started to get up. "We should do this again sometime."

Mia laughed out loud. "Yeah, okay, I get it. We're *always* the bad guys, I've gotten used to it." Jake laughed as well. "You know, it's kind of like being an orthodontist or something. You help people, and yet they still hate you for it."

Jake giggled guiltily. "Sorry, yeah, I know. The stigma is strong. It's just that everyone gets annoyed by the stupid number of rules these days."

"The funny thing is, we probably save more lives through our work than firefighters and policemen combined. But people just find us annoying. No kid wants to work in OHS when they grow up" she joked. "Where's the occupational health workers' calendar?"

"Well, if all your co-workers looked like you, I'd buy that calendar." Jake froze, the phrase had just fallen out of his mouth. The tension in his chest was back, just like seeing the car's tail lights earlier. There was always a moment in a date, a flash where the conversation went from platonic to flirtatious. If it happened too early, it ruined it. If it never took that leap, the date wouldn't progress. He hated this moment - had he flirted too soon? It had only been 10 minutes since they met. Why hadn't she responded? Jake's mind went in panicked circles.

The pause seemed intolerably long, but he saw the slightest hint of blood rush to her cheeks, and she smiled sheepishly. "Well, thank you Jake."

"How did you get into that field anyway?"

"It kind of just... happened. I started looking into it after my friend had a workplace accident."

"Really?" Jake pried.

Mia paused, struggling to find the phrasing she wanted. "You know how when you're a kid, you want to work in something that helps people? Most of us never end up doing that." She paused and took a sip, as if she was just starting to think deeper, beyond superficial small talk. "When I was in my last year of university, a good friend of mine got killed on a jobsite."

"I'm so sorry" Jake piped in.

She paused momentarily. Jake noticed how her tone had changed. "I was pissed, he was put in a situation he wasn't trained for. It was a preventable accident." Mia took a sip of her beer. "I was a history major, and I didn't really have any plan for a career with that degree. Health and safety seemed like a good choice, and it meant that I could help prevent other people from getting killed. Once I started studying it, I grew to like it, and I felt like I was making a difference, you know?"

"Just sucks you had to lose a friend to find that, though."

"It was a long time ago, it's okay now. I was so pissed off when it happened, though. He was the first friend that I had lost, I had a really tough time with it."

Jake was surprised by the honesty of her answer.

"I actually really enjoy the work, though. You get to travel a lot. And I do feel like I've made a difference. Not at the end of every day, because most of the time it's just endless paperwork, but at the end of a big project I definitely do. And there's a part of me, deep down, that kind of enjoys seeing workers fear me, like I'm a hard-assed vice principal. Although I'm not supposed to admit that," Mia giggled.

"I always suspected that about you OHS folk" Jake replied.

The server came by the table. They both gave their orders, she got a second pint. Mia got the spiciest thing on the menu, it had 5 chili peppers beside the name. "Jesus," said Jake. "A little adventurous?"

"Ah, it's not too bad. And if you think that's spicy, never, ever come out for dinner with my Korean friends," she replied. "So, Shannon said you work at the university?"

"I used to, for quite a while. I'm one of those guys who just couldn't leave school" he smiled. "After I finished my PhD, I stayed on doing various jobs in the department. Eventually, I started working there as a research assistant, and I did that for almost four years."

"And now?" she asked.

"I'm at an off-campus research institute. The pay is a lot better. There's not as much freedom in your work, but we have a lot more resources. Oh, and there's a lot less annoying health and safety like there was at the university."

Mia faked offense. "So, what is your PhD in?"

"Physics."

"You've got me wondering what a physics researcher could be working on that has health and safety concerns."

He gave a suspicious grin. "Quite a bit, actually."

Her second pint arrived. The two chatted about various subjects through dinner. It felt - different. Jake had prepared himself for the usual awkward small talk that filled his first dates, but that didn't happen. The conversation flowed freely, they laughed and told stories, shared views and opinions. She had an amazing sense of humor, and always seemed genuinely interested in the conversation, even though she relished in taking the piss out of him. Talking with Mia was truly effortless, as if they had been friends for years.

The server came by the table to clear away the empty bowls, as well as an embarrassing amount of wet napkins from Jake's side. "Soooo, for someone who likes ramen and sushi and stuff, you really suck at using chopsticks, Jake," Mia laughed.

"I was hoping you wouldn't notice," he said shyly.

"It was hard not to. The server was seconds away from bringing you a fork. I think my 3-year-old nephew is better."

"Yeah, I tried to figure it out by myself when I was a teenager instead of asking anyone how they worked. I only learned I was doing it wrong years later, and it was too late to fix shitty technique."

Mia laughed. She excused herself as if she was heading for the washroom, but made a pit stop at the counter to pay the bill. She returned from the washroom and sat down again. "Thank you - you didn't need to do that," Jake said.

"Well, I've decided something," Mia said, as she took the last swig of Sapporo out of her glass. "It's Friday night and it's still early. And since I covered dinner, I think that you have to buy the first round across the street."

Normally, Jake chose ramen as a first date to keep the encounter short. If things went well, he could line up a second date. If they didn't, at least he could get out of it quickly. But a second venue? That was well outside of his plan, that wouldn't work. He worried about staying too long - what if she liked him now, but she didn't like him in two hours? Had she just taken his parachute away? Jake tried to calm the hamster that was running wildly in his head.

"I'm game," he replied, still half holding back. "I probably shouldn't have any more, though, I drove here."

"Can't the car just take you home?"

"Yeah - ...I'm still in an old manual car. It's actually a gas engine, even" he chuckled, embarrassed. "I'd love a self-driver, but my car just won't die, and I can't justify throwing away something that's been good to me for all these years."

"Wow - how....old fashioned, I guess? Are you a car guy? Is it a muscle car or something?"

"Nope, just a boring old Toyota Camry. My dad gave it to me when I moved south for university. It was already super old then, but the damn thing just keeps going. All I do is change the oil, and it just keeps chugging on like the Energizer Bunny. And it reminds me of him, so I guess I don't want to let go of it until I absolutely have to, as stupid as that sounds." He paused.

"He's not with you anymore?"

Jake looked at her, surprised how suddenly he was talking about this. He never talked about his dad. "No, yeah, he passed away in my second year at UBC. It was an aneurysm, he went quick - I never got a chance to say goodbye. That rusty Camry is the only thing of his I have."

He felt a warm, small hand holding his as he looked towards the far wall to avoid eye contact. It felt nice, he had to admit. Although, he was a little weirded out by how fast this was all moving. He never talked about his dad - with anyone. He thought he would have pulled his hand away by now, but there was something holding it there, like a magnet.

"But it's a really shitty car" he blurted out, cutting the silence. "And it's becoming a real bitch to find a gas station, there's not many left." The intimate moment passed as quickly as it came, but both had felt something, however small it was.

"Well, it sounds to me like no one's going to steal it if it spent the night down here, then," Mia joked. "But no pressure, obviously."

He couldn't really say no - he didn't have plans in the morning. The only reason to refuse at this point was out of routine. Just because every other date stopped at this point, why did this one have to? *'Just let yourself go'* Jake had to tell himself.

"Screw it, why not?" he smiled. They grabbed their coats and walked outside. It had started to drizzle again, as the Pacific coast would do on and off for the next five months. It was a dreary time that was hard to get used to, but Jake had found a way to accept it. The company of both friends and strangers, new challenges at work, and the warm embrace of alcohol all had a way of repelling the long gray dark of that temperate winter. Without that, living the same routine day in and day out, Vancouver could be a very depressing place.

They crossed the street and stepped into a crowded distillery. Mia found the last high-top table near the back wall, Jake followed her and put his jacket on the wall hooks. "What would you like?"

"Surprise me..."

'*Shit*' Jake thought. '*Didn't need that pressure.*' He walked over to the bar and picked up a large, leather-bound menu. The cocktail list was five pages long, he'd have to take a shot in the dark. He walked back to the table with two London mules. Jake was betting in his head that a girl who just downed two pints and ordered the spiciest thing on the menu wouldn't want something sweet and fruity. She looked down at the shiny copper mug topped with a rosemary sprig. "Thank you, looks delicious!"

"Hope so". The mule *was* delicious, fragrant and smooth, but very strong. "So, what are you working on currently, if I can ask?"

She shot him a small frown, as if she didn't quite want the conversation steered that way. "Nothing too exciting. There's a new solar plant being installed in southern Saskatchewan. I'm working on the safety manual right now. They should be up and running by the spring, though, and I'll need to work out there for a few weeks then." She sniffed the top of her mug, enjoying the smell of the rosemary before taking another sip. "But enough about my work - I want to hear more about what *you* do."

"No, you don't" Jake laughed. "Most of my job is on the computer, it's not all that exciting." He took another sip of the mule, it was very strong. He could feel the aroma of it working its way up his sinuses like a hit of wasabi. "But my partner and I are working with some new stuff right now, which may get me back in a lab running experiments for a while. So that'll be a nice change of pace."

Mia looked genuinely intrigued, which surprised him. "Sooo, what's the new stuff?" She wasn't letting him out of this conversation.

Jake sighed. Secretly, he loved talking about his studies, but not right away, and he tended to ramble on about it. "Well, normally we do experiments with various new materials. Basically, we're trying to tweak existing technologies and make them lighter or stronger. It's not all that thrilling, but it pays the bills. I'd love to get back to studying base dimensional theory, though, that was what I did my PhD thesis on." Jake took a sip of his cocktail again. "I actually might incorporate it into our next project.

"Sorry, but - base dimensional theory? What's that?"

"It has to do with the attributes of the universe at a subatomic level, and the variations between our dimensions and the behavior of subatomic particles."

Mia giggled. She was still listening, but she gave him a confused shrug. "Sorry, ummm... what?" she laughed.

Jake laughed, embarrassed. "Well, I guess I'll start at the beginning. You know how everything is made of molecules? And those molecules are made of atoms?" She nodded. "Well, if we go smaller than that, much smaller, we know the atom itself is made of pieces. The protons, the electrons, the nucleus, you know..."

As she sipped her cocktail, he found himself having to speak louder to overpower the ambient bar clatter.

"The thing is, at that size - smaller than an atom - nothing follows the rules. The rules of physics that govern how things move and interact don't apply at that scale. The universe doesn't make sense, it's never made sense - because large physics doesn't line up with small physics. Things get weird when things get small."

"How small are we talking?" Mia interjected, smiling lightly over the table at him. The jarred candle on the table flickered slightly when her breath interrupted the flame. Jake was enjoying the ambience, although it seemed weird to be talking about science in such a romantic setting.

"It's a little tough to comprehend. It's all theory, these things are too small to ever hope to see. Atoms and molecules are behemoths compared to the subatomic particles. And we still can't really even see atoms properly, never mind past them. See, if we look at a hair," Jake rolled his sleeve up slightly to point at one of the hairs on his forearm. Mia leaned in. "One of these hairs is one million carbon atoms across. Hairs are so fine that our eyes can just barely see them, and yet there's a million atoms across that tiny width. Like, if every atom was a basketball, this hair would be as wide as Vancouver to Seattle."

Mia looked closely at the hair, leaning over the table to get a closer look at it, only slightly to take piss out of him. "But, I mean, like - some hairs are a *lot* thicker than others? Are there more than a million atoms in those?" she asked, serious, but trying to hold in a smirk.

"Don't make it dirty," Jake laughed, realizing where her joke was going.

"Sorry, I'm listening, I swear," she smiled.

"There's no way of seeing down to the size of an atom, because they're ridiculously small, but that's just the start of the... smallness." Jake paused to take a sip. "If we took one of those tiny atoms and blew it up to the size of the earth, some of the subatomic quarks within it would still be smaller than a golf ball. That's how small these particles are, and they only exist for a tiny fraction of a second. They don't live in the same rules that we do."

"What!? That's crazy!" she excitedly giggled. Maybe the gin was starting to set in on her, he never had women giggle excitedly when he talked about subatomic particles. And, somehow, here they were, joking about pubic hair and physics.

"That's what base dimensional theory is. Basically - that there is a dimension that we can't interact with because we're too big. But that dimension is where the quarks, the electrons, the photons - all those other pieces live. And that's why they act differently.

"Ok, you're losing me," she spoke up over the crowded bar. "I'm with you so far, I think. But what do you mean by dimension? Like the parallel dimension that Evil Spock lives in?"

Jake laughed. "No, that's not quite what I'm talking about. You know how we live in a three-dimensional space? We have the x, y, and z axis of our physical surroundings. We can interact with those three dimensions. I can move this mug through them, for example" Jake picked his gin mule up and moved it through the air, as if he was trying to feed a baby with a pretend airplane. He suddenly realized what he was doing, got embarrassed, and put his drink down. He definitely wasn't going to drive home; this drink was strong.

"Some consider time another dimension. It's a dimension that we interact with but have no control over. I can't move forward or backward in time no matter how hard I try, but I am interacting with it. It's constantly flowing in a forward motion, dependent on many factors such as our current speed through the universe, gravity, and so on. There is no stopping time, there's no changing its course. I can't affect it like the way I moved the mug through the other three dimensions. But it does affect us, and we are totally aware of it, even though it's out of reach. This night is progressing forward out of our control, and it will come to an end, regardless of whether or not you and I make a choice to not let it."

Mia smiled. *'Ok Jake, reel it back, don't try to be Don Juan when you're talking about this shit'* Jake thought, although he did think that was quite a smooth line. At least he wasn't going to try some flimsy shit about 'not wasting the time you have left'. That might get a 20-year-old in your bed back in college, but not anymore.

"So, those are the 4 dimensions that we're all familiar with. Now, theories have proposed many other dimensions that we don't interact with, dimensions to explain the great mysteries of the universe, mysteries such as dark energy and gravitational singularities. Some mathematicians believe there's as many as eleven distinct dimensions, but it's all theory at this point. What I'm studying is called Base dimensional theory. Basically, that there's a dimension at the subatomic level that all other laws and dimensions relate to, but that we can't detect or interact with, simply because of our size."

"Ok, ok," Mia stopped him, touching his forearm lightly. "I kind of wish we were talking about this two drinks ago. My head is swimming here - how can there be a dimension there that doesn't affect us?"

"I'm not sure anyone truly grasps it, to be honest." He glanced at the window briefly, collecting his thoughts. "Brian Greene had an interesting analogy for it. Picture a tight clothesline strung between two trees. When you stand at a distance and look at it, it's a one-dimensional line. It's just a thin line connecting two points, and because of your size and distance there's no immediate reason to think of it as a three-dimensional object. But if you were an ant crawling on it, then it's an immense tube that you can walk around and across and down. So, because you're smaller, the other two dimensions become relevant to you."

"Hmmmmm, ok, --- I think. So, if there was a subatomic ant, they'd have another dimension to play in that we can't see."

Jake could hear the ice rattling against the copper sides of her mug. *'Jesus, this girl can put em back'* he thought, feeling the weight of his half-full mug. Hopefully that meant that she was enjoying herself, and not trying to drown the tedium of this conversation.

"Ok - so the ant dimension thingy is the base of everything."

"The base dimension, yep. The dimension that everything else is built on top of."

"So, kind of like the 'Sauron's ring' of dimensions then?"

Jake smiled. "Thank you."

"For what?" Mia asked.

"I was really worried that I was getting too nerdy for you." he laughed. Mia smacked his arm playfully. "I like to think of it this way. Space, time, energy, gravity - it's all a big blob of pizza dough. Space itself is being stretched out all the time, just like a pizza chef stretching it out to put the sauce and cheese on."

"So, the base dimension is ...the rolling pin?"

"No, the base dimension is the countertop that the dough is sitting on. Never moving, never changing, but always a base for everything else on top of it. It is where all of the rules of our universe don't apply. It's where space, and time, and energy are all invalid. It's the very foundation of everything. That's what I studied, and hopefully what I'll be working with again soon."

Mia didn't say anything. The bar seemed to quiet down into a lull. Neither one of them spoke for a few seconds, but for Jake that awkwardness felt like hours. He hoped this didn't scare her off, he'd had other dates that got very intimidated when he talked about his job. He really liked this one, they were getting along great. Had he just finished the evening pre-maturely? *'Damn it Jake, stick to other topics'* he thought.

"I think I caught most of that, but I'll take your word that you do important work, Jake. It definitely doesn't sound boring."

"Well, you say that now, but most of my job is just figuring out how to make a sheet of carbon fiber two grams lighter, it's not all mind-bending shit." he sighed. "To be honest, most days I'm really bored, it's just a lot of data entry and processing. And I haven't worked with base dimension theory at all since I started at my new company." Although he tried to pass it off lightly, she could hear a note of genuine dissatisfaction in his voice.

"Well, I still think it would be a little weird to ask you how your work went each day, I feel like I'd need to smoke a joint first."

They both shared another awkward pause, and Jake continued to describe a couple less 'sciency' things about his work. They continued talking until Jake finished his cocktail.

"I'll just be right back," he said, excusing himself to the washroom. As he stood up, he felt his head swim a little, in a pleasant way. "Christ, those were strong" he muttered, almost unaware that he said it out loud.

She laughed. "You're adorable." He felt his cheeks go red. "But yeah, those had some kick."

When Jake returned from the washroom, Mia was putting her coat on. "What do you say? Change of venue? It's a little loud in here."

"Sure!" he replied, fighting the urge to instinctively check his watch. They walked out the front door, feeling the cool outdoor air. The distillery had been slightly warm and muggy, and the brisk evening air felt stark in contrast. It woke Jake up. He had been reeled in by this evening, he was breaking all of his own rules. He should have left after dinner, before she had a chance to get bored by him. He started feeling the small ball of stress in his stomach. He had no idea how to entertain this amazing woman he was with; he had no clue of what to do next.

"So, where to?" Jake broke the silence. Mia didn't respond, instead he felt her hand softly grip his forearm and spin him towards her. Her other hand grabbed his jacket, and she pulled herself into his chest, pressing her lips softly into his. She held them there for a little more than a moment, enough that his head was swimming, but not long enough to be awkward in public. She pulled her head back and stared up at him, still holding him close to her.

"Sorry, I've just been wanting to do that for at least an hour now. Didn't want to be trashy and lean over the bar table."

"Yeah, wasn't really that kind of place. But, thank you --- " Jake said, awkwardly, trying to get control of himself again.

"How do you feel...." she started. Jake knew where this was going. That small ball of stress in his stomach was growing, gurgling up into a panicked anxiety. Was she going to ask him back to her place? Part of him wanted to say yes, definitely. Well, a particular 'part' of him wanted to say yes. But this night had been so great, she was the first person he had connected with in such a long time. Could going back to hers and getting physical already ruin that? There was nothing wrong with it, they were both adults, and definitely able to make their own choices. And who was to say what was too soon and what wasn't? He knew he was attracted to her, very deeply, but the logical half of Jake was screaming at him to turn down the offer. The stress ball was growing larger and larger, and getting dangerously close to his vocal chords.

"How do you feel about vintage video games?" she asked, still holding him seductively.

"Ummmm, hell yeah," Jake responded. This girl was amazing, she was working him like a marionette. He was surprisingly okay with it, though.

"There's a place about two blocks from here that's stocked with Nineties arcade games. I haven't been yet, I've been waiting for someone to check it out with. You in?"

"Let's do it!" he responded, without any hesitation.

The two of them walked east down the damp street, chatting and laughing and enjoying themselves thoroughly. They stayed up late playing Double Dragon and Street Fighter, barely noticing the clock ticking slowly forward.

2.

Mia stayed in Jake's thoughts long after they parted ways that night. In fact, he thought about her all weekend, and constantly fought the urge to message her. His mind raced with the options - would he ruin things if he messaged too soon? He didn't want to seem too eager or desperate. Would she lose interest if he didn't message right away, though? He didn't want that to happen either. Even though the night had been amazing, Jake felt stressed about the date's aftermath all day on Sunday. He was locked in indecision.

She stayed in his thoughts all the way into Monday. He was still weighing the options in his head as he pulled his car into the parking lot for Hachiro Industries. Although Vancouver was a very transit-friendly town, Jake still had to drive to work. Hachiro was located in an industrial park way out in Richmond, near the airport. It was too far to bike, and not accessible by bus.

The drive itself was short, but he had to walk eight blocks each morning to get to his car. Newer A.I.-driven cars could be summoned to pick up their owners, so his apartment building had gotten rid of their parking lot, like most residences in Vancouver had. Cars parked themselves in large, centralized lots in order to leave more room on the streets for pedestrians. Jake knew how much time he'd save with a new electric, self-driving car, and how much easier his life would be, but he still couldn't let the old one go. He stared blankly into the windshield long after he twisted the keys out of the ignition. 'Get a hold of yourself, Jake.' He shook his head awake and grabbed his coat from the passenger seat.

Jake locked the Camry and walked across the road. His office was in a very unassuming building, wedged between a carpet warehouse and a wholesale distributor. It was a new build, but very plain - just a beige box with blue highlights. It was huge for the relatively small staff, however, with a high-ceilinged warehouse space stretching well behind the abundant office frontage. The signage was small, just a stenciled window reading "The Hachiro Institute" on the door.

The unassuming exterior gave way to a very lavish interior, however. The two sets of doors entered you into a large reception area. The alcove near the front was outfitted with modern, designer furniture, with marble and jade sculptures sitting on custom log tables. The carpets were deep and plush, as if the designers had never anticipated much traffic through the area. The walls were hung with a mixture of both Japanese and West Coast Indigenous artwork, on top of a slate gray textured wallpaper. The opposing space, to the right of the front desk, was an enormous 'green wall', with tropical plants and flowers growing thick up to the thirty-foot ceiling. Entering the space smelled a bit like entering a flowering greenhouse, not overly humid, but fragrant and earthy in a natural, relaxing, way. The sound system played soft jazz music, and it was just barely audible over the trickling water making its way down the lush wall of flora.

Michelle, the receptionist, sat at an ornate carved desk - originally a large cedar tree, but in which an artist had carved a coastal landscape. From the left of the desk, breaking ocean waves made their way towards a forested beach, which transitioned into a range of mountain peaks towards the right of the carving. Jake loved that desk, he often caught himself staring at the intricate detailing in the wood, preserved behind a light coating of shellac to retain its color.

Behind the desk was the only part of the lobby he didn't like. Instead of a simple sign or carving to keep with the natural theme, they had installed a glowing green hologram, about 15 feet wide, with a simple font reading "The Hachiro Institute" and a smaller subheading - "Science for a Better World". The colors matched the room's decor, but it just seemed tacky compared to the rest of the room. It was technology in contrast to the surrounding nature. That was very much like Harada Hachiro himself, however, so maybe it did work. Although the unassuming exterior of the building was meant to hide what was happening inside, Mr. Hachiro wanted to impress any and all invited visitors, that much was clear.

"Morning, Michelle!" Jake waved at her as he walked towards the security door.

"Hi Jake. Heyyy…Any chance you're ever going to RSVP to the Christmas party? I just need to get numbers for the caterers." Jake had been waffling back and forth about going, he definitely wasn't looking forward to it. Not that he didn't like his co-workers, it was just the pomp and circumstance of the whole affair. The management always booked a fully formal dinner, black tie only, as that's what Mr. Hachiro wanted. Jake hated dressing up for anything. Renting a tuxedo for his work Christmas party wasn't really his cup of tea.

He had gone to it his first year at the company, but had skipped it last year. The formal nature of it also made it quite a weird event to attend solo.

"You know what, yeah, I will come this year," Jake replied, his distracted mood this morning taking over his decisions. "Oh, and Michelle, can you put me down for a plus one?"

"Interesting…" Michelle pried, smiling suggestively. "Will do, thanks Jake."

Jake walked to the door and pressed his thumb into the scanner. *'Whoa, what was that?'* he thought. *'You haven't even called this girl back yet. Slow the F down, man…'* He stopped in the middle of the hallway. He wanted to go back and change his booking with Michelle. But now that would be awkward, she would have a lot of questions. What had he just done? *'Get a hold of yourself, Jake'* he thought, again, continuing the walk towards his office.

Once through the security door, the office spaces of the Institute were more conventional. They were well appointed, with soft lighting and plush carpets in the hallways. The lavish elegance of the front lobby stopped, however, with the exception of the boardroom and Mr. Hachiro's office, both of which were elegantly designed, but almost always empty.

Jake's office was at the end of the hall, close to the break room. It was cozy, windowless, with just enough room for a large desk, one extra chair, and a wooden filing cabinet. Jake had hung a few pictures around the walls, mostly from various hikes in the Rockies. There was a framed picture on his desk from his sister's wedding. Kyla had stayed in Smithers, which helped Jake with the guilt of being so far away from his widowed mother. He tried to go home to visit when he could, but it seemed like he was getting there less and less each year.

There was a shipping notice on Jake's desk. For security reasons, the institute never used any printed info, or even emails, to send certain information. All that was on the desk was a small paper slip with a code to scan. He could tell it was a shipping notice by the color of the paper. He took out his phone, scanned the code, and was prompted for a thumbprint scan. Even after that first screen, he was required to enter another password. He always found this method of getting communication tedious, it seemed like security overkill. But when he saw his shipping notice, he felt the security was justified.

RECEIVED: 100 GRAM BERLINITE SAMPLE x 10.
ATTN: JACOB ANTHONY CRAWFORD, % THE HACHIRO INSTITUTE

They had come in! Not only had his request been approved, the samples were at the office! Jake excitedly went over his purchase orders. It had been a long time since he'd gotten a chance to run experiments, or even gotten away from his desk for that matter. Now he and his lab partner would get the chance to book time in a lab, and work with cutting edge physics once more.

The received samples would be locked up in the secure area of the laboratory wing. Jacob had requested these months ago from Freie University. They were extremely expensive, but he had finally convinced his manager of the experimental potential of berlinite, and they had agreed to fund a small shipment of the material.

Berlinite was named after the city it was created in. Researchers at the university had been making new alloys with combinations of rare earth elements. A certain combination of iridium, titanium and bismuth was stumbled upon, mostly by accident. It had a curious reaction to the ambient light in the room - it reflected a purplish hue into the room, no matter what colors of light they projected onto it. If they used a red light, or green, or blue, it still appeared as the same shade of purple. On further experimentation, the researchers had discovered that berlinite absorbed a great deal of the electromagnetic spectrum, but that the energy wasn't being transferred into the material - it just vanished. Berlinite seemed to break all the laws of thermodynamics, and it caused quite a buzz in physics circles when it was first discovered four years prior. Freie University was tight lipped about the 'recipe', however - the exact proportions of the metals necessary to cause the reaction was not known outside their labs.

Ordering these samples was extremely expensive for a couple reasons. First, the iridium needed to create it was acquired at a high cost, being one of the rarest elements in the Earth's crust. Second, the discovery of this material had still not been announced publicly, and it was only experimented with in very controlled circles. The potential for berlinite was still largely unknown. Several people had already hypothesized about its possible military uses. If they could figure out which bands of the electromagnetic spectrum were being absorbed, a vehicle could be made completely invisible to radar, and possibly even invisible to the naked eye.

Jake was sometimes concerned with the military research side of what he was doing, but he wasn't ignorant, either. The salary he was making, the fancy parties, the elegant office - all this money had to come from somewhere. Hachiro was betting big on several research projects, in the hopes that future patents would pay back handsomely on those investments. But he wasn't going to experiment with military radar. Jake had other plans for it. Plans that were more in line with his own goals.

He had speculated that the missing energy was somehow being transferred to the base dimension. Most scientists still dismissed the idea of the base dimension, as no research had ever proven its existence. If the missing energy that hit berlinite was truly being transferred to the base dimension, proving that reaction would be a milestone in his career. So far, only a select few wavelengths had been shown to 'disappear'. But what if the frequency of radiation was so high that its wavelength would hit the berlinite on a subatomic scale? Would all of the energy disappear from this dimension? Jake had ordered the samples to find out, under the guise of doing radar research for Mr. Hachiro.

He sat down in his chair, and spent an hour or so going over the emails and memos that had come in over the weekend. There was yet another cyber security course to do when he had the time, there was a memo about parking rule changes, and this week's safety bulletin - "Drink at least 500ml of water every 2 hours." He thought about Mia when he read it, hoping that her work was more fulfilling than this bullshit. At least it wasn't like the university, where he had to fill out ten forms to lift a pen off the table. Reading it did make him thirsty, however.

Jake walked down to the break room to fill his water bottle after catching up. Michelle was near the coffee machine, with her hand on the back of Olivia, one of his fellow researchers. Olivia had her hands on the counter, and her head down. Whatever they were talking about was intense in nature.

Jake had never really gotten along with Olivia. He found her to be a bit too dramatic about things. He quietly tiptoed to the water cooler, trying not to get involved in whatever was happening. He couldn't help but eavesdrop, however.

"I'm just saying, Liv, think it through before you make any big decisions, ok?"

"How can I keep working here, Michelle!? Could you?"

"It's not...right, I know. But it's how things are done, here. It sucks."

Jake tried not to look over, but caught himself doing it anyway. He caught eyes with Michelle briefly, but quickly turned back to the water cooler.

"This was it, Michelle. This was my big break, my discovery - and it's gone. The bastard sold it from under me."

"But that's how we afford all this, though. This place sells patents, Liv, you know that."

"I know!" Olivia huffed in reply. "I just think it's cruel that they have us on such a strong non-comp agreement on top of that. So, all my research is gone, and I can't go work for the company that bought it, and I'm..." Olivia started balling. "Fuck this place. I'm stuck."

Olivia sobbed into Michelle's shoulder. Jake, suddenly realizing that he had taken an unreasonable amount of time staring at the water cooler, started quietly sneaking away. Michelle smiled at him over Olivia's shoulder, mouthing "Sorry" under her breath.

He had never been one to get involved in office drama. This scene intrigued him, though. Rumor had it that past researchers experienced the same scenario as Olivia, long before he had started with Hachiro. He'd never worried about it, simply because nothing he had ever worked on had been exciting. He'd never had research that he would be afraid to lose.

He dismissed what he had overheard, attributing it to Olivia's usual overreactions as he walked back along the empty hallway to his office. A large, curly haired man in a short-sleeved plaid shirt was waiting for him when he arrived. "Did they come in?" he asked.

Jake squeezed by him and entered his office. Turning around, he just smiled and nodded.

"Yes!" the man yelled, hugging Jake and lifting him off the ground, making an undulating, caveman-like noise as he bounced him up and down. Travis did this often - he got very excited about things. It was well outside the realm of what both Jake's personal space, and company HR, would accept, but Travis was such a genuine and happy person that everyone went along with it.

Travis was a large person, in every sense. He was six feet tall and built like an ox. His plaid shirt barely contained his arms and chest. He didn't wear a tight shirt out of vanity though, more out of necessity and habit. He didn't work out much. He was just a big farm boy from rural Saskatchewan, and that corn-fed upbringing had stuck with him. Travis was one of the most gifted and intelligent physicists Jake had ever known, but his rural Canadian accent disguised his inner genius. He'd call everyone 'man' or 'bud' irrespective of gender, and the societal norms of the academic world had always been foreign to him. He would be just as comfortable riding dirt bikes or shotgunning beers as he was delivering a dissertation. Travis had also specialized in base dimensional theory, and he and Jake had been good friends since University, long before either of them worked at Hachiro.

Travis often went on about how much he missed the wide-open prairies, but he had grown to love Vancouver. Although he was from Canada's flattest province, he had learned to embrace the mountain lifestyle. His weekends were filled with snowmobiling, rock climbing, kayaking, and various other outdoor sports. He'd often show up to work with battle scars visible, bandaged evidence of his most recent adventure.

    The women at the institute all loved Travis, and flirted with him constantly, but he was largely ignorant to it. He just thought they were all as naturally friendly as he was. There was a youthful joy and innocence to him that was addictive, and women were definitely drawn to it. The fact that he looked like the cover of a western-themed romance novel didn't hurt, either.

    "How many did we get?"

    "10 samples. I'm not going to have much of a budget left for anything else this year, it's a damn good thing it's October already."

    Travis was almost shaking in excitement. "Fuck yeah, man! I'm stoked! They in the evidence locker out back?" He was referring to the shipping lockup where they kept the highest valued assets, the most secure location in the building.

    "Yep. And I think that for now they're going to have to stay there, until we get some lab time booked. Even then, we'll probably just check out one or two at a time, depending on the experiment."

    Travis grinned sheepishly. "Well, it's a good thing I already booked us the Harrison Warehouse."

    "Jesus, Trav, you did that before we even got the samples in?"

    "I was betting on it. Coulda gone either way, yeah, sorry man. I didn't know how long it was going to take before they'd give us access to the site! But shit, it worked out, we can have it til March if we want, there's no one else out there until early April. We're out there starting Thursday, so pack your shit, cause you know what that means."

    Jake nodded.

    "We get to use the hulk gun…." Travis' eyes opened wide and devilish as he continuously tried to contain himself. The 'Hulk Gun' was what they had nicknamed the facility's gamma ray emitter.

Jake laughed excitedly, then stopped himself. "I don't know, Trav. You didn't need to rush it this much. How the hell are we going to get everything prepped in time?" He could feel that same ball of stress growing in his stomach. "You should've asked me. What's the rush, anyways?"

"I'm bored as shit, dude! I can't just keep doing these spreadsheets every day. I need to get in a lab - I thought you'd be stoked?"

"I am…just…" Jake smiled. "We've got a lot of prep to do. Thanks, this'll be sweet."

"Let's give 'er!"

Jake spent the remainder of his day trying to finish all the loose ends that he'd been putting off. It was easy, however, because the mundane repetitiveness of October had been ignited into a flame of excitement. He stayed very late that night, trying to clear his plate and prepare for what was to come.

3.

The sun was getting lower in the sky. Sunset would be a welcome relief for Marcela, she felt her skin getting crusty and cracking underneath the relentless rays. As was the usual here, there wasn't a single cloud in the sky, just a sea of endless deep blue. Far away on the horizon, she could see a wisp of steam rising from a volcano. Between her and that billowing cone in the distance lay an expanse of rock and red hills, stretching out as far as she could see. It was an alien landscape, devoid of life, but it had a stark beauty that she appreciated. She made her last few steps to the summit of the rolled mountain top in front of her and sat down on a small boulder.

Marcela struggled to catch her breath as she took out her water bottle from her backpack. She calmly sat and let her heart rate settle, and eventually her breathing slowed back to a relaxed rhythm. Her panting wasn't surprising, she had to use supplemental oxygen for her first two weeks at this site. It was tough to breathe here at the best of times, never mind climbing up the hills above the dormitories. Her supervisor wouldn't approve of her going out on her own, it was against the camp rules, but she figured she had acclimatized by now. It had been two and a half months since she'd been down out of the mountains to Santiago.

As the sky started to change from the stark blue of day to the pink of twilight, Marcela was jogging back down the mountainside, eager to make dinner before the kitchen closed. There was no official trail to speak of, but enough of her coworkers had been up and down that peak to scar a line in the scree of the slope. She descended quickly, getting jagged little stones into her boots as she went. Once the slope leveled off, she took her shoes and socks off to drain out the pebbles. In the fading light, she saw her camp in the distance. It was small, a couple of trailers surrounded by fencing. And behind them, a trio of enormous radio telescopes.

The Atacama Desert had become a hotspot for astronomy. Since the ALMA array had proven so successful earlier in the century, several other radio telescopes had been established to take advantage of the incredibly dry air and remote location. Marcela had been working on and off at this location for six months. Not many astronomers got used to living at over five thousand meters above sea level, but it didn't seem to affect her as much. She liked to joke that it was her Chilean blood that allowed her to do it, even though only her mother was from there. Her father was British, and she joked that she needed a lot of tea to keep that half going.

She reached the camp just as the last light was fading. She dusted herself off, hung her jacket in the foyer and headed straight to the mess hall for her breakfast. She wasn't in a huge rush, tonight was just paperwork and review, but she always tried to start her day at sundown regardless. A career in astronomy meant getting used to graveyard shifts - waking up in the afternoon and sleeping through the day. Unfortunately, the camp cook still had to wrap his head around that concept, and still prepared full dinners each evening. Lasagna was a bit heavy to have for breakfast, so Marcela opted to just have a couple slices of toast and a hard-boiled egg instead.

She was only a few bites in when she felt a hand on her shoulder. "Where you been?" Owen asked as he made his way to the other side of the table and sat down, coffee in hand.

"Oh, I was just doing a bit of yoga in my room" Marcela lied. She wasn't going to let her supervisor know that she had been solo hiking again.

"Did you get my message?"

"Noooo...sorry, must have had my phone on silent. What's up?"

"Diego had to go home today, family emergency. So, that dish is yours tonight. You'd better get moving soon, I don't want to get audited again for down time."

'Shit' thought Marcela. Not that she didn't enjoy her time using the telescope, she just liked being a bit more prepared for it. And she liked being at her station before sundown when she had the opportunity. "Sorry Owen, yep, I'll head over right now."

"Thanks Marcela. Sorry for the short notice, I appreciate it. I just want to stay on the right side of the board. I know it's a pain when you're not prepped." Owen got up and walked over to the dinner station and helped himself to a heaping plate of lasagna. He was a very safety conscious manager, and was always harping on at everyone about the health risks of working at extremely high elevation. He definitely didn't look healthy, however, and Marcela couldn't help but think that he could benefit from a bit more walking outside, and a little less of the buffet.

She finished the last bite of her toast and grabbed a coffee to go. She walked briskly towards the control building, almost in a jog. It was frustrating - she could only hope that tonight didn't cut her dish time later in the week. She had only received funding for her project on the agreement that she could meet targeted deadlines. It was easy to get university funding if your research had to do with black holes or dark matter. It was much harder to get funded to scan the cosmos for signs of intelligent life.

She reached into her bag to grab her flashlight. The site was kept very dark for obvious reasons. Even though the main telescope at the site was a radio dish, there was also a traditional observatory built nearby with a large Newtonian reflector. Any unwanted light could interfere with both systems. Marcela knew the path well enough to find her way in the dark, but she didn't want to get in trouble, again, for breaking safety rules. Especially after going on a solo hike above the installation earlier in the day. The flashlights they were issued gave off a soft red light, just enough to navigate by but not enough to interfere with the telescopes. The red beam gave her the creeps, she kept thinking there was going to be a demonic face around the next corner when she used it.

      The control facility was quiet this evening. One researcher was hunched over a station in the far corner, his long ponytail draped down and partially hiding a ripped 'Imagine Dragons' t-shirt. "Buena noches Matias!" Marcela half-yelled as she made her way to her station. He responded with a subtle grunt and turned back to his station. She knew that he wasn't trying to be unfriendly, he was just a socially awkward person. She wondered how often he had left the site in the past year, or if he had left at all? There were several researchers at the site who succumbed to cabin fever at this remote location and gave up on the finer points of etiquette. And personal hygiene, for that matter.

      Marcela spent the first twenty minutes loading her project on the computer in front of her. *'Shit, I've already lost two hours tonight'* she thought, frustrated at the situation she had been placed in. Dish time was precious - if she had known she had it tonight she would have lined up the proper star systems ahead of time, and even maneuvered the dish while the sun was still up to save time. Other researchers could use the dish during the day, especially for elements of astronomy with very powerful energy outputs. She needed the nighttime, she was looking for miniscule signals, and any interference in the atmosphere could upset the readings. Now, she was wasting precious minutes determining which system she had finished on last time, and on top of that, the dish could take up to a half hour to position where she needed it.

Her long-term project was to scan individual star systems on a long radio exposure. It was time consuming, but she had programmed an automated algorithm for her PhD. It could cut through the radio noise of the star's nuclear fusion and listen for distinct frequencies at very, very small power outputs. Each night that she could use the dish she ran her algorithm on a new system, sometimes two if the night was long enough. Analyzing the data took much longer afterwards.

Between the three sites that she had worked at over the last four years, Marcela had now scanned 162 systems. As she got to further distances from the Earth, the process took even longer, so she sometimes needed to return to the same star multiple nights. It was demotivating. She knew that the work was important, possibly the most important thing that a person could do. But each day she continued to find nothing but background radiation and stellar noise. Which either meant that each and every star system that she scanned was empty of intelligence, or that the algorithm she had spent years developing didn't actually work.

Each day she became a little more disheartened. She sometimes lay awake in the morning asking herself the same question Enrico Fermi had famously asked a century earlier. *'Where is everybody?'*

Although, sometimes she worried about success just as much as failure. What would she do if she actually found something? Nothing in the scientific community drew more skepticism and ridicule than claims of extra-terrestrial intelligence. Each time a discovery was made, or a theory proposed, the pundits would spend an exorbitant amount of time and energy to refute it and make the researcher sound like a crackpot.

One of her university professors had scared her with his experiences. He had taken a massive hit to his early career for proposing that an interstellar object that was drifting through the solar system could be an intelligent probe. The media jumped on it to sensationalize the story, and his proposal was ridiculed by the academic community.

Some claimed he was looking for his 'fifteen minutes of fame', and wasn't representative of true science. She didn't want that to happen to her, she knew that she was basically searching for bigfoot, but she also knew that her work was vitally important.

The dish was still slowly moving into position. Setting her frustrations aside, she went over her readings again from the last system while she waited, drinking tea and listening to the quiet hum of exhaust fans. Once the dish had aligned, she started her custom program on the control computer and let it run through the frequencies.

The door slammed shut behind her, startling her. Matias had finally gone to bed. Letting out a sigh of relief, Marcela put some instrumental hip hop on the stereo and kicked her feet up on the desk. Once the program was running, there wasn't much to do until it finished. She pulled out her holotab, read the news for a while and waited.

At a little after 3 am, the computer gave a gentle beep, bringing her out of a doze and alerting her that the program had completed. She lifted her head up to check the findings. She expected more of the same - similar results to the last 162 times she'd done this. But this looked different.

The readout showed something she had never seen before - there was a big spike in the signals from 8 to 11 gigahertz. It was very faint, but something was there that wasn't just background radiation. She expanded the signal, looking for a clue as to what had caused it. Her algorithm was supposed to isolate individual signals from the background, but it was really struggling with this.

Marcela leaned into the screen, fascinated and excited. 'Don't get your hopes up' she told herself, even as she stared at the most promising result she had seen yet. The computer kept trying to isolate individual signals, chugging along and spinning its working symbol. Her algorithm would usually pick apart frequencies in a matter of seconds, but this was taking hours. When the cursor finally changed back to a pointer, she examined the 8 gigahertz frequency closer.

"Holy shit…." she whispered. The computer algorithm was struggling to pick apart individual transmissions because - there were millions of them. She couldn't tell much about them, except that they were a patterned, encoded RF. An intelligent signal? It was tough to say, there was so much data to pick through, she couldn't quite be sure what she was looking at. They looked very different from the Earth's satellite signals, but there was definitely something in the readout that looked like binary code. Had she picked up another planet's communications grid?

Marcela stood up, not sure what to do first. She left her program running and went over to the station Matias had been at. She needed to see more about the star she was checking - it had just been the next number in the sequence until now. Her feet tapped on the ground with anxiety as she looked up the data.

It was Cepheus HD314. 132 light years away. One and a half solar masses. A preliminary survey using the James Webb space telescope had shown 4 planets, but didn't note the system as a frontrunner for life potential. It didn't take long for Marcela to read everything that was known about this star. Out of the millions of stars that had been surveyed, it was quite average in every sense. But not for long, if her readings were correct.

The sky had rotated her star behind the horizon by the time Marcela sat back at her station. She was shaking with anxiety, her mind racing. Where did she go from here?

It wasn't the time to tell anyone about this, not yet. It wasn't time to slap a folder on the desk of the oval office with her 'earth shattering discovery'. No, to avoid the ridicule and skepticism, it was time to study her findings in depth, and book more dish time. She needed to be absolutely sure about this before anyone else could know what she had just seen. She carefully covered her tracks, closing all of her windows on the computer and cleaning up her notes from the far station.

    The door behind her opened as the day crew made their way into the building, chattering and laughing as they went. Marcela finished gathering her things and quietly snuck away back to her bedroom.

4.

Jake got home late on Wednesday evening feeling exhausted. Travis had put a brutal deadline on the new project, the workload he had to get done in just a few days felt overbearing. Jake was trying not to be resentful, because he was just as excited as Travis. He just didn't have a limitless supply of cowboy energy to draw on. He usually enjoyed the walk from his car to his apartment, but tonight he just wanted to be home. He felt his feet yearning to go into a slow jog instead of a walk, just to be on his couch a few moments sooner.

Jake walked up the stairs to his apartment. He couldn't bother with thinking about dinner yet. He kicked his shoes off, grabbed a bottle of beer from the fridge, and flopped into the couch. He closed his eyes, sinking down into the soft leather, happy to be away from the stress of preparation, if only for an evening.

He barely got a sip into his mouth when he felt a message vibrate in his pocket. "I swear to god, Trav, we can talk about it tomorrow…" he muttered. Jake drew in a long breath, and reached his phone out on the exhale.

"Hey, I'm heading to Mystic Realms tonight with a few friends. I think you should come and meet us."

Holy shit, he had forgotten how many days it had been since his date with Mia. He always tried to subscribe to the "rule of three days", as he didn't want to scare her off, but now he's left it five full days! He had been so wound up with planning the experiments he'd completely forgotten about messaging her. Now, the extra days would have baggage attached to them. The first conversation after too long of a communication delay would be awkward, he had been in this situation before.

Yet, there was no pretense to her message. Just a simple invitation. No apologies, no acknowledgement of the five silent days since their amazing date. He smiled thinking about it. Mia didn't seem to play by the rules at all, she just did what she wanted. She just knew how to bypass his defenses so easily.

"*Mystic realms, eh?*" Jake typed in reply. The phone buzzed again a few moments later.

"*We're both nerds Jake. The sooner you admit it the more fun you'll have ;)*"

She was right. There was no denying their nerdiness, especially after a first date spent discussing astrophysics and playing Mortal Kombat until 3am. There was no point in pretending to be anything else now.

Mystic Realms was a virtual reality experience in downtown Vancouver. There were several of them, everything from beach vacations to steam-punk futures to pornographic fantasies. Mystic Realms was definitely the nerdiest of them all, though. It was a Tolkien-esque world, complete with warriors, elves, trolls and wizards.

Jake had never been to one of the VR bars. Home VR systems had only ever given him a headache, and he'd never had an excuse to go to one. But he really didn't have the energy to go out tonight. How could he get out of this without letting Mia think that he wasn't interested in her?

He racked his brain for a magic excuse to use - where he could just stay home tonight, and yet still see her again. He stared blankly at a picture on the far wall of his living room, contemplating how to proceed. That stress ball in his stomach was rising up again. Just as his confusion reached its breaking point, his phone bounced on the coffee table from a new message.

"*Don't overthink it, Jake. I know it's a school night, but I promise to get you home on time. All good if you're busy, but we'll be there in an hour if you want to come."* It was as if she'd read his mind.

'Damn. Ok, why not' he thought. He put the beer down on the coffee table, stood up, stretched his arms out and tried to wake himself up.

"Alright, I'm sold. I'll meet you there :)"

He didn't really like VR much. It kind of freaked him out. The VR bars were different though, there was a limited area, limited time and only a few people inside. The equipment was always top notch as well, which meant that he might not get the pixel headache he got from home units. He'd give it a shot; he could use a diversion to take his mind off of work.

Jake went to take a quick shower and get dressed. He tried to find something different than what he wore on Friday, but still fashionable and presentable. What would Mia like?

Walking swiftly towards downtown, he started rehearsing his excuse for not texting her earlier. Was it a cliche to blame work? Then again, she may not have noticed the delay, she just seemed too laid back to care. And she could have texted him on an earlier day as well, right? The onus wasn't only on him. He decided to just not mention it, and have fun, as clearly that's what Mia wanted to do.

He arrived early. The business was fairly plain. It looked like a converted retail storefront, in an old Yaletown building. The lit sign out front had a vintage look, with neon lettering straight out of the seventies, and even a slight flicker in the purple 'Realms' tube. He couldn't see inside, the windows were blacked out, as well as the door.

After a few minutes waiting out front, he saw a group of four walking down the street towards him. He tried not to strain too awkwardly to see if it was Mia. They were chatting and laughing loudly, but not at a rude level. As they got closer, the streetlight above them finally threw some illumination on the group, and he could see that the short one was Mia. She smiled widely and waved at him.

Her friends were all done up in dress coats. Jake felt a little underdressed, and he started to worry about it as he was just in a softshell hoody. Luckily, Mia was wearing a rain shell as well, a very nice, hooded jacket in a bright yellow. Most people would look like Christopher Robin or Paddington Bear wearing a bright yellow rain jacket, but she pulled it off well.

Mia walked straight up to Jake and hugged him, just briefly. "So glad you came! Jake, this is Abby, Liam, and Jeung." Jake waved, ineptly, then changed his mind and decided to shake all their hands, making it even more awkward. Abby was a bit taller than Mia, with red curly hair and a round face. She looked very Scottish; it would be tough to think she was anything else. Liam towered over the other three, he was four inches taller than Jake, and was at least a foot taller than the three girls. He had blonde hair with a side part, and a sky-blue collared shirt was visible behind his business coat. Jeung was about the same height as Mia, with dark hair, but she had dyed the tips bright green and had a hooped nose ring.

"Nice to meet all of you. Ummm, you done this before?" Jake asked. "I've only tried VR a few times. Gotta say, this is a little intimidating."

"Oh man, nah, it's nothing to worry about. It's just fun," Jeung replied. "There's nothing to it. But the graphics at this one are crazy, you completely forget where you are sometimes. Or at least I did," she said with some embarrassment. The other three laughed at a shared memory.

"Yeah, just don't think about it too much. It's only 90 minutes, and you can always exit early if it gets too crazy for you. We can meet you in the bar after" Abby replied.

"Should we go in? It's not all that warm out here" Mia chimed in.

The five of them went through the entrance doors. Jake was very surprised when he saw the interior. He was expecting a sterile, doctor's office sort of environment to check in, but it was just a pub. An old timey beer hall, complete with a holographic fire in a roaring hearth. Mia walked over to the reception desk. "Hi, I made a reservation earlier for four, any chance I could add a fifth on our time block?"

The receptionist was in full costume, dressed up like a beer wench with a white puffy blouse and a deep green ankle length skirt. "It shouldn't be a problem, I think, we're pretty slow tonight. The interface room you're in only has 4 beds, though, would it be ok if the fifth was down the hall? You'd all meet in the game right away anyway." Mia looked at Jake. He shrugged in agreement, as if to say 'sure'. "Ok, perfect, we'll have you in there in about forty minutes, feel free to grab a table and a drink."

The five grabbed a long wooden bench table and placed their orders with the server. "You see, this is how they get you," Abby whispered, with an evil grin. "No matter when you book for, they always put you in the bar for a drink or two, and the drinks ain't cheap."

"Yeah, but they're good" Liam replied, smiling. "And they know that you accept the interface better after a couple. Your mind doesn't reject it as much when you're just a little tipsy." The server brought over three steins of beer and two glasses of wine, and they clinked a cheers together.

So, the interface works better with alcohol Jake thought. *Makes sense, I guess*. Virtual Reality had evolved a lot in the last decade. The omni-directional treadmills that he had used as a teenager were long gone. The new interfaces had two pads that stuck to either side of your neck, and intercepted the brain's signals to the muscles. The interface could also provide basic sensations of touch and pain, which helped the user interact with objects in the virtual space. It provided a very immersive experience when done right, and a jerky, downright scary experience when it was done wrong. Jake had experienced the latter more often than not.

The visuals and sound were still provided by a helmet and headphones. There was no way to send that much information straight to the brain. Although certain companies had made advancements sending very basic images, like a gray box, or a red circle. The current brain stem interface was only used to control the character in the game, the same way a hand controller had been used to control video games in the past.

He had used one for speed dating once. The unit had eventually worked okay, but it took ages to get his avatar calibrated with the motions he wanted. He left the experience with no dates and a two-day migraine. But the headaches still weren't the worst part. His biggest fear of VR was using the interface when it was connected to the internet.

No one had figured out yet how to send visuals and sound to the brain, but hackers had figured out how to send very basic messages through the neck pads and implant them in the user's subconscious. It was an internationally condemned practice and extremely rare, but it did happen. As far as Jake knew, it had never been used for political or criminal reasons, just advertising. Only the lowest contingent of advertisers would think of hacking someone's brain, though. So, every now and then a user would wake up after using the console with the insatiable urge to buy penis growth pills or get a home equity loan.

Mystic Realms was one of many businesses that popped up after the subliminal advertising became a problem. A home unit needed to connect to the internet, simply for processing power - no home computer could ever handle that much graphical intensity. But Mystic Realms was completely unplugged, they had their own servers that were disconnected from the internet, which meant that it was a safe experience again. There were dozens of operations like this in Vancouver, and most were successful. Some, like Mystic Realms, were franchises that used the same software in cities around the world.

The conversation at the long table strayed between various topics. A lot of old stories and inside jokes between the three girls; they had obviously been friends for quite a while. Mia made a subtle effort to change topics every now and then to include Jake, and he appreciated it. In his head, he was trying to secretly figure out if Abby and Liam were dating, or if it was Jeung and Liam. The idea had crossed his mind that Abby and Jeung could be dating as well, but Liam came across as a boyfriend, not a part of the original group. They may have all just been friends as well, he could be way off. He decided not to think about it too much.

"So, are we heading to Silverstar this year?" Abby asked Mia. "We haven't done that trip in a few years now."

"Oh, I could be in. I had a blast last time" Mia responded. "Jake, do you ski?"

Jake didn't know how to answer. He could hold his own, he'd grown up skiing with his dad in northern BC, but he hadn't gone out once since he moved to Vancouver. "I --- *can* ski. It's been a while, but I was pretty good back in high school."

"Ah, it's like riding a bike, you never forget. But Mia rips, look out for this one," Abby gestured at Mia, who ducked her head shyly.

"Well, maybe in a few weeks when there's a bit more snow, we can get you out there" Mia gently grabbed his sides. It was a cute motion, but slightly seductive. "Always looking for a new ski buddy."

"Well, as long as you don't expect too much," Jake said. "But sure, I'd give 'er a go." Mia was becoming more intriguing to him all the time.

"Whoa!" Liam cut in. He had taken his phone out to check it. "One of the Martian Twelve died today."

"What? Crazy!" Jeung said, almost grabbing the phone out of his hand to see.

The Martian Twelve were the first permanent colonists on Mars. They had been on the planet's surface for about 5 years, using a system of water and air recycling, solar energy, and hydroponic farming. The project was part of Planet 9 Enterprises, a private space exploration firm dedicated to colonizing the inner solar system.

"Does it say which one it was?" Jake asked.

"David Anderson. Looks like it was a heart attack."

"That's so sad, they were just starting to settle in up there. Isn't the next crew leaving in February?" Mia replied.

"Postponed again, believe it or not. This is, like, the fourth time. It's been touch and go, sounds like Dylan's dream is running out of juice" Liam smirked.

Dylan Bishop was the eccentric billionaire CEO of Planet 9. He had made a habit of setting overly ambitious goals for his company, often drawing mockery from the media and general public. However, his company had beaten all other competitors and governments to Mars. Nine years earlier, Yasmina Coskun had become the first human in history to walk on another planet. Her crew of three had stayed for a month, delivering equipment and supplies for the future missions. The Martian twelve left a little bit after Yasmina's return to Earth, with the intention of staying on Mars permanently.

"What a dick," replied Abby. "Dylan Bishop just wanted the glory of getting his people to Mars first. I bet he's more than happy to let them die up there now - especially if it's too expensive to send more support crews. Stupid billionaires…"

Jake had to bite his tongue. He didn't want to get in a debate with Mia's friends ten minutes after meeting them. Although he was a controversial figure, Jake was a big fan of Dylan Bishop. He'd advanced science in countless ways, all without waiting for government money or assistance. People were quick to criticize the ultra-rich on how they spent their money, but Jake had always thought that Dylan Bishop spent his fortune wisely. However, this wasn't the venue to voice his opinion. He nodded silently.

"Wouldn't that suck to be one of those people up there, waiting for the next crew, only to find out they ran out of money and aren't coming anymore? That's like, the worst version of being stood up at a restaurant." Jeung let out a guilty laugh. "I wonder what caused the heart attack? They were all super-screened for health issues before they sent them."

"You'd have to think that five years in lower gravity might play some havoc on your cardio-vascular system" Abby said. "Those poor people, that's a small group to lose one of your own."

"Could you do that? Leave forever?" Mia asked the question of the group, looking around at them over the top of her stein. "Remember when they were running tryouts to find those people? I mean, I get it - the idea of being the first group of people to live on another planet - it's exciting, but - fuck me…" Mia laughed. "I feel like I get stir crazy staying in the house for a full day. I just don't know if I could spend the rest of my life in domes like that, I think I'd go nuts. No way could I do that."

"But what greater thing could you do with your life?" Jake asked. He hadn't spoken much at the table yet, but this was something he felt strongly about. "There's 10 billion people on Earth now. There's no frontier left to explore. It's pretty hard to be special or remembered in a group that big. What more noble thing could there be than being the first humans on a new planet? You'd have a street named after you, for sure." Jake laughed and took a sip out of his stein. "I'd do it, I think."

"I don't think I could. Call me crazy, but I'm really fond of Earth," replied Mia. "It's not like I've seen everything here yet. There's still so much on *this* planet that I want to do."

"I don't know, yeah – maybe... I still don't think I'd want to be in the first group" replied Abby. "Let everyone else work out the kinks in the new technology, then finally get on board when it's nice and comfy."

"I think I'd be an early adopter," said Jake. "If it meant I got that kind of adventure, to be the first people up there. I think that would be worth it to test all the new gear".

"Says the guy who still has a gasoline car" Mia whispered in his ear.

"Yeah, fair enough" Jake whispered back. She was sitting right next to him on the bench, so as he turned to whisper at her, their eyes locked with each other. Jake became aware after a few seconds he was making googly eyes, and turned back from her to his stein, taking a big gulp. Mia giggled quietly at his awkwardness.

"I do hope they send more people up there. What a raw deal for the twelve if not. Well, the eleven, now... Dylan Bishop owes them - he's got to make this right. " Liam was still reading on his phone as he talked.

The twelve had been global celebrities since they were chosen nine years ago. The world had watched the competition, their training, the construction and launch of their ship, and eventually their landing and settlement. It was like an ongoing reality show, except that it held the fate of a now multi-planet species. The death was unsettling news to hear, for sure. The group had an unintentional moment of silence at the table, as they all struggled to find something to say.

The bartender dropped off a piece of paper in front of each of them, which was a welcome distraction. It was printed in an Olde English font and tied up in a scroll. It described the rules of the game they were entering.

You are about to enter the Realm of Tharion. It is a Kingdom in crisis. Orcs and goblins are creeping in from the dark woods, and the Evil Sorcerer's armies lie in waiting. There are many heroic quests to undertake, which can be found in the town square. If you wish to banish the evil from this realm and save its people, you must obtain the crystal amulet from the cave of Skarlax the Dragon (win a free year's membership).

The paper went on to describe a few more of the available quests and their estimated completion time, as well as some of the rules and controls. Jake started laughing when he read it. "Oh man, this is awesome. And hilarious."

"It's everything you want it to be," laughed Abby. "It's so, so cheesy, but it's actually super fun in there."

"So, are we gonna give 'er and try to get that Dragon?"

"There's no way to do it. You just die right away, then they try to sell you more time to get back in there. There's a couple good quests in the town square. Sometimes, it's just kinda fun to go out in the woods as a group and fight orcs," Jeung replied.

"Alright, fair enough, I can be in on that," said Jake. He really had no idea what to expect, hopefully the others would help him get started once they were inside.

The server returned and gave them a five-minute heads up to finish their drinks. Jake had been too focused on the conversation, he still had two thirds of a stein to finish. Mia had one gulp left. The server returned and guided them through a large wooden door at the back of the bar, where another employee met them. This part of the business looked more conventional, like the hallway of a dentist's office. She called out Mia's, Abby's, Jeung's and Liam's names outside the door for room 3.

Jake looked at Mia. She shrugged her shoulders. "You'll be fine, we'll all spawn in the same spot. I'll see you in there, sorry..." she called out as he was escorted down the hall.

The Mystic Realms employee took Jake further down the hall to room 6. She opened the door and let him in. "You've been here before, right?" she asked.

"Nope, first time. Only really done VR at my friend's house" Jake responded.

"Oh, sorry. Here, let me show you a few things." The room was very simple. There were 4 large "bean bag" style chairs for the users to recline on, each with a rack beside it containing the helmet and console. "Here's the fresh neck pads." She took a sterilized ziploc bag out of a drawer in the closest rack. "They plug in here on the console - have you used these before?"

Jake nodded yes.

"Okay, so you should know what placement is going to work best for you. Once you have the pads on your neck, plug them into the console. Lay back before you put your helmet on, make sure that your arms and legs are clear of anything around you, just in case the interface fails. Once your helmet is on, everything is voice command. Remember, once you're in Tharion, there's only three ways to exit the game - you get killed, your ninety-minute timer runs out, or you can say 'command exit'. Got it?"

Jake nodded along as the assistant rattled off the rules, slightly overwhelmed. He wasn't sure if he remembered any of what she had just said.

"Okay, have fun!" She quickly left the room. Jake looked around, wondering what he had gotten himself into. Giggling a bit at the ridiculousness of it, he took out the neck pads, stuck them to each side of his neck vertebrae, and plugged the wire into the rack on the console. He leaned back into the puffy ball of chair that was waiting for him. It was very comfortable, and for the first time in hours he remembered how tired he was, sinking deeply into the soft embrace of it.

He shook it off. The other four were waiting for him to spawn next to them in the game. He reached above his head, grabbed the helmet, and slid it on. Everything got very quiet, even the slight background noise of the cooling fans was gone. He was in a black void, with a single bit of text floating ten feet in front of him.

You are about to give your muscle controls and some of your senses to this game for a temporary period. Speak 'Begin' to start calibration, or remove this helmet to cancel.

Jake took a deep breath in. This was the part that freaked him out the most last time. He braced slightly and said "Begin".

A slow, crescendoed noise started, and the black surroundings faded to white. As the noise quieted, he felt a slight tingling in his neck, which slowly moved down his spine out to his fingers and toes. When it subsided, he looked down, and saw a gray body beneath him, laying in the same position he had been in. A woman's voice gently said "*Welcome. Try wiggling your left fingers.*" Jake looked to his left and wiggled the gray fingers that he saw.

"*Great. And now, your right fingers.*" Jake did the same. The voice asked him to do things for the next two minutes, such as holding both hands over his head, straightening each leg, and so on. Eventually, it asked him to get up, and try walking. Jake got up from the reclined seat and walked away from it. His body was involuntarily moving in a jerky motion, like a zombie in Michael Jackson's 'Thriller' video. His back was tweaking to one side or the other. After a few seconds, the voice chimed in "*correcting...correcting*". He felt himself start to straighten out, and after thirty seconds, he was walking normally. The voice asked him to do ten jumping jacks. He did, and again, he could feel his form correcting itself. He smiled - this was a far easier process than he had gone through last time. Much, much smoother than Shannon's setup at her house. The voice asked him to sit in the reclined chair again. He did.

"*Synchronization complete. Entering game in 4...3...2*"

The crescendo noise started again, but this time faded slowly to the sound of a forest. He could hear the calls of a robin, the light rustle of wind through the trees, and a brook nearby. He was reclined and looking straight up. The white faded slowly to a blurry green, and as it started to focus, he could see that it was actually a canopy of leaves, and that he was lying in a thick wooded area. The leaves blew lightly in the wind and revealed a hint of blue sky behind them. To his left, pillars of dusty sunlight were breaking through to the forest floor.

He sat up, put his right hand down and propped himself up to his feet. He had been laying on a wide tree stump, which was covered in a thick, soft moss. Looking around, Jake was both amazed and bewildered. This was a much different experience than he had tried before. He couldn't make out the pixels in anything around him, the trees and plants looked incredible. If anything, the only thing holding the visuals back from feeling completely real was that they looked 'too' good. Too ideal. He walked over and reached his hand out to touch the oak tree trunk next to him. He could feel it! It didn't feel exactly like bark, but it was close enough.

He walked to find where the sound of the creek was coming from, and found a clearing, with high grasses in between weeping willow trees. A terraced creek trickled through the middle of it. As he approached it, the breeze picked up from behind him, and his long blonde hair blew in front of his face. 'Wait a sec' Jake thought. What was he? He looked down at his clothing. He was wearing tight green trousers, a vest made of woven leaves, and some sort of tight green layer beneath it. He was an elf! He felt around his chest, and he discovered a bow and quiver on his back. Jake took the bow in his left hand instinctively, and an arrow appeared in his right, without him reaching for it. He drew it back easily in the string and fired a shot high up over the willow trees.

He had to find a reflection of himself. Bending over a calm pool in the stream, he saw a thin, blonde, young looking man with long hair and pointy ears. His eyes were vividly green, almost glowing. "No shit!" he said aloud, and his face in the reflection mouthed the words along with him, albeit with a creepy lack of expression. Jake was completely sold on this experience now - he could see why Mia liked this place so much.

Mia! Where were they? Jake thought he would spawn right next to them, that they'd work as a team. He walked back to where he'd woken up and saw that there were four stumps alongside each other. Shit. He'd started in a totally different area of the map.

Jake walked through the woods again until he came across a road. He could see a trail of smoke curling up the sky to his right, and he assumed that would be where the town was. It would make sense that the other four would head for the town square as well, so he started in that direction. The dirt road, again, was beautiful. The treetops curled over the top, creating a green tunnel perforated with the occasional beam of sunlight. He was starting to understand how Jeung lost herself in here - it really was impressive.

Something was moving up ahead. Jake started jogging, thinking it might be one of them. As he got closer, he saw a grotesque creature in the middle of the dirt road. It was human-like, but disfigured with oversized arms, covered in warts, and it carried a large club. "Holy shit, it's an Orc!" Jake laughed. The creature snorted and turned to see the noise. It roared when it saw him, and started running at him, limbs flying about in a disjointed manner. "Shit!" Jake screamed, not sure what to do. He remembered his bow and grabbed it. The arrow appeared in his right hand, but this time, as he drew his hand back, an aiming bullseye appeared on the orc.

He loosed the arrow. It struck the Orc in the shoulder, stopping him for a few seconds, but it soon continued its run at him. He looked at his right hand, there was no more arrow. *Shit*. He started running away. As Jake ran, he reached behind himself again, over his right shoulder, and an arrow appeared in his hand once more. "Ahh, game on, motherfucker!" he laughed, spinning around and loosing another arrow into the Orc's chest. He reached his hand back over his shoulder and fired another, and another - he was getting pretty fast at it. After the fifth arrow stuck into his forehead, the Orc groaned and slowly fell over.

Jake's heart was racing. He walked up to it and crouched down to double check that it was dead. The level of detail was amazing. There was no blood, just the arrows still stuck into its flesh.

Puffed with himself, Jake continued his walk towards the town center. After another two minutes, he heard an Orc roar behind him, and he put him down with arrows once more. *'This isn't too hard'* he thought. *'I'll bet I could get that membership coupon from the dragon with a bit more practice'*. He walked a bit quicker down the dirt road, and his stride changed from a hesitant tiptoe to a cocky strut.

Something was glimmering far up the road. Something shiny. Jake braced himself for another Orc encounter; he reached behind his right shoulder to pre-load an arrow. Slowing his pace, he prepared to take it down again, wondering if he could do it stealthily this time. As he got closer, he saw that it was not an Orc.

A knight in full armor stood in the middle of the road. He was at least a foot taller than Jake, carried a large broadsword, and wore a shining helmet with full visor. He was standing in the middle of the road, facing Jake, but he didn't move. Jake wondered if this character could see him, if maybe he had to interact with it to progress the game. He carefully walked closer. It was a very intimidating scene to approach. As he was about fifty feet away, Jake called out to it "Ummmm...Hello?"

The knight charged at him. "Shit!" Jake yelled. He fired an arrow, but it bounced off the chest armor. The knight didn't slow down at all. Jake fired another, and the knight swatted it away with his sword. "Oh, jeezu…." Jake's yell was interrupted, as the Knight was on him, knocking him in the chest and throwing him backwards to the ground. He felt a little pressure from the impact, but it wasn't too painful. He reached back for an arrow again, but it was too late. The Knight had his arms pinned to the ground. A huge knee set down to his right, and another to his left - Jake braced for a finishing blow, and closed his eyes, hoping that dying in this game wasn't too painful. Or embarrassing.

He heard the helm creak open above him. As he wondered where the knight's sword would finally land, he felt a beard touching his face, and then lips pressing against his. "What the fuck!?"

"I mean, I'd take this further, but I'm pretty sure this place is PG." Jake opened his eyes and realized this enormous soldier was actually straddling him. The man's face had a grungy red beard and intense brown eyes. The voice that had come out of him was Mia's. The shock faded after a few seconds, and Jake started laughing uncontrollably.

"I've gotta say, you looked a lot better on our first date. There's something different about you, Mia, I just can't put my finger on it."

"Yeah, I'm trying something new with my hair" Mia said. Her voice was bubbly and feminine, but it was coming out of a steely eyed giant with no facial expression. The contrast kept Jake laughing.

"You got me good there, holy shit. I was not expecting that."

"Well, I just saw you in those green tights and got all excited. I mean, what's a girl to do?" The knight reached his hand down between Jake's legs and rapped his fingers back and forth against the insides. "But, nothing down there, unfortunately. Like I said, PG."

She was right. Jake's elf was a Ken doll from the waist down. He laughed again and swatted her hand away. "Don't get fresh," he said, faking disdain.

Mia laughed and got up off Jake. "I'm sorry, by the way. I don't know why they told us you would spawn in the same location. Hope you weren't worried."

"Nah, I've just been figuring stuff out. This place is wild, man! I heard some of the new VR bars were realistic, but I had no idea. This is friggn' crazy…"

"Yeah, it's pretty awesome. We were blown away the first time we tried it. I mean, they could use some better writers, but whatever, it's just cheesy fun."

"So, where's everyone else?"

"They were in the town square the last time I saw them, we spawned pretty close to it. I went off to find you. Command, display." The knight stared straight ahead; Mia was seeing something he couldn't. "Oh, they took that boring quest with the tainted well. Command, display off." She looked back at Jake. "We can join them, or we could go do something fun by ourselves?"

"I'm easy either way. But do you want to ditch them?"

"Bah, we do enough together. I'm kind of enjoying the company I have right now," she smiled. "Hey, if we walk north on the map, there's an area where you can save the town's unicorn from a goblin attack. I figure with an archer and a knight we'd have a decent shot."

"Okay, I'm in!" The two of them started walking down the road, towards the direction Mia had come from. "So, how did you get to be the big, tough knight and I'm this dorky woodland elf? I couldn't even make a dent on you when you charged me."

"Oh, we always sign up for random characters, it makes it more fun. I saw on my display that you were an elf, but I wasn't positive it was you until you talked" she laughed. "Oh, and friendly fire is turned off, your arrows can't hurt me, and my sword can't hurt you." Mia poked him with the sharp end of her giant broadsword, it felt like a pool noodle. "Could still knock you down and get frisky, though." The steel glove of the knight pinched Jake in the butt.

Jake found the situation very strange, but hilarious. The forest was opening into rolling meadows. They reached the top of a hill, and he took a moment to look at the scenery. The town was down to their left. He could see a couple small buildings with wisps of smoke coming from the chimneys. In front of them, snowcapped jagged peaks rose sharply into the sky. To their right, an ominous black tower loomed over the horizon, as if the CN tower was rising out of a woodland. Behind him, Jake saw a vast sea, and a golden sandy beach along its shore. "This place is huge!" he exclaimed. "You could spend a long time in here, eh? There's so many places to go."

"Some people come in and spend the whole day in here. We put a cap at ninety minutes, and only on weeknights. It's too tempting otherwise. About a year ago, we spent a whole Saturday in here, and Jeung came out of it acting really weird. She refused to leave the game. We had to get the front desk to stop adding extra time and boot her out. She spent at least a week adjusting to the regular world again. It was like she forgot who she was. So, yes, ninety minutes is a fun amount, but you have to stop after that. They really should have warnings about it."

They continued strolling through the meadows, talking casually, even as they were in their strange avatars. "I'm really glad you decided to come tonight, Jake. I was hoping I'd see more of you. I had a really great time last Friday" Mia said, behind her steel face shield.

"Me too. I'm glad I came, it's been a crazy week, I really needed this."

Up ahead, a hill rose slightly higher than the one they were on. Standing majestically on the summit was a white unicorn, its mane blowing in the breeze. "Whoa, cool!" exclaimed Jake. "Can we ride it?"

"Only if you can fend off the goblins. And if it doesn't get scared off."

Jake went into a stealthy crouch as he approached the unicorn. His elf body seemed to blend into the high grasses. The unicorn stared off into the distance, blissfully unaware. As he got closer, Jake heard a piercing shriek from the nearby woods, almost chimp-like. He turned and saw dozens of monkey-sized dark figures running from the woods, all holding daggers and charging headlong towards the unicorn.

"Wooooooo! This is it, start firing Jake!" Mia grabbed her broadsword and charged straight into the horde of goblins. Jake loaded an arrow, aimed for the closest goblin and fired. It missed, he was too far away, and they were moving too fast. He charged forward, grabbing an arrow as he ran, and shot another as he was diving to take cover behind a boulder. It struck and killed a goblin.

"Holy shit!" he yelled. He took cover at a boulder and started rapid firing into the crowd. Mia was in the middle of the horde now, swatting them away with her sword, and beginning to retreat as the crowd started to overwhelm her. Jake was getting good with the arrows, pinning off one goblin after another, but a stream of them kept flowing from the woods. He couldn't keep up, and eventually they were at his boulder. One leapt over and stabbed him in the shoulder. He felt it, but it was more like a light electric shock than piercing pain. He grabbed the goblin by the arm and threw it to the side, but suddenly there were two more of them on him. As they started to dogpile him down to the ground, he heard Mia yell "Oh crap, haha, I'm coming!"

She charged through the group and got to Jake, who was now covered in six shrieking goblins. She swung hard and knocked two of them off with her sword, and the other four retreated. As she helped him back up to his feet, they heard a loud 'neighing' noise from the top of the hill. The goblins had reached the unicorn. It stood up on its hind legs, crashing its front limbs down to crush one of the attackers. As more of the goblins rushed towards it, the unicorn turned and ran towards the forest. All the goblins chased, shrieking loudly with excitement.

The sound faded slowly. They could hear the chaos of the scene disappearing into the distance. The cracking of branches as the hooves trampled through them, and the excited shrieks of the pursuers eventually gave way to a peaceful stillness once more. "Damn, I really wanted to ride that bastard" Jake smiled.

"Well, you'll just have to come back and try again one day. Liam got it once."

"Where to now?"

"Well, we don't have too much time left. Like I said, we keep these things pretty short these days."

"Whoa, it's already been an hour and a half?"

"Almost, yeah. That's how Jeung gets so lost in here, you really do lose track of time."

"So, what do we do?"

"Well, I think I'd really like to make out with you again, Jake. But maybe not when I'm this big gross Viking guy."

"Yeah, I enjoyed our kiss last Friday a lot more. No offense...."

Mia did her best to bat the big knight's eyelids at him "So, what do you say, do you want to get out of here?"

"Do we need to find the others first?"

"Nah, I'll text Abby and let her know later. I live pretty close to here, if you want to come have a drink at my place."

Jake smiled. The realm of Tharion was incredible, but he really wanted to see Mia in person again. "I'm in, but there's a problem." Mia shrugged in questioning. "How do we get out of here? I didn't listen to the instructions."

"You'll figure it out eventually. Command, exit".

The knight vanished and Jake was left alone on the hilltop where the unicorn had stood. He turned around to enjoy his surroundings once more and took a deep breath. "Command, exit."

5.

The alarm went off entirely too soon. There was no time for a snooze, unfortunately. Travis planned to pick up Jake in a work van early in the morning. It made sense, he lived closer to the office and could pick up the vehicle, and the two of them were going to have to carpool out to the Harrison lab anyway. It was a hefty drive, at least ninety minutes each way, but Jake had brought his tab and keyboard to get a bit of work done on the way. Hachiro had spent the extra money for fully autonomous vans - most likely to save money on their fleet's insurance, but Travis refused to do anything else while the car was driving. He sat at attention, ready to take over at all times, not quite ready to trust the computer at the wheel. Once they hit the highway, he seemed to relax a bit, even checking his emails briefly.

"So, you going to the Christmas party?" Travis asked. He was drinking his coffee out of a dented steel thermos tumbler that must have been thirty years old. The stereo was softly playing a mix of country and alt rock.

"I RSVP'ed. So, I guess I am going this year," Jake said with some trepidation. "Just hope it's a bit more fun than last time. I'm not great at the whole formal networking thing. I just feel a bit awkward, I guess."

"Fuck, you're telling me, bud," Travis replied, taking a swig of coffee. "The old parties at the college lab were so much more laid back! Just a keg and some pizzas, you know? I'm a purist, all you need is some booze and music, and people will have a good time. You don't need ice sculptures and shit."

"Mr. Hachiro is super into that stuff, though. I don't think the phrase 'business casual' means much in his world."

"Yeah, I don't know what he'd say if he saw what I wore to the office most days. But at least it's not the ripped t-shirts I wore to the lab back in college."

Jake had been trying to figure out what the faded stickers were on the side of Travis' mug for at least a half hour. There were a couple of Stihl chainsaw labels and a Fox racing logo. He'd just realized that a couple of the other old stickers were Pokemon characters, which made him chuckle to himself for a while. It was a hilarious juxtaposition, just like the mug's owner. "Yeah, I guess I've got to rent a tux again. There's something just kind of gross about it."

Travis nodded in agreement and seemed to subconsciously nudge his testicles to one side with his left hand, as if protecting them from the dangers of rented pants. "You going stag?"

"Uh, well…." Jake had put off that thought for a few days, he'd forgotten about the 'Archie-esque' scenario he had created for himself. "I signed up with a plus one, and I've been on a couple dates with this new girl - she's pretty awesome. Like, she's incredible. But..."

"What's the problem then?"

"I haven't actually asked her to go to it yet. And we've only been out twice, it's weird. But for some reason I reserved it with Michelle, and now it's all confirmed and shit, and.." Jake's speech had sped up, he was obviously stressed out about the situation.

Travis let out a belly laugh. "Jesus, you can be awkward still. Just living up to the scientist stereotype, Frink." Jake agreed. "Well, I don't know what to tell you there. You don't want to scare her off, I get it, and that's an *intense* party. But it's not for a month, maybe ask her after a couple more dates? But, dude, don't take woman advice from me. I'm terrible with that shit."

"And if it doesn't work out, though…"

"Just tell Michelle on the day of the party that your date isn't feeling well. No more questions after that, you know how much of a germaphobe she is."

Jake nodded - it was a good plan. They were getting close to the facility now. Once the road turned to dirt, Travis took over driving from the computer. Another 5 minutes up the dirt road, they saw the University's logo on a small sign, and saw the hangar up ahead. There was almost nothing in the parking lot, a shipping container and a couple skids had been left behind. The only other car was from the University's security department.

The Harrison Lab had been built this far out because of what it contained - an FEHFR ray. It was a "Focused Extremely High Frequency Radiation" emitter - essentially a laser beam capable of generating gamma rays at the upper limits of the spectrum. Travis insisted on calling it the "Hulk Gun", as it was, in essence, the same device that transformed Bruce Banner.

Although the radiation emitted was very focused, and the university had looked at what precautions should be taken to work with gamma rays, there wasn't a single municipality closer to Vancouver that would allow such a device to be used. Eventually, a location was chosen on a country road well out into the Fraser Valley. It was far from any residence or business, which allowed them to build the facility largely unnoticed.

Essentially, it was just an airplane hangar with a large working and warehouse area and a smaller control room. The real advantage to the location chosen wasn't in its remoteness, however, but in its surroundings. The hangar backed on to the mountain, so if the lead barrier or cement wall behind the 'Hulk Gun' failed to stop the gamma radiation, it would go straight into the heavy igneous rock of the coast mountain range and dissipate harmlessly. Jake had always thought it was overkill, the sheer amount of energy required to create gamma radiation meant they were producing harmless amounts. But the general public knew the word, and much like nuclear energy or particle colliders in the past, were terribly frightened by the idea of a 'gamma ray lab' in their own backyard.

This was his first time seeing the building, however. The location was beautiful. It was the last bit of flat land in the river valley, and the mountains rose sharply directly behind it. Thick trees grew on the steep slopes and worked their way down into a forest that surrounded the property. The morning mist still hadn't lifted, and a gentle rain was falling. The place had a slightly eerie feeling. It was well maintained, but the remoteness of it gave it a creepy aura.

Opening the back doors of the van felt like being a roadie for a rock concert. They had packed a dozen or so industrial road cases of their equipment. In addition to two samples of berlinite that he had checked out from secured storage, Jake had brought a particle detector, an array of cameras for different parts of the EM spectrum, and a high-speed camera for detecting quick changes. They had platforms to construct, cleaning equipment, and special personal protective equipment to use.

Travis met with the security guard and got the access codes, safety protocols and other housekeeping out of the way. The guard left shortly afterwards, leaving the facility completely in their hands.

They spent the majority of the morning getting unpacked and checking out what was inside. The front half of the building was a large warehouse space with empty racks running in straight aisles through the room. The back half of the building had a kitchen and a break room, a couple of offices, and a computer server room. It had obviously hosted a decent sized staff back when it was being used regularly.

Beyond that area, at the back of the building was the lab itself. It was a clean room facility, with an air scrubber and a neutral 'green' room bordering the space with the emitter. The walls were pure white, with LED lighting, and minimal shelving or objects. They peeked as far as they could into the gamma room without suiting up in PPE.

The emitter itself didn't look anything like a gun, which disappointed Travis immensely. It was more like two black fridges stuck together. The power cables feeding it were enormous. It was close to the control room, and the other side of the room had an area that was elevated, where the students had placed various experiments back when the facility was in use.

Travis was busy hauling the crates of PPE into the prep area. In order to go into the room with the Hulk gun, they would have to put on full radiation suits. *'Mia would love that'* Jake thought. It was all a bit ridiculous. They wouldn't do much against high amplitude gamma radiation anyways, and the materials they were touching were not radioactive. It was safety for safety's sake, nothing more. At least they were easy to use, and the suits were pre-sterilized and cleaned.

Jake had to work hard at containing himself, and had to work harder to contain Travis, who couldn't wait to power up the Hulk Gun. It was a new shiny toy, a machine capable of doing things they'd only dreamed of in their undergraduate days, but they had to wait. There was a process, a set of rules that needed - unfortunately - to be followed. And as much as the 10-year-old in him just wanted to fire up the damn laser gun, he had to be patient. As much as it sucked, there were hours and hours of bureaucracy and scientific method to be done before they got there.

By the late afternoon, Travis was growing impatient. "Okay, dude, I think we're good to go," he muttered, as Jake continued adjusting his instrumentation.

"Not quite yet. The particle detector isn't aligned quite right."

That conversation repeated several times, every half hour or so. Finally, when Jake powered up the FEHFR emitter, Travis practically ran to the storage area and grabbed a sample case of Berlinite.

"Not yet, man, you know that. We need a control."

"Do we? Jesus, we know what happens when Gamma Rays hit titanium, or copper, or whatever else you brought. And we can always do it later."

Jake smiled. "Don't rush it, Trav. Let's do it right. We're out here for months, I want to get it done the right way." Travis did have a point - they could start with the exciting stuff and switch to the control experiments later. But that wasn't the proper way to run the process, and it wasn't what they had planned. Travis begrudgingly put on the radiation suit and placed a sample of titanium on the sample pedestal.

It was anti-climactic when they finally fired the Hulk Gun. A slight whirr of electric current was the only noise. There was no unexpected response from the control sample. Travis kept the suit on to change each metal cube, waiting to see the berlinite arrive on the pedestal. But they spent the first day and a half just running controls. By lunch on the second day, Jake had made some progress on his checklist, but still had days of calibration work left to do.

"Alright, we can get back to control tests later. I want to see the real shit! " Travis jumped up off the break room couch and walked over to turn down the stereo. Jake argued for a second, but Travis was already out in the warehouse. He wasn't waiting any longer, and Jake was forced to oblige.

The two samples were in pelican cases, with padlocks through the latches. Jake entered the code he'd received from Germany, and they opened the first case.

Inside was a small metal cube. It was shiny, like they'd expected, but it wasn't a silver color, instead it shone in a rich magenta. It almost appeared as if there was a protective, plastic film over it, but there wasn't. "Shit, I heard it was purple, that's friggn' wild" Travis commented. "So, it's absorbing half the visible spectrum?"

"From what I've read, yes. But the energy isn't being transferred to it, at least not in any of the ways we know. So, it looks magenta because it's basically 'eating' the spectrum between red and violet."

"So, you still think that this stuff is sending part of the spectrum to the base dimension? That's where the energy goes?"

"I mean, I don't know for sure - but no one else has looked at it from that angle. I could be way off, but I think it has something to do with the molecular structure that sets up between these elements. I've seen representations of it, and I think certain frequencies of energy cause it to vibrate, and those vibrations dissipate their energy into a different dimensional space." Jake closed the case again to bring it to the staging area. "That's why we had to work so hard to get it. That's why Harada let me spend all this money, he really wants to get a juicy patent for military use."

"Well, that's not really what we're going for here, but I guess he doesn't have to know." Travis smiled deviously. "We can run some tests with microwaves off this as well, I guess, and do our due diligence for him." He stared at the shiny purple cube once more, losing his focus into it. "I'm stoked, man. Even if this doesn't turn into anything, it's been so long since you and I got to work with new stuff."

They closed the case and brought it to the prep room. Jake donned the radiation suit this time and started cleaning any contaminants from the sample. When he was satisfied, he entered the gamma room and removed the previous sample of iron from the pedestal, bringing it out of the room before replacing it with the berlinite.

He sealed the room, took the suit off, and returned to the controls with Travis. "Okay, let's start off easy, no one has hit this with anything smaller than soft x-rays so far. Why don't we set our wavelength at 50 picometers to start, and see if we get any strange reactions?"

Travis took about twenty minutes lining up the target again, dialing in the frequency of the emitted wave. When he was ready, they fired the emitter again. Jake spent the next half hour reviewing the results briefly, checking the particle detector, the IR, and so on. The results were exactly the same as the titanium sample. "Well, that's not very exciting" he muttered beside Travis.

"Well, let's see if it absorbs a shorter wavelength? We haven't even touched what this thing will do yet."

They ran another test at a 25 picometer wavelength. They were being ever more cautious as they decreased the wavelength. Again, the test showed nothing of note, it was reacting as expected.

They stayed late and continued firing at ever higher frequencies. Nothing of note was happening with the berlinite, however. The energy reflected off of it, just like it had with the titanium. It wasn't responding the way it did to the optical spectrum - it was just a normal metal now. Jake was fighting to hold off his disappointment, he had hoped to have a wealth of data to go over when this week was done. But, so far, berlinite was no different than anything else.

Each step up in wavelength required an increase in energy, so the large power cables feeding the emitter were starting to get hot with the hum of electricity. Travis turned to Jake in the control room to discuss the plan.

"We're reaching the end of what this thing can do, unfortunately. And it's getting super late. None of the energy is disappearing, man, I'm sorry. It was an interesting theory, I guess, but..." He stopped. He could see the disappointment in his friend's face. "...A couple more rounds, and we'll just have to take a break for a few weeks and review the data."

"Yeah. I really thought we'd find something, I'm sorry we did all this, Trav. Maybe Hachiro's right, we'll just see if we can work it with radar shit."

"Well, we'll try a bit more, then come back next week." Travis decreased the wavelength to .25 picometers, and they started the countdown for the next test.

The emitter cables hummed; the lights flickered ever so slightly with the power surge. Jake expected to have very similar results as the rest of the day and wasn't even watching the monitors this time. He read the news on his holotab while the test was running, disappointed with the tedium and repetitiveness. He looked up a few minutes after the hill gun powered down again.

The sample was gone on the monitors. "Dude, did you move the berlinite?" Jake asked, wondering if this last test had just been firing into a blank wall.

"No, man, I haven't been in there since this morning. Is it skewed to one side or something?"

"It's...gone" Jake said, not hiding his confusion well. The monitor just showed an empty pedestal where the purple cube had sat a minute earlier.

"That can't be right, maybe it fell - you get some tremors out here near the mountains sometimes. I'll check it out." Travis took a few minutes to put on the protective suit, and then entered the emitter room. He walked over to the platform where the sample was, and looked all around the area for it, ducking his head down near the floor to check. "I can't see it. Did...did we just vaporize twelve grand?" he laughed uncomfortably.

"Is there any powder, or residue? Anything?"

Travis came back to get some tools, checking the area thoroughly for any dust that wasn't there before. "Yeah, man - there's nothing here. Whatever we just did to that sample, it was thorough. She gone, bud."

"What?! That's impossible!"

"I ain't lyin, man!" Travis was still chuckling.

Travis was one of the smartest and most analytical people he had ever met, but Jake couldn't believe this until he saw it with his own eyes. He put on the second protective suit and double checked the sample platform. Nothing. "Jesus, whatever that ray did to this thing, it left absolutely nothing behind."

Back in the control room Jake checked the particle detector, looking to see if it picked up the moment the sample was vaporized. It picked up nothing the entire time. He was breathing heavily as he moved to the next instrument station.

"This is crazy, dude." Travis said to him, in a slow, stoned manner. He wasn't looking up from his monitor, as if he was possessed by the images. "We're onto something bigger than we thought."

"What did you find? I'm not seeing shit!"

"Okay, so the high-speed camera was recording at 30,000 frames per second, right? I had to check it again to make sure this wasn't a glitch." He pointed at the screen, flicking between two frames. "That thing disappeared in less than one frame. In this frame, it's here, and in this next frame, it's completely gone. In a tiny fraction of a second. We didn't vaporize the bastard, it just...ceased to exist."

6.

Saturday morning found Jake poring over the data he had downloaded. He hadn't slept much, his mind kept racing about. He tried watching old cartoons, reading boring books - nothing worked. He had eventually fallen asleep but woke up early to thoughts of the experiment once more.

He had three strong cups of coffee, sitting on his couch in his underwear, flicking through the different recordings of the incident. No matter what he looked at, he kept returning to those two frames. One frame showed the berlinite, the next frame it was gone. In less than .00003 of a second, it went from this universe to somewhere else.

Maybe they had found a frequency of gamma that caused an increase of energy - a vibration through the molecular structure? Jake continued going through his research, restraining himself from texting Travis each time he found something. Although, he was pretty sure Travis was doing the same thing. It was hard to take a day away from the project after causing something so momentous.

Jake's stomach began to rumble, and he realized he hadn't eaten since the lab. He got up off the couch to make lunch, only then seeing a clock and realizing it was 4pm! He had spent the entire day running his brain on overdrive. He needed to step away.

Picking up his phone, Jake sent a text to Mia. They had chatted briefly since he had left her house on Wednesday, but not much. He'd been so busy with the work out at Harrison that he hadn't had time, and she'd noticed how tired he looked on their holo-chat.

Somehow, he felt more comfortable though, he wasn't over-thinking every move anymore. Normally, he would have planned out every word of a message before he sent it. She was so easy to talk to, even when she had a beard and was a foot taller than him.

"Sorry, I know it's last minute, but any chance you're up for dinner and a movie tonight?"

Jake put his phone down and went to grab a towel for the shower. His phone buzzed on the counter.

"Oooohh, old fashioned, I like it"

"Well, we can't rescue unicorns on every date. Would eventually get monotonous, I think..." Jake responded.

"What's your address? I'll come over in a couple hours."

Jake smiled. Again, there was no dance, no game to the way she acted. She wanted to come over, and she made it clear. It was so refreshing. He texted his address back to her and set the phone down again. Looking around his apartment, he had a moment of bachelor panic. It wasn't filthy, but it definitely wasn't date ready. He turned up his music and power cleaned for an hour, sweeping the mess under the rug wherever he could.

Mia turned up at his door with a meal ready to go in tupperware. "You didn't need to do that, we could've ordered in. Or gone out somewhere." Jake was embarrassed that he hadn't planned their dinner yet.

"Well, you seemed pretty stressed the other night, and overworked. I know you don't like talking about it, but it was obvious. And I was already going to make this at my house, I thought you could use a break."

"Yep, well that's for sure," Jake laughed.

"I thought I could take care of things tonight. Next time, it's your turn, okay?"

Mia had brought all the ingredients for quesadillas. She made him sit at the counter while she poked through his kitchen looking for utensils and frypans. She laughed at how poorly organized his kitchen was, as she hunted for everything in the wrong drawers and cupboards. "My mom would have a field day in here. You'd never hear the end of it," she joked. Jake opened a bottle of wine and turned the music back on.

They sat at his kitchen table to eat, drinking wine and gossiping about her friends. He realized, as they were sitting and enjoying their dinner, that it was the first time he had eaten at his table, ever. He was enjoying the conversation a great deal; it was a welcome diversion for him. Topics came and went like passing cars, and Jake loved talking about everything with her. Everything except work, he would immediately change subjects if it came up. He intentionally chose a terrible old monster movie for them to watch after dinner, so they could keep talking and laughing through it.

Jake awoke the next morning, feeling very comfortable in his bed. The sun was just starting to peek in through the shades. He had slept in much later than usual. October in Vancouver was a transition to the dark months, the sun took forever to rise, and it was usually hidden behind dark gray clouds. A blue-sky sunrise was so rare this time of year. It was like a delicious restaurant meal - one that took a little too long to arrive at your booth. He had a brief moment of pure, blank bliss, before his mind inevitably started wandering back again.

'Where the fuck did the berlinite go?' His head was back where it was yesterday, to the same mystery.

He looked over and saw Mia on the other side of the bed. She was still radiant, not a hair out of place, like a Hollywood actress who had been prepped for a movie shoot. He shook his head in amazement and looked down to his side of the bed where he had left a puddle of drool on the sheets, and the pillows were thrown haphazardly to the floor. He felt a like a dirty hobo lying next to an angel. He snuck quietly out of the room to make coffee in the kitchen while she slept.

An hour later, Jake was sat at the counter, on his second cup, relentlessly going over the recordings once more. He heard a yawn behind him and turned to see Mia slumbering into the kitchen. She was wearing one of his hoodies, a bright blue one with a local brewery logo on the front. "Working again?" She hugged him from behind and gave him a kiss on the cheek before she helped herself to a mug from the cupboard.

"Sorry, yeah. Man, I wish I could still sleep like you. I'm up at six every day, work or not."

"Your bed was comfy. And you've got to take advantage of Sundays, they only happen once a week," she spoke through a wide mouthed yawn. "Soooo, what's got you so stressed anyway? Enough that you left a pretty girl by herself in bed?" Mia could see by the look on his face that his mind had gone straight back to his work.

"I can't really talk about it," Jake said abruptly. He immediately regretted his tone and felt he should elaborate a bit more. "It was - an unexpected result from an experiment."

"What was it?"

"I can't really describe it, and we have to sign strict NDA's at Hachiro" Jake replied, trying to be tactful about it. He hadn't told anyone about the missing sample yet. He didn't know how he would explain it anyway. Travis had agreed with him to not submit results until they knew what they were dealing with.

Mia put her coffee down on the counter. "Can you recreate it this week? Was this out at your office in Richmond?"

"Yep. In the lab out back." Jake lied. He could tell her about the Harrison lab, that wasn't protected in his NDA. The lie had just come out of him, and he didn't know why.

Mia gave him a slightly strange look, as if she knew that he was hiding something. He had started acting so strangely as soon as she brought up what he was working on. "Well...You're not gonna, like, blow up the world, are you?"

"I honestly...don't know" Jake laughed.

Mia clasped her coffee mug and walked over to his window, looking down on the quiet Sunday streets of Vancouver. "I'll make you a deal. I'm going to use your shower, and then you have to put the tab down and take me for breakfast. After that, you're free, you can nerd out over your warp drives and stuff as much as you want, I'll leave you alone, I have shit to do myself." She hugged him again from behind.

"It's a deal. Sorry, I can usually leave my work at the office, I swear - I'm not always like this. But this week's been nuts, Mia." Jake put his work away. "Thank you so much for last night," he said as he returned her embrace.

They walked to a diner down the street and had breakfast together. After Jake paid the bill, Mia kissed him lightly and said goodbye. "Don't be a stranger, OK?"

Jake stood still, watching her leave. As she walked away down the street, he started looking for a flaw, something that made her less perfect than she seemed in that moment. He couldn't find one, and although he was sure that a flaw would one day present itself, he decided to relish that moment. To enjoy this brief point in time where she was, indeed, perfect. If she was to turn around, she'd see him still creepily leering at her from the front of the diner, so he shook himself out of it, and started walking home.

Although it was Sunday, Jake decided to drive in to work at the Hachiro offices anyway. Most people worked from Monday to Friday, but the office still had a skeleton crew in on the weekend. There was a security guard who usually sat at Michelle's desk in the front lobby when he wasn't doing his rounds. A couple other offices had lights on, but the majority of the building was dead and quiet. Jake took the opportunity to use his stereo speakers, he didn't have to worry about his music bothering his neighbors today.

Jake went over his findings again and again, still not finding any reason for the disappearance. Staring at the results wasn't going to change anything. He had to accept that he had no idea where the sample had gone. And that he had definitely lost a cube of metal worth thousands of dollars.

He decided to finish the rest of his clerical work for the week instead, so that he could head out to the lab again in the morning. He crushed through his requisitions, timesheets, safety minutes, and various other bits of paperwork that had been piling up. Once finished, he grabbed his bag and his holotab and walked out of his office down the hall, feeling very unfulfilled. He had hoped that working through the whole weekend would get him closer to an answer. He was no closer than he had been on Friday night, and he'd just wasted his day.

There was a smell in the air - smoke. It was faint, but definitely there. It wasn't the smell of an electrical fire or burning wood or nylon. It was... cigarettes. Jake knew there was only one person who would dare smoke inside at the office, only one person who could get away with it. Walking out of the break room in front of him was a tall, thin figure in a designer gray suit. It was Mr. Hachiro.

Harada Hachiro visited his company very infrequently. He kept an enormous personal office in the back corner of the building where the morning sun hit. He used it once every few months when he flew in from Tokyo to check on things. Someone always got fired during one of his visits, you could set your watch by it. It was well known to lay low and stay hidden when Mr. Hachiro was in Canada. If you were doing your job well, sometimes it was safest to just blend into the walls.

"Hello, Mr..." He reached his hand out to shake Jake's. He was six and a half feet tall, skinny with a gaunt face, and had a glowering expression that looked as if it had never been graced with a smile.

"Crawford, sir. Jake Crawford." It had been a long time since Jake had called anyone 'sir', but Mr. Hachiro's demeanor commanded respect. Jake was very intimidated.

"Crawford. You were one of the researchers on the Richardson project last year, correct?" Jake nodded in agreement. "And now you're working with this new alloy we've been hearing about?" Jake nodded again, feeling like a child who had run into the school principal.

"That's right, sir. We've only just received it, and are hoping to start our experiments soon," he lied.

"Well, I look forward to seeing what you find."

Harada continued walking past Jake down the hall towards his office. Jake's chest was heavy with stress, he could feel the weight of it crushing into him. He wasn't sure why he had just lied. Mr. Hachiro would have been thrilled to hear of a potential breakthrough. Something felt different. There had always been something about Hachiro that he didn't trust. Or, maybe, he just didn't want to tell his boss that he'd lost a very expensive sample. But, for the second time that day, he'd openly lied - and for the second time he didn't know why.

7.

"You're kind of being a wuss, dude."
"A wuss!? You don't seem to get it - we lost twelve grand on Friday! You're not the least bit worried?"

Travis and Jake were staring at the second case of berlinite. Travis wanted to bring it into the gamma lab first thing Monday morning, when Jake objected. "Yeah, but...who cares?" Travis frustratingly replied. "You do remember what we're dealing with, right?"

Jake looked at his endlessly impulsive friend. Yes, they needed to repeat the experiment, but he didn't want to rush. He couldn't lose another sample. "I guess - I want to try it again? But we only have one sample left out here, and if the same thing happens with no explainable results, we're screwed, at least for a bit. We'll have to check out more samples, and file the disappearance with the office," Jake said, staring out the window at the low, gray clouds hanging over the Fraser Valley.

"Yeah, bud, about that..." Travis had a sheepish look on his face. Jake realized right away what he was hiding.

"You bastard, I knew it. That's why you were late this morning." Jake shook his head, only half angry.

"Sometimes, you're a little too nervous about these things, dude. I didn't want to come all the way out here to only run *only one* more test, so I grabbed 4 more berlinite samples this morning at the office. I know we're supposed to write our results paperwork and turn it in first, but..." Travis took a long sip out of his dented coffee tumbler. "I just feel like we're on to something big, man. I really wanted to figure this riddle out before we submit any findings."

"It's just sketchy, it's not how we're supposed to do this! Yeah, we're both stoked here, but you just checked out fifty G's of shit that we may never bring back. I've never lost company property before, I'm just not sure how we're supposed to handle this." Jake stared at the pelican case in front of him, avoiding looking Travis in the eyes. "Seeing that cube disappear was very cool - fuck, it was mind blowing, I'll admit that. But we lost a lot of money already, and, Jesus…. neither one of us has reported it yet!" Jake wasn't overly upset, but he had worked hard to get this job, and he didn't like breaking any of the rules, no matter how basic.

He stayed, guarding the case while Travis walked away to power up the control room. Jake's objections weren't doing much to slow him down. In fact, he seemed largely unphased by them. Travis carefully tiptoed back into the room ten minutes later, to find Jake still looking at the Pelican case.

"It hasn't clicked yet with you, has it?"

Jake looked up at him. "What do you mean?"

"That last wavelength we used on Friday. A quarter of a picometer. Do you remember the last time that number came up?"

Jake paused to think about it. "I don't think we've used that wavelength before, have we?"

"Not for a wavelength, no. But back when you and I were doing base dimension theory, that was the transition length."

"Holy shit, how did I not remember that!?"

"Everything smaller than that is out of our dimensions, and everything bigger than it is out of the base dimension. I think we may have gotten the result we came here for - we just have no idea how to measure it." Travis grabbed his notebook from his bag. "We have to run it again, you see? With the exact same parameters, or else we won't know if it was a fluke."

Jake thought about it. Travis was right. The result was too momentous to ignore, and they couldn't verify if they actually caused the disappearance unless they repeated the exact circumstances of the original incident. They had to control the variables. "I just don't know, man. I get it, for the scientific process, it's the right thing to do, I'm just a little hesitant about doing all this so fast." Jake took a sip of his coffee and stared at the wall blankly. "I ran into Mr. Hachiro yesterday, and I...full on lied about our progress. I don't know why I did it, and I feel like if we lose more berlinite, I'm just digging us in deeper."

Travis gave him a look of solidarity. He poured himself a mug and tried to cool his excitement. He took a few moments to gather his thoughts. "Yeah, that's a weird move, but I get it. I've only seen him a couple times in the three years I've worked there, and he always gives me the creeps. Most other research foundations are just tax write-offs and shit; they're in it for the glory of the discovery. But ol' Hachiro just wants the patents. He's in it for the money, period. And that's hard to trust sometimes."

Jake agreed with him. "Well, at least we're on the same page."

"Well, why don't we compromise? The incident on Friday happened when we hit that exact frequency with the beam. That's when the berlinite reacted, and vanished, right?"

"Yep, that's what I got. Nothing happened at all until we reduced the wavelength to half a picometer."

"So, what if we set the emitter to put out a wave of gamma at that same frequency, but cut the amperage in half? Maybe we'll get more data on what's happening, maybe it won't vanish, or maybe it'll happen slower?"

"So, same frequency, but half the power? Worth a shot, I guess," Jake agreed.

They laid out their plan in detail, Jake taking the time to put every parameter into his holo-tab, making sure that he was backed up in his decision making. Travis spent an hour double checking the recording equipment and making sure everything was still calibrated from Friday. Although he was sure that he was ready to go, Jake insisted on running a dress rehearsal on a sample of platinum first. Jake barely had time to take off the radiation suit and enter the control room before Travis fired the Hulk gun.

They checked the recordings; everything was working perfectly. "Okay, I guess, let's do this," Jake said with nervous excitement. Travis grabbed a pelican case from the storage area, suited up, and brought the sample into the emitter room. He took extra care to make sure it was in the exact same position as Friday's test, he didn't want any extra variables. Once set, he ripped the suit off excitedly and came back to the control room.

"Okay, big guy, give 'er! Let's see what happens this time." Travis spun in his chair to face the monitors. Jake checked the instruments one last time, took a deep breath, and fired the emitter.

A brief hum of electricity was all they heard, just like before. Jake had his eyes closed this time. He looked at the camera monitor after the hum died down. The pedestal was empty, the berlinite had vanished once more.

"Fuck!!!" Jake shouted.

"Wooooooooo! Fuck Yeah!!" Travis yelled. "Ha ha ha, we're on to something here, bud!" He was beaming a grin from ear to ear. He had obviously hoped to repeat the result.

Jake's face was not a grin. It wasn't quite a frown either. It looked more like he had witnessed a bus crash. "Oh Jesus, that's what I was worried about. I really hope we have some data this time, I just fried another twelve grand. We are totally getting fired." He rested his arms on the table and bowed his head into his chest. He took a few deep breaths and closed his eyes. Before he opened them, he felt a large hand on his shoulder.

"Jake, you've really got to keep perspective on this, dude. Yes, that chunk of berlinite we just smoked was worth more than your car, but this could be a big, life changing discovery." Travis was still laughing with excitement as he talked. "In the grand scheme of things, this amount of money is not going to matter, you have to trust me on this. Do you think that when Ben Franklin discovered electricity, he freaked about losing his house keys?"

Jake lifted his head and opened his eyes. Travis was right. They didn't know what they had discovered, but it was worth the lost money. There were no mirrors in that room, no magic hat, no trap doors, no trickery. For the first time in history, a person had genuinely, authentically made an object vanish.

"You're right, man. I know it...you're right," Jake sighed. He took a step back and scanned the monitors around him. "Let's review the footage and particle detectors and see if anything is different from the last time."

They spent the next few hours comparing results from the test to Friday's findings. Jake pored over every detail. Travis suited up in PPE and went to check the pedestal. Again, there was no residue, no dust, no evidence that the berlinite had ever been there. It was fully gone, as before.

The two ate their lunches in the break room and discussed their findings. "The amplitude made no difference" Jake said. "It was still here in one frame and gone in the next. The only difference I can find is..." He motioned for Travis to look at a slide on his holotab display. "There's a miniscule increase in temperature before it disappears. Now, that happened on Friday as well, but the increase today was less, almost undetectable. Other than that, the results were identical." Jake put his tab away and took a bite of his sandwich. "Do we report our findings now? Start writing papers and release findings next year sometime?"

Travis knew that Jake was still stressed about losing the samples, even if he was trying to hide it. "I really don't know what to report yet, man. I think we still need to run more trials."

Jake stared at him. "This is getting awful pricey. Too pricey to run without authorization."

Travis took a second to himself, spooning beef stew into his mouth from a large bowl. "We haven't found the lower energy limit yet. We don't know how much energy it takes at that frequency to, well...Houdini that shit, you know?"

Jake still wavered. "We shouldn't risk another one, man. Not without releasing findings to Hachiro."

"That's gonna take months, though, to get through all the bullshit approvals, and we might get reassigned in the meantime. You can't tell me you're not curious. This was tearing me up all weekend." Travis finished the last spoonful of stew out of his bowl and pulled a fruit roll-up out of his bag. "My emotions are somewhere between excited and downright creeped out. Like, how do you handle this? We genuinely sent that thing somewhere, man, whether it's antimatter now, or in Oz - I don't friggn' know. I'm still having a tough time just getting my head around the magnitude of all this."

Travis' excitement was infectious and despite his cautious exterior Jake did agree. He laughed at the craziness of the situation. "It is pretty nuts. Maybe I'm just stressed about the money and Hachiro because I don't want to admit that we maybe....... sent a piece of our office equipment to another dimension?"

"I'll tell you what, let's see how low we can turn the amperage on that waveform. We'll run it at the lowest power we possibly can. I doubt anything will happen at such low power levels, but maybe we'll get a bit more data off the detectors - maybe just the start of the reaction?"

Jake thought about it for a few minutes. He was indeed curious, even though he was sure that they were proceeding in error. But Travis' idea was sound. He needed more data to try and explain what had happened, otherwise it was all, indeed, a fluke. "Okay, I'm in. We check the settings on the FEHFR, we keep the magic frequency, but we turn the amplitude as low as that thing will possibly go. Hopefully we get something out of it, I don't think it will even register on the particle detectors."

Travis hurriedly cleaned his bowl while Jake packed up his lunch. "It's already 4:30, if we're getting home tonight, we've gotta do this now."

"It can wait til tomorrow, man. There's no rush," Jake replied.

"Fuck that! I don't mind getting home late, let's do this." Travis went to grab the next case of berlinite without waiting for Jake's agreement. Once again, he suited up again in the radiation suit, and brought the sample to place on the pedestal. Realizing that he didn't have a say anymore, Jake modified the emitter's settings. He turned the amperage down as low as it would go, a miniscule fraction of the energy that they had released on Friday. As was routine now, he double checked the instruments and monitors, then waited for Travis to come back in the control room.

"Okay, bud, do the honors." Travis stared intently at the monitors, not at all sure what he was even looking for.

Jake fired the emitter. The hum of electricity was inaudible this time. Travis was locked in a deep focus, like a cat getting ready to pounce on its prey.

If the hum was louder, they may not have heard it. If the air conditioner was on, or the exhaust fans of the computers were blowing, they wouldn't have heard it. But the control room was whisper quiet as they stared at the monitors. That silence was sliced by a metallic sound -not from the emitter, or the computers, or the sample, but there, in the control room behind them.

"*TINK*"

The two spun around in their chairs, and saw, laying by itself on the clean, cement floor, was the piece of berlinite.

Silence hung over the room like a heavy blanket as they stared speechless at the cube of purple metal. The quiet stillness lingered well into the point of awkwardness, until Travis finally lifted his head to look at Jake.

"I think I need a beer."

8.

At a small biker bar in the town of Mission, Jake and Travis sat drinking king cans of Budweiser. They hadn't chosen the venue. The work van had driven them there after Travis asked it to find the closest bar. The air stunk of old liquor-soaked carpets, and every now and then a waft of urinal cake would hit Jake's nose. The furniture was at least fifty years old. Blinking lights gave it a depressing Christmassy glow, though the lights were just emanating from the old pull-tab gambling machines that were hung about the walls. None of that mattered to Travis, he was just happy to have a beer in front of him. Neither one talked, just sipped their cans in deep thought, struggling to explain what they had just seen.

"Okay, dude. Soooo, did that thing really just...teleport?" Travis blurted out finally, in an uncomfortable laugh.

"It's the only way, isn't it? The remaining samples are locked up in pelican cases still, aren't they? Unless you're fucking with me for fun. Which, seriously, screw you if you are…" Jake responded.

"Well, I'm not messing with you, you're not messing with me. It must have…. actually happened. This is shit ass crazy." Travis took a long gulp, and his gaze seemed to disappear into an old, dusty television behind Jake. It was showing a broadcast of the Canucks game.

"So, other researchers have teleported sub-atomic particles. We know that's happened, right? But not to this distance. And our sample is what, a trillion times bigger?"

"This is different, man. That's just a variation of quantum entanglement, isn't it? Nothing in history bigger than the quantum field has ever done what just happened. I have so many questions, my brain is exploding." Travis tilted the can back, shook the last drop into his mouth, and swallowed. "This helps" he said through a burp.

Travis got up, letting out a quiet groan as he straightened his back, and walked over to the bar to get another round.

Even with everything else on his mind, Jake still felt uncomfortable in this redneck bar. He felt like a city slicker who didn't belong. Travis was a natural though. This environment didn't faze him in the least. The bar had only a dozen patrons or so tonight, which was good. He didn't want anyone hearing their conversation, especially the rough looking crowd standing around the other high-topped tables.

Travis returned with another two cans and plunked them down on the sticky table. Jake was only half done the first, but obliged anyway.

"Are we going to address the elephant in the room here?"

"Ummm, aren't we already?" Travis laughed, confused. "We teleported something, I don't think elephants get much bigger than that."

Jake stared at him. "That thing, that sample. From where it began, and where it ended up - it passed through *us*."

Travis put his beer down on the table, wide eyed. "Holy shit, dude, I hadn't thought of that." He thought for a second, then laughed out loud. "So, you're telling me that you penetrated me with your sample?"

Jake laughed. "Real deep, man. Went right through ya."

"Well don't I feel special."

"But seriously, we don't know if that has any health effects, we should be careful."

Travis nodded in agreement. "Do you think that's what happened with the first two that we lost? Did they teleport? We hit them with way more power, maybe they reappeared out in Kelowna or something? Maybe watch the news to see if a kid finds a strange purple rock out there."

They went over their theories for round after round, shot after shot, bouncing ideas off each other as they had in their university days. Jake was happy to have Travis with him, his mind would have been racing all night without Travis' practical focus.

He woke up to Travis nudging his shoulder. It was well past midnight, and the van had driven them all the way back to Vancouver. It was parked in front of his house.

"Oh, sorry man, I feel like I passed out as soon as we hit the highway."

"Yep. Snored too." Travis hadn't slept, he didn't trust the computer enough. "Hey Jake, what do you say we skip the lab tomorrow? Head into Hachiro, make a game plan? I really don't know where to go from here, and I don't think leaving for the lab again in five hours is going to help us any."

"Yeah, that sounds good. Oh, and Travis..." Jake looked at him as he was stepping out of the van. "Let's keep all this quiet, eh? At least until we know what to do."

Travis nodded. He knew. It didn't have to be said.

Jake woke up at his normal time, but with a pounding headache. He made a glass of Gatorade, started the coffee machine, and got in the shower. The water trickling down his forehead helped, and he cycled the temperature from hot to cold to wake himself up. It took several minutes under the torrent of water before his memory kicked in, and he remembered what happened before the bar.

At the office, Jake avoided the break room and walked briskly to his desk. He knew that keeping such a huge discovery secret from his colleagues would be difficult. His strategy would be to hide - to avoid all social interaction until Travis and he knew what they were dealing with.

Jake tried to get some work done, but he wasn't at all productive. In their haste to leave the lab, they hadn't downloaded any of the sensor results or recordings. He just found himself staring blankly at his screen for hours at a time. Finally, one of his long, hungover daydreams was interrupted by a knock at his office door.

Travis looked perfectly fine, as if he had drunk nothing but kale smoothies all night. "Hey bud, how's the head?" he laughed at an uncomfortable volume.

Jake stretched his arms over his head, crinkling his forehead in pain as he did. "Guess I broke my school night rule. Should've called in sick."

Travis nodded, although he was obviously unaffected by their evening. "I don't know about you, but I can't get fuck-all done today. Feel like chicken wings for lunch?"

"Ohhhh, yeah, I could go for that." Jake had a feeling that Travis just wanted to leave the office and needed an excuse to do it. But fries and gravy sounded like the right prescription for him anyways.

They took Travis' truck for a short drive towards the airport. There was a small pub called 'The Flying Beaver' that they both liked, out on the water attached to the seaplane docks. They sat on the patio, overlooking the Fraser River, watching the occasional plane descend through the hazy clouds and plow to a stop on the still water. A propane heater radiated heat down on the table and kept the winter chill away.

"Okay, here's how I see it. I've spent the whole morning thinking about this." Travis stared out over the river. "This is big. This is definitely the biggest discovery you or I will ever make."

"No argument there," Jake agreed.

"I just don't want it taken away from us. That's what's been ringing in my head since that first sample disappeared - I really don't want to lose this. And I feel like Hachiro would take it away from us." Travis kept looking out over the river, avoiding eye contact as he spoke. "You've seen it happen on much smaller stuff than this. One of the juniors starts the project, makes a finding, then it gets passed to the seniors, the exec team files the patent, the sales team goes to work, and boom!" Travis lightly pounded his fist on the table. "Your life's discovery goes to Lockheed Martin."

"We don't know that would happen for sure this time..."

"Remember Martin Krazinski last year? Slaves for years over bullshit research until he makes his big breakthrough - figures out how to halve the energy needed on those new MagLev trains. Reports it properly, files his reports, Hachiro sells the patent on the findings, and suddenly it's gone. And he can't even go to work at CJR to keep going with it. All because he signed that stupid non-comp - just like us! Now he's just waiting at his desk doing boring reports while someone else runs away with his baby."

Jake hadn't heard of Martin's problems, but the situation was familiar. "Yeah, I think Olivia is going through something similar."

"Dude, why do you think you lied to Japanese Lurch the other day? You said it was because you were worried that you lost the expensive berlinite sample. But you know it wasn't. You're worried that he's gonna patent and sell this shit from under us, just like I am, and we're back to doing desk work six months from now."

"There's not much we can do, Trav. We work for him. He pays us. He funds all of this. Hachiro *owns* the research."

"Fuck that! We're not set up to run with this stuff. We're just supposed to pass the puck and head back to the bench while someone else takes it up to the goal." he said angrily. "I hate that shit, and I don't want to pass this one. I guarantee that if we submit our findings this week that berlinite teleportation is sold and gone by January. And we're back at our desks."

Their drinks arrived at the table. Jake had gotten a coffee and an orange juice. Travis had ordered a double shot Caesar, which had a prawn skewer garnished on the top. He ate one of the prawns, took a sip, and looked back out over the river.

"At the end of the day, Jake, he's got our balls in a vice. But the longer we keep this to ourselves, the better."

"And what if it gets out? I can't lose this job, man."

"What, you think they're going to fire the two genius employees who figured out fuckin' teleportation? Not likely."

Jake was reluctant. He thought about it more while they gnawed on their buffalo wings. If they *could* keep working in secret until they had a feasible hypothesis, it opened up a lot more options. "I still don't know, man. How do we keep something that big from getting back to them? Anybody could blab about it. What if I slip up and tell the wrong person?"

"If we're going to do this, we can't tell anyone." Travis put his cutlery down and gave Jake a serious look. "For real. You and I know about this, and no one else. Not your friends, not your grandma - no one. We just keep it to ourselves until we figure out what to do."

"You know I'm bad at lying. Real bad. I grew up Catholic, Trav. Every time you lie you have to add another Hail Mary at confession. I'm fuckin' awful at it."

"You're not lying. You're.... just not telling anyone the truth. Surely baby Jesus is ok with that?"

Jake silently considered the angles. He wasn't convinced, but the prospect of keeping this discovery in their lives was enticing, no doubt. "Well, I'll tell you the worst part of large-scale quantum teleportation...."

Travis shrugged.

"The commute. It's gonna start feeling long."

"How do you feel about grabbing motel rooms out there a few days a week? I think if we keep it cheap, we can expense them?"

It would be great to not spend four hours a day in the van, but Jake's thoughts went immediately to Mia. He stuttered as he tried to respond. Travis cut him off.

"I think that new lady friend would understand. At least I hope she would. Only on weekdays. We'll get so much more done, man."

Jake agreed. It didn't make any sense for the two of them to spend so much time commuting. Every day at the Harrison Lab, it felt like they had to choose between getting their work done and getting home at a reasonable hour. Travis planned to look for accommodation when they returned to the office.

The afternoon went faster. As Jake's hangover weakened, however, his paranoia increased. He didn't open any of the berlinite research on the office computer. He worried about the security cameras, that their progress would be documented somewhere. Travis had considered that as well, but he was sure that no one would bother checking the recordings unless an alarm went off or something was reported missing.

Jake spent the rest of the day puttering with various unrelated tasks, trying not to leave his office unless necessary. He walked to the washroom at one point and had to pass the open door of the executive boardroom. Glancing in, he saw his manager and the sales director talking with Harada Hachiro. Harada's steel gaze met his glance. Jake felt his body seize up, his chest tightening. The ball of stress in his stomach was on fire. He panicked and turned back down the hallway. He began walking faster towards the restroom, almost in a slow jog.

He had to leave the office early. His poker face was pathetic, and the stakes were too high now. This idea was terrible, he'd be found out for sure.

Jake packed up his things from the office and waited until the hallways were quiet. He walked briskly out towards the front lobby. The front doors were in sight, he just had to get to his Camry and drive home, away from inquisitive eyes.

"So, you and Travis are up to no good, I see." Jake froze in terror, hearing a woman's voice behind him.

"It's OK, Jake, your secret's safe with me," Michelle simpered from behind the reception desk.

"Oh Jesus, you scared me," Jake said nervously.

"Go have some Advil and a nap" Michelle assured him. She wore a judgmental smirk. "Never seen you guys show up late before or take such a long lunch. Travis is a bad influence, Jake. Those Saskatchewan boys can drink."

Jake's stomach dropped down from its position on top of his tonsils. He breathed a sigh of relief. "That obvious, eh?"

"Ahhh, you guys work hard, you deserve it. Just don't let Hachiro catch you unshaven and smelling like booze, you know how he is. But I can cover for you if he asks."

Jake tried to imitate Travis' carefree tone. "I owe you one, Michelle."

Jake left the building, started his car and drove away. Once he had gone a few blocks, he pulled over to let his breathing slow and his heart settle down. He would avoid the office from now on, as much as possible. He was terrible at keeping secrets.

9.

Spring in England was a magical time. Everything seemed to be saturated in green. Flowers were blooming, the air was warm, pollen floated through the air, and people were everywhere enjoying the break from a long, rainy winter. Marcela found herself glued to the window of her cab as it drove her through Durham. It seemed to be the most magical sight she had ever seen, as if color was jumping out of the world at her. She was reminded of the first colorized scene in 'The Wizard of Oz', when Dorothy steps out of her black and white house and into a mystical fantasy world.

She had spent half her life in Northern England, but it seemed she had never truly appreciated its beauty until now. Marcela realized that spending the last year in the stark, dead environment of the Atacama Desert had set her bar quite low. Anything green, or alive for that matter, was now the most beautiful sight she could imagine.

The last few months had gone quickly. She'd continued taking readings from Cepheus HD314 each night that she was given the array. She was very nervous about revealing her findings to anyone, just in case she had made an error. She'd gone over every scenario repeatedly, desperately trying to find a mistake. But there was none. Still, Marcela worried - if word got out of her discovery, the world would go mad for it. And if she had made a mistake, she'd be a household name forever - for all the wrong reasons.

Marcela needed advice. She needed to consult someone she trusted, someone who could counsel her on her next steps. So, in combination with a trip to visit her parents, she had come to her alma mater, Durham University. She was too excited to wait. She had stepped off the plane and straight into a cab for the campus. Twenty-two hours of travel was weighing on her, but she shook it off. It was too exciting to see Professor Miles again.

Her cab pulled up to the Ogden Centre building. Marcela pulled her bag from the trunk and released the cab contract on her phone. She had expected things at the university to be different, but it was the exact same as she remembered. It *had* only been five years, and the University was well over two hundred years old at this point.

She walked through the wide halls of the physics building to Dr. Miles' office, but it wasn't her name on the door. Marcela looked up her name in the directory and saw that she had moved across the building. Marcela glanced at the time, hoping that she wouldn't miss her before she left for the day. She walked hurriedly across to the new office and knocked on the door.

"Come in," she heard, behind the frosted glass window.

Marcela opened the door and saw Professor Miles sitting behind an elegant oak desk, with her head tilted down on top of a stack of papers. The desk was an antique, and it was matched with a green incandescent lamp and an antique fountain pen. The scene could have been from a hundred and fifty years prior, had it not been for the large holo-screen projected along the right-hand side of the desktop. Miles lifted her head to see who it was.

"Marcela!" She stood up as soon as she saw. She was an older woman, dressed in jeans and a wool sweater, and wore her graying brown hair in a loose bun. Her running shoes squeaked on the hardwood floor as she ran around the desk to give Marcela a hug.

"It's good to see you, Professor Miles."

"Oh, get off it. I haven't been your teacher in years. It's Priscilla."

"Ok. Priscilla." Somehow, the first time using an authority figure's given name always felt wrong. Like, somehow, it was undeserved. No matter how old she got, it still felt wrong to use any name but 'Professor Miles.'

"Have you moved back? You were in New Mexico, the last I heard?"

"No, I'm just back visiting my parents. But...thought I'd swing in and see you."

"Oh, it's so good to see you" Priscilla smiled.

"I'm actually working out of Chile right now. One of those new dishes in the Andes."

"Fun!" Priscilla walked over to the sideboard cupboard of the office and turned on her kettle. "So few of my students actually go on to work in radio astronomy. It's so refreshing to hear when one of my favorites still is." She opened a ceramic jar on the sideboard. "Tea? I'll make a pot."

"Sure, I'd like that. Yes, the facility in Chile is great - brand-new equipment, nice accommodations. It takes a bit to get used to the thin air, but I've gotten there. This English air feels thick, like pool water now." She blushed a little at being referred to as a favorite.

"You still have family in Chile as well, right?"

"Yes, but I work in such a remote location I don't really see them. May as well be back in the States, really."

"I see, that's a shame."

"And you're still doing well?"

"Oh yes. My husband keeps pressuring me to retire, but I'm not ready. I still feel sharp, I don't see the need. I think he just wants someone to be around, the bugger retired too early."

"You can't retire! What would this place be without you?"

"Thank you, Marcela. I know." She poured the boiled kettle into a teapot, carried it back to the desk, and sat down again. Marcela sat in the opposing chair, considering how best to broach the subject that had brought her halfway across the world.

"I didn't...I didn't just come to visit. I did want to see you about something."

"What is it?" Priscilla asked, noticing the tone in Marcela's voice change.

"I've found something. Something amazing, and I need your advice. I don't know ...what to do. Can I show you?"

Priscilla was intrigued. "Of course," she said, calmingly.

Marcela pulled her holo-tab out of her bag. She set it up on the desk perpendicular to the two of them, found the appropriate file, then increased the screen size so that Priscilla could see properly. "My thesis - what I've been working on..." she struggled to find the words, not knowing where to begin. "I made an algorithm that works with radio telescopes. It can filter out the noise to find extremely weak signals. Intelligent signals. I've used it for years now, in New Mexico, Germany, and now down in Chile. I've been scanning hundreds of systems without much luck. Until a few months ago." She loaded up a frequency profile on the display.

Priscilla cleaned her glasses with a small lens cloth in her desk drawer. She spent a few minutes going over the profile, pinch zooming on sections of the display and scrolling through the data. "Oh my..." she said, reading the data with a look of fierce concentration. "This is incredible, there's so many of them. Where is this?"

"Cepheus 314."

Priscilla looked up the star on her computer. "Interesting, there's no mention of a Goldilocks zoned planet there. Just a couple of gas giants."

"It's never had a detailed survey, though. It's the right solar mass. I bet there's a rocky world in a closer orbit."

"And you're sure? You've eliminated possible errors in detection? Gone through your checklist?"

"For months now, yes. Exhaustingly. The only thing I need now to verify it is a second set of eyes on it, from a different dish. But..." she trailed off.

Priscilla had been standing with excitement, face into the holo-display. She took two cups and poured the teapot carefully into them. "Milk?" she asked.

"Just black, please."

"Shameful" Priscilla joked as she passed her the cup. Marcela accepted it and put it on a coaster in front of her. Priscilla added milk to hers, stirred it slowly with a spoon, then took a sip. The silence of the room was like a lit fuse.

Priscilla was remarkably calm for having just heard about an alien civilization. She always kept a calm demeanor, no matter the circumstance, and usually Marcela had respected her for it. But she needed an answer, even some sort of recognition. She started squirming in her chair as the spoon slowly rotated the cloud of milk through the cup of Yorkshire Gold.

Finally, Priscilla spoke. "So, I take it, you don't know what to do now. If you involve anyone else, you risk these findings getting out before you have the chance to properly analyze them."

"Exactly" Marcela exhaled, relieved to hear her speak again.

"And, if this did get out, the media would hound the story relentlessly. It would be one of the greatest discoveries in the history of mankind. Marcela Reyes, the woman who proved once and for all that we're not alone! And if you were wrong..."

Marcela nodded along eagerly, smiling in recognition.

"If you were wrong, you'd go down in history as either the world's greatest fraud, or an idiot, or both..."

"Thank you. There was such a big part of me that wanted to shout this from the mountaintops. A part that wanted the world to know, that wanted the fame so bad."

"It was very responsible to hold back. You're sitting on a very big secret, my girl."

"You have no idea. You're the first person I've told."

"Well, I'm very flattered." Priscilla changed her gaze back to the frequency profile, clasping her teacup with both hands. "Have you been able to decipher any of the signals? They're so faint, I can't imagine we'll get too much."

"It's not my field of expertise. I can tell that they're using some sort of binary coded data system, but nothing beyond that. To be honest, I don't even know where to begin. How do you get usable data from an alien code? Unless you have a galactic Rosetta Stone kicking around."

"It's true, that will be an incredible challenge. I know someone who could be up for the task, though, one of my students from a long time ago. We can trust him. If anyone can figure out what's in these signals, he can."

"Do you think that's a good idea?"

"If you do. This is yours, Marcela, and I'll go along with whatever you want to do."

"Well, I *don't* know what I want to do! That's why I'm here."

Priscilla took another long sip, leaning back in her chair and looking up at the ceiling, deep in thought. "The way I see it - we don't know what this is yet. We don't know what they are, who they are, what their civilization is, what their motivations are. I don't think the world should know anything about this until we have more answers."

"No? Don't you think the world would be a better place if people knew we weren't alone?"

"No, as a matter of fact, I don't. Not unless we know more about them. Think about how divided the world is now, how tribal we've become. Political and social divides have never been greater. If people only know that this is out there, but not what it is, we throw more petrol on a raging fire. How many people would claim to know what to do next? How many religious zealots would rise from this info? How many con artists? How long until the conspiracy nuts of the world are rising in the streets, claiming to know everything about the aliens?"

"I guess. I hadn't thought about it that way."

"Ambiguity is a dangerous weapon in our world. I hate to say it - but there's just too many fools out there. They deserve to know, of course, but only when we have a better idea of what we're dealing with. I think that now is the time for careful study and analysis, but we *will* have to bring certain people in on it."

"To decode the signals?"

"Yes - then we can start figuring out who they are. What they breathe, what they think, what they build, what they destroy. Only then should this get out." Priscilla paused, deep in thought again. "And I guess we still have a bit of time. Not much, but a bit."

"What do you mean?"

"What if we announced this to the world? What if some of those zealots insisted on trying to contact Cepheus 314?"

"I'm not following, Professor Mi…Priscilla."

Priscilla smiled knowingly. "Have you thought about the distance of your planet? 132 light years…"

Marcela shrugged, confused.

"We only started broadcasting *our* 'intelligent' radio signals into space in the 1930's and 40's. They've been traveling outwards into the universe ever since. So that means…"

"We can see them, but they can't see us" Marcela responded.

"Not yet. Not for another decade or two. Not that they necessarily will, mind you. They may not have a Marcela Reyes working for them with her amazing algorithm."

Marcela smiled. It felt so good to finally have this conversation with someone.

"Who knows what their intentions are, or their ability to gather information? But in twenty years, if they have a telescope as powerful as yours was, and they're pointing it at our system…"

"They'll pick up our radio signals too," said Marcela. She hadn't thought of that angle. In fact, she hadn't considered the radio waves coming from Earth at all.

"Now, I know that I'm fairly new to inter-planetary relations. In fact, I only started working in the field five minutes ago" Priscilla chuckled at her own joke. "There are theoretical pros and cons for contacting alien worlds, no doubt. All I know is, if our two planets will know about each other from now on, throughout the centuries and into the future, these next few years will be the only time when we on Earth have that small advantage. We should use that time to crack their code, if that's even possible."

"So, we should keep this a secret?" Marcela was getting confused again.

"I think that this info doesn't help humanity being out there in public knowledge. The world will tear itself apart, unfortunately. But - it also doesn't help humanity sitting on my desk, with just the two of us knowing it."

"Then - some people will have to be told."

Priscilla nodded, wisely.

"What do you suggest? I'm a little lost."

"I think we should bring it to my old student, Ben. We'll see if he can cipher anything from it. I trust him, he'll carry this to the grave if I ask. He started working for MI6 shortly after he did his Masters here."

"MI6? Seriously?"

"They've been decoding secret signals since the Nazi U-boats were in the channel, love. I can't imagine anyone more suited to the task. And they can keep a secret better than anyone. But don't worry, when we do learn more about the residents of Cepheus 314, whether it's next month or next decade, we'll make sure the world knows that Marcela Reyes discovered them. You deserve that."

Marcela was relieved to share the burden and happy to have somebody with a plan. Somehow, Priscilla seemed to see their path so clearly. She wasn't as sure, though, and was feeling very overwhelmed. "I... I don't even know where to start. It's a lot. Thank you so much Professor Miles."

"Priscilla" she retorted back. "And thank you!"

"For what?"

"For saving me from retirement" she laughed. "Now, have you even celebrated your find yet? Has it really been only you who's seen this?"

"Just me. I only came down from the desert two days ago."

"Well, we have to remedy that, post haste!" Priscilla stood up, powered down the screen on her desk, and grabbed her coat. "Earth's radio waves aren't going to reach them tomorrow. I'm pretty sure I have enough time to take you to the pub."

10.

Jake had spent weeks being mentally drained, but this time he was physically exhausted. Every muscle ached as he walked slowly up the stairs to his door. Jake had only been gone a few days, but something felt different about the apartment, it felt smaller and cozier than it had before. He put his bags down, flopped down on the couch, and didn't leave it again til the following morning.

The Harrison Lab was too small for their experiments. It was too dangerous to teleport the samples from the tiny gamma room, and they were concerned about using the control room within a dangerous range. Travis had come up with the idea of moving the Hulk Gun to the warehouse portion, in order to get more clearance and a safe control distance. Unfortunately, that meant moving all the shelving out of the warehouse, a brutally physical job that had taken the two of them all week. Travis had been keen to work longer, and move the equipment all weekend, but Jake had put a stop to that. He didn't have that limitless energy that his friend did, and he needed the weekend to recharge.

Saturday was beautiful, a sunny break in the depressing drizzle of the week. Mia messaged him to see if he was back in town, and they took a bike ride near Deep Cove. Jake was still quite tired, but the desire to spend time with her far outweighed the exhaustion.

Although the sun was out, the trails were muddy with deep puddles and tire ruts. They were both speckled in thick mud from their hair down to their ankles. Mia laughed in a high-pitched squeal every time she went through a puddle, charging through them with reckless abandon. Jake followed behind, struggling to keep up, and taking extra care to balance in each muddy spot so he didn't go over the bars.

They spent the night at Jake's again. This time, he did the cooking. Mia pried into what was going on at his work, but each time he would steer the conversation away. He had told her that he was working out in the Fraser Valley, but he didn't divulge much else. After the third time inquiring, she gave up.

"What are you hiding?" she smiled.

"I told you, I can't talk about it. The NDA agreement."

"Yeah, that. Sure, Ok."

"I'm sorry Mia, I know I'm acting strange. I just really can't talk about my work right now."

"But it's obviously all you think about."

He dropped his shoulders. She could see that he was frustrated.

"Jake, I know it's all super-secret out there, and it's not my business - I just want to make sure that you're safe. I hope your company is taking good care of you guys. I just find it odd that they have you and Travis working with dangerous equipment in such a remote location. But, if you tell me that you're actually being safe out there on the Manhattan Project, I won't keep digging."

Jake nodded. He knew they weren't being safe, not in the slightest. But he also knew that the risk was worth it. "We're following all the safety rules, just getting into some easy experiments now," he lied.

She gave him a judging smirk. "Jake, you're making the face my nephew makes when he's up to no good. Like when he just finished playing with matches in the garage."

"Up for dessert?" Jake asked, trying desperately to get out of the string of interrogation. It only worked for a few minutes. He could tell that Mia was bothered by his elusiveness. Hell, he was bothered by it. All he could think about was the teleporting sample, he wanted so desperately to tell someone about it. To tell Mia about it. But he knew he couldn't, it wasn't time yet.

The following days at the Harrison lab went quickly. Jake committed himself to doing a deep clean of the new experiment space before they went any further. Travis began examining the hulk gun, trying to find out what was involved in moving it. He started working in the room in his jeans and flannel shirt, until Jake insisted that he wear the protective suit when unplugging a gamma ray emitter. Travis muttered something along the lines of *"okay mom"* and agreed.

Jake was trying to do the impossible - getting the warehouse as clean and dust free as a laboratory space was not an easy task. He swept, vacuumed and mopped repeatedly, but he kept finding more dirt. The building had been lying empty for years and had accumulated a thick layer of dust on every surface. Moving the shelving around had only disturbed it more.

Once Travis had laid out the wiring to the warehouse, including the control cables and the five heavy copper power lines, he asked Jake to help him move the emitter. Jake suited up in protective gear and stepped into the old lab.

"No man. Hell no." He looked at Travis, who was waiting in the room already. "I'm not moving a four-million-dollar piece of equipment with a fridge dolly."

"It's heavy as balls, man. I think it's the only way."

They agreed to find another way. Jake ended up renting an air cushion furniture mover, and they very carefully jacked the machine up onto it. Travis had planned a spot for it, where they could aim at the pedestal, the rays would still dissipate into the mountain behind, and the two would be safe from the control room. Moving it was very stressful, knowing that the machine was worth more than they would make in their lifetime. They very gently placed it in position and spent the afternoon reconnecting the emitter to the control room.

Once they had tested the connections, Travis began explaining his part of the plan to Jake. "Okay, so I've placed three high-def cameras in the lab room, instead of one. We'll be able to triangulate the exact position that the berlinite reappears. Judging by what we saw a few weeks ago, if we emit the exact same beam, from the exact same distance, it should end up somewhere in this area." Travis had marked a square on the floor in painter's tape.

"So that's the 10.7 meters, on a 9.5 degree clockwise angle from the beam?" Jake confirmed. They had measured the exact distance that the cube had teleported 2 weeks earlier, but they didn't know how high off the ground it had re-emerged behind them.

"Yep. And I did some quick math. From the floor to the ceiling of the control room gives us a 22 degree variable on the Z axis. So, it should drop somewhere in the taped lines."

Before turning the emitter on, Jake put on a radiation suit once more. Travis took his coffee to the control room and waited for the signal to turn the system on. The monitors and control computers hummed to life. Jake took the used berlinite sample from its protective case and placed it on the pedestal, taking care to position it to the beam in the same way it had been weeks before. Before removing his helmet, he went to the control room to check in with Travis, who was lining up the crosshairs of the gamma beam on his monitor.

"All good?"

"I think we're good, bud. Looks to be the exact same distance and angle as it was before. Ready to rock!"

Jake took his helmet off and took his seat beside Travis. "We didn't check it with a control sample this time."

"For f….Just shut up and hit the button, will you?"

Jake grimaced, then spun back to his keyboard. He checked the recordings, the high-speed cameras, and the particle detectors one more time. "Okay, here goes nothing!"

He fired the emitter. Travis watched the video monitor in an unblinking stare and smiled in satisfaction as the sample disappeared from the pedestal. He couldn't wait, as soon as the machine powered down, he rushed out to see the berlinite resting in its targeted zone.

But it wasn't there. "Fuck me, did we lose another one!? The settings were exactly the same...."

Jake shook his head, not knowing what to say. He stared at the markings on the floor in frustration for several minutes. "Well, I guess we were wrong? Another twelve grand, friggn' hell." Looking up from the ground, finally, he saw a glimmering cube of purple metal sitting in the opposite corner of the warehouse. "Oh, shit, it's way over there!"

"I don't get it, dude," Travis muttered, walking over to the berlinite. "It went in a completely different direction this time."

"It's really weird, for sure. The distance looks pretty close, maybe we missed something in the calculations?" They triangulated where the cube had reappeared, and it was 10.2 meters away this time. Much higher off the ground as well, and at a completely different angle. Jake took a couple hours to record every detail of the experiment, while Travis grew ever more impatient.

"Okay, I know it's dangerous - and we can't fully guarantee it won't jump into the control room. But I *need* to run it again. Pretty sure it'll drop into this new spot - I'll replicate the conditions."

Jake agreed to fire the emitter at the cube again. The two watched the cameras from the control room, waiting for it to appear where it had an hour earlier. It didn't. The two walked out to the warehouse once the hulk gun had powered down, and found it in a new corner of the warehouse. Jake and Travis stared at it in confusion, wondering what to do next.

Once again, they checked the footage and triangulated the distance. 10.4 meters, and at an entirely new angle. They ran it again and found that the berlinite moved to a fourth location, and had traveled 10.5 meters this time.

"There's gotta be a pattern here, but I sure as shit don't see it," Travis muttered.

"I have no idea. It doesn't make any sense. I don't understand how it could be this random. This isn't much use to anyone if we can't predict where the damn thing will end up."

Admitting defeat for the day, they packed up and retreated to the hotel.

11.

Mia felt uncomfortable. She didn't dress up much, and she always felt a bit like an imposter when she did. Jake had certainly been impressed when he picked her up that evening, he was stammering awkwardly for a while. Glancing around at the assembled guests in the Fairmont Ballroom, she knew she certainly wasn't underdressed, it was a swanky affair. But she was still uncomfortable.

Maybe if she had been given more warning. Jake had invited her to this event only four days earlier. But that was Jake - he was just a lovable, oblivious idiot sometimes. Just because he could spend a half hour renting a tuxedo and combing his hair, he assumed it would be that easy for her to prepare. She felt that men sometimes assumed that all women had a closet of formal gowns to choose from. But that wasn't the case. And now, the stress of finding evening wear on top of navigating the social complexities of a formal office party had made her irritable. But when she turned and looked at Jake, she was just happy to be there with him. He had cleaned up nicely, although he looked just as uncomfortable as Mia felt. It was nice to finally see him in something other than jeans. He wasn't looking back at her, however. He was sitting at attention, listening to every word that Mr. Hachiro was saying up at the podium.

In fact, everyone at their table looked uncomfortable. No one dared take a sip of wine or look away from the podium in any way. The speech had gone on uncomfortably long, in Harada Hachiro's deep, unexciting, monotone voice. They were sitting at a round table near the back entrance of the Fairmont's ballroom. The plate ware, cutlery and linens had all been upgraded from the hotel's normal stock. The room was decorated with white and red flowers, ice sculptures and even holographic snow floating down from the ceiling. Hachiro spared no expense on the annual Christmas party.

Their table had three other couples at it. Sharon from accounting sat across from them with her husband. Ermanno from marketing was to their right with his girlfriend, and Camilla from research was on his left with her wife. They were all intently listening to the speech - or at least pretending to as much as Jake was. She had been told about the company's notorious and unpredictable owner. The whole room was obviously terrified of this man. Harada was droning on about the following year's forecasts, the new satellite office in Kyoto, and the success of several projects over the year. He listed all of the research projects currently in progress, of which there were over a dozen, ranging from battery technology to surgical materials to acoustic temperature conditioning.

Mia gave his knee a gentle nudge under the table. 'Which one is yours, he didn't say anything about Harrison?' she whispered at him. He shook his head, trying to convey *'don't worry about it'*. It was a strange dismissal. And there was something behind his eyes that she had trouble placing - it looked a lot like fear.

The speech finally ended, and the band started up, filling the room with upbeat jazz. "Well, if that was any longer, I think it may have stretched into next year's Christmas party," Ermanno joked, leaning over the table to ensure his voice didn't carry.

"As long as he's footing the bar bill, he can talk as long as he wants," Camilla replied. The servers were unleashed into the room like a line of lemmings, bringing salads and appetizers to each table. Jake leaned to one side to let them reach a plate through, but it wasn't a server that was behind him. "Buy you a drink?" Travis said. He was in a rental tuxedo, just like Jake, but he was unshaven and badly needed a haircut.

"Ummmm, sure." Jake quickly got up to go with him, and they hurried away before Mia could say anything. Jake was normally well mannered, and it was very unusual that he didn't invite her or excuse himself. In fact, he seemed to have completely forgotten that she was there.

"Thanks for leaving me with a group of strangers" thought Mia. For the first time in their relationship, she felt sidelined. She was just a piece of arm candy tonight, not his partner.

The rest of the table was talking about the various projects that were mentioned in the speech. Mia wasn't listening to them at all, though, she was still watching Jake. He walked briskly across the room to catch up to Travis. She could tell from his body language that it wasn't a social drink - something was up. She strained her eyes, trying to discreetly watch the interaction from her seat.

Jake and Travis were talking near the bar, but it didn't look like they were laughing or having fun. It looked more like a quieted argument. Mia wished that she could read lips. After 10 minutes Jake hurried back to the table and donned a fake smile as he sat down to his salad. "Everything OK?" she whispered at him. He smiled and dismissed the question again, placing his napkin in his lap and looking across the table away from her.

Sharon was trying to steer the table's conversation away from work talk as her husband looked quite bored. Mia sympathized. They talked about weather, politics, and the Martian Twelve for a few minutes, before the group inevitably returned to shop talk once more. "So, Jake, haven't seen you at the office for a while now, are you on the road?" Ermanno asked.

"Oh yeah, you guys are out using that weird Harrison place, right?" Camilla said through a slurp of soup. "Haven't seen any green monsters terrorizing Chilliwack, so you must be using the gamma rays properly."

"Mostly. Just a heads-up though, try not to make Travis angry tonight. You won't like him when he's angry" Jake joked.

Mia was intrigued by the casual nature of the exchange. Jake and Travis had been extremely secretive around her. She had even driven out to Harrison Hot Springs to see them, and they hadn't let a single detail slip. Even the fact they were working with gamma rays was news to her. But now Jake was talking about it openly and loudly, in the middle of the Fairmont Ballroom?

"How is it going out there anyway? You're working with that new German alloy, right? Anything fun come up yet?"

"Nah, pretty standard, no different than I was expecting. Maybe one day we'll find something worth a continuing study, but nothing fun so far." Jake took a long sip of the red wine glass in front of him. "How's your new hydrogen cell coming? Feels like half the company's working on that." Jake smoothly changed the subject and listened to Camilla give an update, and laughed when she complained about her coworkers.

Mia looked at him again, trying to figure out what the hell was happening. Jake had spent the last two months obsessing over his experiment. He returned to the results on his holo-tab at every opportunity; she had once woken up in the middle of the night to find him poring over it. He was constantly tired, and it seemed that Travis and Jake were both stressed out. She admittedly hadn't known Jake for a long time, but this did not seem like the behavior of a man who had found 'nothing'.

She had thought that he was simply keeping her out of the loop because of his non-disclosure agreement, or, as much as she hated to admit it, because the experiments were too complex to explain to her. But he had just dismissed his work to another researcher. Everyone else at the company seemed to talk openly about their projects with their partners, and there was no mention of NDA's.

The way he'd been acting - he was obviously on to something, but he avoided any talk of it. Something else was going on with Jake. And he was getting much better at lying. Mia knew how to spot a liar.

Dinner went by uneventfully. Mia couldn't shake the bad feeling, though. Every time she looked over at Jake she saw only questions, and a larger question started to form in her mind about their future together.

As the desserts were being cleared and the band increased volume, she decided she had to leave. Maybe she was overreacting, but she wasn't going to get over this anxiety and suspicion, at least not tonight.

"I'm sorry, Jake, I'm really not feeling well. I think I'm going to get going." Mia leaned over and talked into his ear to overpower the music.

"Oh, I'm sorry - let me take you home." Jake gave her an authentic look of concern.

"It's OK, it's your party - you should stay and have fun."

"I have more fun with you."

Mia mustered a smile, despite the obvious secrets and lies. He was still Jake. "I insist. You stay and have fun, I'll talk with you tomorrow, OK?"

With that, Mia exited the ballroom and retrieved her coat from the coat check. She summoned her car to pick her up at the lobby.

Questions still bugged her all night, and she didn't sleep much. Why was she the only one who didn't know the truth? Was he lying to everyone?

After breakfast she went for a run in Queen Elizabeth Park. Exercise usually cleared her head, but she couldn't shake the odd feeling today. Mia knew she was crazy about Jake, and she loved spending time with him. She liked his awkward shyness, and how it turned to absolute confidence when he was talking about his passions. He might not think it about himself, but he was fun and funny. He was a great person, and he was great for her - but she absolutely couldn't deal with dishonesty.

It had been two years since her breakup with Seth. Seth had been fun and funny too, but he had also been a pathological liar - it was an unfortunate fact that Mia didn't realize until it was too late. The problem with dating a compulsive liar was the seismic scale of the eventual heartbreak. Little lies had eventually led to big ones, to infidelity, and to misery. Their breakup had been brutally hard on her. She lost a partner, an apartment, a way of life. After picking up the pieces of her life, she made a resolution. She wouldn't deal with dishonesty, in any fashion, from anyone.

Mia thought she had put that phase of her life firmly behind her, and meeting Jake had felt like a fresh start, but maybe she was just repeating the same mistakes. Maybe Jake's work really *was* so important he couldn't share it with anybody, but Mia doubted it. The question was, was she comfortable committing her whole self to a relationship when the other person kept such a large part of themselves secret?

She returned home and showered. The cool water brought clarity. She wasn't ready to give up on Jake, they had something special - she knew that. But that didn't mean she would accept being lied to either. Not again. It was time to address it. She picked up her phone to text him.

"*Sorry for leaving early last night.*"

"*That's totally OK :) Are you feeling better?*"

His instant reply made her smile. "*Much. Just needed a good sleep. Hey, I was thinking of getting out for a backcountry ski day tomorrow. It's going to be a bluebird day up in the mountains. Wanna come?*"

A few minutes passed. She pondered what the delay was. "*Sure, I guess. But I haven't been since high school.*"

"*I'll take you on an easy one. Go rent some gear, I'll pick you up at your place bright and early tomorrow morning.*"

Jake had been so fearful of Mr. Hachiro and of all the prying ears that were around him at that party. Perhaps, if she got him alone, in the middle of nowhere, the real truth would come out.

12.

Jake was already waiting on the sidewalk by quarter to six the next morning. He knew that something was definitely off on Friday night. Even if she hadn't said anything, she was upset with him, he could feel it. He didn't want to risk anything else upsetting her further, even something small like waiting for him to come downstairs

    Mia pulled up at 6am, on the dot. He loaded up his skis in the back, grabbed his coffee and got in the passenger seat. She smiled at him, and their talk was surprisingly friendly as the car drove through Vancouver.

    The traffic was very light at that time of day, and soon they had crossed the bridge over Burrard Inlet and were making their way towards Squamish. Jake looked out the windows, trying to remember the last time he'd been out of the city, or up into the mountains. He loved to drive up the Sea to Sky highway, although it was still dark at this time, and they couldn't see much past the headlights.

    As they headed north, Mia explained the plan for the day. She took her time, describing in detail what the distances were, the potential hazards, and the weather they could expect. They were heading up into an area near Garibaldi Park, where the snow had fallen deep earlier in the season. Jake started feeling more comfortable about the plan, but even more worried about his skill level. He had only been ski touring twice in his life, when he still lived in northern BC. He may have exaggerated his experience a bit in conversation with Mia, and he was sure he would be found out soon.

Mia took control of her self-driving car as they left the highway. They started driving up through a thick forest of cedars and hemlock. The gravel road was hazed in a mist that nearly concealed the large ferns lining the sides. As they climbed, the wet rainforest started getting a light coating of snow and ice. The higher they drove, the deeper the snow got. When they reached the trailhead, the snowbanks around the car were as tall as houses. It wasn't quite daylight yet; the sky was a milky gray and the stars were disappearing. They could just barely see their surroundings.

Mia hopped out of the car and started putting her boots on. Jake fiddled with his equipment first, struggling to get the climbing skins to clip on to his rental skis. By the time he had figured out that first step, Mia was standing beside him, ready to go. He still hadn't prepped his avalanche gear, packed his bag, or put on his ski boots. She smiled and offered to help.

Mia wore her same bright yellow shell jacket, but with black waterproof bib pants and a bright blue toque. Jake looked at how prepared and professional she looked, compared to his old, ripped hiking backpack and green fishing jacket. "So, you must do this a lot? You sure look the part," he commented.

"I used to, for sure. I don't get out nearly as much these days, but I do really love it."

Mia helped him with the rest of his preparation and showed him how his ski bindings worked. They checked their avalanche beacons and the rest of their safety gear. Once they were finally ready to leave the parking lot, the morning sun was glowing behind the mountains to the east.

Mia skinned comfortably up the track in front of Jake. They kept a conversation going while the trail stayed flat. Jake made a lot of jokes at his own expense, as he clacked his bindings awkwardly through the trees. Soon the track turned uphill, and they began ascending steeply up the cedar forest.

Jake realized he had overestimated his fitness as well. Soon he was wheezing and sweating trying to keep up with her. He took off his jacket and tried to stuff it in the top of his pack. He hadn't left enough room, so he found a way to clip it to the outside and started running up the trail again after Mia. She was comfortably striding along up the trail, not a bead of sweat on her.

After an hour, the trees started to thin. As they made their way through the subalpine fir, the sun finally rose above the mountains and bathed their route in a friendly yellow light. Jake turned around for the first time and enjoyed the view. Each switchback revealed more of the coast mountain range around them, and he found his motivation to keep moving, to try and keep up with Mia.

Eventually, the two were skinning through an alpine bowl, making their way to a col between two jagged peaks. "See that?" Mia asked him, pointing her ski pole at the pass. "That's our turnaround, that's where we'll have lunch." She took a swig out of her water bottle. "How are you feeling?"

"Awesome!" Jake lied. He could barely see her, his eyes stung with the salty sweat pouring off his brow. She laughed and flung her left ski into a kick turn, continuing her ascent. Jake tried to delay the look of pain on his face until she was safely turned away from him.

By lunchtime, they were on their final push to the col. Mia saw the end in sight and started skinning faster, leaving Jake huffing up the slope behind her like a hot bulldog. By the time he crested the final rise, she was comfortably seated at the top of the pass, bundled up in a down jacket and getting supplies out of her pack. Jake looked at the view down the far side for the first time. They were far above the cedar forests, the rolling mountains, the fjords, lakes and rivers of British Columbia.

"Wow," he exclaimed, keeled over and leaning on his ski poles, trying to catch his breath.

"Quite the spot, huh?"

"I need to do this more." Jake finally admitted his exhaustion. "I'm ummm...I'm fuckin' wiped."

"You did good, Jake. This is a big one." She stood up, squeezed him in a hug and gave him a kiss on the cheek. She didn't seem to care that he was a sweaty mess.

The wind was low, and the sun beaming down on them was warm. They relaxed, leaned back on their packs, and ate their lunches. Mia took out a small stove and boiled some snow into tea for them. For a while, they sat in silence, enjoying the serenity of the mountains.

"So, Jake... We have a problem." Mia broke the silence and the warm comfort of the moment. She had worked herself up to this conversation, she had planned this as the spot to have it.

Jake didn't say anything, just gave her a scared and confused look.

"I like you," Mia continued. "I know it's only been a few months, but I really like you. You're super smart, you're funny. I think we're so great for each other, and I love spending time with you, but...."

"But what?" Jake asked. His sense had been right. There was something off. Had she brought him all the way up a mountain to break up with him? That didn't seem right.

"We're not being honest with each other. And that's OK for a couple dates, maybe some fooling around, you know? It's okay to have secrets from each other early on. But I can't keep going forward with this, Jake. I can't keep dating someone unless I know we're totally truthful with each other."

Jake nodded. He was sick of lying, but knew it was necessary. "I...." he stammered.

"I'll go first" Mia cut him off. "We're both at an age where you deserve to know this.... I don't want kids." Mia paused to let the comment sit. "I've never wanted them, I can't see myself as a mother, and I don't think it's a necessary part of my life. I usually don't tell that to guys I'm dating because I don't want it to be a problem; I don't want it to scare anyone off." She paused to think about what to say next. "But there it is, it's out there. And before we get any more serious with each other, I need you to be okay with that, so that you're not surprised by it down the road."

Jake nodded in agreement. "I get that, yep. And, yes, I feel the same." He knew that wasn't why they were up there, however, there was definitely something more. "Was that all you wanted to tell me?"

Mia took a sip of her tea. She wasn't looking at him anymore, rather she was staring off down the valley, lost in her thoughts. "I had a serious boyfriend a few years ago. We lived together. I thought we were gonna get married, the whole nine yards, you know?"

Jake nodded, scared to say anything in reply yet.

"I was naive. I took everything Seth said as his word. But as time went on, the truth started cracking apart. He lied about so many things, Jake. Not just who he was with, but his finances, his career - everything. One lie led to another, and to another, and when the web finally broke apart it was really painful for me. My whole life fell apart."

Jake said nothing, he just looked at her, seeing a beautiful, tough and yet vulnerable person. It was rare that Mia would show a weakness to him.

"Seth was cheating on me the whole time we were together. I can't look back at a single thing that he told me without questioning his motives. He broke my heart, and I can't go through that again. I can't deal with people lying to me, every lie makes me wonder if anything they tell me is the truth." Mia was still staring off into the distance, but she returned her gaze to him and made eye contact once more. "I know you haven't told me what you're doing out there with Travis. I know you've signed things with your work that make that impossible. I thought maybe I wouldn't understand it, or it would go over my head. And I was okay with that, I know that an NDA is serious. I accept that you may have to keep certain things from me. But you're also lying to your company and your coworkers, Jake - you made that obvious on Friday. Which tells me, basically, that you're full of shit."

Jake looked at his boots, fiddling with a buckle in anxiousness. "I may be keeping certain things secret, I guess."

"It's a lot, Jake. I don't know what it is, but you're holding back a lot from me. And I won't date someone who keeps things from me. Never again. I know that might not be fair to you, but it's what I have to do. Maybe it's just my weird insecurities that have brought us to this point, but I need to address it before we go any further." Mia paused, turning back to look him in the eyes. "So, I brought you up here today. There's no one around us for miles, our phones are turned off. It's just, you, me, and the mountains. And I'll give you this choice." Mia took another sip of her tea. "Either you can tell me what's going on, and we can share that secret, or we can just….be friends going forward. And that's okay as well, if that's what you want. I really like being with you, Jake, even if we're just friends. It might not seem fair to make you choose, but I just…. I can't be in a relationship with secrets. Never again."

Jake was taken aback. He knew he was bad at lying, he just hadn't realized how it was affecting her. He took a deep breath, and sighed it out slowly, staring down at the waters of Howe Sound in the distance. It would feel so good to tell her everything, regardless of whether it was the right choice. "I never thought that hiding what I'm working on would hurt you, Mia. That was not my intention, and to be honest, it wasn't really even on my radar."

Mia looked at him with compassion, not anger. "I know it's not that you've *intentionally* hurt me, Jake."

"Okay, well…where to begin?" he sighed.

Mia grabbed his hand. "If you want to tell me, start at the top. But again, you don't have to…"

Jake thought for a few seconds, then started. "So, you met Travis? A few months ago, he and I got permission to experiment with a new alloy. It's crazy stuff. It reacts strangely to all forms of radiation. Some of the radiation is reflected, some is absorbed - just like everything else in nature. But with this stuff, a portion of the energy just disappears."

Mia nodded, happy that he was finally ready to open up, but trying her best to follow along as well.

"Different scientists are using it to play with invisibility, or cloaking planes from radar systems. But I had a different theory about the alloy, and about what was causing the strange tendencies. I started wondering if the disappearing energy had anything to do with the 'base dimension'. Like, maybe the disappearing energy is vibrating its way into that smaller dimension, somehow transferring away from ours.

"We needed to see what happened if we hit it with very small wavelengths of energy, smaller than an atom. Wavelengths small enough to vibrate the alloy at a quantum level. Gamma rays. We needed to get samples of this alloy, berlinite, and hit it with gamma radiation to test our theories."

"Ohhhh kay. So that's why you're in that Harrison lab, way out in the sticks."

"Yeah, for safety reasons we can only fire the gamma emitter out there. Travis booked that facility from the university, and I convinced my company to spend a small fortune on samples of berlinite. Anyways - we keep increasing the frequency of the rays that we're hitting this shit with. We were trying to see what happens to gamma radiation when it bounces off berlinite, to get readings of energy variations. We keep increasing the frequency, and get nothing for results, until suddenly - the sample itself vanished. The cube of metal didn't disintegrate, it didn't vaporize. It just, simply - vanished from existence."

"So, that was your 'unexpected result' you talked about way back in October? When I came over and you were all stressed."

"Well, yeah, but believe it or not, it gets crazier. First, I lied to my company's owner about the results right after they happened. I'd been stressed because we lost a couple samples doing this, and each of the cubes of berlinite is worth about twelve grand. I wanted to report our findings before we went any further. But Travis wanted to keep going until we could measure the reaction, or at least figure out what happened. He convinced me to lower the power of the beam as much as I could, and we hit another sample. And..."

"And?" Mia was absorbed.

"It reappeared in a different part of the lab, behind us. We fuckin' teleported it." Jake paused, taking a bite of the chocolate bar from his pocket. It felt good to tell someone besides Travis. "We've transported dozens of these samples through the warehouse now. Travis and I are the first people ever to - teleport something," Jake laughed. He looked at her sideways trying to gauge her reaction. Did she believe him?

"Holy shit" Mia responded. "That's...wow." She took a minute to absorb what he was saying, it didn't sound believable. "So, would that fancy ray-gun work on anything? I can't help but think of Charlie and the Chocolate Factory, and that cowboy kid who gets teleported."

"No, it needs to be this berlinite stuff."

"Do you know why?"

Jake paused, trying to think how to explain it. "Do you know how a microwave oven works?"

"To be honest, I've never really thought about it. My grandma thinks they're evil, though, she won't use them."

"Well, there's an exact frequency of microwave radiation that interacts with the H_2O molecule. With water. It vibrates the water molecules when it hits them - only the water molecules, and the friction of those molecules vibrating at a tiny level cooks the food. That's why your food gets hot, but not the plate."

"Ohhhhh, huh. Never knew that. So, you think this is the same?"

"We think a similar thing happens with berlinite. It has a distinct molecular structure that interacts with radiation in weird ways. But, when that magic, exact frequency of gamma radiation hits it, it vibrates."

"Just like the microwave oven, then."

"Except that the microwaves reheating your lasagna have a wavelength of about twelve centimeters. The gamma rays we're using have wavelengths smaller than an atom. Which means that when the berlinite vibrates, it's such a small movement that it would happen both in our dimension and the base dimension. Aaaannnd - crazy shit happens, I guess. We just haven't figured out exactly what's happening."

"Whoa. That's heavy stuff." Mia searched in her pack and produced a small flask of whiskey, took a long sip, then passed it to Jake. "That's insane! Okay, but two questions. First, why aren't you telling your company about this? Wouldn't you guys be, like, the heroes of Hachiro Industries?"

"For a couple weeks, yep. But then we'd lose our chance to work with it. Our company just fishes for patents and sells them. We make decent money, but it's not…." Jake took a second to collect his thoughts, still unsure of his decision to disclose all this to her. "Every time someone makes a big discovery, they sell the research. And because we have a very strong non-compete clause in our contracts…"

"You and Travis would be cut out from the biggest discovery you ever made" Mia said. "Are you sure that's what would happen? You're taking a huge risk. I mean, Jesus, if you got caught hiding something of that magnitude…"

Jake nodded. "We've seen it happen before. We've seen our colleagues lose their big finds. I mean, it was Travis' idea to hide our work, and I wasn't quite sure about the decision, but I went along with it."

"Second question. And I say this as your friend, but also as a health and safety professional - what happens if that sample of this magic alloy reappears inside you? You could die, Jake."

"Yeah, we did think about that. Well, *I* did. We've made a lot of changes in the lab to compensate, but it's not a hundred percent safe, really. We remodeled the whole lab, moved multi-million-dollar equipment, all without telling Hachiro or the University anything at all about this. None of what we're doing would pass a health and safety inspection though, for sure," he laughed.

Mia gave him a judgmental stare, which melted into a smirk. "Just be careful, *please*. None of this will matter if you're dead next month."

"We're taking precautions. As much as we can."

Mia stared blankly ahead. "That's all...crazy!" She started laughing, thinking more about what she had just heard. The sound of her laugh filled Jake with relief. "I just thought you guys were stealing office equipment or something. I didn't realize you were sitting on..."

"Maybe the biggest scientific discovery of the last hundred years, yeah." Jake cut in. He was relaxed again, leaning back and absorbing the sunshine. He smiled and closed his eyes, and took a swig of whiskey out of her flask. It felt amazing to finally tell someone.

Mia put her hand on his. "Thank you for telling me, Jake. I could tell how much it's been weighing on you. I'm sorry for pressuring you. At least you don't have to lie to me anymore, even though I guess you're still lying to everyone else. And I won't tell a soul, I promise."

"Yes, please don't." Jake replied.

"What's your guys' plan, anyway? What do you do now? Where do you go from here?"

"I honestly don't know. We thought we had it figured out, but we really don't. So far, the technology is cool, but it's useless."

"How so?"

"The berlinite moves in random directions. We can't figure out how to predict where it's going to end up. It always moves a distance between 10.1 meters and 11 meters away from where it started, but we can't predict what that distance will be. Or which direction it will choose to move in. We've hit the same sample with the exact same amplitude and frequency 89 times now, and have gotten it to reappear in 88 different locations. We lost one, and I can only assume that it reappeared somewhere in the bedrock below the lab. So, there's twelve grand down there somewhere, I guess, if someone wants to dig for it. Another sample went straight vertical, and we had to pick it off the roof."

"So, there's no pattern to it?"

"Not that we can figure out. We've been at it for over a month. We've both been working crazy hours checking every equation, every recording, trying to figure it out. And we can't. There's simply no way to predict which direction it's going to move in."

"Weird."

"Yeah, and teleportation is cool, but it would be a lot more useful if you knew where you'd end up," Jake laughed. "It's almost as if the berlinite is acting like a subatomic particle, we can only predict a range of where it will be. But, shit, that can't be it either, the math just doesn't support it."

Mia looked at Jake again. "So, you won't tell anyone or make a plan until you figure that out?"

"We're going to try for a bit longer, but we'll have to file reports eventually. We both wanted to be the ones to solve the mystery of it, but it just - may not be in the cards. And without a functional theory, it's just playing with science. We may as well turn it over to someone else if we can't solve it. As much as I would like to be the one who did. If we can't figure it out in the next few weeks, we'll report all the research to Hachiro. And they'll most likely sell it, and who knows, maybe fire us for hiding the results as long as we did."

The sun went behind a cloud. They could see the shadow sweeping up the snowfield towards them. Mia's mind started to move to the practicality of the ski descent. She got up and took Jake's sunglasses off before she kissed him. "You're amazing, Jacob Crawford. I'm pretty friggn' into you. And I'm sure you'll figure it out."

"Thank you" he replied, shyly. "I'm so sorry if I hurt you, I really hated all the lying. I won't keep anything from you anymore. And - I'm pretty into you too, Mia."

"You promise?"

Jake looked up at her as a light breeze kicked granules of snow between them. "I promise." He held up his fingers like a boy scout. "No more lies, I'll let you know everything." He looked around at the white peaks and their long track up the mountain side. "Look, we'll probably have to own up to all of it soon anyway, and I hope we don't get in too much shit. I just can't figure out the pattern of movement."

Mia smiled. "Well, I'm about as good with physics as you are with chopsticks. So, I don't think I'm the person to help you with it."

"It just helps to tell someone, really."

"But - maybe you just need to change the way you look at it, like, maybe you're too close to it. Remember a few weeks ago when we ate those weed gummies? And you rambled on about the theory of relativity for hours?"

"Oh god...barely" Jake said, embarrassed.

"Well, I was pretty high, I didn't get most of it. But you kept going on and on about how I have to change the way I think about things. That speed or space isn't the variable in the equation - blah, blah, blah," she said in a mocking, nerdy impression of Jake.

"Yeah?"

"How sure are you that you're looking at the right variable? Maybe you just need to change the way you think about it."

"Huh...." Jake replied, eyes glazed in deep thought.

"Anyways, we've gotta get going." Mia started packing up the stove and peeling the skins off of her skis. "It's a long ski down to the car, and you can't teleport there, yet. You just have to try to keep up." Jake laughed and started packing up, happy to leave the conversation behind.

They skied one at a time down the alpine bowl, both feeling relaxed and free beneath the wide-open sky. They descended towards the heavy cedar forest and home.

Jake didn't reveal to Travis what he had told Mia. He knew that Travis would disapprove. The car ride to Harrison the following morning was quiet, and his mind kept returning to what she had said about changing the variable. What could be changing each time they fired the hulk gun? The parameters were all exactly the same each time, what could be different?

Suddenly, it struck him. "Holy shit...." he muttered under his breath. Travis had his toque pulled down over his eyes and his headphones in, reclined beside him. Jake got his holotab out and started furiously entering different angles and equations. "Could that be it? It's so simple," he muttered again. He didn't want to get Travis' hopes up, so he let him sleep while he worked. They pulled into the lab just after ten.

Jake walked straight to the emitter. He found the mark on the floor signifying where Friday's berlinite had fallen. Travis watched him run excitedly around the room, thoroughly confused as to what was going on. Jake took out his holotab, grabbed the laser measure, and did a bit of math in his notebook. He checked the positions from the last few experiments as well, plugging the math into his holotab. The pattern began to emerge, finally. Travis watched his friend scurry about, muttering things under his breath while he excitedly scribbled.

Finally, with confidence, Jake strode across the warehouse, measured once more, and marked an 'X' on the floor in masking tape.

"I think I've got it. I'm Babe Ruth'ing this shit, bud! I'm callin' it right here!" Jake shouted across the lab, excited.

"What are you up to, man? Are you gonna let me in on your psychosis this morning?" Travis yelled back.

"If I'm right!"

Jake ran and got the radiation suit on, Travis headed more slowly to the control room with his coffee. After he had lined up the sample, Jake returned to the control room. "Okay, ready to fire?" Travis asked.

"No, not yet," Jake responded. "It's 11:12, we need to fire it at exactly 11:20."

"Umm, ok, sure," Travis chuckled. He was very curious, but he didn't pry. They waited another eight minutes, while Jake double checked every instrument one final time. At 11:20, Travis fired the hulk gun. Jake had his eyes closed and his fingers crossed.

As soon as the unit powered down, the two ran out to the warehouse. The sight waiting for them was beautiful. Jake threw his hands in the air and screamed in exhilaration.

The cube of berlinite had fallen exactly where Jake had predicted, a beautiful shimmering purple pebble sitting on an 'X' of masking tape. "Okay, man...H-how?" Travis was speechless.

Jake relished in the satisfaction of the moment. "We've been looking at it all wrong. I lined up my equations with where the earth would be oriented at this exact time and date. I had to figure out the different trajectory of each experiment we've done, cross referenced with when we did them. But I was right! Holy shit, I was right!"

Travis was still trying to figure it out. He didn't say anything, just looked at Jake and shrugged his shoulders. "Ummmm...what?" he laughed again, thoroughly confused.

"It's not teleporting. The berlinite isn't moving through space at all!" Jake said. "It's moving through time."

13.

Dylan yanked his hand back from the fish hook. He had hastily pushed it through the bait and rammed the pointy end into his thumb in the process. He looked at the end of his thumb and saw a small globe of red forming in the middle. "Shit" he muttered as he stuck it in his mouth, sucking on it like a toddler in a crib.

Not letting the throbbing pain in his thumb stop him, he cast his line behind the boat, let out a few hundred feet and stuck it in the rod holder. "Computer, increase speed to 7.5 knots," Dylan said loudly, grabbing his coffee and sitting back down in a white leather armchair. He faced backwards, keeping an eye on the rod tip and waiting to hear the joyful 'spreeeee' of the reel unspooling if he got a hit. Seven knots was too fast for most fish in this zone, but since he only had a couple hours today, he'd have to be back in his office for a meeting by 9:30. Why not go for a big one?

The sun was just beginning to crest over the horizon, igniting a thousand glittering diamonds of light in the gentle waves. This part of the Caribbean stayed very calm in the morning, as if the world itself was still yawning and waking up. Dylan pulled his sunglasses down off of his faded baseball cap and put them on. He rested his feet up on the transom and enjoyed the moment, trusting completely that the boat's autopilot would keep him on course. The electric motors were almost inaudible, the only sound was the swish of the thirty-foot flybridge boat moving through the still water.

It wasn't that he couldn't afford a pilot for the boat. Or a seasoned fishing guide. Dylan could pay for a thousand fully staffed boats and barely notice the expense. The auto-captained electric boat gave him something that was much harder to find in his life. Solitude. The Planet 9 campus kept him very busy, and there was nowhere to hide from his staff and supporters. The only option for privacy was the open ocean. Dylan made a point to leave all of his communication devices behind every time, taking only an SOS beacon. He didn't chart where he would be going or tell anyone when he'd be back - he just wanted the occasional morning completely to himself. That did mean waking up at 4 am, unfortunately.

The warm sun was hitting his face now. He closed his eyes and leaned his head back. As the relaxation took hold, he almost fell asleep when the reel suddenly sung out in a high-pitched squeal. Dylan shot up to his feet, grabbed it with both hands, braced his feet and set the hook. He could feel the fish fighting back. He let it have more line, and the reel spun out as it swam away from the boat. "Computer, two knots!" he yelled, and the boat slowed down to crawl. If it was a marlin on that hook, he'd have to yell careful commands to reverse and chase it down. Unfortunately, he could feel right away that it wasn't. It was a decent fish, but definitely not a marlin.

Dylan reeled it in, letting it have some line occasionally and playing with it. His boat had an auto-reeling rod holder, so as it came close, he placed the rod in the computer's hands, letting it bring the fish close to the stern deck. He grabbed a long net, ready to scoop as soon as he saw it. A flash of bright green appeared, and a dorado jumped out of the water. It still had some fight, but it wasn't a trophy fish. And it didn't look like the computer would lose it or snap the line. "Computer, neutral!" The dorado came closer, and the auto-arm holding the rod brought it in, close to the deck. He reached the long net out and scooped the dorado into the boat.

Dylan had owned this boat for a couple years now, and had yet to catch a marlin. All the computers and fancy gadgets in the world were still no match for the local fishing guides. He did often wonder what he would do if he actually hooked one. He was a moderately strong man, but there was not much chance he'd get a big one into the boat by himself. A Dorado would have to do - at least it was good eating.

Dylan looked at the time and changed course to head back towards the dock. He baited his line again and cast it back, increasing to a fast troll once more. He didn't get any more bites, but he was happy with his morning regardless. The fishing was just a side dish, his main course had always been simply getting out on the water. He loved when the mainland disappeared, and all that remained was the unknown sea in every direction. At least it felt that way. With satellite maps, communication networks and computerized boats the 'frontier' of the ocean had been sterilized.

The rolling, tree covered hills of the mainland were getting closer, so he reeled in his line, threw out the bait, and walked up to the captain's chair. The boat was fully capable of docking itself, but he felt foolish pulling into the harbor on autopilot. His private dock was to the north of Planet 9's shipping port. In the far-off distance, just poking their noses above the treeline, he could see the tops of two rocket platforms. He slowed the boat down to a dead crawl and pulled behind the marina barrier into his berth. It was a covered berth to keep the boat safe from the consistent tropical rains. The roof pulled double duty, as it was built with solar panels which recharged the boat for his next run.

Dylan packed up his gear and stored it on board, then took his catch and loaded it in the back of his waiting golf cart. It was still cool outside as he drove up the hill, enough so that he was still in pants and a sweater. A dirt road carried his electric golf cart up the hill, through a loose palm forest, and eventually onto a grassy plateau above the coast.

The Planet 9 complex was huge. It would take a full half hour to drive to the other side. The launch areas were kept well inland as a protection from tropical storms. The assembly bays and ship storage areas were also further from the ocean. The research areas, administration, staff accommodation and Dylan's residence were very close to the eastern shore, however, to make to most of the beach. He had moved all his operations to Costa Rica just under a decade ago and hadn't regretted it once. Come for the sun, stay for the tax breaks.

Dylan drove through the security gate and passed central administration on his way home. Parking the golf cart out front of the house, he grabbed the bagged fish from the back and carried it inside. He took off his boots and changed into flip flops, then walked into the kitchen. His personal chef, Edgar, was reading a book in the corner, and having his morning coffee. The smell of fresh bread was coming from one of the ovens. "Morning Edgar!"

"How was it, Mr. Bishop? Any luck?" Edgar straightened up and stifled a yawn.

"Got a decent guy here." Dylan dropped the bright green dorado on the counter. "I think I've got my technique down for these ones, but god help me if I hook something bigger out there. At least when I'm going solo, that is."

"You should really hire that old Jorge guy down the coast. He's a magician, we all had a marlin on the line last month. Only got one in the boat, but still."

Dylan nodded in polite agreement, but he had no intention of getting a guide. It would defeat the purpose. He walked over to the large stainless-steel fridge and opened it. Edgar had left a smoothie for him inside. "Any chance you have enough limes on hand to make ceviche for the staff?"

"Of course, Mr. Bishop. I'll fry up some fresh chips, too."

"Great, and remember, you can call me Dylan," he smiled. "I'm heading into a meeting upstairs in a bit, if you wouldn't mind sending some of it up at noon or so?"

"Not a problem."

Dylan took the green smoothie and made his way upstairs. Looking at his watch, he realized how close he had cut it for time. He had hoped to shower and put on something more professional for his meeting, but he was running far too late. Jeans and an old t-shirt would have to be enough.

People would wait for him, no doubt. He was one of the wealthiest and most powerful people on the planet after all, but that wasn't the point. Dylan still judged other people by their punctuality, and therefore he would always hold himself to the same standard. He'd just have to show up to his meeting in a stained 'Margaritaville' t-shirt, unfortunately.

His office was in the top corner of the house. His living quarters were fairly modest, at least by billionaire standards, and he kept that corner of the building very private. The rest of his sprawling residence was used by Planet 9, and both he and his wife kept offices on the top floor. An open-air staircase led him up to a foyer, where his receptionist sat at a desk. The room had rolling walls that were open to the warming breeze. "Morning, Roldan!" he exclaimed as he walked into the room.

"Good morning, Mr. Bishop. How was the fishing?"

"Quiet" he smiled. It wasn't worth reminding Roldan to call him by his first name. He was professional to a fault, and always smartly dressed. "And beautiful, as always."

"Good. So, I've tried to keep your day as slow as possible, I know you've been swamped. But... the botany department wants a meeting at some point today. And some of the rocket engineers would like you onsite at the propulsion lab this afternoon. Some kind of new problem with the Mark 6 engines."

"Shit" Dylan said. He didn't want to hear any more bad news about the new engines. They were already years behind schedule. The failure of those engines was holding up every plan that the company currently had. "One day, I would really love to hear some *good* news from propulsion." He chugged the rest of the smoothie and left it on a side table. "And this meeting now, this is the Canadians? These guys just wouldn't let up."

"Yes, that's right. I've asked them to keep it brief, but they did just fly down from Vancouver last night, so they probably expect at least a little bit of your time. I've let them in the boardroom already, they're waiting for you in there."

"Perfect, thanks Rolly. How's the weather this afternoon? More showers?"

"Looks to be sunny, but that might change."

"Can you schedule the botany department meeting on the marina terrace? Would be nice to be outside for it."

"Of course."

Dylan went into his office, picked up his holotab and a notepad, then grabbed a fresh espresso before letting himself into the boardroom. It was a beautiful space, open and airy, with a floor to ceiling picture window that looked out into the jungle canopy. The table was a long, polished slab of ceiba wood surrounded by a dozen leather chairs. On one side, two men sat waiting. They both stood up to greet him as he walked in.

"Mr. Bishop?" one asked, as he reached his hand out to shake. He was in dress slacks, a white shirt and a blue tie. He was tall and thin, with a neatly trimmed beard and short dark hair. He had thick rimmed glasses on. The other man was wearing a short-sleeved plaid shirt and linen pants. He was clean shaven, with curly auburn hair and a muscular build.

"Yes, nice to meet you…." Dylan trailed off.

"Jake Crawford, sir."

"Travis Strickland," the other man also reached out and shook his hand, very firmly, almost to the point of being painful.

"Well, have a seat. Can we get you anything? Coffee, tea?" They both politely declined. "Okay, well then, first things first. Don't worry about formalities here, I honestly just find them annoying. Please call me Dylan. We keep things fairly casual. As you can see" he laughed, gesturing to his fishing clothes.

"Okay - thanks Dylan. Our current company is pretty formal, but I've always preferred a more laid-back environment as well." Travis said. "Oh, and I think I speak for Jake and myself when I say what an absolute honor this is. I've been watching Planet 9's progress since I was in high school, it's amazing."

"Thanks Travis. I'm sure you've heard of our ups and downs. For better or worse, we have people on Mars now, which was always my goal. And, no matter what happens, playing with rockets is just a lot of fun." Dylan had a sip of coffee while he looked down at his holotab. "Soooo, you two have had virtual meetings with our HR department, our R&D department, my procurement officer, my head propulsion engineer - and each time it's just to try and get a meeting with me. With *me*, personally." Dylan sounded annoyed. "We have a very large company down here, guys, with a lot of brilliant people. A *lot* of them could give you better answers than I can. I'm impressed with your persistence, but I really don't have much time to give you. Why the big insistence on talking with me?"

"We both agreed that what we had to discuss with you was too important for anyone else. And we are sorry that we were so insistent on that," Jake replied.

"Sorry, eh?" Dylan said, in an over-the top Canadian accent, chuckling at his own joke. "But - I would never have taken this meeting if my head of propulsion didn't urge me to. What the hell did you tell Nick to get this appointment?"

"We told him that we had a technology that could put your ships in space for a tiny fraction of the energy you're using right now," Travis said confidently. Dylan did not look convinced.

"We've come a long way on our own dime to see you. I can only imagine how busy you are, Dylan, so thank you so much for hearing us out" Jake added, gulping with nervousness. He had anticipated skepticism and annoyance. He knew that their relentless nagging to get a meeting with Dylan Bishop would most likely be met with frustration. The room was well air conditioned, but there were still small beads of sweat forming along the top of his brow. "We have stumbled upon something in our research. Something big, and the reason we wanted to talk to you, personally, is that only a handful of people know about it. No one in our company, or even outside of this room - knows what we have discovered."

"So, you guys work at an independent institute up there, right? If you have something new for our rocket tech - efficiencies or what not, I guess I can point you in the right direction. Or are you selling some new material for the builds? I can get you the right meeting if the tech is worth it. But guys - I'm not the guy to talk to, seriously. There're people down here who know our rockets much better than me. And I'm very busy, I don't really have the time for a sales pitch..."

Travis cut in. "What we've got, what we've discovered - it could mean that your rockets aren't necessary anymore. That they're now all obsolete."

Dylan gave a skeptical look at Travis, almost laughing at the brazen statement. But he was curious, no doubt.

Jake took out his holotab and loaded a video clip, then drew his hands apart, expanding the screen display onto the wall behind him. "This is footage taken from our temporary lab in the Fraser Valley." The video showed Travis in a protective suit, loading a sample on the pedestal.

"What's the material he's holding? Is that plutonium or something - why the suit?" Dylan asked.

"The suit is for the gamma ray emitter in the room. The material itself that we're using is perfectly safe, it's not radioactive" Jake responded. The video sped ahead to the firing sequence, as the hulk gun powered up. The feed went into four separate screens, showing a close up of the sample, the gun, and two views of the room. The sample disappeared.

"You vaporized that cube of metal, ok. Impressive?"

Jake realized that his video wasn't illustrating his point, at all. He stuttered, flustered that he hadn't given Dylan Bishop a 'jaw dropping' reveal like he had hoped. Jake rewound the footage to the beginning again. Travis pointed at the wall holo-display this time. "Keep an eye on this quadrant here." The cube reappeared about fifteen feet off the ground and fell.

Dylan finally put his coffee down. "What!? Can you rewind that? Let me see again." Jake started the footage over. Dylan watched it intently. "You teleported it?"

"We didn't teleport it. But - it did travel through space," Jake replied.

"When we found this reaction, we *thought* that the cube was teleporting" Travis continued. "We struggled for weeks trying to figure out what was happening. We thought we were dealing with teleportation, but we were very wrong." Travis stood up to point at features of the holo-display. "It always traveled a similar distance from its origin, but in random directions. One experiment would put it in the corner of the warehouse, the next one in the other corner, the next on the roof. It seemed random, and we couldn't find a unifying pattern to it. Each experiment had the exact same parameters, the same sample, the same gamma frequency, but the cube would move in a new direction each and every time. It was Jake that finally figured it out, so I'll let him explain."

Jake took a deep breath. He was nervous as hell, but he'd rehearsed his explanation a hundred times now. "Are you familiar with base dimension theory?"

"Not nearly as much as I'd like to be, but yes" Dylan said. "From what I understand, it means that another dimension exists at a subatomic level, but that's about all I know."

"Yeah, that's the start of it. The basic idea is that this other dimension doesn't have any of our rules. Space, motion, energy - they're all elements of the dimensions that we exist in. But our dimensions are all built on top of the base dimension. My favorite analogy is to think of our dimensions in the Universe as a blob of pizza dough - you can move them, you can stretch them. But the base dimension is the countertop that it sits on. The base for all other things."

"Okay, I'm with you. What does that have to do with what I'm seeing?" Dylan asked abruptly, forgetting his manners in his confusion.

"We believe the cube is traveling through time - in the base dimension. Basically, we're changing the time coordinates of the sample cube with a precise gamma ray frequency. And because motion doesn't exist in the base dimension…"

Dylan was keeping his face a studied blank. Jake had trailed off, intending for him to finish the sentence, but he just shrugged instead. "I don't think I'm following here, Jake. How is it moving through time? It looks like it reappears at the exact same time that it disappears."

"So, you know that even though it feels like we're sitting still - in this boardroom, we're always in motion. The earth is rotating, which means we're constantly moving in a circular motion, just under half a kilometer every second. The earth is orbiting around the sun at 30 kilometers per second. The sun is revolving around our galaxy at over 200 kilometers a second. But all of this pales in comparison to how fast the Milky Way galaxy is moving, which is thousands of kilometers per second. It gets tricky at that scale - we don't actually know how exactly fast we're moving."

"So, when the cube moves through time…"

"It changes time in the base dimension. And the base dimension has no such thing as space, or motion. Which means that what you're seeing…" Jake paused, struggling slightly to find the words. "That cube stayed perfectly still. The earth itself is what moved."

Dylan was quiet, trying to process what he had heard. Jake reveled in the moment, happy that he had finally gotten the 'jaw-dropping moment' that he flew down to Costa Rica for.

"So, when it was moving in random directions, that just had to do with where the Earth was in its rotation at that time of day." Travis continued, showing a new diagram on the holo-display to illustrate. "Or where it was in its orbit around the sun, which would also change the direction. The Earth itself would move away from the berlinite in a different direction at nine in the morning than it would at four in the afternoon" Jake continued.

"So, you didn't invent teleportation. You invented...time travel?" Dylan asked.

"You see, we've always thought about time travel the wrong way" Travis started in. "All of our science fiction about it was wrong. We thought that Marty would go back thirty years in that DeLorean and reappear in the same spot in Hill Valley. But he wouldn't have come back anywhere near Hill Valley. In actuality, that broken clock tower would have drifted billions of kilometers away from him. And the DeLorean would now be floating in deep space."

"Holy shit" Dylan whispered. He was mesmerized by the video footage and took a long time to ask his next question. "How - how far forward have you sent something? How far did it go?"

"Well...we're not quite sure. What we've been able to determine is that the amount of time traveled depends on the amplitude of the ray we hit it with. We lost a few samples at the beginning because the beam was much too powerful. By our rough estimates, they're well beyond the solar system."

"So, two Canadian guys in a warehouse accidentally sent an object further into space than NASA ever has? I love it!" Dylan laughed. He stared at the display again, smiling, then looked upwards in thought. "Give me a sec here, guys." Dylan got up and walked over to the window, taking a small phone out from his ripped jeans pocket. From the back, Jake could see that his curly black hair was a bit disheveled under his ball cap and had gone half gray. He didn't look anything like the Dylan Bishop that Jake and Travis had seen in the news for decades, the well-dressed CEO of multiple tech companies. "Hi, can you come meet me in the boardroom?" Dylan said into his phone. "Well, I know, I remember that's today, but just make an excuse - please? You really, really need to hear what I'm hearing right now." He walked back to the table, leaving Jake and Travis curious as to who he was talking to.

"We...kind of just wanted to talk to you, Dylan. You, specifically - no one else. Not to be rude." Jake said as Dylan was walking back. "We're dealing with confidential research, that's why we didn't show this to anyone else at Planet 9, we can't risk it."

Dylan sat back down at the table. "I get that, I do... but you'll want her to see this." He took a sip of his coffee and stretched his neck, waiting for the other person to arrive. "I'll be honest, I'm great at running a company, but I'm not great at everything. I get a reputation as a space travel genius in the news, but I'm definitely not. Not as much as I'd like to be, anyways."

Jake and Travis nodded in agreement.

"I'm an MBA, not a scientist, no matter what the internet says. Really, the only way I got to Mars was to surround myself with truly brilliant people. And the smartest of all of them - I married."

14.

The door to the boardroom opened a few minutes later. A brunette woman walked in. She was tall and attractive with straight brown hair flowing down over her shoulders. Her designer sunglasses rested above her bangs like a headband. She wore a long, navy-blue skirt which flowed elegantly as she walked, and the beaded necklace she wore over her white blouse clicked softly as it swayed. She smiled at Jake and Travis as she walked over to greet Dylan.

"What the hell are you wearing?" she laughed in a whisper, looking down at Dylan's unkempt outfit.

"I was late coming back from the boat this morning - I didn't have time to change" Dylan responded.

"I know we say we're casual, Dyl, but there's limits. Christ, we live a hundred feet away," she responded through a heavy Irish accent.

"Jake, Travis, I'd like you to meet Jessica, our CSO" Dylan cut in, trying to change topics. Jake and Travis both stood up to shake her hand.

"Nice to meet you gentlemen," Jess replied. "Sorry my husband looks homeless this morning. Things aren't that bad down here, I swear." The boys laughed obligingly. "At least he's not trying to grow a beard anymore. No amount of money could fix that damn ugly thing."

"Alright, alright, I'll change in a bit, I promise," Dylan cut her off, his embarrassment becoming more pronounced.

"How was the flight in?" Jess asked, turning her attention to her guests.

"It was fine, yeah. The car that drove us up here from San Jose might have had a software glitch, though. It was flying - we were doing 260 clicks in the outside lane at one point. I was hanging on for dear life hoping we wouldn't crash."

"I do wish they would warn people about that," Jess apologized. "When we built the compound down here, Dylan completely funded a new four lane highway for Costa Rica. On the condition that they removed the speed limits on that section. Like the Autobahn…"

That appealed to Travis. "Oh man, that's awesome!"

"Still scares the bloody shit out of me, and some of the locals, but he loves it," replied Jess.

Dylan smiled. "Those cars are perfectly safe at 260, you have nothing to worry about. My '67 Stingray, on the other hand…"

Jess shuddered when he mentioned the car.

"I just don't like wasting time if I don't have to, and on that note…" Dylan looked up at the wall projection impatiently. His wife could small talk for hours. "Jess, you really need to see what these guys just showed me."

Travis rewound the video once more. Jake and Travis explained their experiment once more. Jess listened attentively, and was even more shocked than her husband at the results. She seemed to understand why they had come to Planet 9 right away, whereas Dylan hadn't.

"Bloody hell, that's unbelievable! How much power did the gamma wave take?" she asked. Jake showed her a graph, showing both the power they had used in the original experiments and their reduced wave. "It's remarkable, it's almost nothing…." Jess trailed off and went silent, before regaining her thoughts. "Have you been able to determine any kind of speed of travel? Do you know exactly how far you sent it forward?" Her joking demeanor had disappeared for the moment.

"We need bigger resources to test that more, but in that video clip it's going forward roughly 2300 nanoseconds. So, if you put the math together, you can figure out the speed. That means that the earth travels - against the base dimension - at about 4500 kilometers a second."

"Wait - so if you sent it forward in time, just two minutes..." Dylan started doing some quick math in his head. "It would reappear somewhere past the moon."

"How did you manage to measure it? I'm just curious, I can't figure it out." Jess asked.

Travis cleared his throat. "We really didn't want to come down here until we knew for sure what we had. This material that we're working with - it has a lot of peculiar qualities. Strange ways that it interacts with light and radiation. We had no idea that it would do this though, we were just looking for the gamma rays themselves to disappear. We had no idea that the material would jump ahead in time."

"But - if it was just this material that could time-jump, then this technology wouldn't be worth all that much," Jake added.

"Yes, I see that," Jess responded. "It's still just a parlor trick unless you can send other material along for the ride."

"Exactly. If that's all it was - just sending a chunk of metal a few nanoseconds through time - we'd be going to a scientific journal. And we definitely would have released our findings to our institute. We wouldn't have bothered coming down here, to see you two," Travis said.

"Travis had a theory," Jake said. "The gamma rays were causing the molecular structure of the material to vibrate; vibrations so small that they would be interacting with both our dimension and the base dimension simultaneously. This would create a field of space that would temporarily jump into the base dimension and back out at a different time. The big question we had was whether that field would only work within the material itself. Or... if we encased an object in it - would that object jump into the base dimension as well?" Jake was gaining more confidence by the minute. Jess was more approachable than Dylan, and her excitement was rubbing off on him. "We had to test it. Somehow."

"And so... I'd like you to meet the world's first time traveler," Travis said triumphantly. He reached into the breast pocket of his plaid shirt and pulled out a tiny green army man. He stood it up on the boardroom table in front of Jess and Dylan.

Jess had a smile that was beaming from ear to ear. She was in her element, her excitement breaking through, and she didn't know what questions to ask first. "So, did you mold the material into a casing? How did you do it? Was there any structure change to the specimen?"

Jake turned his focus to Dylan again. He looked sheepishly embarrassed about his answer. "One of the reasons that we're here to see you, Dylan, is that we have no funding left to play with. We're low on our sample material, and it's very expensive to acquire. Our company knows nothing of what we've been up to, and we've had to improvise all of our procedures. We'd love to work more with this stuff, and shape it into all sorts of vessels to send through time, but it has an extremely high melting point. As it stands, we can't even change the shape from the original cubes we received it in. We're at the limit of what we can do up there, as we don't have the resources to make anything else out of this stuff."

"Wait, so how did you encase the toy soldier in it then?"

"Had to get a little Red Green on that one," Travis replied.

"Like, stop and go? I don't follow...." Jess asked.

"Sorry, I think Travis forgets that we're not in Canada sometimes," Jake cut in. "Red Green was a famous comedian back in the 90s. His schtick was that you could fix anything in the world with duct tape. Travis convinced me, reluctantly, to carefully tape together six of the cubes around G.I. Joe here. It was nerve wracking, and definitely a Hail

Mary. But it worked. The little army man appeared, with the cubes, across the warehouse." Jake smiled at the memory.

"Wait, wait." Dylan put his hand up. "Let me get this straight. You two created the world's first functioning time machine - with duct tape?"

"You got it, bud," Travis replied.

Dylan let out a howl. "Oh man, this just keeps getting better." Jess was laughing too, but regained her composure much faster. She looked back at the charts that Jake had given her, still fascinated.

"The field created by it is extremely precise," said Travis. "In fact, most of the duct tape got left behind on the pedestal and didn't time shift. Just a tiny bit of the ol' tape goo in the cracks of the shape I made, that's what made the trip." Travis switched to another video, showing their apparatus of six berlinite cubes and tape sitting on the pedestal, then falling separately to the floor across the warehouse, with a green army man sitting in the middle of the pile.

"Eventually, we borrowed an atomic clock small enough to fit in that gap and sent it through. That's how we could determine how far it had traveled through time, and what speed the earth was traveling at while it was gone. We have a rough idea now, but we want to test more and refine it," Travis continued. He could feel that they were amazed, but it was time to get to the real heart of the matter. "We know now that this discovery has big implications.

"The first application we thought of, and the most important for this technology, is a launch system. Send a ship a few seconds into the future, and boom! You're in space. No rockets, no boosters, no muss, no fuss."

Jess and Dylan shared a look. It was skeptical, but optimistic. Dylan took the lead. "I have too many questions to count, guys. But let's start with the big one? Why me? Why all the secrecy? Don't you *want* to be in a scientific journal for this? Wouldn't your company be thrilled to know about what you're working on?"

Jake felt his chest tightening, the ball of stress in his stomach starting to form again. The lies. The fucking lies. He was so sick of them, and just wanted all of this to be in the open. Jess watched him struggle to find his words. Her eyes met his and seemed to dive right into his conscience. She nodded quietly with a reaffirming smile, as if to say, '*I know why you're here, and we can help you*'.

Before he could open his mouth to respond, Travis spoke up to fill the awkward silence. "This is the biggest thing we'll ever work on. Jake and I - we work for a company that..." He struggled mid-sentence as well, trying to remember the words they had both practiced. "They just sell patents. We've both seen colleagues who have had their life's work sold away from them. If we were to bring this to Hachiro, there's very good odds that we'll lose our chance to work with it. They'll sell the research, and we're both stuck with a very strict non-comp agreement. Because they don't want to lose their best researchers, we're bound, by law, to move on to their next project."

"And because Hachiro doesn't have the resources to fully develop this, you'd be stuck on the sidelines while someone else runs away with it," Jess completed his thought.

"Exactly," Travis responded.

Jake found his confidence again. "We first sent that little army man through about three months ago. I can't tell you how many conversations Trav and I have had over what to do, about how to proceed…"

"There's been a *lot* of pints in this decision process," Travis joked. "We've considered hundreds of options. We didn't make the decision to come down here lightly."

"This is the biggest breakthrough since, maybe…" Jake thought out loud.

"Probably since atomic energy," Dylan mused. "Maybe bigger."

Jake nodded in agreement. "Yeah, and it would be easy to just file our report, accept the fame, and move on. But then who knows what happens with it? Who knows how long it takes to develop this into usable space travel? I want to see that happen! In the grand scheme of things, we're only alive on Earth for a very short time."

Travis took over. "At the end of the day, more than anything else, we want to see what can happen with this technology in our own lifetimes. Honestly - that was the number one priority for both of us. This has the potential to help people travel between planets, maybe even between stars! With the right team and enough resources, there really is no limit to how far we can go. And we want to *see* that. We want to be a part of it. I don't want to die knowing that some future generation will reach the stars. I want *my* generation to do it. Because even if we become rich and famous from this, it would always feel like a letdown if we died before that happened, you know?"

"A lot of my life has been based on a similar idea. I know the feeling," Dylan said.

"There's a river that runs through Vancouver - the Fraser," Jake replied. "When I was growing up, we learned about the life story of Simon Fraser, a fur trader and explorer who was the first European to navigate it. He spent the majority of his life mapping and exploring North America, and ended up retiring there, along the banks of the river that held his name. When he was offered a knighthood from Queen Victoria, he was far too poor to sail back to England and accept it. The great tragic twist of his life was that, only a few years after his death, huge fortunes of gold were found in the Fraser River - right where he lived for years. He died a very poor man, never knowing that he could have been a wealthy elite if he had just looked down in the river he explored - that was the tragedy of his life. I never saw it as a tragedy though. I mean, the guy got to explore the new world. He had adventures most British would never have thought possible. Who cares about being a rich knight after experiencing that?"

"So, before my partner gets too carried away with this" Travis cut in. "Yes, we want to be a part of this. But we don't necessarily want to give it away to you for free," he laughed.

"Of course, that's only fair" Jess was all seriousness again. "So, what are you looking for?"

"Jobs. And we want to be heavily involved in the project. In charge of whatever team you give us" Jake was ready with an answer. "We know you have the best engineers and physicists in the world down here. We just want to work with a team that can get things done quickly. The reason we chose Planet 9, and not NASA or another space firm, is that you guys always seem to do things in years that others do in decades. I know we're young - but we're not that young, and we'd like to get moving with the experiments as soon as possible."

"We know this is extremely valuable tech. We know its worth. We don't need to be billionaires, though" Travis said.

"You sure? It's pretty cool" Dylan joked.

"I mean, we wouldn't mind being millionaires" Travis smiled. "We'd like enough of a salary so that money is no longer a concern in our lives, ever. I think, compared to the amount of money you're spending on rocket fuel right now, that's really not all that much."

Dylan and Jess shared another look. Jake couldn't tell what this one meant - was it excitement, or skepticism, or both? "Fellas, we'll be back in a few minutes, okay? Make yourselves at home, I'll get some drinks brought in for you."

The couple stood up and walked out of the boardroom. The heavy wood door closed softly, but definitively, behind them. The room became deathly quiet.

Jake exhaled loudly and flung his neck back on the chair. "What do you think? Do they believe us? I can't read this guy, I'm not sure we made the right call," he whispered to Travis. "What if they figure out what material we're talking about? Shit, what if they just figure this out on their own and kick us out?" Jake's mind was racing.

Travis didn't say anything, just nodded his head absently.

"What if they choose not to trust us? I mean, we *are* screwing over our previous employer, hard - and I saw Dylan's face when he realized that. We're probably not making the best impression. Fuck, fuck...fuck! I don't know if this was the right choice...."

Travis had gotten up and was looking out at the jungle canopy through the window. "Holy shit, is that a toucan? Dude, come check this out!"

Jake looked at him in confusion. He was on the verge of hyperventilation, while Travis serenely looked out at the world beyond the boardroom window. "How are you so friggn' calm right now? We just spilled our biggest secret to one of the richest, most powerful men in the world. How can that not stress you out?"

Travis didn't turn around; he was very intrigued by the birds flying through the dense jungle in front of him. "Jake, there's nothing we can do but our best. We're in this now. The decision's already been made. We've already told him. So why stress about it? Second guessing yourself isn't gonna do you any good." Travis pulled his hands back off the windowpane, realizing that he'd left a greasy smudge on the immaculate glass. He started trying to wipe it off with the sleeve of his shirt.

"I can't think like that, Trav. I can't just dismiss the feeling that we made the wrong choice in coming here."

"You ever been whitewater kayaking?"

Jake shook his head, confused at why that was relevant at this moment. He felt the comment was a bit rude, as if Travis was just trying to change topics and shut him up. "What? No, never tried it. Just went on a rafting tour once."

"Nah, man, rafting's different. You have a team with you, and a guide. It's not the same." Travis sat back down at the table. "When you're in a kayak, it's just you and the elements."

"Like skiing."

"Not at all. It's not like skiing, or biking, or any other sport that I've tried. You can't stop once you're in. With skiing, there's time to plan your next turns, time to rest, time to catch your breath. You can pull off the trail on your mountain bike and plan your next move. But with kayaking, once you're in the river - you can't stop. There's no time to second guess your decisions. Once that current takes you into a rapid, all you can do is your best. And …. the river decides if your best is good enough. That's all there is to it. It's real simple.

"You get nothing from panicking, you'll just end up in trouble. If you second guess your choices, you'll end up in trouble. You have to make fast decisions, and you have to hope they're the right ones. If they're not, you deal with the consequences, you paddle hard, and you hope for the best. But, at some point, you have to take a step back and recognize that you, really, only have a small bit of control. Eventually that river is going to take you where it wants. Your best has to be good enough, or that's it for you. And - it's fuckin' weird, man, but there's a peacefulness to that.

"I guess what I'm saying is…. you're stressing out way too much. We're in the current now, and for better or for worse, and it's going to take us where it wants. All we can do is our best, and - we have been, right? Just accept that there are many, many things that are out of your control and you'll stop having these panic attacks all the time. Who knows, maybe, no matter what you do, no matter which way you go or how hard you paddle, that current is going to drag you into a strainer anyway. So why stress out? Just do the best you can. I'm pretty damn sure we've made all the right turns on the way to get here, but I'm always ready to paddle hard if they weren't."

Jake was silent. He'd always respected Travis' positive attitude, but he never realized that his 'happy-go-lucky' nature was a conscious choice. He began to see his friend in a new light.

"Anyways, sorry for rambling. But we'll find out soon what they have in mind. This would be one hell of a cool place to work, though" Travis said as he stared out the window once more.

Roldan entered the boardroom with a drinks tray. A french press of coffee, freshly squeezed papaya juice, and a teapot were all on top. "Sorry, Ms. Bishop wasn't sure what you wanted."

They each had a coffee and a juice. It tasted unlike anything Jake had drank before, sweeter and more flavorful than any papaya he had ever known. "I'm sick of lying to everyone, Trav. So god damn sick of it," Jake muttered between sips.

"We'll be done, eventually. Just need Dylan Bishop on our side, right?" Travis smiled reassuringly, but Jake wasn't having it.

"I'm stressed about the decisions, for sure. But - I can't keep hiding all this shit from everyone. From our company, our coworkers, my family. Even my girlfriend. Mia thinks I'm in Sacramento right now, not Costa Rica."

"I can only imagine how tough this situation is in a relationship, man. I'm sorry." Travis took another sip of his coffee while he thought. "Wait, I thought she knew about the time jumping? You came clean to her about it. Why wouldn't you just tell her that you were meeting with Planet 9 then?"

"I don't know. I can't keep things straight anymore. I think I lied this time because I was worried I'd have to move away if this deal comes through. Who the fuck knows anymore? Sometimes, I don't even realize that I'm hiding the truth in our conversations. I suck at this."

"We're close to the goal, man. If we can pull off our plan…."

"It's a big if…"

"It'll work out. And Mia's awesome, by the way. If she already knows about the berlinite, I don't know why you're still hiding other things from her."

"Me neither."

They sat for another fifteen minutes in the quiet boardroom, anxiously waiting for the Bishops to return. Each minute felt like an hour to Jake, and although they did their best to fill the time with small talk, he was still having a hard time keeping his stress in check.

Finally, the door opened, and Jess walked back in, followed by Dylan. She was in the same outfit, but Dylan had changed into a pair of khakis and a pressed polo shirt. "Sorry to keep you waiting, gentlemen," Jess remarked as she sat down again.

"It's a big thing you just threw at us, guys" Dylan said. "So, first things first - I'm very, very stoked about this. So is Jess. Regardless of whether or not this works out for Planet 9. You guys have changed the world, even if the world doesn't know it yet."

Jake smiled politely. He was waiting for the 'but'. Billionaires didn't become billionaires from being this nice. Dylan Bishop had been a cutthroat investor in his younger life, had been involved in multiple hostile takeovers in the tech industry, and had countless enemies in the business community. Enemies which may have been a factor in his move to Central America. The Dylan Bishop he knew from his research was definitely not this laid-back beach bum he saw across the table. He wanted to trust him, but he couldn't shake the feeling that they had made a mistake in telling Planet 9 their secret. Jake glanced over at Travis, who was still calmly sipping his juice, listening intently to Dylan speak. *'You're in the current, Jake'* he told himself. *'There's no point in second guessing yourself now'.*

"So - we're at an impasse, guys, unfortunately. I want to believe you. I want to believe that this works. But the only way to prove that it works is for you to give us the material you were using, and the magic frequency."

Jake braced. He knew it, they were gonna get screwed. Shit.

"But I also understand that if you give us that, then there's no reason for me to give you anything back. We can run away with it and give you jack squat. Especially since Hachiro hasn't filed a patent on it, and no one in the world knows about it," Dylan continued.

"Well, it's a good thing I have all of our research dated and stored away, bud. And that I've been recording this meeting just in case. Sorry." Travis replied, taking his phone out of his pocket. His tone had changed. It wasn't aggressive, but it wasn't the jovial tone he had before.

Dylan didn't seem phased by the revelation. In fact, he smiled. "Good. That was the right move." He took a long sip of his coffee, glanced at Jess to give her a chance to speak, then turned back to Travis. "You guys took a big risk coming here, and I respect that. And no, I don't want to screw you out of this. In fact, Jess and I are very excited to work with you."

"I appreciate that. And yeah, it was a huge risk, but we were fairly sure that Planet 9 was our best option." Travis was taking over the negotiations. He had seen Jake freeze up when Dylan put out an empty threat. "Like I said, Dylan, Jess - we're willing to share this with you. But we want what's coming our way. And a guarantee that we're on the Planet 9 team, developing the time travel department."

Dylan looked to Jess. She hesitated, then looked at him and nodded, subtly. "Alright, sounds like we have a plan. I'll have my lawyer here draft up an agreement that keeps you on staff at a management level, for as long as we're using the time travel technology. You won't have to worry about money ever again if this stuff works, I can promise you that. And to secure the deal, to get you here…." Dylan paused, trying to read their faces. "Would a ten million dollar signing bonus get us you and the research? Each?"

Jake's eyes fired wide open. Holy shit, it had worked! He was rich! He broke into a huge grin and started rising from his chair to shake Dylan's hand.

"I'd feel a lot better about it if it was twenty" Travis replied from his seat. Dylan paused, and the room became deathly quiet. Jake's stomach shot into his throat - the stress ball was about to explode. Dylan stayed quiet. "C'mon, bud, that's still less than it costs you to launch one rocket. For tech that's gonna completely change the space race."

The room stayed eerily quiet. Jake couldn't tell if they had stayed in that stalemate for a second or a month. He gripped the armrests of his chair in panic, as if he was sitting in a jetliner being rocked by turbulence. *'Damn it Travis! What the hell did you do?'* He looked for anything around the room to hold his gaze, anything to avoid the conflict and the eyes of Dylan and Jess. He stared deeply into a wall sconce between their two faces and waited for the moment to be over. Travis sat calmly and looked across the table, as if it was a normal request. No more stressed than if he had asked for extra tartar sauce at a restaurant.

Dylan's emotionless poker face eventually melted into a confident smile. "It's a deal." He stood up and walked around the table to shake their hands. "Let's make history."

Jake and Travis stood up, excited and relieved beyond words.

"How does everyone feel about lunch? You guys like ceviche?" Dylan asked.

15.

The steel racking was heavy. Not as heavy as it had felt in November, but heavy nonetheless. And the time demands were so much greater than they were before. Jake and Travis had to rebuild the warehouse - the exact same as it had been - so they could secretly leave Hachiro and begin working for Planet 9. They had to ensure they didn't leave any breadcrumbs, any clues to what they had been truly working on. Jake had taken detailed pictures of the warehouse prior to rearranging it back in November, but they were still struggling to reference them. Perhaps it was the stress, or maybe the excitement of the scenario.

It had only been a few months since they had built their improvised gamma laboratory, but to Jake, it felt like years ago. So much had happened in such a short time. He'd done the best, most intense scientific work of his life. He'd snuck away to a foreign country to sell his research to one of the most powerful couples on the planet. He'd become a multi-millionaire. All the while, managing to keep a relationship going with the most amazing woman he'd ever met. But here he was again, in a ripped t-shirt and old work gloves, trying to piece back together the warehouse racking that they had torn apart. Trying - desperately - to cover their tracks before it was too late.

The decision to go to Planet 9 had not been made lightly. They hadn't exactly *lied* to Dylan Bishop, but they had left out a big piece of the puzzle. If they were to get the research out of that warehouse, if they were to leave that hangar snuggled away in the rainy mountains of British

Columbia, they would need a big wing to hide under. Befriending Dylan was their emergency plan in case things went wrong. In case Harada Hachiro ever discovered what had actually happened out in the Harrison lab.

Even if they got the funding to start their new 'dream' lab in Costa Rica, and Planet 9 provided them with mountains of berlinite, they could still be sued for intellectual property theft at any moment. Maybe even arrested. After all, they were effectively stealing their company's research and selling it on the side. Even though Jake and Travis had made the discovery, they were using Hachiro resources at the time, and they were being paid for every day they spent in that warehouse.

Although he had learned to accept that they had made the right choice, Jake was still very worried about the legality of what he was doing. Just because his decisions were the right ones to advance humanity, it still didn't make them legal - he was still, technically, a thief. And it would be tough to enjoy his newfound wealth from a prison cell.

He often felt bad for Mr. Hachiro. If they got away with this, the company's most lucrative discovery would slip away from them. Harada Hachiro had paid Travis and Jake quite well, at least for young scientists. He gave them good benefits, flexible work schedules, and a comfortable working environment. All for a gamble - a bet that his investment would pay off with a highly profitable patent. In fact, if it wasn't for the ridiculously strong non-comp agreement that he had signed, Jake would have released his findings to Harada himself. It would have been a massive win for the company, and Jake would have been a hero to his co-workers. If there was any way that he could let Hachiro make a profit, and still continue on with the berlinite research, he would.

But unfortunately, they were backed into a corner, and they needed an escape route. Dylan had figured out most of the problems in their scenario. He offered them as much legal help as they needed, but warned Jake and Travis that he may not be able to protect them if things turned sour.

Their best option was to cover all traces of their experiments and slip away from Hachiro under the radar. And for that, they needed a plan.

The first task was to reset the Harrison Lab. They needed to move the FEHFR emitter back to its original room and wire it up again the same as it had been. They needed to remove their cameras and instruments and return them to Hachiro, making sure to wipe the memory cards and hard drives of everything that was going back. The control room needed to be reset the way it was - Jake had taken a lot of liberties with the layout and monitor arrangement. All the markings and measurements needed to be wiped from the warehouse. And, finally, the warehouse racking needed to be re-built. Time was of the essence, and they had gotten started immediately after stepping off the plane from San Jose.

Phase one of the plan would be complete in just a few days. Phase two would be much more complicated.

They had released a report back to their management before Christmas, showing their various experiments and, conveniently, omitting every experiment with the time travel frequency. Travis would need to forge more than three months of new reports and submit them. He was furiously working on that task from the control room, while Jake finished cleaning the warehouse. Basically, he'd need to substitute every experiment undertaken with the berlinite samples with results from the titanium. If it worked, the only question the office should have was *'Why did you spend so much time and money to re-do the same experiment eighty times with no new results?'*

Once they returned to the Hachiro head office in Richmond, Jake would give his notice to the company. He would cite family health issues back home, and apologetically ask to waive his last two weeks so he could take care of his 'sick mother'. It was a decent cover, as it would also give an excuse for him to leave Vancouver.

So as not to arouse suspicion, they would not quit at the same time. Travis volunteered to stay on at Hachiro for a few more months while Jake started getting set up down in Central America. Jake had argued that plan with him, feeling guilty that he would get a head start while Travis twiddled his thumbs at home. "It's the only way this'll work bud," Travis had told him. "You keep secrets as well as I keep New Year's resolutions. You'd crack like an egg in the first week." Jake had to admit the truth of that.

Travis also suggested that they have a fake 'falling out'. He would request to not be put on a project with Jake again, should he ever return back from northern British Columbia. If he could keep the act up, it would cause even less suspicion when he left Hachiro in the early fall. He promised to slag Jake to all the cute girls in the office and make him sound like a pretentious douchebag. For the plan, of course.

Since they returned from Costa Rica, Jake had made a lot of progress in packing up the lab. He'd been in contact with Planet 9 to begin ordering equipment, and he'd even begun packing up his belongings from his apartment. There was just one more item to accomplish in Vancouver. One more big mark on the checklist, and it was the one that he had been dreading since they left their meeting with the Bishops.

He had to tell Mia he was moving away.

He hadn't told her anything about the Planet 9 meetings, his plans, or his newfound wealth. From the moment they had decided to contact Dylan Bishop, he had a dreadful feeling about their future. He knew that the research would pull him away from Vancouver. He knew that berlinite was going to take him away from her, and he didn't have the guts to tell her.

The secrecy of what they were doing was weighing on him so much. Since Christmas, Jake felt progressively guiltier about his decisions. Mia was such a good person, and he felt like he was involving her in a criminal conspiracy. He'd have long discussions with Travis at the bar about future plans, but intentionally wouldn't invite her. He knew that the next step in his career would definitely be away from Vancouver, and he wanted to put off that discussion as long as humanly possible.

The week had flown by out at Harrison, and they were ready to wrap up and lock the doors by Friday morning. Travis needed the weekend to continue writing his fake reports, but he insisted that Jake take the weekend off. "I'm fine, man, I'm as cool as hell with all this shit. But you take a couple days, and get ready to resign next week, you know? You need it, you look friggn' stressed out. Stop thinking about all of it for a bit."

Jake got home in the late afternoon. The stress of the corporate espionage was waning, but the stress of telling Mia was rising. It had to be done. He decided to put it off for another night and grabbed a beer out of his fridge.

He hadn't decided what to do with his Vancouver apartment yet, whether he should keep it, just in case, or sell everything and get a fresh start down south. The rent wasn't cheap, and it seemed like a waste to keep somewhere that he wasn't using. Even with the signing bonus that had been wired into his account, Jake had a tough time wasting money unnecessarily. A lifetime of thriftiness is not forgotten easily. He needed to blow off some steam. He needed to splurge.

Jake took his phone out and sent a message to Mia.

"Hey, I'm so sorry I haven't been around much this week. I finally have a chance to come up for air. Any plans this weekend?"

He went and changed out of his grubby warehouse clothes and came back to find his phone buzzing on the kitchen counter.

"I'm heading out with some friends from work tonight. But I'm free tomorrow? Have anything in mind?"

Of course she was busy. He'd been absent for a week; he couldn't expect her to just be waiting at home for him to call. His plans to go out for an elaborate, expensive dinner were shot.

"Still good skiing out there for a couple weeks yet. You up for it? My treat, we don't need to skin up the mountain this time."

"Ummm - sure. Yeah, I could get out :)"

"Awesome, I'll pick you up in the morning"

"Sorry about tonight, Jake, we'll hang out tomorrow. I know you and Travis have been killing yourselves out there, we'll have some fun."

Jake was set. He picked up the phone again to text his friend Gary to go for a beer, then changed his mind and put it down again. He was carrying too many secrets, and he hadn't let his friends Shannon and Gary in on any of them. Changing the history of science was a lonely endeavor, it turned out. Even with the ever-growing ball of stress in his stomach, he fell asleep early.

Jake was surprisingly cool on the drive north to Whistler the following morning. He didn't mention anything of Costa Rica, or Planet 9, just that he and Travis had made great progress. Mia had landed a new safety contract and was very excited about it. She apologized to Jake for being distant, as she'd been very busy over the last two weeks. This calmed Jake immensely, as he realized that she wasn't going to press him about the events of the last ten days. She, in fact, had her own life, and it didn't completely revolve around him and his experiments.

The sun was rising much earlier than the last time they drove the Sea to Sky highway. It remained well hidden behind the towering North Shore mountains as they neared Squamish. But the sky over Howe Sound began to glow. The water was perfectly still in the channel near Gambier Island, enough that they could watch the morning ferry waves ripple their way north. It was another beautiful day on the coast.

The speed limit lowered as they neared the turnoff for Whistler. Jake continued past the town and continued north on the highway.

"Ummmm - I think you missed the turn. You can make a U up here if you need," Mia commented.

"We're good, we're not going to Whistler," Jake smiled secretively.

He continued another 10 minutes north, then turned left onto a gravel road. Spring was in full force in the valley bottom, the only snow left was in the high banks off of the highway and deep into the shaded forest floor. They started driving up a switch backed road, gaining elevation quickly. The snow got deeper, the forest got thicker, and Mia's curiosity peaked as they ascended.

Eventually, the well-maintained road showed a large billboard.

Welcome to SKYPOW
Guest parking 200 meters ahead

"No way! Is this drone skiing? You're fuckin' kidding me!" Mia yelled at Jake in excitement. She punched his right bicep playfully, but hard enough that it throbbed after.

"Yep, I booked it last night. They're only running for one more week this season."

"Isn't this, like, crazy expensive?"

"It's not too bad," Jake lied. It was outrageous for a day of skiing. "I've always wanted to try it, and I've come into a bit of money, so I thought I'd treat you."

Mia squealed and kissed him on the cheek as they parked. "Oh man, and it's sunny, this is gonna be sweet."

"Well, we're running a little late, so let's get in there."

The Coast mountains of Canada had always been a mainstay of wild, deep backcountry skiing. People would access them by hiking up with skins, by snowmobile, snowcat, or helicopter. The 2030's had seen helicopter skiing fall out of favor in Canada, however. It still existed in many parts of the world, but the climate riots of 2032 in North America saw helicopters reduced to emergency work only, as they used a ridiculous amount of fossil fuels to operate.

Around the same time, though, battery powered drones had become powerful enough to carry people long distances before recharging. In recent years, operators had taken over the abandoned heli-skiing lodges of the past and re-opened them as drone facilities. As each skier needed their own individual craft for the day, it was a prohibitively expensive activity for most people, and was usually reserved for wealthy international travelers. Most of the new operations named themselves after some clever pun combining robots and wintersport, like "Ski-Net" or "C3PSnow".

A young Australian girl swiftly greeted them, took their bags and directed them to the training room. The lodge was beautiful, constructed of huge cedar trunks and finished with polished copper fittings. Some guests would be staying there for several days, even weeks. Jake and Mia were just on a day trip, however.

Entering the grand room of the lodge felt like traveling back in time. There were no screens, no holograms, just a smoldering fire in a river stone hearth surrounded by plush leather seating. There was a breakfast of fresh fruit and cheese laid out for them, and another Australian took their coffee orders. Soon, their guide, Kyle, entered the room, wearing full mountain gear and an oversized safety harness.

They spent the first twenty minutes going over avalanche safety and learning how to use their beacons and other equipment. Jake used it as a refresher, but it was very simple for Mia with her mountain experience. She was bored and anxious to get started. Eventually the guide started explaining to them how the drone flying would go.

"I hope you're not afraid of heights," he joked, getting polite laughs from the six people going out that day. "Anyone done this before?"

Two people raised their hands. "Good. For those who haven't, there's not much I need to tell you, it's pretty simple. Once Sarah and I hook you to the drone, it will fly you up there by itself. They're very safe, don't worry. The octocopter design will keep a three-hundred-pound person in the air even if one of the engines fails."

That thought started to scare Jake a bit, but he wouldn't admit it. A small grain of fear planted itself in him and began growing.

"I'll be flying to our drop zone first, and Sarah, our tail guide will fly up last. The AI flies your drone, so you just hang there and stay calm, OK? Sarah and I can override and take control if we need to, but in four years of running this operation, we've never once had to do that. You'll fly up clipped into your skis, with your collapsible poles stowed in your bags. So, make sure the DIN on your bindings is set right, or your skis will spend the winter in no man's land." Everyone giggled, while trying to remember if their bindings were in good order. "The only big thing I need you to know, and this is essential - orient yourselves, as you descend, so that your skis are across the slope. *Across* the slope. Otherwise, you'll just start sliding down the hill until the drone lifts you back up to me again. Capiche?"

The 6 nodded, eager to get started.

"Awesome. We haven't had much new snow this week, but I've got some north facing stuff that should still be skiing really well. Let's hit it!"

Jake and Mia hurriedly put their boots on downstairs, giddy with excitement. As they walked outside the lodge, the tail guide Sarah was waiting to put their massive harnesses on them. She explained that they felt weird to ski with on the first run, but that they wouldn't notice them afterwards. Once they were on, Sarah double checked them, and made them hang from a pulley outside. "Trust me, Jake, you don't want to find out that it pinches your balls when you're five hundred feet off the ground," she laughed, as she cranked him off the ground. The harness was different from what he had climbed with before. It was much heavier and more industrial, but the shape of it kept him hanging straight up and down, which surprised him.

They were the last in line. Once Mia had been tested, they rejoined Kyle and the other four skiers at the drone pad. Kyle had his skis and backpack on. "Alright folks, here we go!" he yelled. He gave a command into his radio, pressed a button combination on his wrist, and thirty seconds afterwards eight large, loud octocopters drifted in above the pad. Each was attached to a short length of thick green rope, with a smaller red rope beside it. The first drone lowered down to hover above Jacob, and he clicked the large green carabiner into his harness. "MAIN!" he yelled over the deafening hum. "BACKUP!" he yelled again as he clicked the red carabiner in as well. He hit a switch on his wrist control pad, and the drone began lifting him in the air. Eventually, he stopped, floating in midair in wait roughly 200 feet above the lodge.

One by one, Sarah hooked each guest to a drone with surprising efficiency. In just two minutes, the four guests in the front of the line were all hovering above the lodge with Kyle. The drones kept them in a line, ready to go once the whole group was in the air. The precision was incredible, the skiers hung so steady it appeared they were standing on an invisible platform. Mia skied up to Sarah, beaming a huge grin at Jake as she went, and whooped so loudly as she lifted off the ground that Jake could hear her over the motors.

Finally, it was Jake's turn. He glanced up at the six suspended skiers far above the lodge and froze. He had been trying to keep the fear in check today, but, suddenly, it was crippling him. "Hey! Your turn, let's go!" he heard Sarah yelling. *Shit!* Was it too late to back out? He was glad that Mia was having a great time, but the thought of being lifted by a drone over the mountains was secretly giving him a panic attack. He honestly didn't even enjoy flying on airplanes. Was it too late? Could he still back out of this? Would Mia respect him if he did?

"Hey, come on! Let's go!" Sarah yelled again.

Jake looked down at his shiny new powder skis that he'd hurriedly bought the night before, and breathed deeply.

'You're in the current now, just go with it' he told himself. He looked up, skied to Sarah and yelled "Sorry!"

"All good. You OK?" she yelled back over the whirring of the drone

He summoned all of his acting skills and gave her an enthusiastic thumbs up. She clicked the two dangling carabiners into his harness, hit the switch on her watch, and the drone above started to ascend. The harness tightened, and suddenly Jake's skis began to lift off the ground. The ball of stress in his stomach was on fire. He closed his eyes and huffed breath in and out as if he was taking a Lamaze class. When he opened them, he was hundreds of feet above the ground, peering over the ocean of trees around him. In the distance, he could see the signature shape of the Black Tusk near Whistler Village. He started to calm down, the flight was very smooth, it felt like being picked up and dragged around by some friendly giant.

Jake barely got into line behind Mia when Sarah joined them at the rear. He saw, hundreds of feet ahead, Kyle's drone started flying rapidly towards the southeast, climbing in elevation towards a small alpine bowl. One by one, the skiers dangling from their drones in front of him began to follow. Mia, roughly 50 feet in front of him, spun around to wave at him, still smiling and laughing. *'Damn, I wish I could enjoy it that much. She looks like she's done this a hundred times'* Jake thought. Mia's drone suddenly started off to follow the pack. His moment of happiness ended and switched back to terror.

The tone of his octocopter changed pitch, gaining several tones as the engines spun up. It tilted itself forward and started accelerating to follow Mia. Jake closed his eyes again, gripping the main line so tight that his hands hurt. The wind on his cheeks started to feel colder. *'Just get through it'* he thought. *'It'll be over soon, you can do this. Just hang on...'* He felt the wind increasing on his cheeks, getting colder by the second as the drone gained velocity and altitude. His hyperventilating wasn't helping at all, he tried slowing his breathing to calm himself. It didn't work. There was still a boiling ball of anxiety inside him, panicking, trying to scream its way out.

At last, after what felt like hours, but was most likely a few minutes, Jake squinted his eyes open, eventually opening them fully in wonderment.

He would have several sights in his lifetime that would imprint themselves on his personality forever. Seeing his mother crying with joy at his graduation. The northern lights dancing across the skies of the Yukon Territory. The first time he saw Mia with her clothes off. And the scene he saw at that moment.

He was soaring over the glaciated granite peaks of BC. He could see from the Tantalus Range down to Mount Garibaldi, and a hint of deep blue in the far distance where the mountains met the sea. Far beneath his skis, the rainforest of cedar and hemlock stretched out like an endless carpet. Above him, on his sides, pillars of ice hung off the mountain tops. And, like a convocation of eagles, six dangling skiers hung in front of him, flying peacefully into the yellow morning sun.

16.

"I think my favorite run was those burnt trees. They had the best snow, nicely spaced, I had a blast in there" Mia reminisced.

"Yeah, you whooped my ass on that one," Jake replied. "That was the steepest it got all day, I was a little out of my element. It was a little embarrassing."

"You did fine, that old Swiss couple was still way behind you when you got down." Mia paused to take a sip of her wine. The appetizer plate was empty, but the two were still famished from their day. Servers bustled around the steakhouse, wafting delicious smells to their table each time they passed. Jake's stomach growled in anticipation.

"I think I liked that long glacier run the best. Mellow turns, but holy shit, was that ever a view. Mind-blowing..."

"Yeah, that was pretty incredible. Even the flight up to it would have been enough for me. Cold, though, I'm glad I wore my big mitts today."

"Yeah, as amazing as that was, I don't know how people do it when it's -20 outside."

"I think they have heated vests in the lodge you can borrow. And heated mitts. Would probably help in that wind."

"Definitely. Would still be rough, though. And even scarier" Jake said. "Not gonna lie, I was pretty nervous getting strapped to that drone the first time."

"No...." Mia said, very sarcastically. She laughed out loud.

"Yeah, yeah, I know you're a badass. I'll admit it, I was shitting my pants until we got dropped off on that first run."

"I saw you behind me. Eyes closed, hanging on that strap for dear life. You're adorable."

"I deserve that," Jake laughed. "I got better after that first takeoff, but Jesus, that was intimidating." He picked up his glass of wine and raised it to cheers hers. "I still haven't said a proper congratulations, by the way. You've been working on that Brentwood Resources proposal for months!"

Mia smiled sheepishly and clinked her glass with his. "Thanks Jake. Yeah, it should be exciting. My boss was very happy, we've had a pretty slow spring for new contracts."

Their entrees arrived shortly after. Neither one of them ate red meat often, mainly because of the staggering cost of it, but Jake insisted that they go for steaks and treat themselves after their full day of powder skiing. They barely talked through dinner at that point, enjoying every bite for the exceedingly rare treat that it was. Mia took the time to describe what she'd be doing at Brentwood, and Jake caught her up on Travis' latest dating exploits.

The plates were taken away as the two leaned back in their chairs in delighted satisfaction. The server dropped dessert menus as he walked by. Mia picked one up in curiosity. "Oooohhhh, crème brulée," she moaned, but then her eyes shot wide. "Holy crap, this place is expensive. Thank you, Jake, for everything today. It's been so awesome."

"My pleasure. I've always wanted to try drone skiing, I was just happy to have someone to do it with," he smiled.

"Do you mind me asking… I know it's none of my business" Mia started, before trailing off, "Do you mind me asking where this new money came from? You must have come into a fair bit of cash, I saw you were on a set of brand-new K2's today as well."

The day had, indeed, been amazing. But now the time had come, he couldn't procrastinate any longer. Jake would have to tell her about Planet 9, there was no other option. He'd almost forgotten about it in a blur of blue skies and untracked snow. "A lot has changed in the last week. A lot."

"Ok?"

"Travis and I have... Well, we have new jobs." Jake glanced around the restaurant nervously. The chances of someone from Hachiro being in that room were astronomically low, but he still felt the need to double check. "We managed to get into a meeting with Planet 9. We sat down with Dylan Bishop himself! And his wife, she's awesome. They're going to build us a huge lab to continue our work and give us all the resources we need. We'll have a team under us, unlimited berlinite."

"Wow, Jake! That's amazing!"

"It's everything we wanted. With their fabrication equipment, we won't need to keep duct taping things together. We'll be able to build berlinite coated vehicles, probes, everything. They completely agree with us about the potential, it could be used to put satellites in orbit in just the next few years. After that, who knows?" Jake took a sip of the Irish coffee he had ordered. He knew that he was broaching a difficult subject, but he still couldn't contain his excitement. "It also comes with a pretty crazy salary, to be re-negotiated when the tech is proven further. And Trav and I both got multi-million dollar signing bonuses."

Mia smiled widely. "Jake...that's so awesome! So, you could totally afford that today, I don't feel as bad" she laughed, giddy with excitement for him. "I know I said I'd chip in for dinner, but, you know, I was thinking Mongoli Grill or something cheap. Didn't realize I was dating a millionaire" she laughed. "I mean, you're cute enough that I'd fool around with you anyway. But hey, money helps."

"Yeah, there's one more thing, though" Jake gulped. "I, ummm...need to move to Costa Rica. Next week."

Mia's smile slowly descended. "Next week?" she whispered in shock.

Jake pushed on. "We really want to get a jump start on it. Travis is staying in Canada for a while, and will continue working at Hachiro to keep suspicions down. We agreed that I would go down to the Planet 9 launch site to oversee the new lab's construction."

"Why you? Can't he go down there, and you stay here for a bit? Travis is single, and he loves traveling."

Jake opened his mouth to speak but stopped the words as they came out. He didn't want to explain that Travis was a better liar than he was, it wouldn't go over well. Not with Mia's issues with honesty. "It just...worked out that way, it's a really complex plan. He'll be down in Central America with me by the fall, hopefully."

"I guess. Okay." Mia sighed. She didn't hide her disappointment well. "Maybe I'll come visit you down there. Do you know how long you'll be down there?"

"No idea, unfortunately. As long as it takes."

"As long as it takes?" she repeated. "That's pretty ambiguous, Jake."

Jake's fear had come true. The conversation that he desperately wanted to avoid. They had only been dating six months, could they justify a long-distance relationship from that? He had rehearsed this conversation in his head a dozen times. He knew every line he wanted to say, every response to every question she could have. But it was all gone now as he stared across the table at her deeply disappointed face. She had changed her gaze to the far wall, trying to avoid eye contact. "I love you," he blurted out.

Mia looked back and stared at him angrily. "Really?"

Jake said nothing, just kept his look of intent.

"Are you really going to say that to me for the first time, right now? Thirty fucking seconds after you tell me that you're moving to another country?"

"I've known for a while now, Mia. I'm crazy about you. I've never met anyone like you, or known anyone in my life that I got along with so well."

Mia's eyes were glistening. She wasn't yet crying, but she was definitely struggling to hold it back. "I think I love you too, Jake, but," she huffed a breath out and collected herself, leaning her head back to look at the ceiling. "But... I can't, just... are you breaking up with me? Or do you expect me to like, wait here forever while you go build time machines?"

Jake again forgot every angle that he had rehearsed. He had screwed this up somehow. He struggled to find anything to say, and just muttered "I can't choose. I can't choose between this and my life here with you. This is my chance to change the world. I have to do this Mia..."

"I know. I know you have to."

"Come with me." The words came out of Jake so confidently that it surprised him. "Move down there with me." He had briefly considered this as an option, but dismissed it. But it was out of his mouth now, somehow, lying awkwardly on the table.

Mia was taken aback. She thought about it briefly while waving down the server to order more wine. "Jake, I... can't. I mean, I have a life here! My friends are here. My whole family is in Canada. My grandmother is old, and my sister has just had a kid. I can't just pick up and move to Costa Rica with you!"

"It's not like you couldn't come back. I'd have enough money for you to fly back whenever you wanted."

"My job's here, Jake."

"Planet 9 is huge, they have thousands of employees. Maybe Jess can find something in Health and Safety down there for you? I'm sure if I asked..."

Mia cut him off sharply. "Jake, I'm really happy for you. You've worked really hard, you've achieved incredible things, and that's paying off - it's great." Jake could hear a definitive anger behind her voice this time, overpowering the sadness. "But I've worked really hard to get where I am too. I've put years into my career! You might think it's boring, but I care about it. I don't want to go down there and get some bullshit job thrown at me, just because I'm Jake Crawford's girlfriend. That is not who I am."

"It doesn't have to be like that. It's an amazing facility, you could do good work there."

"I know Jake, I just... I just don't like the idea of handouts. I've worked hard for everything in my life, just like my mom and dad did."

"I get that, I do." Jake struggled to find a response. "Just, think about it, will you?"

She relented slightly. "I will, but..."

"Who knows, you could be making safety regulations on interplanetary spaceships," Jake joked.

Mia didn't smile. The server brought her another glass of red. She took a long sip, avoiding eye contact with Jake. "It's a lot to process right now, Jake. Just give me a few days, okay?"

"For sure. I'm sorry, I didn't know how to tell you."

"Thank you again for the skiing. It was an amazing day. And... I love you too, Jake."

Jake smiled with relief. As rough as this conversation was - it felt great to hear it back. Although he was nearly positive the feelings were reciprocal, the nagging doubt would've worn on him. "So, where do we go from here?"

"I don't know." Mia took a long pause. "Have you started packing?"

"Just small stuff. I think I'm going to keep my apartment here for a while. I can afford it, and it'll give me a home base when I come back to visit."

"Are you planning on visiting a lot?"

"Depends how tonight goes, really" Jake said coyly. "But I *am* moving there in secret, by the way. Until we get things sorted in the fall, I really don't want anyone knowing that I'm going to Costa Rica."

"Because of Hachiro?"

Jake seized, glancing around the room again. *'Don't use the damn name'* he thought. The secrecy and anxiety were killing him. "Yes" he whispered. "It's part of a plan, it was the only way to get our research and ourselves out from there."

"I don't know, Jake.... You guys sure about all this? It just seems so sketchy."

"Just don't give up on us, ok?" Jake pleaded. "We're great together, you know that. Don't let a couple thousand kilometers come between us. Please."

Mia smiled cautiously. "I guess. I do...kinda like you." She took another sip of her wine. Her shoulders seemed to drop, the tension releasing as she began to consider the upsides of their new future. "Maybe I can come visit you."

"Damn straight you will. I'll fly you down to San Jose first class! Whatever you want."

"Well, that doesn't sound too bad."

"Wait til you see this place, Mia" Jake said excitedly. "Dylan's built a paradise. The offices are built right into the jungle, there's a white sand beach right near the accommodations, there's fresh fruit and seafood all the time. Oh, and the top minds on Earth all working together in one place."

"Do you have a plan? Where are you going to stay?"

"They have a staff accommodation building that I think I'll start in. But just to get settled. When we were heading back to the airport last weekend, we passed a couple beautiful oceanfront homes that were for sale, really close to the compound. I don't think I'll have any problem affording one of those" Jake said excitedly.

"Last weekend?"

Jake's smile instantly dropped. *Shit*. "Yeah, Travis and I flew down there to meet with Dylan Bishop in person. It was too important a meeting to risk talking with anyone else."

"You didn't meet him in Sacramento?"

Jake's face wore his guilt. He couldn't pass this off. "No, we had to meet him at the compound in Costa Rica. It was the only way."

"Yeah - you told me you were in Sacramento, Jake. What the fuck?"

"I... I" Jake stammered. "I was just nervous about telling you my plans with Planet 9. I didn't want to have this conversation. I didn't want to have to tell you I was moving away."

Mia frowned and put her wine glass back on the table. "You said you weren't going to lie to me anymore, Jake. You promised!" She was whispering to keep from yelling in the restaurant, but her anger seethed between her teeth as she talked. "I know I'm fucked up, I get that. I have serious trust issues, but I just....... you can't lie to me!" Mia was trying her best not to raise her voice, but she was furious.

"I just didn't want to hurt you, I was trying to do this in secret. I didn't want to let you know. I knew it might end up in me leaving Vancouver."

"I don't get it. I thought you were confiding in me. Keeping your secrets from the rest of the world, but keeping me in the loop. But you're just getting pathological now, you can't stop! I know you've still been hiding things from me all winter - it shows. Were you planning to leave for Planet 9 this whole time? How am I supposed to believe anything you say anymore? You won't even tell me what country you're in! Your whole life is just lying and secrets, and you're leaving me out of it again."

Jake was silent. He didn't know what to say. His mind was racing, but nothing was reaching his mouth. He sat and looked at his wine glass instead.

"I'm happy for you, Jake. You're going to do great things - shit, you've already done great things." she said bitterly. "I just don't know if I can be a part of them, I don't know if I can trust you. I know you're always hiding this stuff from me, it's not just the Sacramento trip." Her tone faded from anger to a defeated sadness. "I can't take anything you say as the truth anymore, Jake. You've never *once* stopped lying to me. Even after you promised me last December."

"I was going to tell you, I just..." He had no words left. His mind was blank in panic.

Mia stared at him while he drowned. She had lost the glistening in her eyes, and now seemed to look right through him with a frightening sense of purpose. "I think I need some time, Jake. I don't think that this is going to work out. Promise me that you won't message me, or call me, or show up at my place. I can't..." she trailed off and stopped.

And with that, she took the napkin off of her lap, stood up, and walked toward the front door. Jake followed her with his eyes but made no attempt to stop her. Mia got her jacket from coat check and, without looking back, walked out of the restaurant doors into the cool evening air.

17.

"Jake!" He heard an excited yell from the roadway in front of him. Jake was standing at the security gates of Planet 9, struggling to convince the guard to issue him a security badge. He looked up and saw Jess parking a golf cart. She was much more casually dressed this time, in jean shorts with a white tank top and a 'Planet 9' ball cap.

"Hi Jess! Sorry I'm late, got a little held up at the airport, and again here. I don't think they have me on the visitor list."

"No worries at all. Let me help." She talked with the security guard briefly while Jake waited on the sidewalk. "Okay, I think we've got it." She passed him a security badge on a blue lanyard.

"Jacob Munford? I think you got the wrong name on it."

"That was Dylan's idea. Just in case, until we get you guys both down here and settled. Never know what paper trails will come back, right?" Jake knew it was a good idea, but it was still unsettling. Yet another lie.

"Sure, as long as we take our real names back soon. Once Travis is here and everything's settled."

"Anything you want there, Harold" Jess winked. "Where's all your stuff?" she asked, seeing that he just had a backpack.

"I just left it all in the car for now, back at the gates. I wanted to get my bearings and see the place first."

"I can help with that, hop in! You can put your rucksack in the boot if you like." Jake got in the passenger seat of the golf cart. "You may want to buckle up. I know it's strange to put a seat belt in a golf cart, but they go pretty fast here." They started driving down the tarmac towards the facility. She wasn't joking, the cart could move near highway speeds in a straight line.

"So, where are we going?"

"I'm so excited you're here, Jake. Dylan and I have been talking about this non-stop. We can't wait to start testing. I have so many ideas…"

"I'm stoked too! It'll be really great to work with the team here. But - where are we going?"

"Oh right, sorry. I thought I'd show you around a wee bit. We're going to take a look at your new lab, then I thought I'd take you on a full tour of the site."

"Do you have time, Jess? You must be busy, look at the scale of this place!"

"To be truthful, I don't do this for every new hire, Jake. But this situation's a little different," she smiled.

They arrived at a bank of enormous buildings. Jake could see the tips of the launch towers off in the distance, far away from the rest of the compound. The building in front of them looked more like an international airport terminal. "Wow, I had no idea how big this operation was."

"For sure, yes. I'll bet it's pretty daunting the first time you see it. We've been doing our own ship construction, designing new engines, testing camp designs for the Martian surface - you name it. We have departments experimenting with human hibernation, virtual reality recreation, even cybernetic enhancement. Dylan has his fingers in a lot of pies right now. Probably too many, honestly."

"What's that?" Jake asked, pointing at the largest building in the area, a collection of glass domes and connecting tunnels.

"Exo-planet agriculture. They're genetically modifying crops to grow in the conditions we have on Mars.

As well as testing for other planetary conditions. We want to be able to grow the food we have at home, but in any alien soil that we can find."

"It's huge!"

"The original plan was to have thousands of people on Mars by now. They need to eat, just like us. The systems we have up there for the Martian Twelve are very temporary, they won't sustain more than a few dozen people. Our long-term goals are sustainable fresh vegetables, grains - even lab grown beef and chicken. We just need to start getting it up there, into bloody orbit…" Jess trailed off. She seemed distracted, as if she was holding something back.

"So, what's happening with the Twelve anyway?" Jake changed the subject, seeing her frustration. "When is the next crew leaving?"

Jess started to talk, then hesitated. "I suppose you're here now; you'll have to sign an NDA at some point. I really shouldn't be talking about this before you sign that. But to hell with it."

Jake's curiosity peaked.

"We bet big on a new rocket engine. A new, extremely powerful, efficient rocket engine. It was meant to replace our entire fleet. It was meant to launch all the components of the Nomad ship into orbit."

The Nomad was Planet 9's design for a reusable transport ship. It was meant to carry up to four hundred people between the Earth and Mars at a time. Dylan had done a flashy reveal of the blueprints at a press conference over a decade ago. As the years went on and on without anyone actually seeing it, questions started being asked. The extended delay had been a big blow to Dylan Bishop's reputation. The media called him a 'Twenty First Century Howard Hughes.'

"Is the Nomad for real? Or was it all B.S.?" Jake asked.

"Oh, it's real. I can bloody show it to you, it's right over there!" Jess pointed at the largest of the buildings.

"The components are all constructed and ready to go, we just need to get the individual pieces into orbit. The problem is that it's all too heavy. Everything we have was built in anticipation of these new Mark 6 engines. Our old engine models won't lift what we've designed and built. We can't get anything into orbit anymore. By the time we realized there was a fatal flaw in their design, it was too late."

"Oh, so that's why the second crew hasn't left. That's why the Twelve are still alone up there."

"We didn't mean for any of this to happen, Jake. When they left Earth, we had full confidence in the Mark 6 engines being ready for the second trip. We took a big gamble, we redesigned everything, and we lost. We're grounded."

Jake was at a loss for words. He thought about the eleven people left on the Martian surface, stranded for years on end. He felt terrible for them, especially after David Anderson's death the previous year. What Jess and Dylan had done felt almost - irresponsible. But the Twelve had known what the perils of settling Mars would be. They had spent years training, going over every possible scenario. They knew that death or stranding was a likely possibility, and they had chosen to leave Earth nonetheless. It was still a shitty deal, though.

"Jesus. I had no idea," he eventually managed.

"That's something that no one knows outside this compound, Jake. And the propulsion team is still working so hard on the Mark 6, but I'm starting to lose hope. We've actually considered rebuilding an older rocket design, and sending another small group up in the same style of ship that the Twelve used. Just so that they don't feel like we've abandoned them. But that really feels like moving backwards to me."

Jess continued her tour of the compound with Jake. He realized then that Travis and him must have appeared like a gift from heaven. They should have asked for 30 million, he thought wryly. People were bustling between buildings. Trucks and carts moved quickly down the roads, and they had to wait several times for traffic to clear before proceeding. It was a busy place. They checked out the various research buildings, moving from astro-telemetry to hydrology to propulsion.

"This is our fabrication division. We make most of our parts on-site now, and only have to order out for some of the more complex engine parts. They can work with steel, aluminum…"

Jake cringed at her Irish pronunciation of aluminum.

"Oh, get off it," she laughed. "Ah-loo-mi-num. Happy?"

"Sorry" he smiled.

"Anyways, titanium, and… berlinite! We can easily get it to the temperatures required to work with it. And we're excited to."

"Have you ordered any from Freie University yet? It got a little held up in customs when I ordered it last time."

"No, we're not going to order it from them. We're going to produce it onsite."

"How? They wouldn't release the ratios, only provide the material? At least that's what I thought?"

"Let's just say that they'll have a new wing being built on their campus next year. Why buy just a slice of the cake when you can get the recipe?"

"Wow…you guys are throwing down a lot of money on this!" Definitely should have asked for 30 million.

"Well, from what you showed us last week, it could be our savior, Jake. It could be another big flop, too, but with the state of the new engines right now, we have to bet big. We have no choice."

"I guess that makes sense, yep."

Jess stopped the cart and looked at Jake. "Dylan took David's death pretty hard. He's been riding the propulsion team to get these new ships in the air, pushing them and throwing out ideas as fast as he can. But we're still no closer, not at all. If berlinite can get us into orbit…"

"Okay, fair enough. Now, I'm no rocket scientist..." Jake chuckled at the absurdity of that sentence. "But even if your ship could re-appear in space, it would still need an engine to push it into orbit. And to get to Mars, am I wrong?"

"Of course it would. But we've never had a problem with our third stage rockets or thrusters. It's the *getting off the ground* part that we can't do right now. And, if it works, berlinite takes that problem away, completely. I've been working with the problem on my computer for the last week. We really only need a tiny bit of propulsion and fuel to get to Mars if this works."

Jake nodded, but was still curious. "What were you thinking?"

"Let's say that this works. Let's say that we can coat a ship in berlinite and send it through time. And let's say that your estimate of traveling 4500 kilometers in a second is right. If we sent a ship forward, say, twenty seconds, at the proper time of day, it would reappear roughly 90,000 kilometers up. The Earth's gravity is still very strong at that range, so it would start falling towards us immediately. A slight steer with our propulsion to swing around the side and - tadah! - we're in orbit. Or, potentially, we could work out the same system to use a gravity slingshot towards Mars."

"You'd still be pushing a massive ship, though, no?"

"Have you ever had to push a stalled car?"

Jake nodded. His crappy Camry had finally been left behind, and now he thought of its inconvenient stalling fondly.

"Think about how much exertion it takes to push a car like that down your driveway. How many people, sweating and panting, just to get it moving at a snail's pace? But when you're at highway speeds, you can turn that two-ton object by pushing the steering wheel with your pinky finger. It's the same thing, if we can use the Earth's gravity as the engine to get up to speed, all we need to do is move the steering wheel. And I have lots of engines that can do that."

Jake nodded in agreement, it made sense. Jess continued with her tour, eventually bringing them to a very large building on the outskirts of the compound.

"This is where we assembled our very first rocket down here in Costa Rica. Over a decade ago now. I can't believe we've been here that long, it feels like yesterday."

"Is it still used for ship assembly?"

"Not anymore. The Mark 5's got moved to a different facility. This place is sitting empty. Or, at least it was…"

"You mean….?"

"This is your new lab. I know you just got off the plane, but I just wanted to show you. I'm really excited."

They stepped inside. Jess's flip flops echoed through the cavernous interior. It was completely cleared out, just a cement floor and a staircase on the far wall leading diagonally up to a control room bank. The lights were off, but beams of sunlight shone through the high windows, and dust floated delicately in the lighted paths. The space was hauntingly large, Jake had never seen anything like it. He was reminded of watching 'Hoosiers' with his dad. It felt like walking into that giant, empty stadium before the state finals, looking around all sides with awe and anticipation. "This is all for the Berlinite trials?" he said too loudly and heard his voice bounce around the space.

"You wanted more resources, Jake. You got 'em. I've got three FEHFR emitters on order, and I've already got a team working on a smaller, more portable gamma emitter."

"You got this all done in a week?"

Jess smiled. "You're surprised? I thought that's what you and Travis wanted? To get right at it? Hit the ground running?"

"I just… didn't expect to have a space to work in already."

"We don't mess around down here" Jess was at least fifteen years his senior, but she really seemed to have the boundless energy of a teenager. It was infectious. "I was going to ask you, Jake, we made the agreement that this is yours and Travis' show. And you'll still be in charge of this lab, for sure. But...."

Jake braced. He had been waiting for the other shoe to drop, this was too good to be true. They'd surely have some way of giving this to one of their more experienced physicists to take charge of, and start him as a junior assistant. He started getting ready to bring up the legal agreement he and Travis had signed - if they threatened to take his baby away from him

"I'd really like to help, personally. Not to take charge, but I'd really like to work on this with you."

Jake smiled, relieved. It seemed ridiculous to have one of the richest women on Earth asking his permission. "Of course! Why wouldn't we want the top mind at Planet 9 working with us?"

"Oh hell, I don't know, Jake. Some people...mostly men, if I'm honest, feel threatened by me. On top of that I am married to the big boss, after all. I wanted to suss it out first."

"Nah, I think I can speak for Travis and myself when I say we'd be flattered. And to be honest, I'm pretty intimidated by the scale of this facility. I could really use the help."

"Fantastic," she beamed. "I know it sounds odd, but being in charge of a place like Planet 9, and being as busy as Dylan and I are, I sometimes get bored. Until the propulsion team gets us back in the air, I feel like I'm in limbo."

She walked Jake through the empty facility and gave her ideas on possible layouts and equipment placement. *'We can do whatever we want in here'* he thought. *'The possibilities are insane...'*

The sun was getting low in the sky by the time the cart got back to the security gate. "I'll let you go now, Jake, they'll let you back through with your new badge. There's an apartment reserved for you in the manager's housing wing for as long as you need it. Just go to the housing office and give them your name, they'll get you checked in. Your fake name..." She reached into a compartment in the dash and passed him a map, circling the housing offices on it.

"Thanks so much for the tour, Jess."

"My pleasure, happy to have you. I've got a small team assigned to start with you tomorrow. They're going to meet you at 9 at the new lab."

"Sounds good. It'll take me a couple days to get them up to speed on the research, hopefully we can start getting equipment in the next few weeks." Jake was worried about the blistering pace this was happening at, but would be happy to start work. It would be a good distraction.

With that, Jess drove away, back north towards the mansion. Jake got his rental car, brought it through the gates and followed the map to find the housing office. The estate was beautiful. Planet 9 had cleared out the forest where the research stations were, and, of course, to install launch pads, but the rest of the grounds were built in harmony with the natural rainforest of the area. The drive through the thick jungle to staff housing took about ten minutes, and Jake rolled down the windows to breathe in the earthy refreshing air.

The staff housing block looked more like a resort. It was perched on a cliff above the ocean and consisted of several large apartment blocks mixed in with houses, outdoor restaurants, and a large swimming pool. Jake checked in at the front and was greeted warmly by the receptionist. She showed him to his private house, near the end of the crescent row of buildings, and gave him the keys.

The house was modern, air conditioned, and comfortable. Not overly large, but he didn't need much. There was a gift basket sitting on the kitchen island, containing fresh fruit, crackers and cheese. Jake picked the note off the top.

Welcome to Planet 9! Sorry I couldn't meet you today, but let's meet for dinner later in the week, once you're settled in. Hope the travel went ok, let the team at housing know if you need anything else. Really looking forward to working with you.
-Dylan

    Jake smiled. A year ago, who would have thought that Dylan Bishop would be sending him fruit baskets. It was all a bit surreal.

    He looked at his suitcases, and the effort of unpacking seemed too much to handle. It had been an extremely long day. But it had to be done soon. This was his only home now. He'd thrown all of his chips into this after Mia left him. His Vancouver apartment had been leased; his father's old car had been donated to the Kidney Foundation. All he owned was either in a small storage locker near the Vancouver airport or here in his suitcases.

    He opened the fridge and saw that it had been stocked with beer, wine, vegetables and other staples. He grabbed a bottle of Imperial Lager and walked out to the porch. He flopped down on a wicker lounging chair and twisted the cap off.

    It was then, taking his first sip and staring out over that vast expanse of calm water, that a profound loneliness first set in. He couldn't see another person down the beach, or in the other houses, or out on the ocean. He was all alone. Truly alone. A small tear welled up in his left eye.

    How could he possibly be sad? How could getting all of this - the lab of his dreams, a beautiful house to stay in the tropics, a twenty million dollar signing bonus - still leave him wanting?

    It had been nine days. Mia hadn't messaged. Or called. Or visited. He wanted more than anything to pick up his phone and message her. He had promised not to contact her, and he was going to keep his word this time. He had sure messed up the last promise that he'd made to her. The last four months re-played in his head, and he questioned every decision he had made with her. A year ago, he couldn't have dreamt that he'd have found the girl of his dreams, had her fall in love with him, then ruined it and lost her forever. He wished he could go back and tell her the truth. If only he had a time machine. Well, if only he had a different *type* of time machine.

Jake had also managed to alienate himself from Travis. He really wished he could have handled their last meeting better. He wished he hadn't yelled at his best friend.

The Monday after Mia left him, Jake walked into the offices of Hachiro to find Travis in a cast and an arm sling. Jake was furious - the plan was to not draw attention to themselves! He cornered Travis in an empty break room.

"Dude, what the hell?"

"Oh, yeah, I know I said we shouldn't spend any of that bonus yet, but I couldn't resist."

Jake knew he couldn't say anything about the spending spree, he'd just dropped a month's salary on a day of drone skiing. But he really didn't want any additional questions to come up. All they had to do was lay low, to stay under the radar until the fall. "What did you do?" he asked, in a condescending tone.

"I thought about renting a snowmobile for the weekend, but I ended up just buying myself one of those new Polaris ones instead. The hundred kilowatt one! Why not, right? I can afford that now, no problem. Fucker's got some kick, it slammed me right into a tree first thing" he laughed, clutching his broken arm. "My buddies had to help me dig it out, the battery's friggn' heavy as shit. Anyways, have to wear this for eight weeks now. Balls."

Jake was furious. "Travis, all we have to do is not draw attention to ourselves. That's all, and we get away with this. Now everyone's going to be asking about your broken arm, and who knows what they'll dig up. And what did your friends say when you showed up with a brand-new sled?"

"Just told 'em I felt like splurging. It's no biggie."

"What the fuck, man? You've gotta keep it together!" Jake was nearly hyperventilating as he talked. "I'm trusting you on this!"

"There's only one of us that needs to keep it together, dude. Explain this to me, Jake. Explain to me what series of questions leads from me having a broken arm to you and I selling top secret research to Dylan Bishop. It's ridiculous. You're losing it."

"DUDE!" Jake whisper-screamed, looking around the room to see if anyone had heard that last comment.

"There's no one here, man. It's all fine. It's...all...fine."

"I'm not in the mood for your redneck Zen bullshit today, Trav. Not today."

"Okay, whatever man." Travis' expression had changed. For the first time, Jake saw the happiness retreat from his face. "I know you're having a tough time with all this, so I'm gonna let that slide. But you need to remember we're partners on this. This isn't just the Jake show."

"I just...I need you to take this shit seriously, man. We're in serious trouble if we get caught. Serious trouble."

"You think I don't know that? It'll be okay. Whatever happens now, it happens. You know?" Travis was trying his hardest to calm Jake down, but it wasn't working. "I thought we were good, what happened to you?

Jake let out a long, drawn-out sigh. "Mia left me."

"Jesus. Did you tell her you're a millionaire now?"

"Yep. But I hurt her, it didn't matter. I'm an idiot."

"Wow." Travis struggled to find the words. "I'm sorry man. I really liked her, she was awesome."

"I know, she was perfect. I screwed up so bad."

"Awwww, man, she called you out on that Sacramento bullshit, didn't she?" Travis laughed. "I warned you that was a bad move."

Jake's ball of stress in his stomach finally boiled over. "You know what? Fuck you, Travis." He started storming away in anger, then spun around to re-enter the argument. "I don't get it man. I don't get you! We're dealing with real world consequences, and you can't afford to be this stupid carefree hick." Jake tried to stop himself, then kept going. It was erupting out of his throat, and he was powerless to stop it. "She won't talk to me because of you! Cause of your ideas. Because of all of this shit! And now I'm in too deep to get out, and too deep to ever get her back."

Travis was taken aback. His face was pale and concerned.

Jake took another breath, his face beet red with rage. "Just... fuck off. Do whatever you want, I don't give a shit anymore."

With that, he walked out of the room, and stormed back to his office. He gave his notice to leave the company that afternoon.

Jake hadn't told his family about Costa Rica. In fact, the only two people in the world who knew that he was down there weren't currently talking to him. He stared out at the turquoise sea and forced that single tear back inside himself.

He had way too much to do. There was no time to let that shit out right now.

18.

The cork flew out of the champagne bottle with tremendous force. Owen ran to the closest sink as half of the bottle came foaming out the top. There were many, many things to take into account when you live at 15,000 feet. Not wasting champagne, apparently, was another one to add to the list.

"Yeah, maybe we'll open the next one outside," Owen laughed as he tried to find some paper towels. He'd made quite a mess everywhere. The camp cook took the bottle from him and began filling glasses. They didn't have champagne flutes, so the water cups from the mess hall would have to suffice.

Marcela picked one up and prepared to toast with everyone. On the table was a large cake, covered in purple frosting with red highlights. It read 'Felicitaciones!' in large, bold letters (congratulations). It was just after dawn, and most of the camp had finished work for the night. The mess hall smelled like bacon. The chef still hadn't adjusted to their work schedule and was cooking breakfast instead of dinner.

Owen picked up a glass when everyone else had one. "Sometimes, in this industry, it's easy to feel forgotten or ignored. You can spend years - maybe decades, chasing something that you may never find. The progress of science can be exhausting, and most of us never make that breakthrough discovery we want."

Marcela glanced around the room. People were politely nodding. Yes, the pursuit of scientific discovery could be a lonely affair, especially in the middle of the Atacama Desert.

"But sometimes," Owen continued, "one of us gets that discovery. Something groundbreaking. Something that changes the way that we look at the universe. And this season, we saw that happen right here! I couldn't be more proud." He raised his glass to the group.

Marcela had just a sip in the bottom of her cup, as did most of the room. The majority of the champagne had foamed out onto the ground. She raised her glass anyway.

"To Matias!" Owen exclaimed.

The group cheered in congratulations. Matias had not only discovered a new black hole, but he had also discovered the closest known black hole to Earth. It was an incredible achievement, the tiny feature was less than one solar mass, and incredibly hard to detect. When his findings were released, it made headline news globally.

"He put his name out there in the world," Owen continued. "But he also put our tiny research station on the map."

Matias still looked as miserable and awkward as always. Even for a party in his honor, he showed up in a dirty t-shirt, and his greasy ponytail hadn't been washed in days. Owen gestured to him to say something. He looked at everyone, and quietly mustered "Gracias, thank you," before quickly sitting down.

It was a tough moment for Marcela. It was hard for her to stand there and congratulate her colleague, all the while knowing that her discovery would completely eclipse his. Marcela had found a definitive answer to one of life's greatest mysteries, and yet she couldn't tell a soul about it. Now it was Matias getting the cake and champagne, Matias getting the respect of his peers, Matias getting the headlines.

She told herself, constantly, that the work was its own reward. She told herself that she didn't need the fame, that she didn't need the recognition. But that was bullshit. The fake smile was becoming heavier to wear every day.

The fake applause she had to give her colleague was tearing her apart.

Professor Miles had set up a meeting with MI6 while Marcela was still back in England. The weeks following had been very intense. Her research was locked down. She was scrutinized heavily by the agency. She was put through medical examinations, psychological tests, and they'd pried deeply into her personal life and finances. Right when it got to be too much, when she was ready to run to the press out of frustration, she was sent back to Chile. Magically, her research had become fully funded for the next 36 months.

Priscilla Miles stayed in close contact with her all the time. She'd been a good friend, and she'd felt terrible about the way MI6 had treated Marcela. Each week they'd have a video chat, and Marcela valued that time immensely. To have someone, anyone in her life that she could be fully open with - it meant a lot. Priscilla wanted so desperately for Marcela to get the credit for her find, but they both knew that it couldn't happen. Not yet.

Attending a party for Matias was hard, but it wasn't the hardest day she'd spent with this secret. When her mother had fallen ill, and they were having trouble covering bills, the temptation grew to reveal herself to the press. One exclusive interview could pay her off her parents' mortgage. She'd given it heavy consideration, especially after the way her contact at MI6 had been treating her. Marcela knew the reasons to keep all of this secret, but it felt an unfair burden to carry.

She told Priscilla about her mother's financial issues, and how much she wanted to help her. The only thing Professor Miles could tell her was to 'stay the course.'

So here she was, celebrating a much lesser achievement, trying to smile. Marcela quietly ate her cake as others chatted around her. She would stay just long enough to make an appearance, then get out of the party before she grew too angry at the situation.

"Marcela, how's the hunt going?" Owen asked, sitting down across from her.

"Still going. Still waiting to find something," she lied.

"I've always thought it was a noble thing - the way you and your colleagues can just keep scanning the sky, never knowing. It's patience that I don't think I have."

"It gets pretty monotonous after a few years, yes."

"I can only imagine. Good for you for sticking with it, Marcela."

Marcela bit her tongue. The search for extraterrestrial intelligence was a very small branch of radio astronomy, and there was always an undercurrent of pity in the way other researchers talked to her. All she heard under their words was *'maybe one day you'll start working in real astronomy like the rest of us.'* She tried to take comfort in the fact she could wipe the patronizing smile from Owen's face with one image from her holo-tab.

Most days she was completely fine. She loved studying Cepheus HD314. She'd been gathering signals for over a year now, and working with a secret team at Oxford to decode them. It was incredibly exhilarating work, and most days she didn't care what anyone else thought about her. Most days she was completely fine. But not today.

"I do have some bad news, though. We have to get more scans of this new black hole. Matias has a new team, and they still have a lot of data to retrieve. So, I have to cut you back to one session a fortnight."

"Owen, you can't do that!" Marcela was stunned. "I have sponsors just like the rest of us. They've paid for this dish time. I still need to submit results, just like Matias."

"Look, it's not forever. And I'm sure your research can wait. They need extra dish time right now. If you ever found something, I'm sure they'd let you have their extra dish time."

Marcela was screaming inside. She *had* found something! If they only knew.

"So, I'm down from two nights a week....to half of one. That's what you're telling me."

"I'm sorry, Marcela."

She stood up and brought her plate to the bussing station. *'If you can't say anything nice, don't say anything at all.'* She knew that if she stayed a moment longer, she risked revealing her secret out of anger. Retreat was the best option.

It was still only 6am, but England was four hours ahead and it was mid-morning there. She placed a video call to Priscilla and explained the situation. Priscilla expressed her sincere disappointment, but said little else. It was imperative that the study of the alien planet remained in secret, no matter what. She made the same promise that she had for months now, that there would soon be 'a larger role for her in all of this mess'.

Marcela struggled to sleep. She felt alone. No one was in her corner. This whole process was brutally unfair. Priscilla wasn't helping, and her complaints seemed to be falling on deaf ears. It was one thing not getting the glory, but not being able to defend herself and her research - that was another.

Again, like so many times before, Marcela fantasized about releasing her findings to the press. She dreamed about her face on international headlines, her name on the cover of Scientific Journals. Marcela - not Matias!

Eventually sleep took her. She slept far later than normal, into the late afternoon. A rapping knock on her bedroom door woke her up. She quickly threw some clothes on, yelling "One minute! Un momento!"

She swung the door open, and Matias was standing there. He still wore the same t-shirt from the party, and she was fairly sure he hadn't showered yet.

"Are you and Owen dating?"

The comment took her back. There was no 'good afternoon'. No pleasantries. But that was his way, he was a very socially awkward man.

"No. God, no, why would you ask that?"

"I saw you in an argument at the party. I thought maybe that's why you got what you wanted. He's helping out his secret girlfriend, or something."

Marcela was confused. "I...didn't get what I wanted, Matias. They're slashing my dish time and giving it to you."

"Not anymore. I just found out my team is getting moved to ALMA. And we're only getting one night a week up there! Something's not right."

"Oh, I'm sorry Matias! We'll miss you down here" Marcela lied. She'd never been fond of him, even before his new discovery.

"Well, I'm just saying, it sure worked out for you." Matias began walking down the hallway. He turned around after a few steps and added "I don't know who your sponsor is, but they're paying for three nights a week now. You got all the time that we were supposed to use."

19.

The next few months went by quickly for Jake. Having resources and equipment made building the new lab much easier than it had been out at Harrison. Instead of grunting steel racks around and improvising every bit of construction, Jake simply had to ask for what he wanted, and it was there within hours. He never had to piece together items, or make things work with the wrong parts. It was all taken care of.

It was awkward at first. He realized that he had never worked like this. For the last year, he and Travis had been building a lab from spare parts and duct tape, all under the radar. But, even before that, at the university and at Hachiro, he'd always had to beg for what he wanted. Planet 9 got everything done so fast that he never got a chance to catch his breath.

The team that Jess had assigned to were from varied backgrounds, and they were all very capable. He had eight full time researchers under him, and could use extra employees from other departments on a day-to-day basis, as needed. The structural engineer helped Jake design a new experiment pedestal. The electrical engineer began wiring the building for multiple FEHFR emitter locations. The radiation specialist prepared the surfaces and walls of the building for proper deployment.

Dylan's new gamma emitters took nearly a month to arrive, as well as the materials for producing berlinite. Jake and his team spent that time going over his results from the Harrison Lab and proposing new variations. It felt good to get fresh eyes on it - eyes that weren't his or Travis'. They proposed new ideas, new theories, and new experiments. Each time one of his team approached Jake, they had already devised a method to test their ideas. He started to feel a little left behind at times. Although he was the most versed in base dimensional theory, different members of his crew were far more versed than him in other realms of physics. There were times when he felt inadequate, as if he wasn't the right person to lead the team.

One evening, as Jess stopped by to check in, he brought his concerns to her.

"I understand, Jake. But you have to learn to let that feeling go. Do you think I know more about every field of study than the thousands of scientists down here? Do you think I'm the world's top expert in every possible field? Hell no. Not even one."

Jake nodded. He understood what she meant.

"I don't walk on water either. I don't think I do, at least." She put a hand on his shoulder. "Your role has changed now, Jake. You're the person steering the ship, it doesn't mean that you have to grease the engine or fix the rudder."

"I guess you're right, yep." Jess' words seemed to help.

"You have to believe that you're the right person for the job, and I know that you are - this is your baby. But I know that feeling that you get - when you think that everyone else in the room is smarter than you, and you're woefully inadequate to lead them. Trust me, it's ten times worse when you share a bed with the owner of the company," she smiled.

Once the berlinite was produced onsite, things started getting very exciting in the lab. The long days helped Jake put emotional things behind him. Now, he could truly bury himself in his work, and forget about all he had left behind in Vancouver.

The team started by reproducing the conditions of the Harrison experiments. They were using new berlinite, a new gamma emitter, and a new lab, so it was important to make sure that the measurements still lined up. Jake and Natalie, his radiation expert, programmed the exact variables of the original hulk gun. He was happy to see that the berlinite moved the same distance, and in the expected trajectory. They spent several days checking their results and repeating.

Soon, they began fabricating small containers of berlinite. The atomic clocks available at Planet 9 were more precise than what Jake had used previously. They made a box shape with a latched door and sent one of the clocks 10.5 meters through the warehouse, getting a more precise time and speed calculation as a result. Tiny increases in the amplitude of the wave allowed them to send the boxes further through the lab. The further they could send the berlinite, the more they could begin to map out the relationship between the wave amplitude and the time shift. Even the enormous lab that they worked in had its limitations, though, and Jake began to realize that after only a few days.

After two weeks of experiments, Jake called a staff meeting to discuss ideas. In Dylan's style, he brought everyone for a drink on the marina terrace. It was a quiet, beautiful spot, and he could see why Dylan preferred it to his boardroom. Once his crew had assembled, Jake let them get comfortable and order drinks before he started. It was a new experience for him. He'd been on many teams in his life, but had never once been in a position of authority, or held a general staff meeting. But he kept that fact to himself.

"I just want to say how amazing the last couple weeks have gone, guys. Thank you for crushing it, I had no idea how efficient Planet 9 was going to be before I got here." They nodded in recognition. "The way I see it, we have long term goals and short term. Our long-term goal is to use a berlinite shell to place a satellite in orbit. But we're a long way off from that. We need to run medium scale tests, I'm still unsure of our scaling on the amplitude models."

"We've got a fairly good idea, though, right? Our latest run gave us deadly accurate numbers" Natalie chimed in. She was roughly Jake's age, and an absolute genius with the hulk guns. Although they'd only worked together a short time, Jake had learned to appreciate her brazen confidence and casual manners. Although she was from Arizona, her personality and sense of humor felt very 'Canadian' to him.

"If we're going to encase a satellite in berlinite, we want to be sure" Jake responded. "It's a big investment, even for this place. I really don't want to accidentally send it a million years into the future, you know?"

Jon, his aerospace engineer, raised his hand. He was young, barely out of University, and very shy. "I've been working on a solution to this, Jake. I drafted a design last week." He pulled out his holo-tab from his shoulder bag, expanded the display so that the table could see, and opened a design document.

"What are we looking at?" asked Jake.

"It's pretty basic. I've designed an atmospheric probe that we could launch forward in time. If we wait for the right time of day, so that the earth is moving in the proper direction, and send it 10 milliseconds into the future, it should reappear in the upper atmosphere. I've included a parachute that triggers on inertia, and an instant GPS fix."

Jake was impressed, this was the first time Jon had brought an idea to the table. It was an easy solution that he hadn't thought of. "So, instead of sending it to space, we send it high up in the atmosphere, get a fix for our calculations, then retrieve it. And we get way more accuracy on trajectory and distance. I like it, Jon - I really like it."

"Has anyone considered where we are? It might be impossible to retrieve it. We're surrounded by jungle and ocean" responded Kushal, the team's electrical engineer. He was struggling in the humidity with his long hair, and beads of sweat were condensing on his bushy beard.

"Yeah, might be tough," said Jake. "Could be a lot of fun, though, too. Jon, you may want to double check how long we'll get a GPS fix on your toy. And that it floats. And - make spares."

Jon nodded and put his tab away, happy that his idea was accepted.

"While Jon is building our next phase, I'd like to continue our work within the confines of the lab. We still don't know what the limits of the berlinite construction are. How much is needed for the reaction? Can it be thin? Does it need to be thick? How are objects affected by the trip through time? By Monday, I'd like an action plan on how we'll begin to answer these questions."

The team nodded, taking notes. Natalie interjected with a question. "What should we begin sending through?"

"I want every material used in the Mars program tested, to see if there's any negative reactions. And, eventually, we should be sending living organisms through to check for ill effects."

"Already?"

"All I know is that Dylan agreed to fund this on the agreement that we move quickly in development. So, yes, I don't see why we shouldn't begin with living trials. Or at least preparing for them."

Jake and his crew spent the next hour going over more ideas, timelines, and theories. Eventually, even the excitement of time travel wore off, however, and they began to change topics as the second round of margaritas came around. The terrace staff began lighting the torches around the tables as the sun went well below the horizon. Jake spent the night learning more about his crew, their backgrounds, their families, and their hobbies. Each time they turned the questions to him, though, he politely changed topics. He still didn't trust his secret from Hachiro here. He also didn't want to answer any questions about the convoluted tornado that was his personal life.

Two months passed before he risked sending a message to Travis. He felt awkward and embarrassed by his behavior when they last saw each other, but he also didn't want to acknowledge it or apologize. He was still deeply worried about Travis running loose in Vancouver, and that someone would find out Jake was at Planet 9. He kept the message short, just an update on what was being built, and what their plans for the next month were. All he got back was "*Cool. Thanks Bud.*" Jake didn't know how to take it, he thought Travis would be more excited. He was probably still upset. Maybe he was waiting for an apology, but Jake couldn't bring himself to do it, even though he was missing his friendship more than ever.

He hadn't heard from Mia. Every day Jake fought the urge to message her. He reflected on it every now and then. He still missed her more than he thought he would, and wished more than anything for her to be there with him. That time was done, though. '*It wasn't that bad*' he often thought. '*Just a few white lies to protect her. And myself.*' He struggled to understand where it had gone so sour, so quick.

Nearly three months had passed since he took over the lab in Costa Rica, when he got a message in the early evening:

Hi Jake,
Hope everything is going well in Costa Rica. I'm sure you're even busier down there than you were here in Canada. I just hope that you're finding time for fun between sessions at the laboratory. And I hope you're staying safe around those gamma rays ;)

I wanted to apologize for how things ended between us. I didn't handle it well, and you probably deserved better. You did make a promise to always be truthful with me, and you were breaking it. I didn't know how to deal with that. But I made a promise to you as well, and I've realized that I've broken it. I said that if you needed to keep these things from me, I'd still be your friend. I know we can't be 'together' anymore, but if you'd still like to be friends, I'd like that.
-Mia

Jake read the message, then read it again. He grabbed a beer from the fridge, sat on his patio, and read through it again, and again. He didn't know how to respond. Jake hadn't moved on, but the pain from the breakup was no longer raw, and he didn't know if he wanted to pick at the wound for the sake of a superficial attempt at friendship. Which is all these things ever were.

No. No, he wasn't going to get drawn into this. He had only done things in her best interests! He hadn't stolen or cheated. He hid the details of his life that were criminal from the woman he loved, and he shouldn't have been punished so severely for it. The more Jake sat and thought, the angrier he became. She was right - he hadn't deserved the heartbreak he was feeling. And that was Mia's fault! Jake wasn't the same person as her cheating ex. Jake's lies were far less consequential. He felt a raging anger towards the ex-boyfriend that he'd never met. This was all his fault, not Jake's.

He sat and stewed in his fury for the evening, and finally landed on the decision not to message her back. *'Let it go'* he thought. *'Let yourself move on.'* He opened his holotab again, deleted the message, and deleted all of Mia's contact details.

20.

"I'm caught up!" Jess exclaimed, as she burst through the doors of the control room. "I delegated the rest of the boring rocket stuff away, Jake. I want to spend time with you folks sending stuff through time!"

Jake had been going hard at the lab. He hadn't taken a day off since he'd arrived, and he was happy for any help he could get. Even if it was the CSO.

At first, Jake found Jess Bishop's continued presence slightly intimidating, but he grew to really enjoy her company. She operated just like one of the other researchers, reviewing results, proposing control changes, and so on. When Jake's positive energy began to wear off, he could be sure that Jess' personality would pick up the slack. Seeing her in her element - seeing her as a scientist and not an executive or a billionaire - was very refreshing for him. Planet 9's success began to look less and less like the work of Dylan Bishop and more the brainchild of Jessica Bishop.

After a week of working in the lab, Jess approached Jake in the breakroom. "How are you getting settled? It's been a couple months now, are you comfortable?"

"Yep, the place is great. Just been working, honestly. I haven't spent too much time away from the lab."

"Yes, some of the crew was saying that. You're allowed to take days off, Jake" she smiled. "In fact, I really do encourage it. There's no point in us living down here in paradise if you don't take advantage of it."

"Yeah, I know. I just don't want to right now. There's too much to do."

"In my experience, when people bury themselves too hard into their work, it's usually to distract themselves from something else." Jess grabbed a teacup out of one of the cupboards. "Are you OK? I know it must be strange being down here without Travis."

Jake nodded, staying silent. His face turned to the floor, in a defeated frown.

"I won't press you. Just know that you have resources down here if you need them. And friends."

"Thanks, I know."

Jess could see that he was uncomfortable with the topic. She changed gears. "So, we're ready to try a higher amplitude wave when Jon gets his prototype finished. That should be next week. And we have the frequency dialed in, the time reaction only happens at that exact frequency of gamma wave?"

"That's right. We determined that back in B.C. It's a very narrow band, nothing happens if you're even a little off of it."

Jess fiddled with the cappuccino machine on the far wall and stomped some freshly ground coffee into the portafilter. As the espresso poured smoothly into her cup below, she turned and asked another question. "I'm just curious - did you ever try the inverse of the wave? Same frequency, but inverted?"

Jake thought about it. They hadn't. It seemed so simple, but they'd never tried it. "I have to say, we haven't. Our machine at Harrison couldn't do that, and I've just never thought of it here."

Jess smiled excitedly. "Ooooohhh. Do you want to try it? I've been thinking about the possibilities for weeks now."

Jake agreed. She was like Travis in a way, finding such simple joy in playing with physics. Somewhere in the last few weeks, he'd forgotten just how fun this all was. He shouldn't need to *act* positive in front of his staff, he should just be having fun. He was playing with time travel; it wasn't a chore.

After she finished her espresso, they returned to the main chamber of the building. The pedestal holding the berlinite was 12 meters high, and the lab assistant needed to load the sample with the assistance of a scissor lift. Once the lift had been parked and the safety checks were complete, Jake gave a PA announcement to clear the room. Jess and Jake powered up the FEHFR emitter from the safety of the control room.

"I'm going to repeat the original parameters from Harrison - the same amplitude that we used that whole time. If we fire it in five minutes, with where the Earth is in its rotations, it should reappear right...there," Jake said, bringing up a large holographic display of the chamber. The projected re-entry point of the dolomite sample was highlighted in pink.

"Perfect. I am going to..." Jess trailed off as she typed into her control station. "Here. It's the exact same frequency, but an inverted waveform." She looked up from her monitor to address Jake face to face. "It might do nothing. Or it might repeat the same results. Hell, it might blow up the bloody building."

"We won't know unless we try."

They waited until everything had charged completely, and the appropriate time was on the countdown. Jess fired the emitter.

It took about a minute for the results to pour in, just as it had before. Jake now had sensors to detect the re-entry, he wasn't clawing through security camera footage to get it.

"No way! It moved again, but not where it was supposed to."

"If my hunch is right," Jess measured the new re-entry point to the pedestal on the holo-display. "Boom! 10.31 meters, just like we predicted. And I'll bet...". She drew a line from the re-entry point to the pedestal, then continued it through. It intersected the original re-entry point. It was a perfect, straight line between them.

"Whoa!" said Jake. "We jumped it backwards!"

"I'd been wondering why the gamma reaction always affected the flow of time in a positive direction. Now we know. We can move the same distance in time, but backwards as well."

"That's big. Real big. That changes everything. Again." Jake was floored. How could he and Travis not have thought of this? His mind began racing with possibilities.

The experiments had started with parlor tricks of 'jumping' a cube across the room. Then, they realized that the cube was jumping forward in time. The applications for a forward time jump had been well established in Planet 9's plan. It was a quick and easy way to send a ship on a one-way trip into space. Into orbit and beyond. But the ship would always have to find its own way home or remain wherever it ended up. Time Jumping had been a one-way cheat code through space. But now…

Now that he saw the potential to jump backwards in time as well - the game had changed. That cheat code, the one that could instantly jump them out into the universe, it could also bring them back. Jake started looking into the future, seeing all the progress, pitfalls, and potential disasters such a technology could bring. It was overwhelming. Exciting. Terrifying.

Jess was feeling pretty chuffed. She powered the unit down. "Well, it's too early to say a hundred percent, we'll need to run clocks through again to confirm the results. But, yes, it looks like that moved backwards, for sure."

Jake couldn't wait to tell Travis. If Travis still wanted to hear from him, that is. "I don't know what to say…" He still hadn't quite brought his jaw up to a normal height. "I'll start putting together a new testing regimen, I'll get on it right away. We really need to confirm what we just saw!" He sat down at a desk and brought up the lab's schedule spreadsheet at a workstation.

"Jake." He swiveled around to see Jess calmly leaning against a desk. "It can wait. Let's go for a walk.

Jesus, you're in one of the most beautiful places in the world, and you barely leave the building. Besides, I do my best work out there. I think I need some fresh air, there's a lot to think about now," she laughed nervously.

They finished powering down the control room, then Jake handed it over to Natalie. He and Jess walked out the front doors, squinting into the bright sunshine. The time travel lab was on the outskirts of the facility, and there was a paved trail that led by a creek towards the ocean.

"I haven't been down here yet," Jake said.

"Because you never leave the bloody lab" Jess responded, nudging him in the ribs. "I'll be honest, Jake, I've been wondering about the possibility of backwards time jumps for a while now. I started working out the calculations shortly after you sent down your research. A lot hinges on it. Depending how the rest of the trials continue, there's so much more we can do now."

"I was just trying to process the possibilities in my head. This tech just got a lot more versatile."

"Exactly. We just opened up the galaxy, Jake. Nothing needs to hold us in our own solar system if this works. If we can get the emitters small enough, we can send probes to explore whatever system will be crossing this spot ten thousand - even a million years from now? And now, we can get those probes back, or at least the info from them."

"I see. Because of the drift, they'll be tough to retrieve."

"We'll have to explore very quickly, yes. But even if we got them back in range to send us the info... Christ! Think of the possibilities, Jake."

"Wow, yeah. We can get close-up views of planets we've never even dreamed of."

"Imagine. We can begin designing probes to send back and forth thousands of years through time! We can see any star system along our line of travel, and jump it back to our solar system to relay the information."

"You're thinking that far ahead, already?"

Jess stopped on the trail and looked at him. "Remember when we met, back in April? Do you remember what your motivation was for coming to us with this? It was because you wanted to see what could happen in your lifetime. How far humanity could go." She paused. "I'm almost fifty, Jake."

"No way, really?" Jake had always thought Jess was in her late thirties.

"Well, thank you" she said, tossing her hair back like a runway model. "But yes, it's true. And Dylan's pushing sixty. We may not look it, but we don't have that much time left. Not in the cosmic scale. If you think that the amount of time left on Earth is an issue for you - Christ, you're probably twenty years younger than me, Jake. Whatever rush you're in to get this working, I guarantee that Dylan and I are in a bigger one."

Jake nodded understandingly.

"Dylan took David's death on Mars pretty hard. He felt terrible about not having the Nomad ready, not being able to send more people, more supplies. The press started tearing him apart, saying he didn't care about the twelve. That couldn't be further from the truth. These damn engines..." Jess paused. "We began to realize that we bit off more than we could chew. That, maybe - we had reached the limit of what we *could* do. Of what rockets can do."

"I had no idea any of this was happening down here. Not before I arrived."

"No one does. The engine problems have been kept very secret. You know all about keeping secrets, right?" Jess stopped to check out a large flower growing from an old stump at the side of the trail. "You may not realize it, but you and Travis breathed new life into Dylan. And me, for that matter. I was so excited to start working on the probes, to start mapping out our next chapter. Dylan is already loosely planning huge settlement ships, not just to Mars, but - who knows where?"

"That's if the trials go well. There may still be problems with scalability. You guys are really getting ahead of yourselves."

"We didn't get where we are by playing it safe, Jake."

The thick canopy of the forest opened up as they got closer to the beach. The creek trickled down a rocky shoreline towards a small cove. It was an amazing spot. Jake hadn't spent much time in the tropics, or outside Canada for that matter. He got excited and started to walk down on the sand to where the waves lapped gently into the shore.

"Not so fast. Not here." Jess stopped him. Jake stopped and turned back, confused. "We stay on the trail in this part. There are sea turtles who lay eggs on this beach. We like to leave it for them. They don't seem to use the beach by staff housing, so we swim there."

Jake smiled. "That's so cool. Yeah, no worries." They continued walking along the cove until another path began leading them back to the compound. "These settlement ships..." Jake started. "How big are we talking?"

"If we can construct them on the ground, and time-jump them into orbit, there's really no size limit. Room for hundreds of people, maybe thousands. And all their equipment."

"We can't make that much berlinite, though."

"We can always scale up production, Jake. Especially if we get more investment."

"No, I mean - we physically can't. There's not that much iridium on Earth. You'd be using more than has ever been mined, even with just a thin veneer of berlinite covering the ship. Surely I can't be the first person to think of this problem?"

"You're right" she nodded. "Again, that's why we need you and your tech. Let me show you something." Jess took out a tiny holophone and summoned a cart to pick them up. They kept walking for a few minutes, until a driverless golf cart appeared on the trail in front of them. It did a three-point turn and waited for them to get in. Jess sat in the driver's seat and drove up the trail back to the compound, eventually stopping outside the second largest building on the site. "You need to meet the dwarves."

They walked inside the cavernous space. Technicians in white clean-suits scurried around from area to area. The space echoed activity, the ceiling arched 150 feet over them, and the room stretched out as far Jake could see. There were rocket components being assembled further down, and he could see what looked like habitation pods as well. In front of them, however, was an enormous machine. It had several robotic arms, two of them extended and the rest folded into its body. There were drills, pincer arms, doors and conveyors all over it. "What the heck is this thing?" Jake asked.

"There's not much money in settling Mars, Jake. It's not a great investment. To help with the colony construction, and to begin repaying our investors, we designed these. The dwarves - the first fully autonomous asteroid mining fleet." She walked up to it, and it towered over her terrifyingly.

"Amazing! Again, I had no idea you guys were doing this. How did you hide all this?"

Jess tapped the side of her nose. Obviously, there were still many things kept secret at Planet 9. "Powered by a small nuclear reactor, they can take their own measurements and observations, and only export back the minerals we want. There's an incalculable amount of money up there, and 'rare earth' minerals like iridium aren't all that rare."

"How many do you have?"

"I wanted seven dwarves, just cause, you know? But we ended up with only five" she frowned. "But, if we send these to the right point in the belt, those asteroids will give us all the iridium we could ever want."

"And they're operational? They're good to go?"

Jess nodded.

"Why the heck aren't you using them yet?" he asked, then realized the answer. "The Mark 6 engines. Ah, you can't get them into orbit."

"You see now - just how important a berlinite transport could be to us. If we could time-jump these robots into orbit, and slingshot them out past Earth, we'd be back on track within a few years. And with what we've discovered today, holy shit Jake...everything has changed again." Jess continued showing Jake more of what they had designed, including transport ships she called 'the buckets' which would bring the raw materials back to Mars or Earth. After well over an hour in the assembly building, her phone buzzed. "Do you want to come meet Dylan with me? I asked him if he wanted to check in and have a drink with you."

Jake thought about it. He was starting to feel completely comfortable with Jess, but he wasn't so sure about Dylan, he was very intimidated by him. He quickly tested several excuses in his head to get out of it, but none of them seemed feasible. He'd have to go. "Ummmm, sure, I guess" he resigned. Jess smiled and messaged back on her phone.

They drove through the last of the afternoon sun towards the marina, discussing the proposed asteroid mining project in more detail.

Dylan Bishop was waiting for them at the terrace over the marina. He got up and shook Jake's hand. "How's everything going?"

Jake shook his hand firmly and sat down. "Good. Really good!"

"Jess told me about today's discovery. It's unreal. We've got so much work to do! I'm thrilled!"

The three sat and speculated over what could be coming, and what they could be capable of. The equations of jumping ships both forward and backward in time, with drifting points and large distances, poured out of all three of them. Jake's brain started to hurt; it was a lot to process. After they had settled down, and he was done with his first

Mai Tai, he thought of one more angle. "I guess - I guess we have to discuss something else, here."

"What's that?" Dylan asked.

"We have to promise not to use this for...evil, you know? Now that we can jump backwards through time, there is a potential to manipulate the future. Or the past." He felt ridiculous saying it.

"I don't follow. If you went any consequential amount of time, even a few minutes - you wouldn't be here anyway. You'd have shifted millions, maybe billions of kilometers away. I don't think that's a concern, is it? I know we can talk about the sci-fi tropes of time travel all day, but this is different." Dylan looked at the other two. "Isn't it?" he asked, hesitantly.

"I know that, but you can still predict the future." Jake started drawing out his equation on a bar napkin to illustrate his point. "We've determined that the Earth moves away from the 'time jumped' object at 4500 kilometers a second, right? So - let's say that you wanted to know the outcome of tomorrow's election. Or who wins game seven in the Stanley Cup. So, you send a probe 24 hours into the future, and it pops out roughly 400 million kilometers away.

"But, as fast as the Earth moves away from the probe while it's gone, that movement is still nowhere near the speed of light. So, it can still receive radio transmissions from the Earth at the time that it pops out, and those transmissions will only take twenty minutes or so to reach it. You let it scan the news for a while, then jump it back in time 24 hours, and have it beam it's results to us. Even with the transmission times, you'd be getting the news..." Jake paused to do some quick math in his head. "....at least 23 hours ahead of its broadcasted time. It's a hassle, but it could be done. And I'm scared of the consequences if we did."

Dylan and Jess looked at each other. "I honestly hadn't looked at what we were doing as regular time travel. I hadn't thought about the pitfalls and paradoxes that could bring up. I thought we were safe from all that with the base dimensional movement. You're... right, Jake" Dylan agreed.

"It's a little far-fetched, but it could happen. And we have to make absolutely sure that it never does. The paradox is easy to see - it would have gotten transmissions from a future that we have the potential to change. With these backward trips through time, this suddenly went from an incredibly useful tool - to the most dangerous thing ever invented."

Jess looked at Dylan, who was still deep in thought. "I have no way of guaranteeing that it can't happen. Except my word. It's a risk, for sure. But I think we can all agree that the reward of having this technology is worth that risk."

"Definitely" Jake replied.

Jess looked at her glass, pensively. She hadn't said much since the topic was brought up, and Jake could see that she was deep in thought, calculating the angles. She finally looked up from her glass and spoke. "The more I think about it now, the more I worry. We're in uncharted waters - we have no bloody idea what we're dealing with. If we did send data to the past, how would that affect things? What if that data were to affect the decision to send the probe in the first place? I think we're running into the same old time travel paradoxes that have been talked about in science fiction since the days of Jules Verne. We have to be extremely careful with this, we're dealing with ideas and forces we can't possibly understand." The other two nodded, unsure how to respond.

Dylan stayed silent for a bit, then spoke in a confident manner. "Okay, if it's that big of a risk, we simply create a hard rule. No messages will ever be sent to the past."

"But we can't do that, Dyl," Jess responded. She started arranging glasses and the saltshaker on the table to illustrate her point. "Say you wanted to send a ship to this planet, way over here. You send it through time, into the future, until..." Jess moved the glass representing the Earth towards Jake, and the one representing the foreign planet into its spot. "until the planet in question lines up with where we are in Space. But the problem is - that will be a very long time. Thousands of years. The only way they could communicate with the Earth again would be to send a probe back in time to relay the message to us."

"And everything to them is the past" Jake chimed in. "So, we would need to make a rule that no message ever reaches the earth in their *relative* past."

"I'm sorry guys, I'm out of my league again" replied Dylan, still looking very confused. "What do you mean by the relative past?"

Jess tried her best to explain it. "So, if you went a thousand years into the future to visit another planet, and you stayed for two years, it would be your responsibility to ensure that no transmission from you reached Earth until at least two years after you left. And when you're sending probes back through time to communicate, that's a tough calculation. Or, in other words, if you send a message home on the 300th day after you left, that message should not, under any circumstances, reach Earth 299 days after you left. We just don't know what we're dealing with, otherwise. I can't tell you how imperative this is. We have no idea, no basis of study on what a time paradox would do to our reality."

"I'm still not following, guys - I don't get the danger. They're light years apart, so how could that possibly create a paradox? The two sides have no bearing on each other," Dylan replied.

Jess exhaled, trying to explain what she and Jake already understood. Jake took over the explanation. "So, let's say that you're living in the future. You've been there for a year, and you send a message back through time requesting supplies. You want to save time, though, so you send the message so far back in time that it arrives the day after you left. Then, because the crew back on Earth doesn't know when you sent it, they ship the supplies to arrive before you ever ordered them. Which would mean that you wouldn't have sent the order in the first place. So why would they have sent the delivery, if the order didn't exist? You see, something as simple as ordering food could create a paradox that could rip space time apart. We just can't afford to mess with that, no matter what. We can't ever, ever send a message to our relative past. Communication has to be continuous, as if we never left. We synchronize our clocks, and we stick with it."

Dylan's furled brow finally relaxed. He understood. "Okay, so we make a policy. A guarantee that we never send a message to the relative past, I'm okay with that." Dylan handled the idea like an executive. As if a simple note in the employee handbook could guarantee that they wouldn't accidentally destroy the universe.

Jess nervously glanced around, realizing that she may not be able to guarantee that. Jake did as well, but the two of them quickly swept their feelings under the rug. The promise of berlinite space travel was too great, they would need to handle this new danger. The last wisp of sunlight disappeared behind the horizon as the three clinked their glasses together in agreement.

21.

The airport was busy. Very busy. Vacationers were flooding out of gates in droves, spreading out to the luggage carousels, gift stores and bars like a zombie horde. The PA had a blown speaker that crackled loudly whenever it was turned on. The announcements boomed through the roar of people every few minutes, repeating themselves in both Spanish and English. A tour guide behind Jake was yelling something over and over, trying to get his group to come around him.

All of this excessive noise was not helping his anxiety. It was strange being out in the world again. Jake hadn't left the Planet 9 compound in six months. Juan Santamaria Airport was, by no means, a scary place. It was well designed, safe, and clean, especially by Central American standards. But it wasn't the Utopian Paradise that the Bishops had built in the northern part of the country. He'd gotten so used to the compound that he'd nearly forgotten what the world was like outside of it. Even a slight nudge from a stranger as they tried to get past him was terrifying. Jake wanted to get out of that building, and as soon as possible.

That wasn't the only cause of anxiety, of course. He'd still barely talked to Travis and any communication had been purely scientific since the spring. He didn't know if Travis was angry at him, or distant, or indifferent. All he knew was the last two words he had said to his best friend in person was "Fuck off." But how mad could Travis be? Their technology was in the right hands, they were both millionaires, and they had their dream jobs in a tropical paradise. He just sorely wished he hadn't lost Mia along the way.

Jake had decided to take a day off from the lab and to come pick up Travis from the airport. Travis could easily have taken a hired car, or rented one, but Jake wanted to show support for his friend and partner by being there when he landed. The noise, commotion, and that damned crackling PA made Jake want to get out of that building as soon as possible. But there was another part of him that wanted to delay seeing Travis for as long as possible.

Just as the tour guide's repetitive yelling became truly intolerable, he saw a straw cowboy hat bobbing behind a large family at the gate. As the family moved to one side, he could see that it was Travis - wearing cargo shorts, flip flops, and an absolutely hideous Hawaiian shirt. *'At least no one will think he's here on business'* Jake thought. He braced for the meeting, still debating in his head how he should address him. A handshake? An apology from the get-go? Strictly business?

Suddenly, a great noise erupted from Travis. It was somewhere between a sasquatch roar and a Chewbacca yell, and it startled all the families around him, some visibly jumping in fright. He ran across the airport floor, snapping his flip flops against his feet like firecrackers as he went. He hugged Jake and picked him up off the ground, bouncing him up and down as his sasquatch yell ungulated. Jake looked around the airport in extreme embarrassment, wondering how long he'd be held in the air before security came.

"Damn, it's good to see you dude!" Travis yelled out as he finally put Jake down again.

"You too, man" Jake replied. *'Shit, that was easy'*

"You didn't have to come all the way down. I could've taken one of those supercar thingies and met you at the compound."

"Ah, I wanted to see you, all good. And I needed a day off. How was the flight?"

"All good. Never flown first class before, it's fuckin' rad! They never let your drink go empty up there, it's wild. And I could put my feet up on this ottoman thing in front of me." Jake giggled to himself, thinking of the wealthy establishment in first class sitting beside Travis in his ridiculous straw hat and his dirty bare feet.

"Yeah, it's quite a difference."

"I just need to grab my bags and we can head out, shouldn't be too long."

They took the bags off the carousel and loaded them onto a cart. Jake summoned his car to the pickup zone, and they began loading the trunk.

"Wait - Avis? Did you rent a car to come get me?"

"No, actually, I've just been using this since I got here. Rented it day one and never returned it."

Travis laughed. "You've been here over six months! You're worth millions upon millions of dollars now, and you're still driving a shitty rental Hyundai? You can have anything you want now!"

"I guess I've just been so busy, haven't really had time to think about it."

"Glad to see you're still the same Jake. It's too bad you couldn't get the old rusty Camry shipped down here," Travis smiled.

The car departed once their seatbelts had clicked in, and it exited the airport parking lot very slowly, dodging tourists and luggage carts as it went. It weaved its way through the city, eventually merging onto the highway north to Planet 9. It steadily accelerated to a blistering pace. The trees and houses on the sides were now just a motion blur of green. Jake was getting used to the speeds on this highway, but it still freaked him out a bit. Travis's face was calm and watching the speedometer in amazement, but Jake could see his right hand gripping the handrail firmly.

After a bit in the car, Travis seemed to settle down. Jake decided that he had to address the elephant in the room, he had to get it off of his chest. He didn't know how to deal with it, or even bring it up. He started feeling the stress rising inside him, until he finally just let it out. "Dude, the last time I saw you. I'm...sorry. I was an asshole, you didn't deserve that."

Travis calmly looked at him. "No worries, man." His face had lost the smile, but he didn't look angry. "It was messed up, for sure. We've got stuff to work out, I know that. But not today, OK?"

"I just wanted to…"

"Just let me get settled here first, man. Let's hit the ground running. We'll eventually work out our shit." He reclined his chair back and lowered the straw hat down over his eyes. "But we're cool, dude. It's all good."

They continued north, the car speeding its way across the immaculate tarmac towards the Planet 9 compound. Travis napped for a while, and Jake took out his holo-tab to check on the experiments he had missed that day. Once at the security gate, Jake brought Travis inside to get his badge.

"Wait, Travis Sudbury? This is someone else's credentials. This ain't me."

"Yeah, Jess arranged that. We're both on fake names for a bit, until we're sure the coast is clear. Doesn't affect your pay, though, that's all good."

"Sweet, I've got an alias then. We should go steal some shit while we've got the chance!"

The security guard gave a concerned look at Travis. Jake waved his hand as if to say, *'it's okay, he's joking.'* They drove into the compound, Jake pointing out the landmarks as they went. "I was thinking we'd get you checked in, get settled, then hit the lab tomorrow. I'm pretty sure they've got you in a management condo near me."

"You're still in the staff accom? You could buy yourself one of those huge villas just south of here and barely dent that bonus you got." Travis asked, surprised.

"I'm definitely not roughing it, man, they're pretty nice places. It's not an Alberta work camp, it's more like a luxury resort. And it's been great to be this close to the lab - I've been going hard. It's been nonstop since I got here."

"Can we go to the lab first? I've been dying to see this place in person." Travis was glued to the car window, fascinated with every building they passed. "I've been stuck doing Stephanie's reconciliation paperwork for months now, on that boring hydrogen cell project. I can't wait to do some real fuckin' science again!"

Jake remembered then that Travis hadn't simply been waiting out the months in Vancouver. He'd had to keep working a dead-end job that he knew was over, all while Jake got to build time travel labs and jump probes into the upper atmosphere. Travis had given up a lot to make the plan work.

Since Mia left him, Jake had always felt like the victim in the arrangement. But Travis had given up six months of exhilarating work in the tropics to stay at home and do basic data entry. "Let's go check out the lab, sure. But we'll need to at least swing by mine so you can change." Travis gave him a disappointed look. "They're laid back down here, for sure, but flip flops in the research area is probably pushing it."

"Ah, yeah, that's fair."

They dropped off Travis' bags at Jake's seaside condo. Travis took a few minutes to enjoy the view and marvel at the size of the staff resort. He then changed in the washroom. He came out in shorts, shoes and socks, and a plain polo shirt. "Much better" Jake said. "But you can always rock the Ace Ventura look again later tonight if you want."

Travis laughed and walked towards the car. They began driving towards the lab. "So, catch me up, dude, where are we at?!"

"You got here on a big week. We've been building atmospheric probes for two months now, sending them up into the upper stratosphere to measure trajectories and timings."

"Yeah, you said you were doing 10 millisecond jumps with them?"

"To start. We've even been doing backwards jumps with them, too. But we had to be at the lab at 2 AM to make that work. It'll change with the seasons, obviously."

"Ah, cause the earth was moving the wrong way."

"Yep, we're always factoring that in. We went up to 15 milliseconds, but it got a bit too high for the parachutes to work properly. And we lost a couple - they're a bitch to find after."

"How'd you track them down? You had a GPS locator on them, right?"

"Yep, and we'd grab most with a boat. But you'd get the occasional one that would sail the wrong way, into the jungle canopy."

"Fuck yeah! Did you go take some quads and machetes and find 'em?"

"Yep. Some of the crew was doing that, but the forest is so thick here, we lost a few that we'll never get back. Crazy expensive, but Jess doesn't seem too fazed by it."

"Oh man! That sounds rad! I want to rip out and grab the next one."

Jake parked his car at the staff lot and summoned a cart to grab them. "Jess is on it, man. Like, really on it. You should hear the plans she has in place already."

"Yeah! You said she wants to launch an asteroid mining fleet?"

"The dwarves, yep. They're already built, they just couldn't put em in space. Once they can time-jump them up there, we're laughing. And she has a team scanning for iridium concentrations already."

"Bad ass, man. Are they going to coat the dwarves in berlinite, then?"

"We're designing a launch vehicle currently. It ain't pretty, just basically a giant egg that opens up in orbit and spits out ship components and dwarves."

"So, it would be re-usable?"

"Yep, that's the plan. Stage two of all this will be using the Egg to get the dwarves and their retrieval vehicles in space. As well as finally assemble the Nomad in orbit and prepare for a Mars departure. Stage three - you won't believe what these guys are looking at for stage three."

Travis was enthralled. He couldn't contain himself. "Stage three! What's stage one!?"

"You're in it, dude. The testing phase. We've got the atmospheric probes to work, the calculations are getting more precise by the day, and next Wednesday…"

"What?" Travis couldn't contain himself or his excitement.

"Next Wednesday we're sending our first probe into orbit."

"Fuck yeah! How far up are you going?"

"Not too far for the first one. About 11 seconds into the future, which'll move the Earth about 50,000 clicks out from it. It'll begin freefalling towards Earth, and we'll use that momentum to nudge it into a high orbit."

"Just like we talked about, sweet!"

"The first supply ships for Mars will jump much further out, hopefully by early next year."

"Ah, so the slingshot will be super-fast when it comes around the Earth." Travis was hanging on the side of the cart, waiting to jump out. "Can we check out the probe? I've gotta see this."

They were pulling up to the time lab. Jake and Travis hopped out of the cart, and it drove itself back to the center of the compound behind them.

"Man, it's like a stadium," Travis whispered, cranking his head back to look up at the building. "You weren't kidding, this is crazy."

They walked inside, and Jake gave him a tour of the building. Kushal and Jon were still there working on one of the atmospheric probes, and Natalie was busy in the control room. Jake called them over once he had toured Travis around. "Hi guys, sorry, I know I said I wasn't going to swing by today."

"You *almost* made it 24 hours away from here, that's a new record" Natalie joked, still absorbed by her holotab. When she lifted her head, she saw Travis standing beside

Jake, and her smile got a little bit wider. She quickly turned around to grab something she had left in the control room. Jake wasn't the most observant person, but he could swear that when she returned, she had taken down her hair and removed her glasses. Travis remained oblivious.

"Just wanted to introduce my partner from Vancouver" Jake said. He realized how it sounded as it left his mouth. "My...my lab partner, I mean."

"He should be so lucky..." Travis said, smacking Jake in the right butt cheek.

'Well, there goes my professional appearance. It was a good six months' Jake thought. He fought through the embarrassment while his team laughed. "Anyways...this is the other guy who discovered time travel. He's finally moved down here from Canada to join our team. Travis, this is Jon, Natalie, and Kushal."

Travis shook all their hands and exchanged pleasantries. Jon winced slightly in pain at the handshake - Travis had a very firm grip.

"Nice to meet you, folks! I'm so stoked to be down here." Travis checked his watch. "What time are you guys wrapped up? Can I buy you all a beer tonight?"

'Endless energy, just endless. He's been traveling for twelve hours now' Jake thought. *'But I doubt they'll go for it, it's been a huge week. And there's so much to do before Wednesday...'*

"Sure! 7:30, poolside cantina?" Natalie said, with no hesitation. "I'll message the rest of the crew if you want."

"Awesome, see you there!" Travis said. He and Jake left and began the drive back to the condos. Jake smiled to himself, thinking about how contagious Travis' energy was. And how it was only that morning he had been so worried about seeing him again.

"You sure that's a good idea?" Jake asked.

"I'm rich now. I could buy them beers every night, don't matter."

"Not the money. I just mean...first impressions, you know?"

"I figure we're going to be spending a lot of time together over the next few years. The sooner we can get to know each other, the better. And we don't want to work in a stuffy Hachiro environment again, right?"

Hachiro. Jake hadn't thought about that name for a while.

He pointed out the other buildings to Travis as they drove along but didn't give him the full tour. It was getting late, and he wanted to get him checked in. Otherwise, he'd end up on Jake's couch that night. Travis' condo was very similar to Jake's. A little bit closer to the beach, a little further from the pool. But they both had amazing views over the bay.

Travis was in full form at the poolside bar that evening. The crew were howling laughing as he regaled them with stories from Canada, including a couple embarrassing ones of partying with Jake. He kept the conversation flowing as fast as the drinks, until Kushal, finally, was the first one to bow out and go to bed. The rest fell like bowling pins soon after that.

Surprisingly, after that night Jake felt more like a leader. Travis had a way of breaking down the most reserved person, and the team, finally, became comfortable with each other. It was a good time, and it had been a while since Jake had actually had fun. He had tried, unsuccessfully, to take it easy on the rounds, and was a bit fuzzy on arrival to the lab the following morning.

Travis had hit the ground running. He was already at the lab by the time Jake showed up. He was sitting in the control room, drinking out of the same, dented coffee thermos he'd always had. Up on the screens he had the experimentation schedule for the previous month. "I think I already see a problem, bud," he said, spinning his chair around to greet Jake.

"My pounding forehead?"

Travis laughed. "You got weak down here. Can't let these Americans and Euros out-drink us! No, I mean…" he pointed at one of the results of the atmospheric probe launches. "I think you guys are slightly off. You factored in the gravity freefall time before the probe gets a GPS fix and used that to take your result. But you didn't look at the circular inertia difference between sea level and that height. It's not a huge difference, but it might significantly change our trajectory later on - once we go further out into space."

'Shit, he's right' Jake thought. "Jesus, man, what time did you get here?"

"Not too early. But I thought about it last night as I was going to bed."

Later that week they re-launched a few probes with his new algorithm, and the results were, indeed, slightly different. Jake and Travis took a skiff out on the sea to retrieve them. They had one probe fall in the jungle, and Travis nearly sprinted to get a quad and chase it down. He was in heaven. The crew was benefiting from the fresh blood as well, Jake noticed a different energy in the air. It hadn't been a negative workspace before Travis, but, as it was in Vancouver, his positive attitude was highly contagious.

They worked straight through until Tuesday, putting in long hours at the lab. Jake continued with the orbital probe team, while Travis revised the math with Natalie on the atmospheric runs. Eventually, Tuesday evening came. Jake and Travis stayed very late at the lab, going over every minute detail of the next day's launch. They planned to hit the probe with a gamma wave at 2:14 PM, so that the trajectory would be straight up from them.

They eventually turned the lights off at the lab at 8:30, realizing there was nothing more they could do. Jake and Travis shared a cart back to the condos. "Feel like a quick one on the deck?" Travis asked as they stopped in front of his house. It was dark, but still very warm outside.

"I guess. As long as it's just one. Big day tomorrow."

They went inside. Travis hadn't unpacked yet, Jake could see a suitcase of clothes torn apart on the couch. *'Fair enough'* he thought - it had been a non-stop week. Travis grabbed a couple bottles out of the fridge and went out to sit on the patio. Jake followed.

"Salud!" Travis exclaimed as they clinked bottle necks.

"It's good to have you here, man. Not just at work, I mean." Jake felt self-conscious saying it, staring out at the moonlit bay. "It's been a tough few months."

"Really?" Travis asked, mid-swallow. "This place is rad!"

"Oh no, it's not that. Planet 9 is awesome, for sure. This is the best place I've ever worked, I'd do this shit for free." Jake paused to take a sip. "I'm just still dealing with the guilt of all the lies back in Canada. Mia never came back. I thought I'd lost you as a friend. My family and friends still don't know where I am. "

"Dude… we're fine. It was a stressful time back then, I get it." Travis paused, not sure what to say. "I *am* really sorry about Mia."

"I'll never find someone like that again, man. Funny, smart, ambitious, hot as hell. And she just got me, you know? She saw right past my bullshit. She knew how to get past all the little quirks and insecurities."

"What happened there, anyway? It seemed like things were great with you two. I honestly didn't think you'd break up over this."

"It was just all too much; I hid too much, I broke a promise." Jake took a sip of beer while he thought. "It was all the fuckin' berlinite stuff. I was lying to my family, to my work, and to her. I couldn't tell what was the truth and what wasn't. She had some trust issues, for sure, but she warned me not to hide anything from her. And I… still did for some reason. I'd still be with her if I took a different project last fall. I told you how bad I was at lying, I'm brutal."

"I never needed you to lie to her, man. I'm sorry if that's what you thought. I'm so sorry if I contributed to that."

"Well, what's done is done. It's in the past now." Jake shrugged his shoulders and put his beer back on the table, trying to hold back tears.

Travis was quiet for a bit, then patted him on the back. "Maybe you'll meet someone down here? There's a lot of gooooood-looking females in this little staff resort."

Jake ignored his comment, choosing to change topics. "It seems like things are finally calming down. I just can't wait to put that bastard in space tomorrow. It feels like everything's been leading up to that.'"

"I just can't believe how fast you guys got things done down here, man. It's incredible."

They finished their first beer and Travis talked Jake, reluctantly, into a second. As he was walking back from the fridge, the doorbell rang. "What the heck? You got a girl coming over or something? It's almost ten o'clock!" Jake yelled into the house.

Travis put down the bottles and walked over to the door. He opened it to find a well-dressed Latino man standing on the stoop.

"Good evening Mr. Strickland, my name is Roldan."

"Travis, nice to meet ya," he replied, firmly shaking his hand.

"I'm the personal assistant to Mr. Bishop. He's asked for you and Mr. Crawford to meet him at the airport immediately. Please pack a bag, you may be gone for over a week."

"Oh....ok. Strange."

Jake had walked over to see who it was. "Roldan! Hey, what's going on?"

"I'm not sure, Mr. Crawford. Mr. Bishop has asked for me to pick you two up and take you to the airport."

"Strange, he didn't message me." Jake had a sinking feeling in his stomach. "And it's super late, he knows we have a launch tomorrow, right?"

Roldan shrugged, saying he didn't know. Travis threw together a suitcase of clothes and toiletries, then put his holo-tab and some extra shoes in a backpack. Jake walked to his condo and did the same. Roldan took them to the airport in a company car, which drove at an even higher speed than the other rentals. Although Jake kept asking questions, he didn't seem to have any answers.

At the airport, they drove through a security checkpoint and stopped at the private terminal. Once inside, Jake saw Dylan waiting for them. He was in a light gray suit, dress shoes, and was clean shaven. Jake immediately knew something was wrong. This wasn't the Costa Rica Dylan that he knew.

"Dylan!" Jake greeted him, smiling.

"Hi guys, I'm sorry we couldn't message you." Dylan didn't smile, and he had bags under his eyes. "It's been a long couple of days."

"What's going on?"

"I'm going to take care of it. You guys brought us this tech, and I said I'd do everything I could for you. Just leave it with me, Ok?"

"What's going on, Dylan?" Jake repeated, getting more worried by the second.

"We chartered a jet, it's waiting out there for you - under your fake badge names. It's going to take you to Caracas. Wait there and don't leave until one of us contacts you, OK?"

"What's in Caracas? I don't get it." Jake was sure he knew the answer, but he needed to hear it from Dylan anyways.

"Venezuela doesn't have an extradition treaty with Canada."

22.

There was a funky odor in the hotel bar. Jake couldn't figure out what it was. It was an old place, but very well maintained. The brass work and the wooden counters were immaculately polished, and every surface was clean. The stools were plush leather and oak, and there was a slight hint of the cleaning agent in the air. But it was still there, something foreign that he couldn't place. He was surprised he could smell anything over the massive cigar hanging out of Travis' mouth beside him, anyway.

It had been three days since they'd fled to Venezuela. They'd checked into a hotel in Caracas to wait for a response from Dylan. None had come. Three days of complete radio silence. Only on the third morning did they start to understand the predicament they were in. They weren't updated from Dylan, or Jess, but from the news.

The large TV behind the bar was still tuned into an American 24-hour news station. They were repeating their top stories, as they did every hour on the hour. It was the fifth run-through since Jake had sat down on that barstool.

Dylan Bishop under fire today. The outspoken billionaire is being accused of Corporate Espionage and intellectual property theft by a small research firm based in Vancouver, Canada. According to Hachiro Industries, Bishop paid two of its employees to steal confidential research worth billions of dollars. They've launched a formal lawsuit against Bishop and Planet 9 incorporated. Details of the lawsuit are still unknown. Harada

Hachiro, CEO of Hachiro Industries has filed charges against the two employees.

Neither one of them said a word, still listening to see if any of the details had changed. It was the same carbon copy story from that morning, unfortunately.

A warrant has been issued for Travis Strickland and Jacob Crawford. However, their whereabouts are still unknown. Dylan Bishop and Planet 9 have declined to comment. This is a developing story, and we'll deliver more details as they arrive.

A picture of Jake and Travis appeared on the TV. It was from the Christmas party, they were dressed in tuxedos and were 'cheersing' the camera with their wine glasses.

"Welp, fuck. At least we look good," said Travis through his cigar. The bartender glanced at the TV, then turned back to look at the two of them again. Travis shrugged his shoulders and shot a guilty smile at him. He put another couple of bills in the tip jar.

"How long til they find out we're down here at this rate?" Jake asked. "This picture's been on the TV all day - while we've just been sat out here in the open."

"I don't think it really matters. That's why we're down here, right? So that they have no jurisdiction to come get us." Travis ashed his cigar into a stained-glass tray while he spoke. "You sure you don't want one of these? I bought a whole box. When's the next time you'll be able to smoke inside, dude? This shit's a novelty."

"I don't know, man. But - we'll probably be able to do that for the rest of our lives. I don't see us leaving Venezuela any time soon."

"Nah, Dylan'll take care of us. He promised."

Jake turned towards him with a very condescending look. "It hasn't crossed your mind yet, at all?"

"What's that?" Travis asked, through his cigar.

"It hasn't dawned on you that we may have gotten fucked over? That the Bishops now have all of our time travel research and that we're stuck here as international fugitives? That maybe, just maybe, Dylan and Jess got exactly what they wanted?"

"Well, that doesn't make sense at all. Why would he have flown us out of Costa Rica then? Why not just let us get arrested and take the research anyway?"

"I suspect to get the two key witnesses out of the picture. So that he can beat the lawsuit and have us take the fall."

"Give him a chance, man. We don't know that yet. I'm not ready to think of them like that."

"What I do know is that he has no *real* incentive to help us now. Jess knows everything about berlinite that we do."

"They'll figure something out."

"Are you sure you covered our tracks?" Jake asked. "You replaced the lost berlinite samples before putting them back in storage? Your falsified reports were believable enough?"

"I mean… yeah! I did everything we talked about, Jake. Every last detail. We both knew there was a chance of Hachiro finding out anyway. And he did. No matter how we played it, both of us leaving in the same year was always going to draw some suspicion. And the security cameras from Harrison may have saved old footage somewhere."

Jake was still staring at the flat screen TV behind the bar. "We're so fucked…"

"I wonder how the satellite test went?" Travis mused, taking a sip of his beer.

"Does it matter?!"

"Of course it matters, dude! Since that day last year when you figured this shit out, that's all we've been working towards. Putting stuff in space. Just because we're not there - that doesn't mean that it didn't happen. It's still important. And I'm still really stoked."

"How the fuck...." Jake started loudly, before stopping himself and staring down at the counter. After exhaling a long, drawn-out sigh, he lifted his head and stared at Travis. "I just don't get how you're still positive about this. I don't get how you're just sitting there, casually passing the time, while all this is going on."

"I don't know" Travis replied. "A year ago, I was sat at my desk, bored out of my skull, finishing my safety reports. And here I am, one year later, worth millions of dollars, on the run from the police in fuckin' Venezuela! It's pretty crazy, man" he belly laughed. "It's not very often that a couple of physics nerds get to live the Scarface lifestyle."

Jake didn't laugh. He blankly looked back at the TV on the wall. He couldn't be so cavalier about the situation. The ball of stress in his stomach had ached since the night they left the compound. His emotions flipped back and forth from anger to depression, and it was exhausting. "So, you're the guy who believes there's no bad decisions, right? Did you see us getting here? Where do your turns take you, Trav, when you've reached the end of the river? When there's no other way out?"

"Christ, man, it's not that bad. Take it down a notch."

"Isn't it?! Am I the only one seeing this? We lost the research. We gave it away. The Bishops have it now."

"But we got paid for it. Big time."

"Yeah, but we have nowhere to spend it! We can't go home. I'll never be able to visit my mom again, or see my friends in Vancouver, or go skiing with" Jake stopped. Mia. He had lost her long before the warrants were announced, but it still stung.

"We don't know that, man. It's too early. And hey, there's worse places to be."

Jake analyzed the previous year in his head. Had he followed Travis blindly in these choices? These choices that had led both of them to a hotel in Caracas, on the run from the law. These choices that had cost him his home. That had cost him his family. That had cost him Mia. Jake felt like he'd been led astray. "Oh my god," he whispered. "I never should've listened to you. I knew it was a bad idea to hide it. It was a bad idea from the very start."

"Hey, we both made that call. You were involved just as much as I was, you were there. And our tech is still going to put people in space, even if we get stuck here in South America. We still made the right decision in the grand scheme of things."

"You're honestly not worried about the fact that you may never see your family again?"

"Of course I am! But all we can do is hope that Dylan comes through. There is literally nothing else that you and I can do right now. And I'm not going to sit here and torture myself over it. There's no point. Why don't you just sit back and enjoy being Butch Cassidy for a couple days?"

"That was Bolivia."

"Splittin' hairs. Same continent. You know what I mean."'

Jake looked at him in astonishment. Travis sat there, puffing on a cigar, calmly watching the news as if he was on a vacation. But Jake couldn't just separate himself from the reality of the situation. The ball of stress in his stomach began to boil itself into a rage. He wanted to punch Travis in the right eye socket, more than anything.

But it would be a bad idea to start a fight with the only friend he had left, especially one the size of Travis. He carefully shoved the feelings down inside himself and stood up off his stool. "Do you mind covering these? I'll grab the drinks another day. I've...I've gotta get the F out of here."

"Yeah, no problem, bud. You OK?"

"Yeah, fine. Just... need to be by myself for a while." With that, Jake left the bar and took the elevator back to his room. He was walking slowly, but his breath was sharp and fast. His legs felt weak. He locked the door behind him, putting the privacy bar across to keep out the hotel staff. And that was it. He wouldn't leave his room again that day. Or the next day, or the day after that.

Each morning, Jake awoke in a worse mood. He didn't leave the room, except briefly to visit the liquor store across the street and re-stock. He laid in his bed, trying to find the motivation to simply get up and shower, but he couldn't. His thoughts drifted each day between planning, scheming and hopeless depression. He was smart! He could figure a way out of this, there had to be a way to un-do what they had done. There had to be a way out of this. But, if there was, for all his brainstorming - he couldn't see it.

Every night, he'd make plans for the next day. He knew that he'd have to leave that room at some point. To take a trip into town or visit an attraction. He'd have to figure out what his life looked like now; he'd have to make a plan. Every day, he'd convince himself that tomorrow would be the day he'd feel better. But he never did. He'd wake up and barely leave his bed. Soon, he lost track of day and night behind the hotel room's blackout curtains, as the depression took more hold of him.

For the first week, Travis would visit his door each day and try to shake him out of it. "Come on, man, let's go out! We're young, we're rich, and Venezuelan girls are super hot!" But Jake never came out. No matter how much Travis begged, he'd stay by himself in the hotel room. Travis' pleading visits at the door reduced from every couple hours, to every couple of days, and then, finally, not at all.

Jake simply sat and watched junk on his holo-tab, ordering room service when the hunger became intolerable. The only interaction he had with the outside world was the daily morning knock at the door from housekeeping. "No, hoy no!" he would yell as they knocked. Afterwards, he would resume the next 24 hours of solitude.

A knock in the afternoon startled him. He yelled at the door, but they knocked again. And again. "Entrega de Correo" the voice said softly outside the door. 'Mail Delivery'. He finally answered, and a courier in uniform passed him a letter. He squinted in pain as he turned the lights on to read it.

Jake, it's Jess. I'm so sorry about what happened, I hope you and Travis are doing okay down there. I suppose we knew there was a possibility of a lawsuit, but I didn't think criminal charges would come up this quick.

The team at the lab has been asking about you guys. I didn't tell them anything on the day of the launch, but they all saw the news eventually. I held a meeting with them to tell your side of the story, and to tell them why you two did what you did. They didn't all understand your decisions, but they do all support you and want you back.

The launch went perfect! Just wanted you to know. I felt terrible that you weren't there to see it with us.

I don't know what's going to happen now. Dylan is in negotiations with Hachiro's legal team, but they aren't going well. I think you guys might have to get comfortable for a while. I don't think we'll be able to get these charges dropped. I'm so sorry.

Anyways, I don't want you and Travis left out of the loop, and I definitely want your help with the upcoming craft trials. You're both still on salary, I found a loophole to use. I've also included login info for another alias email account. Obviously, we can't have you using your existing one while all this is going on.

If you log in to our system with these credentials, I'll see if we can set you up to work remotely for a while. I really hope to hear back from you soon.

All the best,
Jessica Bishop

Jake read it, then put it down and turned the lights off once more. '*Bullshit*' he thought. She got exactly what she wanted. She didn't need to fake concern, he knew that she was just covering her ass. She had the research, she had the resources, and she had his crew. Planet 9 didn't need Jacob Crawford anymore. He didn't see a point in going back to work online. He'd already lost everything.

He put the envelope down on a table and went back to lie in bed. He let the letter sit there for days, never picking up his holo-tab to try the login. Travis came to check on him again, asking if he'd gotten a letter as well. Jake gave his letter to him, saying "That part of my life is done. There's nothing we can do now. The whole idea of us working from here is fucking ridiculous." Travis took it, but gave him a very concerned look as he walked away down the hall.

The housekeepers were getting desperate to get in the room. It had been weeks now. Jake sent them away each day. He didn't want anyone to see how he had been living, it was shameful. The housekeeping supervisor arrived and told him, through the door, that he'd need to let them in. Jake refused again.

They finally arrived with security. "Sir, we need to inspect the room," the guard told him at the door. Jake turned around and saw piles of room service garbage, empty bottles covering every table, and dirty laundry strewn across the floor.

"No. I paid very good money for this room. You can inspect it when I leave."

"I'm afraid we need to see it now, sir."

"No, that's not going to happen. Sorry." Jake closed the door again. He didn't much care if he got kicked out of the hotel. He took a swig of rum from a bottle and laid down in his bed again. A security guard knocked again twenty minutes later, then opened the door. Jake had put the doorstop on, however, and it caught the door after a few inches. The guard yelled something in Spanish, then left.

Jake was stewing in his own anger. His mind was racing now, he didn't know whether to pack his things and leave, or just stay and let them break the door. But, where to go? He laid there for hours thinking about it, and decided that they'd just have to drag him out.

There was a knock at the door again. One of the housekeepers was obviously upset. Jake heard her yelling at the door. "Estoy buscando un apuesto nerd con quien besarme!"

Jake walked to the door. She yelled the same phrase again. "Please, I just want to be left alone" he said. "Please!"

"Estoy buscando un apuesto nerd con quien besarme!"

"I don't speak Spanish, I'm sorry. No entiendo!" he said back.

She pounded on the door this time. "Estoy buscando un apuesto nerd con quien besarme!"

What the hell is she saying? Are the police coming? Jake didn't know what to do. He grabbed his phone, turned on a translation app, and held it up to the door.

"Estoy buscando un apuesto nerd con quien besarme!"

Jake looked at his phone for the translation. It read *'I'm looking for a handsome nerd to make out with.'* "What the fuck?" he said out loud.

He swung the door open to see what was going on. There, standing in the hallway holding a small carryon bag, was Mia.

23.

"Sorry, I just learned the one phrase in Spanish," Mia laughed. "Oh my god, you look terrible. Never mind…" she said, starting to walk away down the hallway. She smiled and came back.

"What…what are you doing here?" Jake asked.

"I was worried about you! You never wrote me back. And now, your face is all over the news, I didn't know what to think."

"How did you find me?"

"Travis messaged me. He's really worried about you as well."

She was just as beautiful as he remembered. She was dressed for the tropics, wearing jean shorts and a sleeveless t-shirt. She had her ponytail threaded through the back of her Patagonia ballcap. Seeing her here, in front of him - everything else seemed to matter a little less. It was as if someone had pulled a drain plug out of his brain. The anger and resentment swirled away, and he suddenly felt naked in front of her. "I'm doing ok" he lied.

"No you're not" she said calmly.

Suddenly, Jake was overloaded with embarrassment. The room. Shit! He closed the door behind him, hiding his cesspit of a hotel suite from Mia. He couldn't let her see him like this. He looked down and saw the dirty gym shorts and the ketchup-stained t-shirt that he was in. "Maybe I'm not OK."

"You think?" she raised an eyebrow. "How long have you been in there?"

"I don't even know anymore. It just - it doesn't matter anymore."

"You still matter. You still have a life, Jake. You're still an amazing person, you still have friends and family who love you. Where you are and what you did doesn't change any of that."

"God damn it's good to see you."

Mia dropped her luggage and hugged him. He held her tightly, remembering the warm smell of her conditioner. Five seconds passed, then ten. He tried to release the embrace. She wouldn't let go. He tried again, but she held him tight. Suddenly, Jake felt it all release. Tears filled his eyes and started streaming down his cheeks. He gasped for air as the emotions began pouring out. Even with everything that had happened, everything he had lost, it was the first time he had allowed himself to cry. Months of pent-up tears flooded out, and he completely lost control of himself.

Mia held him as he sobbed, rubbing his back. A few minutes passed. When he finally stopped, she released him and backed up to see his face. "Feel better?"

"I'm so sorry, I...don't know where that came from."

"Jake, I cry at Hallmark movies. It's OK to cry if you're wanted on international corporate espionage." She rubbed his arm.

"Thank you," he said, drying his cheeks on his sleeve.

"Honestly, you smell fucking awful though," she laughed.

"Ohhh, yeah. I need to shower and change. I'd invite you in, but..."

"Oh, don't worry. I have zero desire to see your disgusting Hunter S Thompson room" she responded. "Tell you what, there's a little cafe across the street. I'll go wait there, you shower and change and meet me there when you're ready."

"There's a nice bar downstairs, too."

"Yeah, let's keep you out of the bars for at least a couple days, ok?" she smiled. "I was thinking we could go for a walk. Here, I'll let you store my luggage, though."

"Sounds good." Mia walked away down the hall. She glanced back and caught him staring at her. Jake shyly looked down, then went back inside his room. Invigorated, he opened the blinds and windows, seeing his mess for the first time in the ugly light of day. He quickly got rid of the empty bottles, bagged up his laundry, and threw out the garbage. His razor struggled to get through the thick growth of hair on his neck as he tried to clean up his beard. He showered, combed his hair for the first time in weeks, and found the last of the clean clothes in his suitcase.

Mia was seated at a street level patio table. Jake ordered a coffee to go and they began walking through the streets of Caracas, taking in the beautiful old-world architecture and street art. Jake hadn't let himself see any of it yet, he'd gone straight from Dylan's jet to his hotel room. Even during the cab ride in, he'd been too preoccupied to see the beauty of the city. They made their way through the narrow streets, stopping in the occasional shop if it caught their eye. Jake caught her up with everything that had happened in Costa Rica. Mia told him about what she'd been up to in Canada since the spring.

They stopped at the National Pantheon to have a seat on a park bench. Jake had made his way through the day without sunglasses, just squinting when he needed. But here, facing the glaring white of the monument wall was a bit too much. "Do you mind if we move to the shade?" he asked.

"You must be getting a vitamin D overload. No problem," Mia replied. They found a shaded spot nearby under some trees.

Jake was relaxed. Perhaps for the first time in months. Being next to her felt so natural, so right. He felt so calm that he didn't hesitate to bring up the tough conversation. He was done procrastinating; he was done waiting to tell the truth. He needed her to know how he felt.

"I'm so sorry about how things went in Vancouver," he said, breaking the silence. "I promised to keep you in the loop. I promised not to lie to you, and I broke that. I guess I didn't want to completely let you in, and I don't know why. I was such a mess with everything going on. I was only thinking of myself, I kept forgetting about how you'd be affected by all the lies."

"Not just me, Jake. How do you think your Mom took it when she saw your face on CBC? Did she know any of this was happening? Or your sister? Or your friends?"

"I know. I wish I could go back and do things over. I wish I could just submit the truth to Hachiro, and none of this would've happened."

"Well, I wouldn't go that far. We don't know how things will turn out. Could still be for the best. But I kind of doubt it." Mia turned from him and looked out onto the street. "I'm sorry too, Jake. I overreacted. Yeah, you shouldn't have broken your promise, but I was pretty damn quick to call things off. I was embarrassed by my behavior after you moved away. I'm still working through my trust issues, and I think I focused them all on you."

"It's okay. It *was* my fault."

"Yeah, but I shouldn't have thrown away what we had just because you hid that meeting from me. I think I just pushed you away... because I thought you would leave me eventually." She turned back to face him. "Why didn't you write me back? I was worried."

Jake got flush with embarrassment. "I don't know. I was angry." He fiddled with his hotel room key as he spoke. "Angry with you, angry with Travis, angry with myself. I just wanted to leave it all behind."

"Why were you angry with Travis?"

"I felt like the whole idea to hide the research came from him. Even though I agreed to it. I blamed him, and it wasn't fair. And he was just so friggn' casual about it, like it wasn't affecting him at all. And after the lies cost me you..."

She smiled at him, shyly. Neither said a word for a few moments. "So, what happens now, anyway?" Mia asked. "Have you had any word from lawyers or anything? Are you stuck here forever?"

"Not a word from anyone. No one knows we're here, officially. There're very few countries in the world who don't share an extradition treaty with Canada. So, yeah, I think I'm here for a while."

"Have you heard from Dylan Bishop? What's their plan?"

Jake felt his right hand harden into a fist. "I think they got their plan. They have the research, they have the lab I built for them. Why would they help us now?"

"So, nothing?"

"Jessica Bishop, his wife - she's the CSO of Planet 9 - she sent me a paper letter by courier. Said they're working on it, that Dylan is in negotiations with Hachiro. She sent me an alias login to continue working with my team remotely."

"And? Have you been?"

"It's a ruse! It has to be. I don't get why they would need me at this point. They're not going to help us. Going to them with the berlinite equations was a massive mistake!" Jake felt his chest tighten with stress again as he said it. He was filled with regret as he spoke.

Mia grabbed his hand. "Jake..." she said. "How can you be so sure of that? How can you be so sure that they want to screw you over? That they don't want you to work with them?" She started laughing to herself as she spoke. "How can the guy who discovered time travel have such low self-esteem? Jake, you're now one of the most important people in history - I hope you haven't forgotten that."

Jake's chest loosened. Somehow, through everything that had happened, he'd lost sight of what he'd actually achieved.

"They're probably doing everything they can to help you," Mia continued. "It's going to be complicated, for sure. But of course, they'll do what they can to get you working with them again. It would be idiotic for them to not want you and Travis back."

"How can you be so sure?"

"You're just……" Mia paused, trying to describe what she meant. "You're looking everywhere for a villain, Jake. You have been for a long time. But maybe your story doesn't have one. Travis has been by your side from day one, and you made these decisions with him. It's not his fault what happened, and he's been a solid friend to you. The Bishops have done everything they said they would do. It sounds like Jess really likes working with you, from what you've told me. They haven't done anything to justify this new opinion you have of them. They're not the villain here, either. Maybe there isn't one."

"What about Harada Hachiro? Travis and I are on the run because of him, he's the reason we're in exile."

"Jake, that man invested a fortune in his company, and paid you well while you worked for him. You discovered a technology worth billions while you were his employee, snuck away and gave it to Planet 9, and he didn't get a dime. You don't think he deserves to be pissed?"

Jake thought about it. Of course Hachiro would go after them. It only made sense to.

"It's your secret opinions of these people that's the problem. It's the way that you over-analyze every situation and everyone's motives. You're not even giving them a chance before your brain goes crazy. Maybe the problem has always been in here." Mia pointed a finger at Jake's head. "But - no judgment. I know the reasons you went to Dylan, and they're noble. It was a tough choice. I wouldn't have done it, personally, but I understand why you did."

"I'm glad that someone does…"

"You guys want to see better space travel in your lifetime. All the choices you made were to get to that goal, but you knew there was a risk that something like this could happen. You guys knew all of that going in. You're paying the penance for that decision, and it sucks."

"I'm having a real hard time staying positive, Mia. Even if it was the right choice, it landed me here. I just don't see a way forward, I don't see a way out of this."

"Well, yeah, but Jake - you're not really trying. Laying in a hotel room drinking rum isn't going to help you."

Jake chuckled. He couldn't believe how much better he felt around her. Just this morning he was completely stuck in a dark cloud. Now he was fully embarrassed by his reactions. "You're right. I'm being an idiot."

"You're stuck in Venezuela. You can't go home, and you're facing serious prison time for what you've done. It's okay to feel down, it's a really shitty deal. But nothing is going to change unless you do. Cliché's aside, you *can* choose to make lemonade right now, if you want."

Jake nodded.

"I usually don't go for the motivational posters. I find them super cheesy. But there was one that I read years ago that stuck with me. It said 'Being positive doesn't mean being happy every day. It means that, no matter what bad things happen, you always know that there are better days ahead.' This time is going be hard - really hard, but you can still make the best of it. You can work remotely with Jess. You can call your family. You can maybe even try to enjoy yourself down here. There's worse places to be."

Jake looked at her. The wind blew her hair onto her left shoulder. She had taken her sunglasses off, and he could see deep into her beautiful brown eyes once again. They locked stares with each other. Something felt right again, like he was in the spot that he was supposed to be. He was with the person that completed him, and he had found that comfortability that had been missing for so many months. He felt himself being drawn in, being pulled into her lips. He leaned in to kiss her.

The brim of her ball cap hit his forehead and threw him off. It scraped back on his head and fell off hers. Mia laughed. He pulled away. "Let's just...not do that" Mia said through a laugh, then stopped and looked caringly at him.

"I just came here as a friend. I don't know about all *that* yet, Jake, I just came here to help."

He laughed as well, suddenly feeling very awkward about the moment. They spent the rest of the early evening making their way back to his hotel. They stopped at a food cart to get some arepas and ate them as they walked. Eventually, Jake summoned an auto-cab when Mia's sandals started cutting into her toes.

"Where are you staying?" he asked after they had sat down in the car.

"I haven't figured that out yet, I came straight to you from the airport."

"Let me book you something. It's the least I can do, you came all the way down here to see me."

"You don't have to…"

"Please. It's not a problem." Jake took out his phone and booked two rooms at another hotel.

"Two rooms?" Mia asked.

"I…don't really want to show my face at the Renaissance again. I kind of want to get the fuck out of there before anyone recognizes me. And now that I'm feeling better, I really don't want to go back inside that room."

"That's fair, I get it."

Mia waited in the bar while Jake packed up his room, leaving a very healthy tip behind for the housekeepers and sneaking away down the hall when it was empty. He loaded up a cart with his luggage and Mia's and rolled it down to the front street. They summoned a cab again, and it carried them to the new hotel.

Jake booked himself a modest room, but got a penthouse suite for Mia. He was so happy to see her, to have her in his life again, and he wanted her to be comfortable. He made a decision to contact Jess the following day to find out how he could work remotely. He would begin looking for houses to rent. He had to get his life back on track.

After dinner at the restaurant, Jake went to his room so that Mia could sleep. Her travel day had been exhausting. He'd barely sat down and taken out his holo-tab before she knocked on his door and invited him up to watch a movie, saying she'd still be awake for a while.

They began the movie as friends, sitting on different couches, and talking all the way through it. Jake ordered some popcorn and candy from room service, and Mia moved to his couch to share it. When the bowl was done, Jake felt her head move to rest on his left shoulder. He could smell the conditioner she used, and the scent took him back to those happy days he had spent with her in Vancouver. He slowly changed positions on the couch, lifted the arm she was leaning on, and she leaned her head onto his chest. They stayed there for a few minutes, both not knowing what the other's intention was.

Finally, Jake heard Mia say "Oh, who was I kidding?" She turned her head up towards him and kissed him. "I missed you so much, Jake."

He canceled the second room the following morning.

24.

Roldan had instructed Jake and Travis to pack for 'a week away' from Costa Rica, but that was a monumental underestimate. Weeks passed, then months. Then years. Occasionally, Dylan would reach out to Jake and Travis to give them an update. It was always something along the lines of *'lawyers are still working on it'* or *'we may be close to a deal.'* Eventually, they stopped getting optimistic each time they heard from him. They began to think about the true possibility of never leaving Venezuela.

Jake was able to work remotely, however. Jess had started off by sending him a new login and a new alias. He could communicate with his team, find out experiment results and join staff meetings. Eventually, Jess managed to send VR rigs down to the two of them in Caracas. They were connected to mobile robots in the lab building, so Jake and Travis could go in and interact with the team for a few hours each day.

At first, the team back in Costa Rica was quite apprehensive about working with the two fugitives. The news had consistently updated the story, and none of the coverage put Jake in a favorable light. He made the decision early on to come clean with them. He decided to tell his team everything from his perspective, and to explain all the reasons why they had come to Planet 9. Travis joined him in a virtual meeting online.

The staff were split. Natalie cheered them on, saying that their choices had advanced humankind by centuries. Kushal didn't agree with them at all, saying that they had broken the trust of their employer. Others fell somewhere in the middle, not taking a firm stand either way. Travis eventually piped in to wrap up the heated discussion, saying "Look, guys. It doesn't really matter what we did, or if you think we're good people or not. The reason we came to you with this shit is that you're the best in the world. We want to see berlinite put people in space within our lifetime. The best way for you to help us is to keep doing your best work. Which you all have been, I can't believe we've come this far, so fast." The team agreed with that, and they made an effort to move on.

Dylan continued to pay their enormous salary, and the cost of living in Venezuela was very low. Still, it took a long time for Jake to lose his thriftiness. He'd lived his whole life with a keen understanding of money and had always tried to make responsible decisions with it. He'd very rarely spend cash impulsively. But now, for the first time, money meant nothing to him. Travis and he were earning massive paychecks, and he'd still barely touched his initial signing bonus with Planet 9.

After four months in the city, Jake finally decided to move out of hotels. He'd be down there for a long time, unfortunately, and he needed to find a life that was more comfortable. He purchased a home in the mountains south of Caracas to live in. It was remote, and accessed only by a gravel road, so he bought a new A.I.-driven Land Rover to access it. It wasn't an ostentatiously large house, but it was new, had a beautiful view from the three separate decks, and had a small pool on the garden terrace. He installed a high-speed satellite uplink to continue his work, and renovated one of the five bedrooms into a home office. Travis bought a similar house nearby and visited him often.

Mia was a consistent visitor. Her company had set her up to work remotely, so she would try to do a month in Venezuela followed by a month back in Canada. He had a great time when she was there with him. Each day was an adventure, however small it may be. They bought mountain bikes and explored the trail networks near him. She convinced him to take an expedition with her to see Angel Falls, and they hiked through the 'lost world' plateau.

They even found out that Mystic Realms had a franchise in Caracas, and would occasionally spend date nights in the city having a fancy dinner - followed by fighting orcs. Jake even convinced Travis to come try it. He was very hesitant to enter the game at first, as he had a tough time trusting VR equipment. But, as luck would have it, the game randomly set his avatar as a sexy wood nymph. He spent the first hour feeling his own boobs and giggling uncontrollably.

Jake contacted his family shortly after Mia rescued him from his hotel room. After getting scolded by his mother for hours about how much she had worried, he managed to sway her opinion to his side. Over the years that he lived in Venezuela, he'd often fly her down to stay at his house. His sister and her kids came down to see him once as well, which surprised him, as she had never left British Columbia before that.

Back at Planet 9, things were moving at a frenetic pace. Their first satellite had successfully time-jumped into orbit the same day Jake and Travis entered exile. After the fourth successful trial, Jess dumped far more resources into the project. By the anniversary of Jake's flight to Caracas, a third of the staff at Planet 9 had changed from rocket science to work with berlinite technology. Somehow, though, Jess and Dylan had kept the project secret from the general public. Even with thousands of people 'in the know', Jake never found any trace of the project in mainstream media. Conspiracy websites talked about strange happenings at the Planet 9 compound, but credible news articles were scarce.

While the Berlinite Egg was being constructed, Jake and Travis were still refining the science with their original team. The atmospheric and space probes had clarified their direction and speed calculations. Now, they worked on studying the effects of the time trip on different materials. They worked out how a thin veneer of berlinite would still cause the time jump reaction, and would shield anything directly behind it from all gamma rays. They played with the width of the beam, the power supply, multiple hulk guns on single targets, and countless other experiments.

Their team was also responsible for testing materials. The full effects of the time jump were still unknown. They gathered samples of every material used in spaceflight and sent them through the jump. Each sample was carefully analyzed afterwards to check for any changes or inconsistencies. It was a very time-consuming operation, but it was necessary for the future plans of the company. Eventually, they began sending laboratory mice through. A team of biologists would spend months analyzing the after-effects of the jump on a variety of different animals. And, eventually, of course, humans.

All of that was simple, though. They weren't pushing themselves. They were simply going through the motions of their earlier experiments. Jess eventually tasked the two of them with something much more complicated.

All the probes had, so far, been launched from their laboratory. It was a one-way trip - whether forward in time or reverse. But, if they wanted to really use this technology properly, they'd need the craft to time-jump itself. The probe would need to fire gamma rays from within itself to trigger its own berlinite shell, cause the reaction, and disappear into time. Not only would it allow them to launch larger ships into orbit, the ships could then jump through time again when they were out in space.

Smaller, more efficient FEHFR emitters were designed and built. Jake and Travis worked with Jon and Kushal to design new 'two-way' probes, from their stations in Venezuela.

A small craft, like their probe, could use one small 'hulk gun' in its core to trigger the reaction. Jake designed a new system with his team, and they sent a new probe 72 hours into the future - a distance of over a billion kilometers. When it arrived out there, the onboard computer was supposed to take a few minutes of scans and pictures, then jump the same amount of time backwards to catch orbit with the Earth.

Unfortunately, their design failed to fire the emitter again for the return trip, and the multi-million-dollar bundle of computers and berlinite was left to drift through the outer solar system forever. They had no way of retrieving it, and no successful way of contacting it. It was a major setback. Jake took full responsibility for the miscalculation, and sent a long, drawn-out letter of apology to Dylan and Jess. He fully expected to lose the leadership of his team.

Dylan had taken a backseat on the project. He was simply there to grease the right wheels and ensure that everyone had what they needed. Jess ran the compound and the research, not him. In fact, Jake had barely heard from Dylan since they left him on the tarmac in Costa Rica, he'd become a ghost. When Jake sent his long-winded apology for losing the probe, however, he got a message back within minutes.

Jake, failure is the best teacher. We all need a bit sometimes. Keep at it :)
    -   Dylan

It was too casual. It was too breezy of a message for such an expensive fuck-up, it didn't make sense. Jake realized that he was dealing with levels of money that he truly didn't comprehend. Back at Hachiro, his budget was limited. Costing the company any extra money back then would risk his career. But now, on the edge of revolutionizing space travel, a 30-million-dollar probe was just a drop in the bucket.

He re-designed the control system with Travis and Natalie's help. Two months later, they had an autonomous probe that could successfully jump years into the future - and return back in time successfully.

After the two-way probes worked, Jess took her rocket team and finally constructed their first berlinite-coated carry ship - the Egg. The concept was brilliant - she could time-jump the Egg into space from the field outside her building, where it would open one side and release a vehicle or component into space. It could then maneuver itself into a low orbit, and, through a very carefully timed series of additional jumps, transport itself into the lower atmosphere above the Planet 9 compound. A series of retrorockets would then gently lower it back to the ground, where it could be reloaded for the next trip.

Within two years of Jake and Travis' departure, the Egg had been constructed and tested. A year after that, Planet 9 was back in the news. They had gotten the Nomad into orbit above the Earth, and it was prepping for a departure to Mars. The massive ship would carry an additional 216 employees to join the Martian Twelve, along with new supplies, equipment and buildings for the surface. What the news didn't cover was that the pieces of the ship, its components, and all the supplies had been sent into orbit using the time-jumping Egg, not rockets.

Jess eventually sent the Egg on trips much further out from the Earth. She had it deliver the 'dwarves' to locations closer to the asteroid belt. They could get close, but the technology still had its limitations, which meant they couldn't get directly to an asteroid using a time-jump.

It was impossible to time-jump their ships directly to Mars, or to time-jump the dwarves directly to the asteroid belt. The sun was following a trajectory around the galaxy, and the galaxy was following a trajectory through the universe. This created a line of travel that the solar system moved in. Because the Egg was staying 'still' during the time jump, and the solar system moved away from it, they could only reach destinations along that line. Jess would often joke about how much more convenient it would be had that line matched the flat plane of the planet's orbits. It didn't, it was roughly 12 degrees off that plane, which created a substantial difference by the time a ship reached Mars' orbital distance.

It was still faster for Planet 9 to build the Nomad at the Earth, and for it to make its own way to Mars. The logistics were easier that way. For the dwarves, though, the asteroids were so far away that it was worth the extra jump. They had a new, fast propulsion system, but it would still take a long time for them to cover the 200 million kilometers from Earth to get to the iridium-rich rocks the team had found. The jump would get them as close as it could, and the dwarves would need to propel themselves the remaining 40 million kilometers 'down' to reach their destination. Still, it was worth it.

While Jess' team worked on sending the Egg, the Dwarves, and the Nomad further out into the solar system, Jake's probe team began looking further. Much further.

It was the most exciting project Jake and Travis had ever worked on. They helped design advanced surveying probes that would time jump hundreds, even thousands of years into the future. Their computer models predicted when a star system would come close to the Earth's current spot, and they would send their two-way probes to those time periods. Once the pictures had been shot, the readings taken, and the survey completed, the probe would jump back in time to beam its findings to Earth. They were finally exploring the universe - just from the comfort of their bedrooms in the South American countryside.

As the months and years dragged on, Jake felt more and more comfortable in Venezuela. His life in Canada began to fade into a distant memory. He made friends in the small village near his house, learned a functional amount of Spanish, and explored the country on his days off. What began as a punishment of exile became a genuinely good life. Jake wondered if he'd ever been as happy in Vancouver as he was in Venezuela. Things didn't seem to stress him out anymore, the ball of stress in his stomach disappeared, and he learned to be content with how his life had gone.

Travis seemed to do the same, but he started to struggle with the delay as the years carried on. He was fine with the fugitive lifestyle at first, and was even enjoying the concept. But as they continued living in those remote mountains, Jake noticed that he was beginning to change.

The upbeat, happy-go-lucky man he'd always known was beginning to fade. Travis would get irritated by petty things at Planet 9, and the news from Canada would anger him into long rants. Most days he'd still have that same joyous energy, but something about it felt forced - like a performance. It didn't feel authentic like it had in the previous years. Jake worried about him and wondered what the difference was between his experience in Venezuela and Travis'.

    The answer was obvious, of course. It was Mia. She had been a supportive partner since the day they got back together. No matter how stressful or dark his days got, Jake could always count down the days until he got to see her again. Travis didn't have that. He had dated plenty in Caracas, but never saw one girl more than a few times in a row. And as the months and years dragged on, he dated less and less. He spent more time at his house. They made an effort to meet up at least once a week, and Jake looked forward to those nights. But, for Travis, anything outside his house seemed like a chore.

    Four years passed. They had worked remotely for what felt like an eternity. Back at Planet 9, Jess had finally sent the Nomad to Mars, the dwarves were all in the asteroid belt, and their team had started sending probes to investigate neighboring star systems. The pace of development was staggering. It helped Jake justify their choices, to accept the path that they had ended up on. He began to accept that they may never leave Venezuela, and prepared himself for that eventuality. Travis also talked about that, but in a much more resigned way. He was an animal in a cage, his soul was being drained away the longer he stayed in those mountains.

    One afternoon in February, no different than any other, Jake heard his doorbell ring. Someone was at the security gate. He stood to attention. Unexpected guests always made him nervous, he always assumed that it was the police coming to extradite him. Mia was in Vancouver, and Travis always messaged before coming over. No one else would come by unannounced. He tried not to panic but carefully closed the file he was working on at his station, and locked the computer with his biometrics. He checked his phone to see if his Land Rover was charged, calculating how far he could get if he made a run for it.

Nervously, he took out his holo-tab to check the gate camera feed. He smiled when he saw a well-dressed Latino man in the image. A familiar face. He ran outside to greet him and open the lock.

"Roldan! Long time no see!"

"Hello Jake. I hope you've been keeping well."

"Well as can be expected. What are you doing here?"

"I've been instructed to pick up Mr. Strickland and yourself and drive you down to the city. I'm not sure why."

"Oh shit. Do we have to pack bags again?"

"I haven't been told anything like that, no."

Jake's mind started to whirl. Was he being taken to another country? Did he have to rebuild his life from scratch - again? "Okay. Can I have a couple minutes? Just need to get changed." Roldan nodded.

Jake got in the car after he put on a clean shirt, and they drove over to Travis' house. He came to his gate wearing nothing but board shorts, and gave Roldan a hug when he saw him. Roldan looked very uncomfortable. They waited for Travis to change, and within ten minutes they were back on the road towards Caracas.

"So, you really don't know what's going on?" Travis asked. "You gotta help us out here, bud."

"I don't, I'm very sorry. I only had instructions to pick you up and drive you to a certain address."

Travis turned to Jake. "I don't know. I feel like if we were getting arrested after all this time, they wouldn't have sent Roldan to get us. Something else is going on."

"I have a bad feeling about this."

"Ah, we could use a shakeup. Let's just see where this shit goes, I guess. If it's our time, it's our time."

Roldan dropped them off in front of a small restaurant. It was a small, cute place, with thatched umbrellas on the patio and an open-air dining room. It looked empty, or at least very quiet. Latin music played softly on the patio speakers as Jake and Travis approached. "What the hell is going on?" Travis whispered.

They opened the front door to see a large table set in the middle of the room. Everyone stood up as they saw them and cheered. They raised their cocktails and wine glasses and hooted and hollered in excitement as the two fugitives walked towards them.

There, sat at the end of the table, were Dylan and Jess Bishop. Jake's entire team was there as well. Jess ran over and gave him a hug, squealing with excitement. Natalie ran right past him to hug Travis. Dylan walked over and shook both their hands, smiling widely and laughing. "Gentlemen! Sorry, I thought it would be more fun to let you know this way. And I had lots of room in the jet, so I brought your whole team."

Tizana cocktails were pressed into their hands as they sat down. Dylan raised his glass to the center of the table to start a toast.

"Wait, so... sorry...What's going on?" Jake interrupted. "Why are you all here?"

"The lawyers took forever to get this sorted out, no matter how much I pushed them. But I own the patent on your research now, finally. And, therefore..." Dylan paused for dramatic effect. "Hachiro has dropped all charges against you two."

"No way! Fuck yeah!" Travis yelled.

"Let's just say that getting that research, and you two off the hook, cost me a few billion dollars, but it's well worth it" Dylan continued. "Either way, though, you guys are picking up the tab tonight, I'm a poor man now."

Jake laughed with relief. It was so good to see people again, and he'd get to work in Costa Rica once more. Happiness washed over him as it sunk in that it was finally over. Travis was shaking with excitement. Jake saw that authentic joy come out in him again, the one that had been sorely missing lately.

They ate and laughed and drank far too much that night. Near the end, Dylan addressed the two of them. "So, gentlemen, sorry for the late notice, but I need you guys back at the compound for Monday. We've only got one week before you, Jess and I have to give a presentation in New York."

Jake was a little tipsy by the time he heard this, but was still intrigued. "Presentation?"

"Oh, that's the best part of all of this, guys. At last - no more secrets. We're going to finally tell the world what we've been up to."

25.

Jake looked out at the sea of faces in the General Assembly Hall. It was very intimidating. The room wasn't completely full, but he estimated there were well over 800 people in attendance. The tables were labeled with their representative countries, and Jake could read the first few rows. As the chairs went further back, he struggled to recognize the flags, and he had no idea who was who. At the back of the room, sealed in soundproof booths elevated above the audience, dozens of interpreters waited patiently for them to begin. He hadn't presented anything to a group since he was in university, and even then, it was only a few professors at a time. Here, he was about to present revolutionary scientific findings to the International Science Council. Being intimidated was justified.

He'd spent the previous week preparing with the Bishops at the compound. Beyond what they had already accomplished, they'd be presenting the future of Planet 9. Dylan had much bigger plans that he was releasing, plans that shocked even Jake and Travis.

They'd taken the private jet to New York and gotten set up at a hotel the night before. Travis and Jake were feeling a fair amount of culture shock. A week earlier they'd been hermits in the mountains of South America, now they were keynote speakers at the United Nations. It was the first time either had worn a suit and tie since that Hachiro Christmas Party so many years ago. They'd watched a few other talks that morning, but their afternoon had been spent making final preparations.

The presentation was about to begin. The lights flashed to call people to their seats. Jake expected to feel more nervous. He expected to feel that familiar ball of stress boiling over in his stomach. But, somehow, it wasn't. He felt strangely calm and collected, and ready to take on the world. Since that day at Harrison when he predicted the landing of the berlinite, when he'd figured out the complex riddle of time travel - all he'd wanted was to explain his discovery.

He was sitting at a table on the stage beside Travis, Jess and Dylan. Dylan leaned over to them and whispered "okay...let's do this." He smiled a toothy grin at the three of them. He got up and stood at the podium.

Dylan started off by addressing the crowd in a very formal manner. He spent a few minutes thanking them for being allowed to speak at the conference, acknowledging the organizers, and recognizing the various other scientific achievements of the year. "But," he said, finally, "You may be wondering why I'm here. At Planet 9, we've never attended one of these before, and have mainly conducted our business independent of the international scientific community."

The crowd murmured softly.

"Planet 9 has advanced our company's position in space by leaps and bounds in the last few years. You've probably seen that our 'Nomad' settlement ship has arrived in the orbit of Mars. We managed to get the different components of the ship into orbit, assembled, and ready to go within a matter of months. We've launched countless new satellites into high Earth orbit. We've even dispatched our first fleet of autonomous asteroid mining machines towards the asteroid belt. They're currently mining supplies of iridium to send back to Earth."

The crowd murmured louder. The existence of the mining dwarves was a surprise to most of them, but much bigger surprises were to come.

"The dark web has been buzzing with rumors of a large, purple 'egg shaped' UFO that has been spotted in

Costa Rica. I can confirm today that that vehicle is *real*, and that we built it at our compound. There's also been conspiracy theories that Planet 9 has been working in conjunction with extraterrestrials. We haven't. Some armchair critics believe that aliens would be the only possible explanation for our rapid progress. I know how the ancient Egyptians feel now," he laughed. The crowd laughed as well, albeit hesitantly. "We're here to come clean today, in front of the world leaders in science. We've been using a technology that we've kept very secret - for legal reasons. A discovery that will, no doubt, change the course of history. After years of legal battles, Planet 9 is finally ready to reveal what we've been working on. All of humanity will benefit from this, and it's high time we shared it with you."

Dylan paused to take a sip of water, then put down the glass slowly. He looked down to read something off of his notes. The audience was hanging in suspense, drooling in anticipation. Jake laughed to himself. '*Still a CEO*' he thought. '*Just a glorified salesman at heart.*' It was the first time he'd seen Dylan in his true element, at least since he'd known him personally. He was still presenting this as if he was a douchey tech executive presenting a new flagship cell phone.

"But, let me introduce my colleagues before we go any further." Dylan changed topics, keeping the audience hanging. "This is Planet 9's CSO, and my wife, Jessica Bishop. She'll give you a more technical rundown later on in the presentation. And let me formally introduce Travis Strickland and Jacob Crawford. Two of the greatest scientific minds of our generation, who have been in hiding for nearly half a decade now. And today, after all this time, they are finally able to take credit for their findings. Gentlemen?" He stepped back from the podium and waved a gesture to the two of them.

'*Here goes nothing*'. Jake stood up and walked to the middle of the platform with Travis. They'd set up a holo-tab and connected to the larger room projection to display their presentation. Jake hit the start key, and the first slide appeared above him, hovering in the open space. He began talking. The room was eerily quiet, there was no applause as they took the stage. "Esteemed members of the International Science Council, we're here today to reveal our findings from a series of experiments we performed over five years ago. A series of experiments that successfully sent matter through time."

The crowd murmured loudly, tables talking between themselves in disbelief.

"Before I go further, I'd like to formally invite questions from the floor as we continue. Now, some of you may be aware of a new alloy called berlinite, and that it has some unusual qualities. That it carries a negative energy balance, and seems to 'eat' sections of the E.M. spectrum. Travis and I were experimenting with berlinite and its reactions to gamma radiation, in an attempt to determine if the missing energy was somehow being transferred to the base dimension. At a certain frequency, our first sample disappeared." Jake advanced the slide to show their original video recordings. "We never recovered it. The experiment was repeated, with the same result. Once the amplitude of the gamma wave was significantly reduced, the samples would reappear, almost instantaneously, in a different area of the lab."

Travis took over and spent several minutes going over their early process, explaining how they had arrived at their conclusions. He displayed the findings from the first atomic clocks that Jake and he had sent through time. "You see," he said, "the berlinite was definitely transporting its contents through time. But why was it reappearing in a different spot?" He switched slides, showing an animation of the Earth moving through space in a spiraling pattern. "The Earth itself is in constant motion. Rotating, revolving around the sun. The sun is revolving around our galactic core. And the Milky Way itself is moving through deep space.

"The berlinite vibrates at a sub-atomic level when hit with the proper frequency. We believe this vibration happens in both our dimension and the base dimension."

A question came from the audience. The microphone from the French table lit up. "Isn't the base dimension just theoretical? There's been zero proof that it exists."

"Maybe this is your proof, then," Travis replied confidently. "We don't have another explanation for what's happening in this reaction. What we *can* tell you is that the berlinite travels through time, and because space and motion doesn't exist in the base dimension..."

The heads in the room started nodding in agreement.

"The berlinite stays still. The Earth itself moves. Along with the sun, the planets - everything else in our dimension." Travis was in full flow now. "So, being gone for just a few nanoseconds will mean that the planet itself will move meters away from the sample. A few seconds gone, and the planet has moved far enough away that our sample would be in orbit. A few *centuries* gone, and you've reached the distance of the stars. Through the last 5 years of research, we've discovered that this isn't limited to berlinite. An item coated in berlinite will make the same trip through time. Even a thin veneer of the material will create a field within itself that transports matter. We've successfully moved thousands of different materials, and yes, even life." He switched the slide, showing a mouse being removed from a small berlinite-coated chamber in the lab. "Only two months ago, we sent our first human test pilots into orbit using a time jump. We're studying them closely, but absolutely no adverse health effects have come up so far." The next slide showed a pair of astronauts emerging from a small floating capsule in the Caribbean Sea.

"Why are we only hearing about this now?!" The question had come from the German table. "Did you not think the scientific community would benefit from this knowledge?"

"Yeahhhh" said Travis, uneasily. "There's been a couple issues with...copyright. I'll let Dylan Bishop speak to that later on."

"This has the potential to let us travel immense distances. We realized that very early on," said Jake confidently. He'd paid for his decisions; he wasn't hiding his choices from Hachiro anymore. "We partnered with the Bishops to develop this technology in a rapid fashion. And they have delivered, more than we could have ever dreamed possible. I wanted to see humanity reach the stars in my own lifetime, and it's beginning to look very possible." The crowd made another murmur, individual whispers combining into a soft roar. "I'd like to pass it to Jessica Bishop to show you some of the amazing progress we've made."

The audience microphones lit up as they tried to ask questions, but they had already resigned from the podium. Jess walked to the stage and took the slide remote from Travis. "I'd like to give you an overview of what we've accomplished in the last few years. We've made incredible strides in space travel. But our next step, folks - that's the truly exciting one. And that's the step that we'll need the world's help with."

She showed demonstrations and videos of the Egg. Some of the clips were new to Jake and Travis, even. There were beautiful shots from space of the hatch opening, and compartments of the Nomad being slowly ejected into orbit. The videos of the controlled time-jump descents were incredible, the onboard cameras catching each micro-jump of the Egg as the surface of the Earth came ever closer, and finally showing the retro rockets easing it into a landing.

"The Egg was our second two-way time jump vehicle," Jess explained. "It has a series of gamma emitters synchronized to fire outwards, vibrating the berlinite hull of the ship and triggering the reaction from within itself. Unlike our first satellites, which were launched forward in time from our facility in Costa Rica, the Egg can transport itself forwards and backwards in time and get itself closer to home in the process."

"How far have you sent it?" one of the American delegates asked, his push-to-talk microphone lighting up in the second row of tables.

"Our furthest trip with the Egg was about 12 hours backwards in time. We unloaded a series of crafts near the asteroid belt, and successfully jumped it back into a high Earth orbit. That 12 hours resulted in it traveling roughly 200 million kilometers. But mostly, we've used it for small jumps to get equipment into orbit."

"If you can go that far in such a short time, why bother with the Nomad project at all? Couldn't you simply time-jump the next settlement to Mars?" he responded.

"It's a good question. We can't use this technology to get directly to Mars, no. Not even if we time it right. It's impossible. You have to think three-dimensionally. The solar system is moving through the universe, and it moves away from the Egg, the Egg doesn't move through it. It would be very convenient if the solar system moved on the same axis that the planets rotate in, but unfortunately, it doesn't." Jess had planned for such a question, and loaded up an animation on the holo-screen above her to illustrate the point. "We can get closer to them, but we can't get directly to any of the planets using this. It just made more sense to send the Nomad from Earth's orbit towards Mars, as we had always planned, even before this new technology."

"Besides the Egg, how far have you sent something? In theory, how far *can* you send something?" This time, the lit red tip of a microphone was on the Belgian table, but the English came from a translator seated above the room.

"With enough power to create a high amplitude waveform, you can go as far forward or back as you want. Billions of years, in theory. But we don't have that much power - yet." Jess paused. "But that doesn't mean that we've stayed in our own backyard, not by any means. And that is where this presentation is going to get really exciting" she smiled devilishly.

Dylan got back up from the table to join her on stage. "Planet 9 was founded on a single vision. To make humanity a multi-planet species. To spread out to Mars and beyond. To buy the human race some insurance from extinction. And we've achieved that! With the new settlers, our Mars colony now has over 200 full time residents, and the Nomad will be sending more every two years to build up the population. But, folks, let's be honest..." Dylan looked out at the audience and took a deep breath. "Mars is quite the fixer-upper."

The audience laughed.

"It's a dead planet. We've been collectively working on this dream of Martian colonies for a century now, but it was never ideal. There's no breathable atmosphere, no life, no easily accessible water. We have a long, long road ahead of us before an independent civilization is even remotely feasible on that planet. When Jake and Travis came to us, and we saw this potential, I started wondering what else was possible. If we can get somewhere better, is it really worth putting all our resources into Mars? If we can go so much further, why settle for what's next door?"

Jess took over again, the couple working together like a well-oiled machine. "We've created three probes to explore other star systems. They have been running autonomously for the past year, jumping forwards and backwards in time by thousands of years. Our stellar cartography team has mapped out the time that certain stars will cross this exact spot." The display above her changed to a moving star map. In the middle, a bright red X showed the location of the probes, and the stars moved across it in a diagonal motion.

"We've set a limit forward, and a limit backward. 60,000 years each way. This means that we can travel to star systems roughly 1000 light years in either direction across this line." She illustrated a line moving its way through the three-dimensional field of stars. "It is possible to go further, much further, but the problems with stellar drift become much harder to calculate."

The audience was doing its best to follow along with the idea. A microphone lit up from the UK table. "Why not go further back? If we could send a probe back billions of years... imagine! Getting a view of the universe forming after the big bang, seeing early star formation, it would be incredible!"

"One day, we may be able to generate enough power to do that. We'd also need to be very quick at taking scans. The drift problem becomes so severe at those timelines - we'd never get the info back from it if it stayed too long."

Jess saw confused stares from the audience.

"Okay, let me start over with that," she continued, attempting to explain what she meant. "So, the probe travels back through time within the base dimension. So, it travels to this same area of space, to.... 10 billion years ago, let's say. Now, if it stays for a couple months, getting readings, taking pictures, and so forth, it does a time jump forward ten billion years to our time. But space was smaller back then, it hadn't expanded as much. So, it drifted a few million kilometers in that timeline, but it jumped back from a sector of space that's now trillions of kilometers away from us. And we never get the probe or its readings back. The technology has its limitations, definitely. We can explore distant times, but very, very quickly."

Dylan jumped in, seeing the audience reeling from the calculations Jess had put in their heads. "That may be something we'll look at in the future, but not quite yet. So, back to our galaxy," he joked. "When we're looking for new planets, this technology does have its limitations. If you were to make a spherical radius around the Earth of 1000 light years, there'd be around 7 million stars within it. Because of this line of travel, though, only a few hundred of those stars will ever cross the exact spot where we are. Or *have* crossed this spot. Only some of those few hundred stars have rocky planets. Fewer of those stars have planets within the 'goldilocks' zone for liquid water. And even fewer still have the chemical signatures of life. But...some do."

"Are you telling us, today, that you've found extraterrestrial life as well as invented time travel?" asked the representative for Japan, through a translator.

"We haven't touched it yet, or fully confirmed that it exists, but all the chemical signatures are there in the atmosphere. On three separate planets, in three different star systems. 2 of them even have a greenish hue that looks a *lot* like chlorophyll." Dylan heard shocked gasps from the audience.

"Can you give us anything more? What sort of environment is this life developing in?"

"We may find life in bizarre, foreign worlds one day. But all three of these planets are fairly similar to our own home. What we've started calling 'Planet C' has an atmosphere so close to Earth's it would be nearly indistinguishable - we could pretty much step off the ship and go for a jog on day one. Planet A would take a slow adjustment, and the atmospheric pressure is lower. Planet B doesn't look breathable yet, but we'll take more readings when we can. But all three have large quantities of liquid water, which is all we truly need to get started."

"Are you sending further probes to study them? When can we see the findings?" The Japanese table asked again.

"We could - but why send probes when we can go there ourselves?" Dylan smiled. He loaded up a slide onto the giant projection above him. The slide was a rendering of an enormous spacecraft. It was round in shape, with a tube-like outer ring surrounding a central structure, and held in place with trussed 'spokes'. "We're calling this the 'Seed Project'. This is our preliminary design, and we're still tweaking it. If we build this ship to these specs, this will end up being the largest human-made vehicle in history."

There were no mutterings or comments from the crowd this time. They simply stared at the rendering of the spaceship in disbelief.

"Anyone who has worked in aerospace knows that the biggest hurdle for spacecraft isn't the actual construction of them. It's - how do you get them to break the bonds of Earth's gravity? We've never been limited on what we can build, what we can seal from the vacuum of space, or what can be shielded from stellar radiation. We've only been limited by what we could push up off the ground. In addition to giving us a route to the distant stars, Mr. Crawford and Mr. Strickland have, effectively, taken that barrier away." Dylan paused momentarily, looking up from his stage facing display. "You know, when these two cocky young physicists from Canada told me that all my rockets were obsolete, I didn't believe them. But it's true. It's very true.

"The Seed Ship will be constructed on the Earth's surface. Once it's coated in berlinite, we'll be able to 'time-jump' it into space. It will hold all the equipment to start a new colony on another world. Housing, food production and much more. It will bring mining equipment, metalworking gear, fabrication, automation - everything the new colony will need to thrive completely independent of Earth. The equipment, housing, energy and food storage will be in the 'spokes' here," he said, using a pointer to illustrate. "The outer ring will rotate at a precise speed to create 1G of artificial gravity. The final ship will hold upwards of 2000 colonists.

"Obviously, this is a project that's beyond the scope of Planet 9. We can take a lion's share of the engineering and technical challenges, but we will definitely need global co-operation to accomplish this. We also want to populate the new colony with a diverse group of people from around the world. We need a huge variety of skill sets and backgrounds to make this idea work." Dylan continued for another thirty minutes, describing in greater detail the plans for the colony.

When he finally finished, the crowd was quiet. It was a lot to absorb, and quite hard to believe.

"Mr. Bishop." The question came from the American table, when Dylan finally paused. "This is all incredible, no doubt. But do you feel like you may be getting a bit ahead of yourselves?" This comment got a restrained laugh from the audience. "You just got a second crew to Mars, now you want to send 2000 people across the galaxy? And all of us in the audience *just* found out about the possibility of interstellar travel. Why wouldn't you start with a small exploratory ship and crew? What's the rush? Why?"

"Why not?" Dylan asked, smiling confidently. "If we have the capability, why not go ahead with it? Fortune favors the bold! That's the way I have always run things, and I think this should be no different. Each day we work together towards becoming a multi-planet species is a day closer to that goal." He looked at Jess for support. She nodded, as if to tell him to continue. "And... the real reason is that we have a very specific launch window. If we want the Seed project to reach Planet A, we would need to be ready to time jump in just six years."

26.

A great rumble of noise erupted from the audience. They were excited and curious, but mostly confused. Jake was worried about this point in the presentation. Was this where their achievements got drowned in ridiculous ambition? Or would the world embrace their idea for a new interstellar colony? He had dreamed about seeing interstellar travel within his own lifetime and fantasized about boarding the first ship. He knew the reasons for the rush, and Dylan had assured him that it was possible, but now - hearing that figure of '6 years' out loud in this setting - he had serious doubts. Judging by the faces in the audience, he wasn't alone.

Jess took the remote from Dylan once more. "I can see some confusion out there," she started. "And that's to be expected. Why would we have a launch window if we're going such a massive distance? In truth, the calculations of this project are immensely complex. We do have a short time available when the stars - for the lack of a better term - align..."

She loaded another animation, showing the Milky Way galaxy slowly moving in a line across the screen. "This is how the galaxy is moving through space. As we've explained, when we time travel an object, the object remains still, and the galaxy, with all of its stars and planets, moves away from it. Now, logic would tell you that if this star will cross our current position in 10,000 years, and it's moving within the same galaxy as us, it will *always* cross our position if we jump 10,000 years ahead." The animation changed, showing a fixed 'X', with a cluster of stars moving by it. A red line extended diagonally outwards from the X. "So, one would think that getting to a different star would be as simple as traveling along this line. But it's not that simple.

"The stars are part of the galaxy, yes. And if they were held rigidly in place within the galaxy as it moved, then we would *always* be able to time jump between systems along this line, no problem. The stars would move by this spot like the cars of a train, and we'd just select which car we wanted to end up at." Jess changed slides and showed another animation, which showed the line moving through stars that were also rotating in the galaxy.

"But it's not a train, that would be far too simple" she smiled. "It's not just about jumping forward and back from one carriage car to the next, because they're all moving in different ways. Instead, we've nicknamed the process 'River Jumping'." Jess loaded a new animation, showing the stars moving within the galaxy. "You see, different stars are orbiting the galaxy's core at different distances, and therefore at different speeds. Their line of orbit may not follow the exact same plane as ours. As well, our ship stays in the same area of space, but that space is expanding over time as well. So that line of travel that we can time jump within," Jess pointed once more to the diagram above her, showing the red line stretching through the galaxy, "...stars and planets will drift in and out of it depending on *all* of those factors. The stars act more like rafts floating down a wide river. Everything is moving in roughly the same direction, but sometimes in a faster or slower current, on one side or the other. The Earth is on its own raft floating down the stream, and so are the other stars around us.

"We call it River Jumping because of that idea. Picture floating down the river, and then jumping high, straight up in the air and coming back down again. You'd only be able to reach the rafts who would cross the exact point in the current that you had jumped from. That's why it's not a train. We don't calculate when a train car passes our station, we must calculate exactly when, and *if,* a raft will cross our point in the river. Our probes that we sent to see these three life-bearing systems were still taking readings from a distance. The Earth hasn't drifted into the right spot in the river to jump to them. Yet."

"So, are there other systems that we've missed our shot on?" asked an audience member.

"Yes, definitely. It all depends on when the Earth is going to be in just the right slot in space. It's tough to wrap your head around, I get it. But just remember that the spaceship is staying still. We need to wait for the Earth to be in the exact right spot in space to line up with our target star system at a different point in time. For Planet 'A', this will be in 6 years. Planet C will line up with our location in just over 8 years. Planet B in roughly 15. And, once the Seed ship lands on any of those planets, it'll have a little under a year to jump back, before the window closes."

A microphone turned on from the German table, and a hand shot in the air. "Wait, couldn't you just jump further back in time? If you're time traveling, why do you have a set window?"

Jess cleared her throat and took a sip of water. She clicked back to her previous slide. "Remember that the river is always flowing. Let's say that 2 planets cross the same point exactly 1000 years apart. We jump ahead in time exactly 1000 years, and because of that, we exit the base dimension beside the new planet. Now, let's say we stay for five years, and decide to go home. We travel 1005 years back in time. But we're no longer at the same point in the river! So, we end up back at the same point in *time* that we left, but we're no longer near the Earth. *That's* the drift problem, that's why the travel calculations are so difficult."

The audience nodded in silence, mostly understanding what she meant, finally.

"So, this is a one-way trip? Do or die? Those people will never get more colonists to join them from Earth once the alignment is over? That seems a little brutal" the French table asked.

"Not exactly" Dylan cut in. "The only reason that this is an issue at all is the pathetically slow speed of our current spacecraft. The Seed ship won't move any faster than the Nomad, about 40,000 kilometers an hour. At that speed, once the launch window closes, the target star will be moving away from the Earth's 'spot' faster than our ship could ever catch it." Dylan went to the holo-tab and skipped through a couple slides. "We're already working on a passenger freighter with a new advanced ion thruster. Once that's operational, it will be able to travel over 250 kilometers a second, which means it would catch up with the target planet, even as it's drifting away from the destination jump location."

"You can get a ship moving that fast?"

"Again, folks, the technology is there, that's not the problem. We've had it for decades. We've just never been able to put it up in orbit. That was the biggest hurdle."

"So why not wait, and equip these faster Ion engines on the Seed ship? Wouldn't you have much less of a deadline that way?" The question came from the Nigerian table.

"The Seed ship will be much too massive to use them. It has to carry all the equipment, housing, fabrication and such. By the time it accelerated using those ion thrusters, everyone on board would be dead from old age. No, if we're sending everything we need for a new colony, it has to be old school rockets pushing the ship. And that means a launch window that isn't very far away." Dylan paused to gather his thoughts. "Trust me folks, we've thought of all the possibilities to give ourselves more time. I wouldn't want to rush it this much unless we absolutely had to.

"But if we can do this...once that Seed ship is on a different planet, it will be able to create its own supplies and technology. Once they're moved into their new house, we don't need to send the couch and dressers. We'll just need to send more people. It's all possible, as long as we can make this first deadline."

The room buzzed with conversation as Dylan awaited the next question. The roar of conversations crescendoed upwards. He smiled confidently at Travis and Jake, who were still sitting quietly at the head table. Jake looked out at the audience, watching people run from table to table to talk to one another. It was chaos. He felt like he was watching a control room in an old Godzilla movie. *'No going back now'* he thought. *'We just opened Pandora's box, the world is about to go mad.'*

"This is fuckin' awesome!" Travis whispered in Jake's ear. "Who would've thought that the shit we were doing at Harrison would lead to this. I think we just broke the U.N.!" he laughed. Jake snickered as well, but was careful not to break composure too much. There were a lot of cameras on the two of them.

"We will send out a full briefing and press packet afterwards!" Dylan shouted, attempting to regain control of the room. People began returning to their seats. Dylan continued on about the berlinite technology, and how they would share it with the world. He offered use of the Egg to interested space agencies. He explained how Planet 9 had nearly exhausted the world's supply of iridium over the last four years, but that their asteroid mining operations would be sending shipments of the element back to Earth shortly. Enough to build the Seed ship and more. Finally, he reached his final slide of the presentation. "So, you can see why we're excited to share this with you. We've been going to space for almost a hundred years now, but we've barely left our own atmosphere. The fastest things we've ever built would still take tens of thousands of years to reach the closest system. It all seemed unfeasible - it was starting to look like the stars were just *too* darn far away to ever reach. Not anymore! With berlinite, we can bring the stars to us!" Dylan hit the last line triumphantly, ever a salesman at heart. "I think we have time for a few questions."

Nearly every hand in the room shot in the air. The red tips of the push-to-talk microphones blinked like

Christmas lights as the system struggled to register each button press.

Dylan laughed. "Okay - how about I take three for now, and then we'll call it a day?"

The first question was about the Seed ship construction. Dylan brushed it off, saying they were finalizing plans for a location. The second question had to do with the Egg, and its landing procedures. They also asked when it was going to be available for rent to different space programs. The third question came from the representative from South Korea. It came to the stage via the monitor speakers, having been relayed through the interpreters.

"These three star systems with the signatures of life - which stars are they?" The audience seemed to all look at their notes, wondering how they had forgotten to ask something so simple and important. Dylan looked at Jess, who took out her notes to verify the answers before responding.

"I'm kind of embarrassed we didn't cover that in the slides, we had so much to go over today" she laughed, getting a small, excited laugh from the crowd as well. "What we were referring to as 'Option A' is a medium sized rocky planet, about 1.1 Earth masses - it's the second planet of star HD75141. It's roughly 94 light years away, and our probes traveled over 6,000 years into the future to survey it. 'Option B' is much further away, as the 3rd planet of TYC-8749-228. One and a half Earth masses, orbiting a red dwarf at close range. It's over 300 light years away, and the least viable option of the three, but we'll keep sending probes to it. It's so far, in fact, that our probe traveled over 18,000 years into the future to survey it."

"Option C is 132 light years away, in the opposite direction. 1.2 Earth masses, orbiting a star very similar to Sol - called Cepheus HD314."

The sea of faces was busy scribbling down the answers and talking amongst themselves. Jake was enjoying the commotion and seeing the excited smiles amongst the scientists. He saw an older woman near the front, however, whose expression was much different. She was talking anxiously to her tablemate while they hurriedly packed their bags. Jake turned his head briefly to check which slide was projecting. When he turned back, the woman and her colleagues were gone. All that remained was the small Union Jack flag on the tabletop.

27.

The reception foyer of the Hall was a zoo of commotion. Jake felt like a rock star leaving a stadium performance. Press surrounded them, camera flashes erupted on all sides. Each time he thought that they were leaving for the hotel he got dragged into another question or a new conversation. It was the most intense hour he'd ever had, and part of him wanted to hang on to Dylan's hand like a lost child at a carnival. Travis was being overwhelmed as well. He had the look of a subdued bear who was about to rage on a group of tourists.

Even with all the commotion, Jake felt a calm deep inside of himself. The secrets were finally out! Everything they'd worked for, everything that they had accomplished - it was all in the public domain now. Although he'd been completely truthful with Mia since their reunion, Jake had still been forced to hide his life from everyone else. He had to hide his work from his family, from his old friends and his industry colleagues. He had told himself so many times that he just wanted to better humanity - that he didn't *need* the fame and glory. But that was bullshit. Seeing the excitement around him, knowing that his name would be in every news headline around the world - that felt pretty damn good.

Dylan was a natural in this environment. He knew how to tactfully deflect questions, how to charm reporters and keep his cool, even while dozens of interviewers were shouting questions at him. Jake glanced over at him, briefly ignoring the Italian ambassador who was talking to him. *'Damn. That's how it's done'* he thought.

Jess had broken free from her conversation and was weaving through the crowd, urgently trying to get through to the other three. Her path was blocked by countless people, but a gentle hand on the shoulder seemed to work to part some of the onlookers. A hard nudge through and a 'Pardon me!' in her thick Irish accent worked on others. When she thought she couldn't go any further, that she was stuck in the thickest part of the mosh pit, she finally saw Jake in front of her. He had a microphone and camera being thrust in his face. She approached him and pulled him aside, smiling and apologizing politely to the reporter. She whispered in Jake's ear.

"Boardroom 4D. Five minutes. Excuse yourself and meet us there."

She weaved through to find Travis and did the same thing. Finally, she found Dylan in the far corner, charming a group of reporters. He had at least 5 cameras on him. She pulled him aside, told him the same thing, and gave a sly wink.

"Sorry folks, when the boss calls, I go. As I said, further details will be coming. Thank you." He smiled and briskly forced himself through the crowd. A couple reporters followed, yelling more questions, but Dylan's personal security team placed themselves in the path, finally giving the Bishops an exit.

Jake had excused himself to the washroom, and was also followed by a reporter. He waited inside for a few minutes, washed his hands, then cracked the door open to check the exit. The reporter was thankfully gone. Jake snuck over to the elevator, scanned his temporary badge, and hit the button for the fourth floor.

4D was a small boardroom, holding a dozen people at the most. It had no windows, one door, and was in a quiet part of the complex. The decoration was simple and bleak, the lighting dim but sterile. Jess was waiting inside, alone.

"Hey Jess, what's going on?" Jake said softly as he approached her.

"I'm not quite sure yet, Jake. I was approached in a hallway by one of the delegates from the UK, accompanied by a member of British Intelligence. They said that something needed to be discussed with the four of us - something of terrible importance. I asked if it could wait, as we were going to be busy with the press releases. They insisted, almost to the point of threatening me. It was quite intimidating." She was sitting at the boardroom table, waiting patiently.

Travis entered a minute later, followed by Dylan. Jess gave them the same answer she gave Jake. A few minutes later, a man and woman from the UN tech department came to the room.

"We've been asked to secure the room. May we please have your phones, tabs, and anything else electronic for safekeeping? That includes watches, and if your glasses are augmented..." she looked at Jake. He was the only one wearing glasses. He shook his head no, and handed in the rest of his electronics. The woman removed the electronics from the room, placing them on a cart and rolling them outside. The man used a sensor to sweep the room for signals. He moved along the walls, under the table, and moved it over the four of them like an airport security guard. Once he was satisfied, he thanked them, left, and closed the door behind him.

"What the F? What's going on?" Travis whispered. The other three were thinking the same, though none said a word.

The door opened and six people entered. A security guard closed the door behind them and stood watch outside. The six sat at the table across from Jake and his companions. They were all formally dressed and much older than Jake, with the exception of a young Latin American woman, who appeared to be roughly his age. No words were exchanged as they took their seats.

An older woman finally introduced herself, breaking the intimidating silence. "Terribly sorry for the cloak and dagger tactics, folks. We felt it was necessary, especially with all the press lurking around today. My name is Dr. Priscilla Miles. I'm with the United Kingdom delegation of the International Science Council. Mr. Bishop, everyone in the world knows *you*, no doubt, and we met several years ago in Zurich, I believe? This is the first time I've met your lovely wife, however."

Jess smiled and introduced herself. The British woman seemed friendly and charming. Jake kept waiting for the other shoe to drop, however.

"And you two gentlemen. I'm astonished! I had heard rumors of Planet 9 working with teleportation, and then there was the stolen tech fiasco a few years ago. But none of us had any idea... any idea at all of what you were actually working on."

"Well, some of us did," a man smirked at the end of the table.

"Fair enough. Those of us that weren't government spies had no idea, I should say. The rest of us here had to weasel our way into today's keynote speech to find out."

"Dennis Webb, MI6," the man said, introducing himself to the four. His manner was much less friendly, and he had a sour look on his face. The other attendees also took turns introducing themselves.

"Lisette Deniel, European Space Agency"
"Taima Asad, CIA"
"Ray Adkins, NASA"
"Marcela Reyes, SETI"

'*Holy shit*' thought Jake nervously. '*This is quite the lineup.*'

Priscilla Miles took over again. "What you're doing at Planet 9, it's truly incredible. I'm personally scared of the vast scale of this 'Seed' project, but I believe that you're heading in the right direction." The other members nodded, some adding their own comments of congratulations. "I'm still wrapping my head around this 'River Jumping' idea, I think I need a strong drink before I think about it again," she laughed.

"Thank you" replied Jess. "And, speaking from experience, yes - it helps."

"The reason we called you in here right away...." Priscilla's tone changed. "I'm afraid, with all that you've been doing in the shadows, you've stumbled upon something that we've been working very hard to keep secret."

Jake's mind raced. "What would that be?" he asked, surprised that he had found the confidence to speak in this setting.

"You mentioned three planets in your presentation, Mr. Crawford. Three planets that you are surveying for life, and contemplating for future human settlement. Just to confirm - the planet you labeled as option 'C', which star was it orbiting?"

"Cepheus HD314" Jess replied, from memory.

"That's what I thought - we just had to be sure," replied Priscilla. She whispered something in the ear of Dennis Webb, the man from MI6. He whispered something back.

"Before we go any further, I need the four of you to sign these" the MI6 agent said. "It is a binding confidentiality agreement. Nothing we discuss in this room can go any further than these walls, understood?"

'Fucking hell' Jake thought. *'Five years of keeping secrets. Five years! I was fully out in the open for less than an hour, now I have to keep another one.'*

They all reviewed the document and eventually signed off. Dylan took extra time to review each line in detail before finally succumbing to it and signing his name. Dennis Webb took the forms back and packed them away. He nodded to Priscilla.

"That star, HD314 - we know it as 'Reyes'. Roughly five years ago, Marcela Reyes here was working out of a remote observatory in Chile. She picked up intelligent radio signals from the third planet of that system. Very advanced signals. Millions of them."

"What!?" spoke Travis, shocked.

"I was using an algorithm that I designed," replied Marcela, softly. "A method that can distinguish very faint signals from the various radiations of interstellar space. I wasn't sure what I had at first, but after countless scans of that system, I'm very sure now. Other experts have analyzed the enormous amount of data that I've collected. There's no mistaking it, the radio signals are of intelligent design. This is our first definitive proof of extraterrestrial intelligence."

Jess looked at Dylan, shocked by the revelation. He looked back, shrugging his shoulders in surprise.

"We didn't see any signals like that on our readings, did we?" Jake asked Jess.

"No, but... we weren't really looking for them, either. The probe was still so far out from the planet - we were just looking for the atmospheric content and a magnetic field. We could have missed this, I suppose."

"Wait, you people have known about this for five years?" Travis asked. "You've known, definitively, that we're not alone in the universe and you didn't let people know? Why would you do that?"

"Why would you hide that you had invented time travel? We all have our secrets." Priscilla smiled at him. "We're not ready to come forward with it. The world isn't ready to know about this yet."

Dennis Webb took over from her. "Only a small group of people around the world knows about Reyes 3. A group of people dedicated to studying the signals, a select few world leaders, and a group of people, like myself and Ms. Asad, who are actively working to keep the knowledge of this planet a secret from the public."

"I still don't understand.... People have been wondering the answer to this question for centuries, yet you won't give them the answer? I don't get your reasoning," Jake said.

"We won't keep it a secret forever," replied Priscilla. "I would love for the world to know this. To show them that once and for all, we are united as a species; that our petty squabbles between ourselves mean nothing. But, realistically, that wouldn't happen." Priscilla took a few documents out from her briefcase and passed them across the table for review. "When Marcela came to me with these readings, my first thought was about how to release it to the press. But then I reconsidered, almost instantly.

"The world is such a divided place now. We can't agree on anything! Every minor detail of our lives is politicized. Every difference of opinion is leveraged for financial gain. The discovery of an intelligent alien race would almost certainly cause that same kind of dissent. Especially with the ambiguity of what we've found. Before the world can know about Reyes 3, we need to know far more about who's out there."

"The problem," added Marcela, "is that we don't know *anything* about them yet. All we know is that they have a very complex communications network. That's it. We've been trying to decode their signals for half a decade, without much success. If we don't know anything about them, just that they're out there..."

"A lot of people on Earth could leverage that for their own gain" replied Ray, the Nasa representative. "Cults. Religious fanatics. Battles and wars fought over whose interpretation of the aliens was the correct one. Conspiracy theorists, social activists, the ambitious, the fearful. They would all clash. Who knows what would happen to society? We simply can't afford to have this info out there, not until we have an idea of who, and what, they are."

"And you haven't made much progress? Can Planet 9 assist at all?" asked Jess.

Ray showed them another document. "It's an immensely complex problem," he said. "If they spoke a language that we didn't understand, but they coded their audio in files like ours, then we would have broken down their language with linguists by now. If they had a different computing system, say, programmed in base 8 mathematics, but spoke English, we probably would have something by now. But we have absolutely nowhere to start with these. They're faded, and missing segments. Ms. Reyes's algorithm is incredible, but it can still only gather so much from such a monumental distance away."

Jess nodded. She had been thinking the same thing. 130 light years was a long way for any sort of radio signal to travel. It was amazing that Marcela had detected anything at all.

"The signals are nothing like anything we've ever seen. We don't even know what kind of transmissions they are. Are they audio? Video? Maybe they're transmitting telepathic thoughts. All we know is that the complexity of what we're seeing is far beyond anything that humans have ever made."

Jake was spellbound. Today was always going to be amazing, but he had no idea that he'd also be let in on a planet wide conspiracy to conceal alien intelligence.

"How on earth have you kept this so secret? Even with all the people working on it?" asked Dylan.

"Luckily, the public is naturally skeptical about anything to do with aliens," replied Ray Adkins. "It's not that hard to discredit information if it leaks out. The dark web has a couple of conspiracy pages about Reyes 3, but nothing has gone mainstream. And that's where we're going to stay for the time being.

"So, what's your plan?" Travis asked brazenly. "If you can't decode the signals, you just keep everyone in the dark forever?"

"At least for the next 10 years or so. Until our advantage runs out." Marcela looked across the table at the four of them.

"Advantage?" asked Jess, confused. She thought for a few seconds, then smiled in recognition. "Ah, I get it! They can't see us yet. *That's* what you're worried about. It all makes sense now."

"Exactly. We weren't sending powerful radio signals into space until the 1930s," replied Priscilla. "Reyes 3 is over 132 light years away, which means that our first signals are still en-route to them. We've been studying their world heavily, trying to determine what they are like. Will they be a threat? Once they know that we're here, will we be a target?"

"And that's the plan we've been working with" added Ray Adkins, the NASA administrator. "We had no reason to suspect that they knew we were here, or could possibly know about humanity. At least, until a couple hours ago. When you told us that you'd sent a probe to their system." His final sentence came out in an accusatory tone.

Dylan and Jess shared a look. She subtly shook her head at him before the conversation continued.

"We must insist that you cease all operations involving that star system," said Dennis Webb, the MI6 agent. "You will immediately release all research involving Reyes 3 to us, and your organization will forget that the star HD314 ever existed."

Jake looked over at Dylan. The billionaire's friendly demeanor had evaporated. He obviously didn't enjoy being talked to in such a manner.

"We are an independent organization" Dylan replied, slowly and coldly. "As far as I can tell, no one in this room is from the Costa Rican government, the United Nations, or Interpol. You have absolutely no jurisdiction over us. So, if you think, Mr. Webb, that you can tell me what to do with *my* research, you have another thing coming."

Dennis Webb's face became flush with anger. His pudgy cheeks turned pink, and the color leaked upwards to his balding forehead. His voice was still calm, although a little strained. "Mr. Bishop, there is only so far you can go without the world's input. You've already, somehow, colonized Mars without international oversight. I'll be damned if we allow you to make first contact with another race as well..."

"I don't answer to anyone in this room! I don't answer to NASA, or the ESA, or MI6. And our technology has made it a million times further into space than anything your countries have done. If I want to keep surveying this star, you have zero authority to stop me." Dylan was angry, but still collected. Jake and Travis were shocked, they had never seen this side of him. They had never seen someone confront him before, or what would happen if he was backed into a corner.

"You may be an independent organization, and we may not have jurisdiction, but if you think that MI6 can't make your life a living hell..." Dennis' voice was steadily getting louder as he talked.

"Okay, okay!" Priscilla put a stop to the back and forth with a loud interjection. "This isn't getting us anywhere."

Jess put her hand on Dylan's shoulder to gently ease him off. She then took over, in a much friendlier manner. "Surely you can see our point of view here. We're planning the largest settlement project in the history of mankind. Our years of work have only given us only three potential options, and it may turn out, with further study - that maybe only one of them is suitable. Or none! Now you're telling us to abandon one of our three options completely. It's a tough pill to swallow."

"It's essential, though. It's very important that you not send anything there, ever again, please!" replied Marcela.

"You don't understand what's at stake. If your probe led them to know of our existence...." continued Priscilla.

"Aren't you kind of automatically assuming that they're evil?" asked Travis. "Seems kinda weird that we wouldn't want to make contact. I don't really understand the fear in this room right now."

Professor Miles took a deep breath, attempting to explain their reasoning. "So, you're all scientists. Which tells me you know about the Fermi Paradox."

"Yeah, of course," replied Travis. "If there are billions of planets in the galaxy, and many of them can support life, logic dictates that there should be space faring civilizations all around us, just by the sheer number of opportunities for them to evolve."

"Exactly" replied Priscilla. "And the paradox is - we haven't seen any of them. Not one."

"Until now" Marcela reminded her.

"Yes - until now. Now there are many possible solutions to the Fermi Paradox, why there are no alien societies visible to us. Perhaps astronomical phenomena wipe the civilizations out eventually, given enough time. Perhaps, once they reach a certain level of technological prowess, they always destroy themselves before they reach the stars." She paused to take a sip from the water bottle in front of her. "But the people in our organization tend to lean towards the Dark Forest theory."

Dylan stopped her. "I'm sorry, I'm not familiar with that one."

"Of all the life on Earth that we know of, it has three universal goals. To survive, to use resources, and to multiply. We have to assume that life on other planets would be similar. No matter how advanced the technology, the simple biology of life is dictated by those three goals. Life takes resources from other life, life eliminates competition for resources, and life defends its own existence. There are no exceptions to this rule.

"If there are advanced civilizations out there in the stars, perhaps they don't want their presence known. Perhaps being 'seen' means being eliminated. In a dark forest, both the hunter and the prey stay hidden, as to reveal oneself is to put oneself in grave danger. No one knows if a larger predator is hiding in the next shady grove."

"The signals I detected are very weak, they were never intended to broadcast beyond their own system" continued Marcela. "It may be a fluke that my algorithm worked as well as it did, maybe we were never supposed to see them."

"We can see them, but they can't see us yet. If the solution to the Fermi Paradox is, indeed, that the Universe is a dark forest, then the result of revealing our presence to Reyes 3 is terrifying. Once our presence is known...." Priscilla trailed off, struggling to phrase what she meant.

Ray Adkins piped in to help. "What she means is.... that the reason we don't detect any other civilizations is that they're either effectively hiding themselves, or they've already been destroyed by a more advanced race."

Jake, Travis and the Bishops all looked at each other. The feeling of the day had changed. Somehow, the victories of their presentation had changed into this. Travis' lower jaw pulled back into his neck as he thought about the possibilities.

"Yeah, I think you might be reaching a bit," Dylan responded. He had a confident but indignant tone to his voice now. "I don't buy into all this philosophical speculation, I *still* think it would be a big win for us to contact another intelligent species."

"But Mr. Bishop," continued Priscilla, "Isn't there enough of a risk to take this seriously?"

"We just need more time" added Marcela. "If we can interpret their signals, and learn anything about them, it helps us make an informed decision on whether to make first contact. And we only have this upper hand for another decade or so."

"Then let me help!" replied Dylan, stubbornly. "I can get another probe far closer to that system, I can get you better recordings! I don't think that completely giving up on river-jumping to HD314 is the answer to this."

"Please, you're not hearing what we're saying" Marcela said, getting frustrated. "It took humanity a hundred thousand years to find out that we're not alone, what's another decade? I'm very frightened that your company has the ability to go to that system, Mr. Bishop."

Priscilla made a huff in agreement. "Yes! If they were to intercept one of your crafts, they would not only find out about the Earth's existence..."

"You would have handed them the technology to jump to our front door," said Dennis Webb, slowly and harshly.

Jess looked at her husband. She understood the risks, and she felt like Dylan did as well. But she knew that he wasn't going to give up, that he despised being told what he can't do. Even when faced with the extermination of mankind, Dylan had a tough time checking his ego. As he prepared to retort again, she gently held his left hand on the table, and stared into his eyes. It may only have calmed him for a second, but at least it would keep him from responding harshly in the moment.

The tension was heavy in the tiny boardroom. Each side had made their points, but no consensus had been reached. Dennis and Dylan were locked in a standoff, each not knowing how to proceed.

Taima, the CIA representative, had remained silent until now. She had a much gentler voice than her MI6 colleague. It was a welcome change to the room, no matter what the content of her conversation was going to be. "Mr. Bishop" she began, "Dylan...this project you're taking on - the Seed ship? It's going to require international collaboration on a massive scale. You're going to need cooperation from many different governments, international organizations, and the private sector."

Dylan nodded yes.

"What I'm saying is - we could work *with* you, behind the scenes, to get through all that red tape. The people who know about Reyes 3 are very powerful. And, depending on your decision here today, they can either work with you, or…" She left the threat unsaid.

Jake saw Dylan's expression change again. It was something that he hadn't seen before. It wasn't indignant, or angry, or ambitious - it was... defeat. Dylan saw the checkmate on the table in front of him, and he slowly nodded in agreement.

"Great. We'll be in touch. An agent from MI6 will visit your compound next week to retrieve the probe's findings. Your organization *will* delete all data regarding Reyes 3. You'll have to formulate a reason why it's been abandoned as a potential settlement site."

Jess nodded. "Yes, I can handle that."

"We may call for your help in the future" added Taima. "Once we have a better idea of what we're dealing with, your time jumping probes may become very useful."

The room all exchanged contact info, and Dennis from MI6 gave Jess a passcode to a secure messaging center. "I think it's been pretty clear, but I just want to repeat - this info does not leave this room. We'll be in touch if the situation changes."

Dennis opened the door and the six walked out, leaving the Bishops, Jake, and Travis sitting in a stunned silence. None of them wanted to speak right away, waiting for the delegation to be further down the hall.

"Well, fuck me, eh?" blurted out Travis, finally cutting the silence. "Wasn't expecting that today."

"It's a lot to process." Jess was still trying to think it through. Dylan couldn't hide his disappointment. Planet 'A' had been the one with the most potential, at least from the preliminary findings. Planet 'C' was the backup destination, but he had very much hoped to still investigate it in a few years' time. But he had to recognize the situation.

"We'll leave planet 'C' alone," Dylan said. "As much as I hate it, we have to. For now. I don't want to give up on it, though. I didn't make any promises to not study it from here on Earth." He was deep in thought, spinning plans in his mind as the situation continued to change.

They discussed for another few minutes, then finally left the boardroom. A sedan service was waiting out front to take them back to the hotel. "You guys want to join us for dinner?" Jess asked.

"I can't," replied Jake. "Not tonight. I've got a flight to Vancouver in just over 2 hours."

"That's a long day. You sure?"

"I've got a date" Jake smiled. "And, for the first time in five years, we're going to *her* place."

He said goodbye to them and got his bags from the concierge. The flight was direct, but he still got into Vancouver International Airport well after dinnertime. Even after all the excitement of the day, Jake still managed to sleep on the flight. A huge burden had been lifted from his shoulders - the world finally knew what he had done. There was a calming peace to it, and it was as if the ball of stress in his stomach finally extinguished itself.

Jake was done with secrets. He wasn't cut out for them. He felt a deep satisfaction within himself. As he was riding in a cab to Mia's, however, another thought crossed his mind. He now had a brand-new secret to keep from her. It made him angry to think about - so much of the last five years had been painful because of holding back information from those he loved. Another secret could ruin everything he'd gotten back.

He got dropped off in front of Mia's building. He had to try not to run up the stairs to see her. He was so happy to be home, but he didn't want to show up at her door in a sweaty business suit. He stopped in the hallway, fixed his tie, checked his hair in a reflection off the window, and knocked on her door.

"Oh my!" Mia said, greeting him. She was wearing a light blue sundress with a black belt, and she had changed her hair since the last time he saw her. "Is that the world-famous physicist Jacob Crawford? At *my* door?"

"Just a poor South American refugee looking for a warm bed, ma'am."

"Sounds like something I can help you out with" she giggled. "Come on in. The news has been non-stop Jake! The coverage is crazy. My phone's been ringing off the hook, I don't know how the media knows that we're dating - but somehow, they do. You and Travis are celebrities!"

"Did you talk to any of the press yet?" Jake asked.

"Not yet. Wasn't sure if you wanted me to say anything, and they were getting annoying so I turned my phone off."

"Good call."

"I know you spoke at the UN, but I had a big day too," she said, laughing sarcastically. "I went to the orthodontist and I cleaned my fridge."

Jake looked at her, remembering how lucky he was to have Mia in his life. He smiled stupidly, put down his suitcase in her bedroom and came back out to join her in the kitchen. *'She's so amazing,'* he thought. *'How did I fuck this up the first time around?'* Then he remembered. Secrets. And now he was carrying another huge one. He was bound by the CIA and MI6 not to tell her.

"So - tell me about it. Was it crazy giving a talk at the UN? Did you meet anyone famous?"

Jake gulped. He couldn't tell her! He struggled to say anything, then made a strange noise and walked to the fridge. Mia could instantly tell that he was hiding something again. Jake started thinking of what he could say to diffuse the situation before it started. His chest tightened once more. He felt the weight of the Harrison lies again, the awkwardness and the pain of it all. For the first time that week, the ball of stress in his stomach was ready to explode.

Jake grabbed a beer from the fridge and looked back at her. The cap hissed as he opened it, taking a well-deserved first sip.

"So?" Mia asked as she walked into the pantry.

'Fuck it' he thought. "Yeah, so... turns out that aliens exist."

28.

Travis flew back to Saskatchewan after their meetings at the United Nations. Although he was excited to get back to work (in person) after so long, he needed some time back at home. He spent nearly a month back at his family farm. Although the whole world knew his name, his small town on the prairies still gave him a brief reprieve from their newfound celebrity status. Jake hoped that some time with family, some dirt biking and late-night campfires would reignite the care-free side of his friend that had been lost.

Jake stayed in Vancouver for a few weeks as well. Only four days after his secret meeting with MI6 and the CIA, he had another meeting scheduled. One of an even higher consequence. Jake prepared himself for it, studying his notes and making a plan of attack. He had to nail the impression. It had been put off for far too long, and it had to be done. Five years after their first date, Jake was finally going to meet Mia's parents.

"You'll be fine," Mia told him in the car. "Just be yourself, and don't hide anything from them. They know all about you already, half the world does."

Jake was anxious as they pulled up to a cozy suburban bungalow in Port Coquitlam. So much had happened in five years - he was such a different person now than he was on their first date. And the situation felt forced and awkward. There were valid reasons why it hadn't happened yet, but it just didn't feel proper to first meet her parents after dating Mia for half a decade.

They were greeted warmly at the door. Mia's mother, Soo-Jin, was all smiles, and looked very much like her daughter. Her father, Jung, gave a quick and polite smile to Jake, then changed his expression to a sort of analytical skepticism.

Eventually, the dinner went well. That is, after Jung grilled Jake for the first twenty minutes. Mia's father had obviously not been thrilled that his daughter was dating an international fugitive for so many years. He let Jake know that right away, and sternly expressed his concerns to him. A moment's peace came when he retreated to the kitchen and left Jake and Mia alone.

"You told him I was a fugitive?" Jake whispered in Mia's ear as they sat in the living room.

"I couldn't exactly hide it; your face was all over the news! What was I supposed to do? And my mom definitely didn't like that I was in Venezuela so much."

"Yikes. Okay, I hope they know the reasons why now."

"CBC Newsworld hasn't stopped their coverage of you and Travis for days now. They've barely covered anything else. For god's sake, the *Weather Network* is talking about River Jumping. I'm pretty sure they know why you did what you did." Mia smiled and grabbed his hand. "You'll be fine. My dad's just a little protective. And a little old school, you know?"

Jake had his work cut out for him to win over Mia's parents. The Canadian news coverage of him hadn't been all positive, after all. A lot of pundits were questioning why he took such a high revenue product away from a Canadian company, and from Canada itself for that matter. Jake still had to convince Mia's parents that he was, indeed, a good person, and that he wouldn't hurt their daughter. When Mia began talking about which villa they were going to purchase near the Planet 9 base, however, her dad seemed to become more at ease.

The conversation switched, eventually, to time travel. One thing Jake hadn't been aware of was how much the topic had been discussed by the general public. By everyone, everywhere in the world. Once the news broke, people in all walks of life had spent countless hours discussing the repercussions. Mia's mother explained how she had been talking with her friends for days about it; how she didn't quite understand the idea of river jumping, but she knew that it was going to change the world. She couldn't wait to tell her friends about how she had Jacob Crawford at her house for dinner.

"No one will believe me that my daughter is going to marry that handsome scientist from the news," she said while looking down at her teacup.

"Uh..." started Jake, before Mia elbowed him in the ribs. He looked over at her to inquire. She silently shushed him and patted his forearm.

Jake did his best to walk them through the technology, and what they were trying to do with it. Soo-Jin asked him questions for hours, hoping to become the new expert in her group of friends. Jung only asked one question.

"I still don't understand why this 'egg' ship is necessary? If it's this berlinite stuff that causes the time travel, couldn't you just coat every ship in it?"

Jake explained the iridium shortages, and did his best to keep everything in layman's terms. He never thought he'd be explaining base dimensional theory to his girlfriend's parents. But it was everywhere now.

Mia and Jake finally left at eleven o'clock. They drove back to Mia's in a gentle drizzle through light Vancouver traffic. Jake had turned his phone off for the dinner, and was greeted with hundreds of unread messages when he turned it back on. "Holy F. This is nuts."

"You're a celebrity now! Everyone wants to talk to you. As soon as you told me about this, all those years ago, up by Squamish - I knew this would happen," Mia smiled.

"I just don't know if I'm ready for all this. I was still hiding in the jungle two weeks ago. I'm feeling a little swamped by it all, and I don't think the big city is helping."

"Well, I'm off for another week, and we don't need to stay in the city if you don't want. Where to next?"

A few days later, they flew to northern British Columbia to meet Jake's family. Mia had far less trouble impressing Jake's mother. Barbara was thrilled to finally meet her. Apparently, she had always worried whether her 'smart but awkward' son would meet someone. Barb and Kyla, Jake's sister, spent hours embarrassing him with old stories. Mia loved every minute of it. She suspected that he must have been nerdier as a child than as an adult, but seeing the proof amused her intensely.

Jake tried to keep his visit home a secret, but word got out in the small town. Soon, people he hadn't seen since high school were begging to meet up at the bar. Even in Smithers, he was constantly having phones and holotabs thrust in his face, and the word 'selfie' had become sickening to him.

This celebrity status was new to him. He didn't quite know how to take it, but he started to adapt to it after a few weeks. Before he went back to Costa Rica to continue his work, Jake hired a PR agent. He had already switched phone numbers and email addresses, but the requests for interviews still seemed to find him. He took a few interviews, but was feeling overwhelmed with the amount that he had to decline.

The public couldn't get enough of the time travel story. The 24-hour news stayed on that cycle for months. They spent hours upon hours explaining the construction process of the Seed ship, when eligible candidates could apply for the program, and what to expect in the years to come. 'Experts' were brought in to explain some of the base dimension concepts in layman's terms. Deep dive documentaries were compiled and released about the history of Planet 9. Jake watched a very inaccurate biopic of himself that had been pieced together hurriedly for Netflix.

Political panels argued endlessly about the implications of the technology. Some called Dylan Bishop an American traitor for bringing the tech to the UN instead of his home country. Many people questioned the morality of bringing the Seed ship to another planet, especially if there was life already there. Comparisons were drawn to Christopher Columbus, the Spanish Conquistadors, and the invasive species problems of Australia. If anything else was happening in the world, you wouldn't know it by watching the news. They played every angle on the story, over and over and over.

    For Jake and Travis, the publicity was nonstop for the following 12 months. They were invited to appear on talk shows. They got to meet the Canadian Prime Minister and the American President, and were invited by the King of England to have dinner at Buckingham Palace. People Magazine Online named them 'Persons of the Year.' They were originally rejected for the Nobel Prize in Physics, mainly because of the shady scientific processes they had gone through. After a public uproar, that decision was upended and they were nominated again for the following year.

    The only honor that Travis received (and Jake didn't) was being named one of the 'fifty sexiest men alive.' Travis laughed about it endlessly, saying 'how ugly the world must have become for that to happen'. Jake was slightly insulted, but accepted it. Travis had been the heartthrob back at Hachiro as well, after all. Jake didn't need to be in trashy magazines. Mia was all he needed.

They both bought properties near the Planet 9 compound. Jake's villa wasn't huge, but it had enough bedrooms for visitors to stay. It looked out over a small cove and a sandy beach, and it had a small infinity pool on the terrace. Travis decided to build his home from scratch, complete with many 'questionable' architecture choices.

    For the first year after his emancipation, Jake and Mia still kept separate residences. She would work from his villa for a month at a time, just as before, and then return to Vancouver. Jake could still work remotely as well, and would spend weeks with her back in Vancouver when he could. Even with the tumultuous events of the previous years, Mia had worked her way up to VP of Operations at her company.

They kept their long-distance relationship alive until, finally, Jake brought her over to the Planet 9 compound to have dinner with the Bishops. Mia was very nervous at first, panicking over what was appropriate to wear when meeting billionaires.

"Trust me, I wouldn't worry about it. You'll most likely be the best dressed person there," Jake joked. He'd gotten to know Dylan and Jess well enough to be fully comfortable around them now.

The dinner was much more casual than Mia had expected. Dylan had them out on his patio and insisted on working the grill himself. There was one attendant who cleared plates and brought them drinks, and she was fairly sure that Dylan hadn't done the prep work, but it still felt like a normal backyard barbeque. She didn't know why, but she had expected dinner to be at a fifty-foot-long table with dozens of tuxedoed servants - she just assumed that was how billionaires ate all the time.

It was that night that Jess, not Jake, convinced Mia to move down to Costa Rica permanently. The two got along very well right away. Jess took an interest in what Mia was doing in Vancouver, and listened to some of the worksite changes she had implemented.

"I'll just say, we could really use someone with your experience on staff. If you're interested," Jess coaxed. "What bigger project could you work on than the construction of the first interstellar ship?"

Mia thought for a bit, taking a sip out of her mojito. "Thank you, I'm very flattered. But I don't want a job here just because I'm Jake's girlfriend, you know?"

Jess looked at her intently. "Forget Jake. I'm offering you a job because of your experience, and because I like hiring people that I get along with. We're starting large scale construction next year, so the HSE team will be expanding. We need to fill a couple senior roles. Just think about it. You wouldn't have to keep flying back and forth all the time this way."

Mia did think about it. As the cart drove them back to their house that night, and she felt the warm evening air rushing over her face, she considered all of her options. Jake's house was paradise, no doubt. And the work would be very fulfilling. The thought of riding on someone else's coattails into a job still bothered her, though.

The following morning, she woke up before Jake and had her coffee on the deck. Watching the sun rise over the turquoise bay, she finally made her decision. Jake joined her when he woke up.

"I think I'm going to do it," Mia said. "I'm going to take the job."

Jake smiled and kissed her lightly. "You're going to love it here. It's the best place I've ever worked."

"There's no snow here, though. We'll have to do something about that," she smiled.

"Pretty sure we can figure that out."

29.

There was a morning chill in the air. Nothing by Canadian standards, it was as warm as most of that country ever got. But Jake noticed his forearms hairs sticking out into goosebumps on the short walk to Travis' house, and he began shivering. *'Man, first I got Vancouver weak, now I can't even handle seventeen degrees without a jacket.'* The years he had spent in the tropics had changed him, he'd adapted to a new climate. It had been nearly 8 years now since he'd lived in his home country.

He and Travis were meant to drive up to Lago Cocibolca today, which meant they were crossing the border into Nicaragua. The roads were meant to be good until the last part of the drive, where they got rough and unmaintained, so Travis had rented a 4x4 to use instead of his Audi E-tron convertible. The large inland lake had been chosen as the final assembly location of the Seed ship, and the two wanted to check out the progress.

It was much faster to take a cart or a quad bike to Travis' house, but Jake enjoyed the walk. It hadn't rained in nearly a week now, and the mud puddles on their rural road had all dried up. It was peaceful, there were only a handful of houses on this stretch, just south of the Planet 9 compound. The forest on his left was an orchestra of bird and insect noises, which seemed to fade as the hot sun finally crested over the horizon.

Travis' house was...interesting. It was mostly patios, and every room facing the ocean could roll a wall completely away to become yet another patio. There wasn't much interior space at all, just a modest kitchen, a small lounge and three bedrooms. The terraced landscaping overlooking the ocean was mostly storage for ocean toys, which included kayaks, sailing sloops, dive gear, and surfboards. There was a small pool and hot tub, outdoor showers, and colorful hammocks hung in every possible location. Each patio and terrace had its own wet bar, and Travis made sure to have kegs of his favorite Canadian beers shipped in and on tap at all times. The house had gotten a reputation at Planet 9, and he'd hosted many, many parties since it had been completed.

Jake liked hanging out at Travis' place. It felt like a clubhouse, very inviting, as if anyone could drop in at any time. He preferred to live in the beautiful house down the road that he shared with Mia, but, somehow, the social scene just seemed to revolve around Travis' place. It was a perfect setup in so many ways. Jake had the peace and quiet he wanted. Travis was back to being his cheery self again. And the distance between their houses was the perfect amount of separation for Jake. An ideal spacing of peacetime and party time.

Jake knocked before cracking the front door open. "Hey Buddy, you ready?" he yelled in the living room. There was no one around, at least that he could see. Travis had left his holo-tab powered on, lying on the kitchen counter. It had locked out the screen, which most likely meant he had some work documents open.

A sasquatch-like noise erupted behind him. Jake turned around to see Travis yawning and stretching out his arms, wearing nothing but his Saskatchewan Roughriders boxer shorts. "Oh shit, bud, what time did we say?"

"Little sleepy, big guy?"

"Shit, sorry man. Give me, like, 5 minutes. You want a coffee?"

"There's really no rush, it's not that far. Take your time."

Travis lumbered his way into the kitchen and poured some coffee beans into the grinder. He put a copper kettle on the stove to boil and continued stretching out his back while it boiled. It was when he groaned loudly and bent over into a forward fold that Jake finally broke.

"Did you...have any plans to put pants on?" Jake laughed.

"Sorry, your highness" Travis replied. He walked to his room and came back out wearing a dark brown bath robe. The kettle squealed out an alarm, and he poured the boiling water over the fresh grounds in his french press. "Cream, Milk? Whiskey?"

"Just milk, thanks man."

"So how far have they gotten with this thing? Do you know what we're checking out today?"

"The components themselves are still being assembled in the States and France. They'll get shipped to Planet 9's port, then coated with berlinite here. I think this is just the first of the assembly camp and heavy haul road that we're gonna see today."

"I still don't get it. It seems easier to just build it here, we could use the east bay. It's right out front, it'd be a hell of a lot easier."

"I guess it's too risky. It does seem like a whole extra ball of shit to get everything up to Nicaragua. But a lake is a lot less liable for storms during the construction phase. Pretty sure, once it's done, this ship will handle hurricanes, no problem. Then it can land in any body of water it wants. But for now, from what Jess says, they need calm water, all the time."

The Seed ship was to be, in essence, an enormous bicycle wheel. It would be a circle over 500 meters in diameter. Or more accurately, an icosagon, as the perimeter would be constructed of 20 straight 'living tubes', each equal in length. 20 support spokes would reinforce the circle towards the core of the shape. The core of the circle would be a large half-sphere that would be used for storage. The reinforced shape of the spokes would also hold cargo, meaning that the entire interior of the shape would be used to transport the enormous amount of equipment necessary for settling a new planet. The storage areas, especially the middle dome, would experience almost no gravity during spaceflight.

Roughly 2000 people would live in the outside ring for the journey. Each of the 20 sections would be constructed with a rigid exterior, but a freely rotating interior tube, running on a bearing system. This 'pipe within a pipe' design was invented for the unique gravitational challenges of jumping a ship from the surface into space. When floating in the lake, the living quarters would automatically orient themselves 'down' to Earth's gravity. Once in orbit, the entire ship would spin slowly, creating 1g of centrifugal force on the outer ring. The interior of each section would then follow the new flow of gravity, and 'down' would be the outside of the ring. It was a simple design, relatively easy to produce, and would solve nearly every health and logistical problem of a long journey in zero gravity. It was a heavy system, however, and would never be possible if they couldn't time jump the ship from the surface into space.

Early in the design process, Planet 9 had struggled with how to land such an enormous craft. Any landing gear or legs would have to support a lot of weight, and the destination would have to be perfectly flat for kilometers in every direction. Jake had been in one of the early meetings, virtually, from Venezuela. One of the designers asked why it needed to set down on land at all, and why it couldn't merely float instead. The immediate response was 'what if there's no water?'. To which Jake himself had responded "Why would we go there then?" And so, their idea for a seafaring and space-faring ship was born.

A large-scale international effort had begun to create the living sections of the perimeter tube. Dozens of nations got on board with the idea, contributing engineers, designers and resources. Wealthier nations were building their own sections and shipping them to Costa Rica for assembly. Planet 9 would have final say on the designs, however, and was responsible for the final berlinite coating, assembly, and installation of the FEHFR emitters throughout the ship. A total of 84 emitters would be installed, ready to fire the 'magic' frequency simultaneously. It was a similar system to the six emitters on the Egg Ship, just on a much, much larger scale.

"It's gonna start getting crazy around here once these sections start showing up. Real nuts. Enjoy the peace-time while it's here, I guess." Travis had sat down at the counter with his coffee. When Jake had told him there was no rush, he'd obviously taken it literally.

"Yeah, the workforce on site is going to triple. It'll be a pretty wild few years," Jake responded. "Kinda glad we're not still up in staff housing for that."

"So, bud. Have you thought about it?" Travis asked, turning away from the view to look at him.

"About what?"

"C'mon man. I know you've thought about it."

Jake knew exactly what Travis was talking about. He'd thought about it incessantly. He stayed awake every night weighing the options, making lists of pros and cons. It was still years away, but it would be the biggest decision a person could make in their lifetime. It wasn't easy.

"Those spots are ours if we want. Nice cozy cabins on the Seed ship. What if we were the first ones off the ship?" Travis took a long sip of his coffee. "Imagine that, bud. Neil Armstrong, Yasmina Coskun...Travis Fuckin' Strickland."

"Whoa, whoa. Who says I have to be the Buzz to your Neil?"

"Because I'd flick you in the nuts and pass you when you weren't looking" Travis laughed.

It was the biggest adventure Jake could think of. To be a part of the first interstellar colony - it was a crazy opportunity. He'd dreamed of being a part of something like this since he was a child. But it was so - final. It was a decision that couldn't be undone. "Yeah, I don't know yet, man. I'm still weighing the options."

Jake heard something move behind him, and it startled him. He turned around to see a woman leaving Travis's room and heading for the front door. She was obviously trying to sneak by without being seen, but caught Jake's eyes mid step. She stopped and smiled, embarrassed.

"Hi Jake."

"Ummm, hi Natalie…" Jake said, chuckling.

Natalie went red in the face and put her sandals on near the front door. "I'll see you guys later on."

"Sounds good, you need a ride?" Travis asked.

"I summoned a car. I'm good," she smiled, finishing her sentence while hastily closing the door behind her.

Jake looked at Travis and laughed. "How long has that been going on? You dog…"

"Ah, she's pretty awesome, man. We kind of hooked up a while ago, just after I moved into this new house. Happens pretty often now. We've been keeping it quiet, though. Don't need the office gossip."

"Seriously? That was over a year ago."

"Yeah," Travis smiled. "Remember that surfing trip I took six months ago? I wasn't alone."

Jake laughed, realizing how good they were for each other. Natalie was quite the wild spirit as well. "That's great, man. I'm happy for you, I really like her."

"Whoa, whoa, dude. It's nothing serious."

"Trav, you've been on trips together, you've been hooking up for over a year. Hate to say it, but it sounds serious."

"Fuuuuck" Travis whispered.

Jake laughed at his discomfort. "Sorry to be the bearer of bad news."

"Yeah, I kind of figured. Hey - by the way, I don't know how the F you kept all the secrets from Mia back in the day. I haven't really had a relationship like this in years, I didn't realize how hard that would be." Travis got up and put his mug in the sink. "I ended up having a bit too much tequila last month and telling her all about Reyes 3."

"What the fuck!?" Jake laughed. He thought about it for a second. He should have been angrier, but he had told Mia on the first day, after all. He shrugged it off, even though they had both broken a binding contract with the world's most powerful intelligence agencies. "You're such a douche." Maybe it was the tropics that had chilled him out, or his work, or Mia, but Jake was definitely less stressed these days.

Travis slapped him on the back. "Well, let me learn from your mistakes. I've always told you not to take my advice with women, I'm an idiot. You know that."

"So, anyways - you're gonna go? With the new colony?"

"Hell yeah! I feel like everything we've done has been leading us there, man. This whole crazy ride has been one long journey to get on that ship. I ain't missing it, that's for sure."

"Jesus, well - wow. Good for you, man."

"Nothing is set in stone yet. The probes still have to get the final surveys of Planet A. It could be an impossible planet to live on still, and we might still have to call the whole thing off."

"That's one of the things that freaks me out. Those surveys are coming back just six months before launch. That's intense - having to commit the rest of your life to something that still may not happen."

"River Jumping is kinda messed up that way. Just gotta go with the flow - no pun intended," Travis chuckled. "But if all those readings look good, hell yeah, I'm gonna do it. I'm planning to take a year-long sabbatical before the launch, though. I'm going to keep working til then, then get outta here for a while. There's a lot of Earth that I haven't seen yet."

Jake finished his coffee deep in thought. It was a great idea. Travis went to his room to get dressed. He came back five minutes later wearing one of his usual outfits, a look that Jake had nicknamed 'tropical cowboy'.

They got in the rented Land Cruiser and started out on the road north.

"I think you should give it more thought, dude," Travis said as they left the main highway. "Just think about everything we've done. It's amazing, I never would've thought I'd be a celebrity scientist - the whole idea of that is friggn' crazy! And we have a pretty sweet life here" he said, gesturing to their surroundings as they drove. "I'd love to stay living here - it's paradise."

"So do I. This is the happiest I've ever been. Living here with you, our friends, Mia - it's hard to think about giving all of that up, you know?"

Travis took a moment of silence to phrase out his next thought. "But…I think of ten-year-old Travis. Everything that he'd want me to be. He'd be really stoked at everything that's happened so far. The money, the fame, the hot chicks. But if he knew there was a chance to visit another planet, and I didn't take it - he'd punch me in the fuckin' jaw."

Jake nodded. It was true. Ten-year-old Jake would think the same, apart from ten-year-old Jake would probably never punch anybody.

"I grew up on Star Trek and Battlestar Galactica and all that shit. Why wouldn't I get on my own star ship, and go on my own journey through the stars?"

Jake stared out the window at the passing jungle as they drove. He felt the heat of the sun and the humid warmth of the air. Life on planet earth was beautiful, and he was in a perfect position to enjoy all of it. He had everything he'd ever wanted. But Travis' words echoed his own thoughts. There was a whole universe out there, and he had the chance to discover it, if he could be brave enough to leave this paradise behind.

The smooth pavement gave way to a gravel road, and the knobby tires of the Toyota kicked up a cloud of dust as the pair sped north into Nicaragua.

30.

Are We Ready For This?

The front-page article of Time Magazine's online edition had an artistic rendering of the 'Dream Team.' It was in black and white, and showed Dylan Bishop's head at the top of the frame, staring off into space. Slightly smaller, and looking the other way, was Jessica Bishop. And, smaller still, near the bottom, their two proteges, Jacob Crawford and Travis Strickland.

Are We Ready For This?
As the final years approach, how are the top minds of Planet 9 dealing with the pressure?

Marcela hissed under her breath and flipped to another page. Planet 9 and the story of the 'two plucky scientists from Canada', it was all overplayed. It had been in the news for years now.

Like everyone else on the planet, she'd been enthralled with Jake and Travis when the story had first broken. The very idea of River Jumping - of being able to transport light years away from Earth for the first time - it felt like humanity had leapt forward by centuries. And the fact that two young scientists had discovered it working alone, with duct tape, in a remote warehouse in Canada; all of it was incredible.

But the news had never stopped. Like a repetitive chart-topping song, the tale of Jake and Travis had outstayed its welcome. Yes, the public still wanted updates. They still wanted to know the details of the Seed ship construction, and who was selected to go aboard. They still wanted to know the results of the new surveys, and the important decisions that had yet to be made.

But it had been three long years. The click-bait stories of the Bishops and the Canadians had grown very tiring, and people wanted to talk about something else. Anything else. At least, that's what Marcela assumed. The only thing that she was absolutely certain of was that *she* was sick of hearing about them.

She was tired of everybody talking about Jake and Travis, and their amazing, world changing discovery. She knew deep down, however, this was because no one, anywhere was talking about Marcela Reyes and her discovery.

She turned off her holo-tab and went for a walk around the office. Although the pay wasn't fantastic, being a radio astronomer had brought Marcela to some amazing places. Besides Chile, she had worked in the remote desert of New Mexico, in the mountains of Germany, and even spent a brief stint in Siberia. The need to get away from light pollution and interference had a great perk; she got to work in remote, beautiful locations all over the Earth.

Marcela had collected signals for from Reyes 3 for 6 years, and passed all of her findings to the coalition of scientists who were working to decode them. Eventually, though, there wasn't much left to collect. If they couldn't determine what the past 6 years of signals meant, the new ones weren't going to do them any good. So, she had been brought back from Chile to England, put under the payroll of the British Government, and quietly buried in bureaucracy. She had swapped the mountains and tundra for a nondescript office in central London, and a draining commute on the northern line.

Not that location should matter that much really, most things could be run remotely now anyway. She could run surveys when needed, and could assist with interpolation. But mostly, these days she worked as a data librarian for the scores of files that had accumulated. It was a job that was way far beneath her skillset, and a complete waste of her time.

It was just a convenient way for MI6 to keep her on payroll. Marcela was being paid to keep the world's largest secret, which she never imagined would be so excruciatingly boring. There was nothing entertaining on her walks through the office. She didn't socialize with anyone in the building, most were not aware of her work and she was contractually obligated to keep it from them. In fact, in this spy environment, very few people ever interacted with each other. She merely walked in circles, breaking up the tedium of the day.

When she returned to her desk, a new email was waiting. It was in her personal account this time, which brought a ping of stimulation to her doldrum morning.

Hi Marcie,

I hope everything is going well in England. I'm sorry we haven't been able to chat for a while, the time difference is much harder now. I liked it much more when you were still here in Chile, but that's just because I like having my daughter closer :)

I would like to talk this week if you can. Your mother's condition is deteriorating. She is still okay, and I think she'll be with us for some time to come, but I've made the tough decision to put her in a long-term care facility. We can't afford to bring the help she needs to our home all the time, and she needs a lot these days. I'll be moving into an apartment closer to her, and I plan to sell the house in the next year to cover the costs.

I know this is a lot in an email, please call when you can. Will you be back in Santiago any time soon? I don't want to get rid of anything before you've had a chance to go through the place.

Love always, and talk soon,
Dad

Marcela held back tears as she read the last few lines. Although she suspected her mother would need additional assistance, she never would have thought that they'd lose their home! She had a little extra money that she could send, but it wouldn't be enough to make a difference. Constant home care would be a massive expense. She cringed at the thought of her mother spending her last few years in a facility.

She closed the email app on her holotab and saw the magazine cover page underneath, still open. She glared angrily at the Bishops and the Canadians. Yes, Jake and Travis had spent time in exile, and they'd had tough times, but they were rich and successful now. Eight years after she'd first detected the alien signals, her finances were the same, her career had all but evaporated, and her parents were struggling.

Regret had been growing in Marcela now for a number of years. She had trusted Priscilla's advice, and had bought into the idea of 'the greater good'. With the reveal of River Jumping, keeping the secret of Reyes 3 had become more important than ever. If someone besides Dylan Bishop used the technology to jump there, Earth's anonymity would be lost forever. She knew the reasons why she was here - but this was the last straw. The 'greater good' wouldn't pay her mother's hospital bills.

Just one interview, one book. If she revealed what she knew to the world, her financial troubles would be over. The Time Magazine cover would be Marcela Reyes, Person of the Year! She would easily be able to buy her childhood home and get her mother all the help she needed. Marcela sat in her chair and thought about her scenario over and over. It was bloody unfair the way she'd been treated. It was ridiculous that she had ended up in that dark, dead-end office. She got up and walked towards the stairs.

Dennis Webb worked in a rather unremarkable office on the floor above. He had the luxury of windows, but the view wasn't great, and the office finishings were bland. That fit his personality, though, there was nothing ostentatious about the career spy. He had spent a lifetime carefully moving up the ranks of British Intelligence, pressing hard on the people he needed to, while treading lightly when required.

Marcela knocked on his open office door. "Come in, then," Dennis said in a monotone voice, looking up from his ledger to see her. His face acknowledged her presence, and almost curled its lips upwards, but it wasn't really a smile.

"Mr. Webb, do you have a few moments?"

He gestured towards the synthetic leather armchair that faced his desk. "What can I help you with?"

Marcela carefully sat down in the round backed chair. It was quite uncomfortable. "Mr. Webb, I've been working with you now for quite a while."

He nodded.

"And... I think I've been asked to make some pretty large sacrifices-"

"We all do, Ms. Reyes," he cut her off.

She tried not to get flustered. Dennis was a stubborn, impossible person to talk to. "I just know that, had I not kept...you know what - a secret, I'd be in a much better position. And I've never been in this for financial gain..."

"We pay you quite well, Ms. Reyes."

Bullshit. It might allow her some basic luxuries, but it was still a government paycheck. "I just need to know... what's the end game? We've been studying this planet together for years now, and we're no closer than we were before. When does it end? When do we go public?"

"We're still a long way off from that. You have to be patient."

"I can't be patient anymore! I've been patient. But my mother is very ill, and they're losing their home in Santiago, and I need more money to help them..."

"I can put a request in for a salary review. Perhaps a slight cost of living increase?"

Marcela was getting frustrated. He wasn't listening. "That's not going to..." she stammered. "I need more than that. I want to know, right now, when this ends. When do we go public? If the world knew about Reyes 3..."

"Ah!!!" Dennis exclaimed loudly. He got up and angrily closed the door. Even in this environment, the name was never spoken aloud.

"If the world knew about what we'd done, I'd not have to worry about money. I wouldn't have to work *here* anymore!" Marcela said, intensely but quietly.

Dennis sat back in his chair. He didn't say anything at first, just let out a long exhale. Finally, he replied in his usual monotone. "What we do, we don't do for financial gain. Intelligence pays my bills, yes, but I've always done what needed to be done for Britain. And you…"

"Yes."

"You know what's at stake more than anyone. Ms. Miles and you have talked at length about it. So why even come to me with this? You know very well that we can't take this information public."

"I just want to be home, Dennis. I just want to help them."

"You're not a prisoner here, Marcela. You never have been. But I will remind you again of your obligations, and the contracts that you're under. You can leave here anytime, but you will *absolutely not* disclose any information of the existence of Reyes 3 to anyone. The only people you are allowed to discuss that subject with - are those who are also contractually obligated to keep the secret safe. So, feel free to leave, but we *will* come find you if this info gets out, I can promise you that."

His last words came out in a slow, intense deadpan. It was very intimidating. As much as Marcela wanted to view him as a harmless, pudgy man behind a cheap desk, she knew what he was capable of. "Fine," she sighed. She wished dearly that Priscilla had never brought her here. "But, if you could please file for a salary review then. I suppose every bit counts."

The walk home was cold, gray, and disappointing. When Marcela arrived at her small flat, she trudged into the bedroom and put her pajamas on. It was much too late in Chile to call her father, and she didn't have the physical or emotional energy left to leave the house. The thoughts of regret and anger reflected back and forth through her brain, and she couldn't stop them. She began looking for a job back in Santiago. If she couldn't help her mother financially, at least she could spend more time with her, and she could leave all the MI6 bullshit behind her. Eventually, she turned on one of her favorite childhood movies and laid chest down on the couch, hoping for the release of sleep.

A knock on her door startled her awake. The movie had ended, and the room was dimly lit by the holo-screen's streaming menu. She quietly took the blanket off herself and tiptoed towards the door. The microwave's clock showed that it was past midnight. *"Who on earth?"* she thought. She quietly looked through the century old peephole, and saw a man in a polo shirt standing at her door.

"Can I help you? What do you want?" she asked quietly through the door.

"Courier, ma'am. Are you Marcela Reyes?"

She thought carefully about her answer. Had her conversation with Dennis Webb inspired this? Was she being intimidated, or even assassinated!? "And if I am?"

"Just a letter to deliver, Miss."

"I'm not opening the door at this time of night. Can you please slip it under?"

The man said nothing else. A letter emerged under the door slip. Marcela's heart was pounding, and she watched through the peephole to make sure he had truly left her alone. When the elevator doors finally closed behind him, she brought the letter to her kitchen counter and opened it.

Marcela Reyes,
We've only met once, but I've been following your work closely. I apologize for delivering a message this way, but I can only assume that your online communications are being watched. I want you to know that I've kept my promise, and I have not sent

any more probes to the area in question. That doesn't mean that I don't want to know more about it, I haven't stopped thinking about that star since we met in New York.

I'm very sorry to hear about your mother's situation, and I believe that we can help. I have a proposition for you...

31.

Usually, ski touring cleared Jake's head. It was one of the few activities in his life where his mind went blank. He could leave all his bullshit at the trailhead and simply focus on getting his skis up whichever mountain he was on. Today, however, it wasn't working. There was too much baggage in his head.

He'd made a decision on the interplanetary journey - or, at least he thought he had. He was still weighing every option, trying to predict the circumstances of each outcome. The scenery around him was stunning, and the climb was tough, but his mind wasn't focused on his aching quads or his pristine surroundings. He barely noticed how hard he was breathing when he caught up to Mia, who was taking a break in a sheltered spot behind a large boulder.

Mia took out a small flask of whiskey and poured a bit into her hot chocolate. The stove had just boiled, so the mug was too hot to drink. She set it in the snow, where it began melting its way down slowly through the icy, faceted crystals. She put the cap on the flask before donning her large mitts again and passing it to Jake.

"Need a leg loosener?"

"Maybe just a little. I'm wiped today."

"Just one more push after this to the summit. You can do it, don't be a wuss," she smiled.

Jake was doing much better at ski touring this year. He and Mia had been many more times since their first trip back in Vancouver. Having his own gear helped, he wasn't struggling to figure out the rental skis and bindings each time. And the lightness of his new skis, boots and pack was a big boost for his mediocre fitness. "I'll be fine" he lied. His legs were already hurting, and they were still 1500 feet off the summit. "Looks pretty windy up there, eh?"

"Yeah, not pleasant. That's why I stopped here for lunch. I just want to get up there, rip the skins off and get right back down. You cool with that?"

Jake nodded reluctantly.

"I think we're going to get a sick view. These mountains are nuts, makes Canada look small!" Mia impatiently picked up her hot chocolate and took a sip, burning her lips a little bit in the process. She was in her happy place.

Mia and Jake shared plenty of adventures over the four years that he was exiled in Venezuela. They hiked through the jungle, scuba-dived in the ocean, and mountain biked - at least when the scorching heat allowed it. There was no snow in Venezuela, though, and that was an issue.

This was where Mia was happiest. On snow, making her way up mountains. Jake enjoyed it as well, definitely. He appreciated the mountains, but not on the same euphoric level that she did. Every time they got back into the alpine, it was like hitting a 'reset' switch for Mia. She'd leave noticeably happier, full of that bubbly charm that Jake had fallen so madly in love with.

"Thank you for suggesting this. It was worth the flight. It's so awesome. I've wanted to come here for years," Mia said, lifting her mug to cheers Jake's, then kissing him gently on the cheek. They usually went north once or twice in a winter, ski touring in the Rockies of Canada or the Chugach Mountains of Alaska. They'd gone drone skiing as well, when the mood struck. Jake didn't like going to the regular 'chairlift' resorts anymore. Even with ski goggles on, his face had become recognizable around the world. He appreciated the anonymity of the backcountry whenever possible.

This time, they'd gone south for a four-day weekend in Patagonia. It was a challenge for both of them. The climbs were bigger, the route finding trickier. It was well worth it, though. The scenery was incredible, and they had hit the season just right for snow conditions. Skiing through snow covered monkey puzzle trees was exhilarating, like exploring a strange fantasy world. They'd gotten the lay of the land from a local guide on day one, after which Mia insisted on going out with just the two of them.

"I think the snow is still gonna get real shitty later in the day," Jake said, feeling the warm sun on his exposed forearms. "Especially below treeline, near the hut."

"It'll be worth it. It'll be an adventure."

"That's what you always say" laughed Jake.

"Because it is. And I like having adventures with you."

Jake swallowed, anxiously. If he was waiting for a moment to bring up the *big* question, this was it. "How... how do you feel about a really big adventure? Like, the biggest adventure..."

Years ago, Mia had pinned him down in the alpine to get the truth out of him, using a rest stop just like this. That day had stuck with Jake all through the years. There was something special about the backcountry. The danger required partnership and comradery, while the solitude brought unmatched clarity of thought. It was the perfect place to discuss the undiscussable.

"You're thinking about it, aren't you?" Mia knew exactly what he was referring to. How could she not? It was on everyone's minds, constantly.

"I am. A lot."

"And?" Mia was being her usual self. No beating around the bush. No games. Just straight up and honest. It was one thing that Jake loved about her, and one of the greatest differences between the two of them.

Jake looked away from her, staring out over the view. He was sitting on his pack, leaning against his skis. "I want to go." There it was. It was out in the open now, there was no taking it back. He gulped, realizing he had phrased it wrong. "I think *we* should go," he said, correcting himself.

Mia looked at him, but he didn't make eye contact. She had thought about it, for sure. But she wasn't so sure. It was a lot to leave behind. "I figured as much. It's OK, Jake. I knew you wanted to go on the ship."

"Am I that transparent?"

Mia shoved her pack closer to him, changing her position so that she could share in the same view and lean against him. She breathed deeply while contemplating her next sentence. "Jake, do you remember why you brought berlinite to Dylan Bishop? Was it so long ago that you've forgotten? *This* was the reason. You always said that fortune and fame weren't as important as this. Now that it's actually happening, why would you even question it? Of course you want to go! I've always known that you wanted to get on that ship."

Jake felt perplexed. He was embarrassed that he hadn't brought it up yet, if she already knew his intentions. "What do you think? Do you want to come with me? Sorry, I know it's a big decision."

"That's putting it lightly! How do I feel about leaving behind everything and everyone I've ever known?" Mia laughed. "I don't know, honestly, Jake. It's super tempting, but - do they even want someone like me? You remember that I don't want kids, right? That doesn't sound ideal for populating a new planet."

"I don't think that's an issue, honestly. The crew will be big enough. We might have to help out with some of the kids, though. 'It takes a village' and all that shit." Jake took the flask and dumped a little more whiskey in his mug, momentarily forgetting about the upcoming ski ascent. "It's supposed to be a sustainable population. We don't want to go there and spread like locusts right away. It's more about setting up the new colony than anything else. And yes, they could definitely use someone like you."

"They're taking the smartest people in the world out there. Physicists, engineers. I just don't see how someone like me would contribute."

"Health and Safety? Hell yeah, you would. You've worked in enough places to know why. Because even if they have three PhD's, these people are still friggn' idiots. And, as much as I hate to say it, they need simple rules enforced - to protect them from themselves."

Mia smiled lovingly. "You've sure changed your tune. You used to think we were the devil."

"I'm just another cog in the corporate wheel now, I know."

Mia took a long, drawn-out exhale through her nose. "I'm really torn. I get the adventure side of it - I get why you're so drawn to the idea. What an amazing experience it would be, to be the first group in the new world. Our generation never really had a frontier, the world was already very small by the time we were born." Mia paused, noticing that the view around them was anything but small. She took another sip and smiled, thinking about the possibility. "But I really like our life now - it's awesome. I've never been as happy as I am in Costa Rica. This is so...final."

"There may be return trips in the future. Dylan's pretty optimistic about the Stingray ship, he says it might even end up faster than they predicted. If it can do the speeds he's talking about, the Stingray might end up working like a ferry between Earth and us, constantly going back and forth."

"Yeah, but - there might not be a Stingray. Dylan's being overly ambitious about that, and no one has proved that it will work yet. I understand that the window for the Seed ship is small, and why it's so big and slow, and why it's only a one-way trip. I get all that. It's just..." Mia tried to figure out how to express her thoughts. "It kinda feels like suicide, almost. Never seeing Earth again. I know the experience would be amazing, it's just a really, really huge thing to commit to. You have to understand that, don't you?"

Jake nodded, taking an energy bar out of his pocket and biting into it. "I know, I've been struggling with how final it is too. But by the time the launch window comes, we'll both be forty. I like to think about it as if.... the first half of my life was in this solar system, and the second half will be out there" he said, pointing his mittened hand towards the sky. "I know it's cheesy and serendipitous, but that's how I feel. I don't know, there's just something that's really drawing me to this, like it was always meant to be."

Mia nodded as well, giving him a gentle smile. "You've been working towards this since day one. I definitely get it." She looked out at the mountains around her. "There's so much I haven't done here yet, though. It's a huge adventure, but we have so many adventures left here on Earth!"

"Not quite the same, though. Even in a place as rugged as this, as wild as Patagonia, someone's been in this spot before. Someone has already been to the top of every one of those mountains that we can see in the distance. We were born too late to truly explore the unknowns of the Earth. And I think that's what's so alluring about this."

Mia nodded as she stared out at the view with him.

"You only get so much time in your life, no matter which planet you're on. And you'll never see everything, no matter what." Jake finished his hot chocolate and dumped the last few drops into the snow. He swept some powder on top of the stain, so it wouldn't spoil the clean, white lunch spot. "I like Travis' plan. He's in, for sure. He's super stoked to be on that ship, no question. But he's going to take a full year off work before the launch. He's got a big list of everything he wants to see on Earth before he leaves."

"That's... pretty brilliant. I like that idea a lot." Mia began packing up her touring bag, putting her jetboil stove away. "Imagine everything we could see in a year. Everything we could do."

"Especially if we blow all our savings" Jake laughed. "I doubt we'll be using dollars up there. May as well have fun with our retirement accounts while we're here, screw it."

Mia stopped packing her bag and got quiet. She stared into the snow, mesmerized by it. "I'd want to spend a lot more time with my family until then. And so should you. That would be so hard to leave them behind, oh my god." Mia took a long breath and stared out at the valley below them. "If we really are going to be leaving forever."

"Does that mean you're..."

A light breeze was the only sound for several seconds. The silence hung over the two of them like a blanket. The wind ruffled the Gore-Tex of their jackets, and a puff of snow blew across the surface onto Jake's pack. He didn't want to say anything else. He wanted her to say yes - he was dying for her to say yes. If she did, then his decision was so much easier. He couldn't go without her, he knew that. Jake loved her far too much to leave her behind.

Mia finally looked up from the ground and smiled at him. "Let's do it. What's the worst that could happen?" she laughed.

Jake took a step closer to her to embrace her, but crunched his right boot through the supportive layer in the snow, sinking in facets to his upper thigh. He'd meant to smoothly walk over and hug her in celebration of the agreement, but now stared at her belly button instead. He still hugged her, while she laughed at the strange alignment of their bodies. "Oh man, this is great!"

"I'm not 100 percent, Jake. But I'll think more about it, OK."

"Neither is the mission, it's all good. It could still get canceled anytime. But if we get signed on officially and start training, we'll be good to board if it actually happens."

"When do they get the go-ahead?"

"75141 is still pretty far out of alignment for the probes to river jump. They won't get close enough to get detailed pictures of the surface and conditions until six months before the Seed launch. That's still three years away. If they get bad news from that survey, we scrap the plans and keep the ship ready to go - just in case we find another habitable planet in the future. But my team hasn't found anything else out there that works for a colony, not within our 500 light year boundary."

"They said it was a breathable atmosphere?"

"Close enough. We'd need to slowly adapt to it, but yes. And the long-range surveys show evidence of photosynthetic life, with large areas of liquid water."

"What would cancel it then?"

"All sorts of things. Anything that could make it unsuitable for human life. For example, if it had no significant electromagnetic field, we wouldn't be able to withstand the radiation. Or if it was too volcanically active, or sitting in a heavy bombardment of space debris. That's why we had to eliminate Planet B from contention. Its orbit is littered with asteroids, enough to have a major collision every few decades. It's too bad, it looked okay other than that, it was nice to have a backup in case Planet A doesn't work out."

Mia nodded. She knew a lot of this, of course, but it was good to have Jake around for reassurance.

"And we can still pull out, even when the ship arrives there at 75141. There will be a short window to change our mind and time-jump the Seed ship home."

"What if - what if it's like the other planet?" Mia asked. "Like Reyes 3? What if we get there and it's already...for lack of a better word...taken?"

Jake had gone so long keeping the secret of Reyes 3, it was still jarring to hear it used in open conversation. "I don't know - I figure we'd have figured out if an intelligent race was living there. We'd have seen something."

"But you guys missed the aliens on Reyes 3, didn't you? What happens, anyway, if there's aliens on 75141?"

Jake was starting to put his skis back on. He was very happy that Mia had agreed to go, but he was hoping to continue the conversation later on at home. The top of the route was still far off above them, and he needed to get moving. "I'll let you know more about the plan later, but, basically, if any animal has evolved to the point where it's self-aware, we jump the whole settlement back home and leave it for them."

"That's a little vague. I hope they have a hard rule to define that."

"I don't work with exobiology much, I have no idea how they'll gauge that."

"And I do hope they stick to that rule once it's set. You've met Dylan - he doesn't like to lose."

"Maybe it's something you should ask about at the compound. I've been too preoccupied with the Seed designs to think about it, to be honest."

Mia was intrigued. It was the first time she'd thought beyond the Earth. She'd been so preoccupied with leaving her own planet behind that she hadn't contemplated what would happen when they landed on the next one.

"Anyways, I've got to get moving," Jake said as he clicked into his bindings. "I'm getting cold. We can talk all about the morality of galactic colonization on the flight home." The two began the last part of their ascent, striding confidently into the swirling snow that was blowing down off the mountain top.

32.

"**C**heap piece of shit!"
Kushal had ripped through his folding camping chair as he sat down, and was now stuck inside the frame. His butt was on the grass, and his legs flopped helplessly above him as he tried to get up. He was swearing in frustration, wriggling around and trying to get his footing. Everyone tried not to laugh for a few seconds, until Natalie burst out in a cackle. She got up and helped him to his feet, as the rest of the group began howling. Eventually, even Kushal started laughing.

"Here man, take mine, I can sit on the grass," said Jake, still chuckling.

"No, it's okay" replied Kushal. Travis said nothing, but handed him a beer from his cooler before tapping on the top, offering it as a seat.

"I hope Jon's okay in there" Natalie said, sitting down again. "How long til the jump?"

"Just under ten minutes" replied Jake. "I can't believe it's happening, it feels like we've been building this thing for half our lives."

Jake and Mia were sat in a double camping chair on a grassy slope, overlooking Lago Cocibolca. Travis and Natalie were there with them, as well as Kushal and Rowena from their Planet 9 team. Jake's mother, Barbara, was sitting near him and Mia as well. They had all driven up to Nicaragua for the day to see history in the making.

Down in the lake below them was an enormous purple tube wrapped around in a circle. From their vantage point, it was tough to make out the round shape. The Seed ship was so hauntingly large that it challenged the imagination. It was half a kilometer off the shore, where it had been towed away from the construction docks by a team of tugboats. Now, as the first test jump loomed closer, all the boats had retreated back to the shore in order to keep a safe distance.

"So, your friend Jon is on there right now?" Barbara asked Jake.

"Yep. It will eventually hold about 2000 people, but they're running this first test with a skeleton crew of engineers. Jon worked with the team designing the landing rockets, and they're on board to test out the first water landing of the ship."

"There's not much for them to do" added Natalie. "Everything about this flight will be computer controlled, but it made sense to have them on the command stations in case things go squirrely."

Travis brought a steel camping-style wine glass over to Barbara. "I know you didn't want a beer, but you have to celebrate this with us, Barb. This is a big moment," he smiled, passing her the cold glass of Sauvignon Blanc. Barbara accepted.

Jake had offered to move his mother down to Costa Rica many times. She'd always refused. Smithers was her home. Jake also offered to buy her a larger house in the small BC town; she'd refused that as well. She did accept a new truck and a hot tub, however, and Jake had paid off the remainder of her mortgage several years earlier.

Barbara would sometimes visit Jake and Mia down in Costa Rica, though. She called the trips her 'all-inclusive vacations', and jokingly said that she had paid for them in diaper changes years ago. Summer was such a fleeting and beautiful time in northern Canada that she never missed it. However, February was a different story and she always jumped on the chance to fly out of the dark, gray, cold of the British Columbia Interior. Jake always enjoyed her visits, except for the incessant encouragement for Mia to give her another grandchild. He cringed every time she mentioned it, while Mia laughed it off.

"And you didn't want to go on this flight? Aren't you worried about it?" Barbara asked her son.

"Nah, I just think I'd be in the way," Jake responded. "They don't need us at this stage, it's a really simple time jump. The complicated science will come in a few days when they bring it down from orbit to land in the Caribbean."

"How far up is it jumping away from us again?"

Jake went to correct her, then stopped himself. Yes, the ship was staying still, but he didn't need to explain it every time. He couldn't blame her, or anyone for getting that wrong. It was a tricky thing to understand, and everyone - including himself - referenced it incorrectly from time to time. "The ship is going to jump backwards in time by 28 seconds. It'll start falling into the Earth's gravity, and the computer will fire onboard rockets to steer it into a high orbit. They're going to stay in orbit for a few days to test the rotational gravity system, and then the real crazy part starts."

"The landing?"

"You bet," Travis cut in. "It's gonna be a hell of a lot of time jumps, but we've simulated it a thousand times. They'll be fine. You see, instead of dropping out of orbit through the stratosphere, the whole ship is going to take microsecond jumps to lower itself." He was waving his beer through the air to visualize the procedure. "Once it's about 15,000 feet up from sea level, a combination of rockets and parachutes will slow it down and bring it gently into the ocean."

"It's the same landing system we use on the Egg, but just on something - huge. And much tougher to balance" Jake replied.

"And Jon - he knows how to pilot that? Sounds scary," Barbara asked.

"It's way too precise for a human to pilot any of that" Natalie said. "It has to be done with a computer, and Jon will be strapped into his seat just like a regular passenger at that point."

It was getting close to the launch time now. This event would be streamed around the world, and it was expected to have hundreds of millions of spectators online. At the lake, however, it was just a few Planet 9 employees and the Nicaraguan locals. They had constructed the enormous ship in the calm waters of the lake, but were planning to land it in the Caribbean Sea off the Costa Rican coast. Now that the ship was fully constructed, ocean weather was no longer a threat to it. Each subsequent test, and its final jump to the stars, would all happen from the ocean now, just off the shore from the Planet 9 compound.

Jake was happy to see it leaving the lake. Dylan Bishop had caused enough disruption to this tranquil environment. If the tests all went well, the temporary facilities at Lago Cocibolca would be torn down, and the heavy haul roads would be cleaned up to be reclaimed by nature. These next few minutes would be the last time that the giant purple 'bicycle wheel' would be in Nicaragua.

Jake's mother leaned over to him to whisper to him. "It still worries me, Jake. I don't like the fact that you two are going on that thing."

"We'll be fine, Mom. It's going to be tested many, many more times before we leave."

"It's the worst-case scenario for a mother, you know. I'm so proud of you, and everything you've done, but watching you and Mia leave is going to be very, very hard. Getting on that bloody spaceship, going to a planet where I'll never see you again…"

"We'll be able to write, eventually," Jake replied compassionately. "Jess and I have been developing a probe system that will jump back and forth and relay messages between the two planets. Even though we'll be thousands of years in the future, we'll still be able to write to you in your time. And vice versa."

"It's not much consolation, Jake. It's better than nothing, but it still doesn't soften the blow of never seeing you again."

Mia reached out her hand to hold Barbara's. Barb held back her tears, not wanting to spoil the moment for everyone there. Mia's eyes misted up looking at her, as she thought of the hard goodbyes that would soon happen between her and her own family. She had no idea how she was going to handle it.

"Here we go! This is it!" Travis stood up, checking his phone. "Less than a minute!"

Time jumping berlinite ships into space lacked the romance of rocket launches. There was no engine ignition, no erupting boom of noise. Jake had only watched one rocket launch in his life, but he would always remember the excitement of that moment. Seeing the structure lift off the ground, the billows of smoke expanding out to the sides, being blown backwards by the noise. It was exhilarating to watch the trail of exhaust curve its way up into the stratosphere - to wait until the noise faded to hear the crowd cheering around him.

He'd seen the Egg jump into space many times now. It was about as different an experience as one could imagine. Whisper quiet, enough to hear the birds singing around him. No noise, no theatrics. Just a building sized object in front of him one minute, and gone the next. Travis liked to say that if you listened very carefully, you could hear the air rushing to fill the void that the ship left behind.

This was different, however. The Seed ship was larger than a cruise liner. It towered over the lake around it. Seeing something of this scale disappear in front of their eyes would be truly incredible.

Natalie checked her phone - she was watching the official countdown. "Here we go - five, four…" Everyone joined in the countdown excitedly.

"Three, Two, One!!!"

It didn't look real - as if an old movie had made a hard cut from cheap editing. One moment the enormous ship was there, the next it was gone. The water rushed to fill the depressed area where the ship had been, causing white capped colliding waves. After a few seconds, the slightest hint of a noise hit them, but it was just the sound of rushing air.

"Oh my god...." Barbara whispered under her breath. It was the first berlinite jump she'd seen in person. "What - what happens now, Jake?"

"Well, they actually arrived in space 28 seconds *before* they left the lake here. We have a hard rule to maintain radio silence until the timeline catches up, so the onboard computer will keep the transmissions off for the first minute that they're up there."

"Why do they do that?"

"Just in case. We don't know what will mess up the timeline or create a paradox. We don't want Jon to be able to read a message from himself, just in case it changes the outcome. It's better to be safe than sorry, especially when dealing with things we don't understand."

"But...." Travis checked his phone again. "Their 28 seconds was over by the time we saw the jump, so...." he paused, checking again. "Jon messaged! They're all good! Fuck yeah!" Travis caught himself swearing in front of Jake's mom, and immediately put on an apologetic face.

The group cheered, clinking drinks together and celebrating the success. Natalie got out her holotab and loaded a live feed from the Seed ship. Its external cameras showed the Earth in the distance, and documented its slow descent into the planet's gravity well.

The whole group was standing now. Jake looked out over the lake, feeling very content. He couldn't have dreamed that his research would ever have led to something of this magnitude. But here they were, watching the ship that would spread humanity through the stars. He felt a hug come from behind. He thought it was Mia, as she liked to do that. But, looking down, he saw that the hands holding him were aged and pale.

"I'm so proud of you Jake. But good god, I'm terrified for you."

Jake turned around and hugged his mother properly. She was softly crying.

"Alright!" Travis yelled. "Game on! Remember, there's a party at my place on Thursday to watch the landing."

They finished their drinks, packed up the picnic site, and drove south once more.

33.

Travis left Costa Rica shortly after the test flight. The calculations were done, and they wouldn't have to revise any of the time jumps until their window was much closer. It was his time to see the world.

Growing up in Saskatchewan had played tricks with his head. The land was so impossibly flat, the prairie sky so endless. It seemed like the whole world was available to you, as if you could just walk away from your house and soon arrive in China, or Africa, or Europe.

Of course, Travis learned at a young age that wasn't the case. That hard lesson was taught to him in the back seat of his parents' pickup truck. Yes, you *could* drive away from home in any direction, but it sure did take a long time to get anywhere. Travis' neurotic energy meant that he'd usually be bored and miserable before they reached the next town over.

Travis had stayed in Canada most of his life, and hadn't left the prairies at all until he moved to Vancouver. Now that he had a taste for traveling, however, he was addicted and he couldn't stop.

He started his year-long sabbatical by exploring the extreme limits of Canada, traveling from Newfoundland up to Resolute Bay, and all the way west to Haida Gwaii. Then he left Canada behind and saw as much of the Earth as he could muster. He trekked in the Amazon rainforest, surfed on the remote beaches of Namibia, and dirt-biked in Northern Siberia. Natalie joined him for several of his adventures, but even her young spirit couldn't keep up with his never-ending ambition. She did convince him, however, to spend some time absorbing global culture as well - instead of just outdoor sports. They traveled to Florence, Xi'an, and Petra before finally returning home to Costa Rica to begin mission training.

Now that he was on the cusp of his greatest adventure yet, Travis was starting to worry for the first time in his life that he was...worn out. He'd packed so much into those last twelve months of travel, staying out until the last possible week before returning to the training camp. He ended his epic sabbatical back at the Planet 9 compound, reporting in with the other colonists who had been chosen for the mission to HD75141.

Five months of non-stop training had gotten him and the other 2,031 astronauts ready for the Seed mission. Most of them had been working for years on their individual disciplines and departments, but the five month 'boot camp' was a much more intense training on the ship's operation, standard procedures, and safety protocols. He and Natalie had the advantage of going home every night, while most other trainees were living onsite at the camp. Still, he hadn't given himself time to recharge, and the unrelenting schedule of it all had left him feeling physically and emotionally drained. Or perhaps he was just getting older, even if he wouldn't let himself admit it.

The final training had started just after the latest probe came back from Star HD75141, which they had renamed 'Mayloz'. The final name of the star had been Jess' idea. It was a combination of 'Mayor' and 'Queloz', the two astronomers who first discovered an exoplanet all the way back in 1995. Now that humans were finally setting out to visit another world, the name seemed a fitting way to honor their accomplishment.

The probe had jumped into the solar system of Mayloz and propelled itself into a low orbit of the planet, surveying the surface and atmosphere. The planet appeared very, very similar to Earth. It had less water overall, but several large salty oceans spread across its surface. They were separated by a large, connected landmass. It had weather patterns, rain, snow and ice in the polar regions, and a stable rotation speed. Each day would last roughly 33 Earth hours.

It was yet unclear if there were any plate tectonics; the oceans appeared to have just filled in existing craters with water. However, the survey did identify several active volcanoes, and mountain ranges ran in fringes along ancient asteroid impacts. It had a strong magnetic field, which was great news. Within that canopy, just like the Earth, the residents would be protected from the worst of the host star's radiation.

The real exciting data came from its lander. The interstellar probe landed a small rover on the surface to take readings. They were right about the atmosphere, it was rich in oxygen and nitrogen, and would be breathable. There was a higher concentration of helium, but it wasn't going to cause any health issues. Travis joked that they'd just sound like chipmunks while they lived there. There was basic plant life as well. It looked very different to the plants of Earth, but the processes were the same. There was organic soil, life, water, and breathable air. They had every green light - the Seed project was a go.

There was a small part of Travis that had wanted the probe to return bad news - to give him an 'out' while keeping his pride. No one could ever be a hundred percent certain about leaving the Earth. Even Travis' perpetual positive attitude had its limits. Now that the trip was confirmed, now that the jump was planned, he'd have to deal with his choices and accept his fate. Luckily, the adventurous portion of his personality still had the winning hand - for now.

Everything came down to this. It was, effectively, his last night on Earth. The following afternoon, he and Natalie would report for their 21-day quarantine with the rest of the colony. After which, they would river-jump over six thousand years into the future. There was a very good chance that he'd never see Canada again, or Costa Rica, or the Pacific Ocean. Here, on Dylan and Jess' patio, surrounded by tiki torches, drinking fancy cocktails - this would be his last experience on his home planet. Like so many things in life that were too serious to truly contemplate, Travis would forget about the situation for hours at a time, simply enjoying the moments he was in. Whenever the conversation lulled, however, or he looked out over the view, the severity of his decision hit him like a freight train.

"I do have to say, there's a big part of me that wishes I was going" said Jess. The Bishops' catering staff had cleared away the desserts, and she was halfway through an iced coffee with Jameson's. "Spending so many years working on this project, just to see it blink away, it's going to be really hard."

"Why aren't you coming?" asked Mia. "I'm pretty sure they could have squeezed you in…"

"We've debated it over and over for the last decade, Mia. Endlessly. You have no idea how much," Jess rolled her eyes. "On our very first date, we kind of bonded over our desire to settle another planet. I'm sure it's a common discussion between many, many people, but when one of you is the richest person on Earth, it…becomes a possibility," Jess laughed. Her Irish accent seemed to get stronger after two drinks, each and every time. One more cocktail, and she'd become incomprehensible.

"It's always been in the cards" added Dylan. "Before river-jumping was a possibility, we'd always planned on retiring at the Mars settlement."

"Truth be told, Mia, there's just still too much to do here. I don't want to leave until I know that the next generation ship is going to work." Jess seemed disappointed in their decision, even more so than Dylan. They didn't say much about it, but it was visible in their faces. "We're so close to getting the Stingray working, and I don't want to leave the compound until it's done."

"And if we can't get that fast traveling transport ship working, you guys are out there alone, forever. I can't let the smartest person at Planet 9 leave - not until that ship is flying," Dylan said, kissing Jess on the cheek. Her cheeks went red, partly from embarrassment, but possibly from the alcohol.

Mia chirped as if she was about to say something, then stopped. She looked at the table and took a long swig out her drink.

Travis roused himself. "It makes sense, I get that. It's just shitty, though. Would love to have you guys with us." It was the first thing he'd said in over an hour, a rare thing at a party. "And, hey, we might see you again? I hope you'll visit once you get the fast ships going."

"Totally," added Natalie, smiling as widely as possible. The underlying mood was too solemn for a party. For 10 years they had all worked and struggled together towards this goal. Jess and Dylan had become much more than just a boss and a bankroll, they had become true friends. Leaving them behind felt strange, and unfair. "It is scary, for sure. I haven't thought about much else since we got back from our meetings in China. I've never been so excited and so terrified by anything in my life."

"The ship is safe, that much we can guarantee" replied Jess. "The landing has worked perfectly, the rotational gravity system works great, and there's been zero adverse health effects from the time jumps. As far as the planet, though…"

"You'll have the safety window. Personally, I wouldn't let the ship go there without that," said Dylan. The 'safety window' was going to be their point of no return. The Seed ship moved very slowly through space. Because of the amount of heavy cargo and the thousands of passengers it was required to use traditional engines. It couldn't move nearly as fast as Jake's probes or the Stingray ship that Jess was working on. Many project considerations had been taken into account because of that simple fact.

The closest alignment of the Earth and Mayloz 2 would be in three weeks, when the Seed ship would jump ahead 6,251 years into the future. Even at that closest point, it would still take 5 months of space travel on the other side of the jump for the ship to arrive in orbit of Mayloz 2.

The plan was to land in a warm, fertile region on the shore of the largest ocean. The ship would slowly start to mix the native atmosphere into the living quarters, letting the crew acclimatize over a period of four weeks. From there, eventually, they would walk out and begin exploring the new world, and building a permanent settlement.

The safety window was the crew's chance to 'pull the chute' and jump back. If the planet was unsuitable - if there was a deadly threat, intelligent life, or any other serious detriment to permanent habitation - they could time jump back that same 6,251 years and get home. The ship was slow, but it had been equipped to support the crew for up to five years in space. The window ended at fifteen months from their departure - at that point, they would have drifted too far from the Earth's point in space to ever get home. The Earth would be moving away from them faster than they could catch it.

"So, we'll have ten months on the surface to decide," said Jake. "That has to be long enough to determine any long-term danger…. you'd think."

"If I find the Statue of Liberty half-buried on that beach, you'll see us again real soon" joked Travis. "I'll hit the fuckin' switch myself."

"Nah, there's nothing smart on that planet, can't be. At least I hope. The angry apes are all on Reyes 3, right?" Jake slurred a bit while he joked.

No one laughed. They all froze. Jess' eyes shot wide, and looked at Jake as if to say *'shut the hell up.'* Even though they all thought about Reyes 3, the name was never spoken. It was a secret that the table shared, but one that was never, ever discussed.

All the Planet 9 staff had been told that the atmosphere was poisonous, and the radiation levels were not suitable for human life. That was all a lie, but a necessary one. Studies had still not been able to decode any of the signals from the alien planet, even 10 years after the secret project had begun. Dylan had kept his promise to not send any further probes, but he now had his own team studying the alien signals as well.

Between Dylan, Jess, Travis and Jake, the name of the Planet had become truly unspeakable. It was like he had yelled 'Voldemort' in the halls of Hogwarts. Reyes 3 was always in the back of their minds, the dirty secret that could unravel everything. There was a certain guilt that came with it as well, the four of them knowing how close they had come to revealing the Earth's presence in a hostile universe.

"Ummmm..." said Dylan, glancing around nervously, and especially looking at Natalie.

Jake caught himself after the joke, realizing he shouldn't have said it. He went red with embarrassment, and questioned whether another drink was a good idea.

"It's all good, guys," Travis cut in. "We told Mia and Natalie about it. Too big a secret to hold onto. That's it, though. No one else, I promise."

A couple more nervous glances shot around the table. The table stayed quiet. Even if they all knew about it, Reyes 3 wasn't to be discussed in public, ever. The silence lasted an awkward length of time.

"Soooo, ten months to make the call on Mayloz," Jake said, awkwardly steering the conversation back on course. He felt like an idiot for his unwanted quip. "That should be plenty of time to make the right call."

"It's still a little nerve wracking" Mia commented. "A lot of hazards don't present themselves until years later. Take air travel, for example - it took decades to make it safe, or asbestos for that matter." She had a very anxious tone in her voice. "I just hope that anything we discover *after* that cutoff is something we can adapt to. I'm having a tough time with that number, for sure. Speaking as a safety professional, ten months isn't that much time."

"Yeah, that's the part I'm having the toughest time with. After that we'll just be stuck out there with no support. Completely on our own," said Natalie.

Mia seemed to shrink into herself at that comment. Travis could hear her rhythmic breathing increase in pace. She disappeared to the washroom and nobody seemed to notice, not even Jake. Travis noticed, though, because he felt the same part of himself screaming inside. Questions and doubts were still flying around his brain. His own point of no return was fast approaching. He looked over at Jake, who, surprisingly, looked calmer and more comfortable than anyone else at the table. How could his nervous wreck of a friend be handling all of this better than he was?

"I don't like the word 'stuck'," said Jake. He had switched from cocktails to Dylan's very expensive whiskey collection. His words had even more of a slur in them now. "Every time I get second thoughts about this, I remember that what we're doing is not unique. Yes, we're the first humans to travel 94 light years away from home, but we're not the first to go settle a strange new world. The Polynesians sailed out to settle far away islands. The nomadic tribes of North and South America spread out across the continents, each one finding new and bizarre environments. They never saw their home again, most likely." He took another sip of his 40-year Laphroiag, two fingers of whiskey that were worth more than his old car. "The colonists who sailed to New France knew they would never see Europe again. I just think we're the next step in this tradition. I'm stoked!"

Travis took his words to heart. So much conversation had been around what could go wrong. There'd been so much negativity and 'what-ifs' in the project for the last few months, he'd lost sight of why he wanted to do this in the first place. "Right on, dude," he replied, softly bumping him on the shoulder.

Jake raised his glass to toast everyone. "Cheers!" They all clinked their glasses together at the center of the table. Mia had still not returned from the washroom.

"To the greatest adventure a group of people can take! To you guys" added Dylan.

They stayed late that night, and the conversation eventually strayed away from Mayloz 2. They reminisced, they joked, and they drank far too much. It was the best way to spend a last night on earth.

Travis and Natalie were the last to leave the party. It was a little after 2 AM. Once Jake and Mia left, the night wrapped up fairly quickly. The auto-drive on his car took them home, and Travis kept the sunroof open as they drove. They reclined their seats, and Natalie put his arm around her. Neither of them said much, they just listened to a Radiohead album and stared up at the stars, dreaming of what was to come next.

As they passed Jake and Mia's house, Travis saw the two of them hugging each other on the front stoop. He smiled. He knew that, even though he was facing an uncertain and scary future, his best friends would be right beside him.

34.

'*Where in the F is the faucet!?*'
Mia had stayed in the powder room of the Bishops' mansion for far too long now. She had to get back to the table, but her face was a mess. Her eyes were bloodshot, and dark mascara had streaked down onto the tops of her cheeks. She needed to get cleaned up to hide that she was crying. She needed to get back to the table, it had been too long. If only she could figure out how to turn the damn water on.

The powder room, like the rest of Dylan and Jess' interior, was very lavishly appointed. A large window looked out into the jungle. The walls were coated in black and white artwork. The fixtures were art deco style, and the large ornate mirror was framed with sculpted silver waves. The sink was on a pedestal, with a waterfall style faucet to dispense water. But there were no knobs, no controls anywhere to be seen.

Mia had spent the last five minutes staring into her own eyes through the mirror. '*Don't be a coward, you're stronger than this...*' but no amount of tough self-talk was working. Tonight's discussion was the breaking point - she knew now. There was no longer any doubt about it - Mia did not want to get on that ship.

For months, she'd felt like she was being swept away. As if she was on a raft heading for rapids, but had no way of steering. All she could do was paddle, but everything was drawing her closer to that drop, and there was nothing that she could do. The tension had been building more and more, and tonight it had boiled over.

The last ten years of her life had been incredible, like a dream. Costa Rica had been amazing, and she loved Jake more than anything. But Mayloz 2 was *his* dream, not hers.

Mia had always thought of herself as the 'adventurous' girl. She didn't wait to be invited on adventures, she made her own. She was tough, and capable, and had never chickened out of anything in her life. But now, here she was, having a full panic attack in the washroom.

Did being the 'adventurous girl' mean that she never got to say no? Mia wondered how she had gotten so far down this road, so close to the zero hour without backing out. Her ego and falsified courage had betrayed her into a corner, and the way out wasn't going to be easy. She knew that she couldn't get on that ship, but her decision was going to destroy the person she loved most in life.

"Fuck, fuck!...." Mia cried to herself, trying to get her breathing under control and gently kicking the pedestal stand of the sink in frustration. She felt a steel pedal with her sandal on one of the kicks, and pressed it. The faucet started streaming a clear waterfall into its bowl. She sighed in relief, cupping her hands into the stream and bringing the cool water onto her face. She splashed over and over, trying to wash the evidence of tears away. Somewhere, in one of those hand bowls of cool water, she found the clarity she needed. The tears stopped, and she toweled her face dry.

Mia fixed her hair and checked herself once in the mirror before leaving. The deck was dimly lit with tiki torches. Her friends were too drunk and boisterous to take notice of her tear-stained face.

For the remainder of the evening, Mia was uncharacteristically quiet. Jake seemed more talkative and louder than ever, while Travis had shrunk into himself as well. Everyone seemed to be dealing with their cold feet in different ways. Even though Jake was having fun, he knew when it was time to leave. He and Mia shared a look, then said their final goodbyes to Jess and Dylan, holding their hugs as long as they could.

The car ride home was quiet. Jake retold some of Dylan's stories, chuckling to himself. Mia stared out the window at the dark forest. Eventually, both of them said nothing at all. They were paralyzed by the nervous energy of the situation.

The car parked itself out front of the house. Jake started walking towards the front door. "Hey, I was thinking we could go to that little cafe down the road for breakfast. The one you like? We'll still have time to do our final checklists after and finish packing." Jake was planning on leaving his estate to his mother once they were gone, on the provision that he would take it back if they ever returned from Mayloz 2.

"I can't."

"Oh, no worries. If you have too much to do, we can just have something quick at home"

Mia stopped on the pathway. "No...Jake...I can't."

He thought he knew all the tones of her voice, but this was different. There was a sadness and depth in it that he hadn't heard before.

"I can't go. Jake... I'm such an asshole for leaving it this late..." Mia started crying uncontrollably.

Jake moved in to comfort her. "We're all nervous, Mia. I bet that everyone going into that quarantine tomorrow feels the same way. You'll feel better in the morning."

Mia looked up. "It's not nerves. You don't get it. I *can't do this*, Jake. I've been pretending for so long - I even fooled *myself* that I was ok with it. But I'm not! I'm so, so sorry. I just can't leave everyone here behind."

Jake was beginning to recognize that she was serious. "Not everyone. Travis and Natalie are coming. Jon, Kushal...you know all of them?"

Mia took a long exhale. She didn't know how to describe what she was feeling. She didn't know how to convince him that she was firm in her decision. "It's so permanent, Jake. And it's so unfair to ask someone to do this. To leave behind everyone they've ever known. It's not fair, I fucking hate it."

Jake's eyes started to water. He began to see that she was serious. She wasn't going to board that ship. "I'll be there with you. You know *me*..." he said quietly, and looked at the ground.

Mia grabbed his hand and put his arm around her. "I love you so much, Jake. But my family, my friends...." she said, taking a second to sob between sentences. "I don't know if I love you more than I love *everything* else in my life. I can't do this, I can't leave it all behind, I'm so sorry. I'm so, so sorry."

Jake took a long exhale while he thought. He couldn't lose her. Not again. He couldn't go through this again. "Well, I'm staying with you then. I can't go there without you."

Mia stepped back from the hug. She stopped crying and looked him in the eye. "You can't, Jake. You can't stay. Don't get me wrong, I don't want to lose you. But you heard yourself talking tonight. You have to do this, it's your dream!"

"It doesn't have to be."

"*Yes*, it does. And if you stay behind, you'll lose me anyway. You'll always resent me for this decision, even if you don't admit or show it. I'll always be the person who held you back, that kept you from settling a new planet."

"I won't resent you. How could I?"

"Yes Jake...you will. Maybe not right away. But it will always be there, lurking in the background, for the rest of our lives. You *need* to get on that ship tomorrow, you won't be yourself again if you don't."

The weight of the situation was beating down on both of them. Jake couldn't move. He was numb. How had this night turned from being so great - to this? How was he about to lose the love of his life?

"I've never met anyone else like you, Jake. And I never will again. I love you more than you'll ever know. And that's why you have to go."

"Please just stop, Mia. Just...stop talking like this is the end. There has to be a way we can figure this out."

Mia repeated herself again, softly. Her face was dimly lit by the porch lights, and her cheeks glistened as she spoke.

Jake stood awkwardly on the dark path. His tears had slowed. His mind was racing, he didn't know how to process the situation. "I can't do this alone..." he whispered.

"Yes, you can. You're strong Jake, stronger than you give yourself credit for. They need you. Shit...You're the reason this whole thing is happening."

"I love you too," he said, blurting it out through tears, as if he'd forgotten that fact.

Mia kissed him, and pressed her head into his chest while she held him. "I don't...." she cried. "I don't know how to say goodbye to you, Jake...."

They stayed on that path for what felt like hours. They held each other. One last night of feeling each other's warmth. One last union of souls, of personalities intertwined. Mia felt safest and most at home being held by Jake, and she didn't know she'd face the world tomorrow without him. She stayed in his arms as long as she could.

Finally, as the still night silence was broken by a faraway boat motor, Mia pulled away from the hug. "I should go," she whispered.

"Do you need to pack anything?"

"I'll come back tomorrow after you're gone. I just... need to go. Now. Please be careful Jake."

"But..."

"Knowing that you're living out there, it'll make me happy. Even if you hate me after tonight, you have to write to let me know you're okay. Promise."

"I could never hate you, Mia. I love you so much."

"I love you too, Jake."

With that, she walked back to the car and got in. She didn't turn around. *'Rip the band-aid'* she thought. *'Just go. Go. Go!'* She sat in the passenger seat and looked at the ground, careful not to make eye contact with Jake, who was still standing dumbfounded in the pathway. The car's headlights turned on, and the gravel rumbled under its tires as it pulled her away into the dark night.

Jake watched until the last red glow of the taillights disappeared from the distant trees. He stood still, processing the shock of what had just happened. Even as the first hue of a purple sunrise lit up the eastern sky, he was still sitting on the stoop of his villa, unable to bring himself inside the house. In every possible sense - he felt cold.

35.

It was Jake's fifth lap of the ship today. He felt restless, and the gym was too busy to get a turn on a cardio machine. Each lap was over a kilometer and a half of walking, though, so he figured he was nearing the end of an 8k hike. It was lot less scenic than the mountains of Venezuela had been, however. The never-ending hallway stretched through living quarters, dining halls, the command module, the recreation section, and various others. It was a strange feeling, walking in a straight line endlessly, and yet continually passing the same areas. His brain had trouble with it and, even though he'd been walking this same route now for months, it still tripped him out.

It would be nice to run the route, but the command crew had banned running after a few injuries. The joints of the ship were tricky to navigate while walking, never mind at a jogger's pace. The Seed ship's living area was divided into 20 straight sections joined together to form an Icosagon shape. Each section was 80 meters long, and was essentially just a free-spinning tube.

When they had boarded the ship in the Caribbean Sea, the Earth's gravity had kept the floor of each tube to the 'down' side of the ship. Once they had river-jumped the ship into space, the thrusters began to slowly push the ship into a rotation. It had taken over 9 hours to gently spin the ship up to speed, all in order to create 1 g of artificial gravity. As that happened, the floor of each section had spun 'outwards' - to the perimeter line of the ship, creating a never-ending loop of living quarters. Once they were prepared for the jump down to the planet's atmosphere, the ship would slow, and eventually stop spinning. When in the final descent, Mayloz 2's gravity would take hold, and the floor would orient itself properly - 'down' - once more.

The problem with running through this endless loop was that every 80 meters, at the 'joint', the floor would angle up by 18 degrees. It was a strange sensation - as you approached the joint, even though the floor was flat, your equilibrium would tell you that you were walking downhill. As you stepped onto the 'ramp', you'd feel like you were walking uphill. 10 meters later, and the sensation would go away, and you'd feel as if you were on flat ground again.

The first few times were tough, and everyone giggled at the strange sensation. It was a bit like being in a carnival funhouse. After you'd done it a few thousand times you got quite used to it. Still, it wasn't a safe place to run.

They'd been on the ship now for 179 days. Three weeks of quarantine while it floated in the sea, followed by 153 days of floating through distant space. The actual river-jump had been so subtle that it was almost imperceptible. Even though Jon had told him repeatedly that he wouldn't feel anything, Jake was still gripping his armrests during the countdown. The only 'real' effect they felt was a sudden weightlessness, as if a roller coaster had taken them over the rise. The entire ship had jumped over 6,000 years into the future, but all that the passengers knew was that they could suddenly float. Once the ship began spinning, many, many people got nauseous as the gravity gradually increased. Jake had been forewarned about the nausea. He had brought medication for motion sickness, and returned to his seat as others were still playing and floating around in the weightless environment. Travis filled 2 vomit bags after he'd spent hours jumping off the walls.

The ship's 2 dining sections were empty at this point in the day. Most of the crew were busy studying the new readings of their destination planet, which they were now - finally - in orbit of. Jake had worked with his team in the morning, but had taken the afternoon off. They were almost off of the Seed ship, almost ready to touch down, and he was definitely feeling restless about the next few steps. He wasn't alone in the feeling - the gym was still busy as he walked through it for the fifth time.

179 days. 179 days living in this windowless ring, wondering what was outside of that thin layer of titanium and berlinite. It was easy to forget where you were sometimes. As if you weren't traveling through space - you were just in some sort of long convention center with no exit. Without windows, the mind couldn't quite accept the insane reality of the situation. Jake could eventually feel normal in the 'MC Escher hotel' he was in, and temporarily forget that he was 880 trillion kilometers from home. From the Earth. From everyone he'd ever known. From Mia.

179 days since the worst night of his life. Somehow, after the emotional steam rolling that Mia had given him, Jake still got on that ship. It was the toughest decision he'd ever made. Leaving Earth was hard enough. Leaving Mia as well, with a low probability that he'd ever see her again - that was even harder. She was right, though, remaining on Earth wasn't an option for him. He had to go. No matter which side of that airlock he had decided to stay on, he knew that he had lost her.

He was so utterly, utterly sick of tough decisions. He was ready for someone or something else to take the helm of his life. The last 10 years had been a non-stop labyrinth of impossible choices. From the moment that the first sample of berlinite had disappeared at the Harrison Lab, every day had been a maze of vague and dangerous turns. But leaving on the Seed ship without Mia - that made every other choice seem easy. His gut had told him on that painful morning six months prior that he still had to go to Mayloz 2. Just like Travis had taught him - trust your first instinct, or the river will swallow you.

Next to the gym was a recreation area. It was simply equipped - some card tables and places to gather with simple, lightweight games. The other side of the room had two dozen VR stations. While planning the ship's interior, the idea of virtual reality was brought up as a solution to combat cabin fever. Jake and Mia had insisted that 'Mystic Realms' be loaded on the control drive during the construction phase.

Travis got Natalie hooked on it. They continually invited Jake to join them in Mystic Realms during their off hours, but he couldn't bring himself to do it. There were other programs and games available to remind people of Earth, from famous hikes to Jet-Ski racing, but Jake didn't spend any time in VR, he didn't want to be reminded of what he had left behind. He preferred walking the halls to pass the time.

Jake's watch buzzed. He looked down at it and pressed the receive button on the right side. A holo-window opened with a message.

"Reminder: Operational Meeting at 1800 hours"

Jake, Travis, Natalie and Jon were part of a small Command Team for the ship. Their expertise in berlinite time travel and the ship's overall design made them an essential part of the leadership hierarchy. From the time of boarding and the initial quarantine, they'd had meetings every 48 hours or so with the rest of the command team. There was also the head of botany, environmental systems, the Chief Medical Officer, the head propulsion engineer, and the Chief Personnel Liaison - a sort of cross between human resources and counseling.

To command the ship, Dylan Bishop had decided against using a scientist. There were several people who put their intent forward from Planet 9, but the Bishops decided on an entirely different approach. It was their intent to form a new society on Mayloz 2, one with a democratic government and fair representation of all people. But that was years away. For now, for a journey this dangerous - democracy wasn't the answer.

They needed someone who had experience in similar situations. Obviously, that was impossible, as something of this magnitude had never been attempted. But they *could* find someone who had led a very large crew in a confined space for years at a time. That was the reasoning that brought them to Captain Victor Carreras.

Captain Carreras had led the largest aircraft carrier in the US Naval fleet for over a decade. The prolonged peace of the 2030's had meant that he hadn't seen much combat, but he still knew how to keep things running in an efficient manner, how to deal with discipline in confined areas, and how to balance crew morale with effective results. Most importantly, he was ecstatic about being chosen for the mission. Victor had been an amateur astronomer since he was a young boy, and had been known in the Navy for bringing his telescope aboard each ship. His wife and daughter were with him. Jake wondered sometimes, jealously, how much convincing it had taken to get his family to join. It must have been a military family thing - they were used to being shuffled from place to place. Why not to a new planet?

It was already a little after 5 pm. Jake turned around after his watch buzzed, heading back to his bunk to grab a change of clothes. It was a very small room, just a single bed with a bit of standing room next to it. The storage was small, efficient, and, most importantly, private. Jake didn't mind the small space, he had room to read and watch films, and it was cozy enough. Even though they were set to arrive on the surface tomorrow that didn't mean they would be living off the ship. It would be years before an external settlement was built.

"Wooooooo! Holy Shit! Last day bud, you stoked?!"

Jake heard Travis yell behind him as he headed to the command module. He turned around to see Natalie and Travis walking briskly to catch him. Natalie looked as pretty as she always had been. Her hair was longer, but still perfectly clean and tied back, and her skin was unfairly radiant for being indoors this long. Travis hadn't fared as well. He'd gone the six months without a haircut. His hair had progressed from curly to a light brown afro, and was now some sort of gross hockey mullet. He had last trimmed his beard months ago, and new gray curly hairs were sprawling out from his chin each day. Jake laughed each and every time he saw his friend with this new look. "Trav, you're the furthest from home you've ever been, and yet, you look more Saskatchewan than ever."

Travis laughed. Natalie smiled politely. She still didn't understand most of the Canadian references they made. She had been born and raised in Arizona. "Just trying to look my best, bud," Travis responded. "You get up to much after we finished this morning?"

"Not much. Just walked laps of the ship again. I tried to nap, but it wasn't happening."

Travis and Natalie exchanged a not-so-subtle look of concern. They hadn't known about his breakup until the final quarantine cutoff, when the airlocks had already closed. It was Natalie who had first noticed Mia's absence, and pressed Jake to tell them the truth. They were shocked and upset that they would never see her again, and that they didn't get a chance to say goodbye. Natalie cried heavily for a few days during the quarantine. She and Mia had grown quite close over the years, and she was greatly looking forward to having a friend with her in the new world.

Travis worried that Jake would lock himself in a room again like he had in Venezuela. He'd seen his best friend at his worst and he knew how hard it was to dig him out of it. But Jake just quietly continued his work. He seemed emotionally numb. Not sad, not angry, not happy. Just numb to all of it.

It had taken three months on board before Travis could make him smile, and only recently had he seen a sliver of his friend begin to emerge again. Losing Mia had hurt all of them, and they were recovering. But Jake would never fully heal.

They arrived at the command module and scanned their watches at the security door. They were a few minutes early for the meeting, but everyone was already there, engaged in small talk. It was an exciting day after all. "I think we're talking about landing early!" Jon called to them as they entered. Although he was now in his early 30's, Jon still looked as if he was in his first year of college. He was still fresh faced and skinny, and his misguided attempt at growing a mustache had resulted in countless jokes from his coworkers.

"Really? Why's that?"

"There's a weather system forming on the Hawking Ocean. It looks like it'll make landfall in three days at our LZ. We want to be down and anchored before then."

"Did you leave your station at all today?" Natalie gave Jon a judgmental look.

"No, I was too excited. And we needed to re-simulate the landing with the new gravity readings. It needed some tweaking."

"You need to sleep at some point, dude" Travis smiled through his furry beard.

"Let's get started everyone" Captain Carreras announced as he walked to the boardroom table. He was carrying his holo-tab and a fresh cup of coffee. The rest of the team followed and took their seats. Jake took a seat in the middle of the table, across from Dr. Pachenko, the Chief Medical Officer. "Well, let's start with the good news" Victor began, quieting the room as he spoke. "The scans are good! We launched a robot lander down to our zone and got great results back. And some pretty wild pics, if I do say…"

The large briefing screen showed a video feed from the lander. It was of a sandy beach strewn with large rocks. Behind the sand line, large fern-like plants stretched skywards. There was green foliage at their bases, but the solar collectors of the ferns were round and bright pink. A ridge of brown mountains was visible in the distance.

"We've got excellent news about the atmosphere. It looks like we'll only be in acclimatization for 20 days, instead of 45!" Victor announced with a beaming smile. The plan was for everyone to continue living on the ship when they landed, as the air supply was slowly mixed with the native atmosphere. By the last day of the mixture, the air inside and outside would be the same, and people could come and go from the Seed ship as they needed. There was a slight difference in air pressure, as well as lower oxygen levels, but the medical team all agreed that their lungs would adapt quickly.

"The bad news" the captain continued, "is that we have a wrench in our schedule. As you know, we were planning on beginning our landing procedure in 34 hours. We're going to move that up - to 12 hours. There's a weather system tracking towards the bay. We have no idea how bad that storm will be, but I'd prefer not to risk it. I'd like to be in the water, anchored at our target shore *well* before it hits. The engineering team has assured me it's possible, we'll just need to fire our maneuvering rockets a little harder to get in position in time. That also means that in the next hour, we'll start slowing down our gravity spin."

"Couldn't we wait in orbit until the storm is over? Instead of rushing it?" asked Liz, the head botanist.

"If there's no danger of landing now, I'd like to get ahead of it. But I'm open to opinions."

Travis nodded in agreement and spoke up. "Time is precious! If we need to pull the pin and get out of here, every day we spend in this system now is another 2 days chasing down Earth on the other end. And that gap is growing bigger all the time, next month it will be 3 days, then 4, and so on. I agree with Captain Carreras, I think we should set her down as soon as we can."

"Well, I know that my department can be ready for landing in a few hours," said Dr. Pachenko. "But I can't speak for everyone."

The captain took visual stock of the table. "Can everyone here be ready, braced, and loaded for a jump within a few hours? I know we were supposed to have a lot more time, but I'm hoping you're all ready."

Everyone at the table nodded, although some were reluctant.

"Okay, perfect! I'll make an announcement. We'll begin slowing our rotation at 2000 hours. Jon, how long will that be til we're at zero gravity?"

"If we do a long burn at 8 o'clock, we can be static in our rotation by 330am. But by midnight, gravity will be so low, it will be functionally gone." Jon brought his navigation diagram up on screen. By 3am, we'll need everyone strapped into the landing modules. The ship needs one more hard navigation burn to line up our time-jump with the Landing Zone. We're already close to the orbit we need, we just need to nudge it into the southern hemisphere a bit more."

"So, if we have more work to do…" asked Liz.

"You'll need to have your department completely secured for landing. If you don't mind 'floating' a bit, you can keep working until 1am. After that we have to lock the ship down."

"Can everyone hit that target? I apologize for the rush. Last chance to object, here, folks." Victor Carreras looked around the room again, seeing the team nodding.

"We'll be rushing, but…yes, we can do it" replied Liz.

"If this goes right, we'll all be having our breakfast on a new Planet," smiled the Captain.

The group looked around the table nervously. No one wanted to address the elephant in the room. Finally, Kenji from engineering spoke up. "Soooo, who's it going to be? Who gets to take the first step?"

Everyone looked around again, curious about who could possibly claim such a right. Everyone *wanted* to be the first, of course, but it was a tough thing to justify. Victor Carreras was looking straight at Jake and Travis, however. "The way I see it, we've all put a lot of work into this ship. Many of you have been with the Seed project since the design phase, and some of you have been with Planet 9 for decades. Therefore, it's a very tough decision to decide who gets the honor of the first step." He took a sip of his coffee, waiting for an interjection. Everyone else was too hesitant to speak. "But it would be hard to argue that any of us would be here without Mr. Strickland and Mr. Crawford. I can't think of anyone more deserving."

Jake tried to think of a self-deprecating reply, as his Canadian modesty took hold. He couldn't, and stuttered.

"Here here!" cried Jon. The ancient expression sounded ridiculous coming out of such a young face, but he was sincere. The other members began to nod. They all knew it was the only logical choice.

"We don't need..." Jake started.

"We'd be honored," Travis cut him off. He looked at Jake and smiled. It was pure elation, simple joy - the kind of smile that only Travis could wear. He winked, and as his left eye closed, Jake noticed for the first time the wrinkled crow's feet in his friend's face. Indeed, they had been working on this project for longer than anyone. Their wildest speculations all those years ago while drinking beers in the Harrison Hot Springs could never have predicted this. Two best friends, with thousands of star systems between them and their home, about to take a historic step for humanity. In so many ways, it was unbelievable, and yet it was actually happening. Jake did something unexpected - he smiled back. It was the first authentic smile he'd worn in 179 days.

Before the meeting broke, Captain Carreras made a ship-wide announcement. *"Your attention please, everyone."* The voice boomed through the corridors of the ship. He waited for people to stop and listen.

"In a few minutes we'll be firing the rotational rockets to slow down our gravity system. An alarm will sound, and you'll feel a bit of shaking as they start, so please brace yourself. The reason we're doing this is that we've moved up the timeline for landing. You'll have until midnight to secure your belongings and workstations for zero gravity, and by 3am sharp, everyone will need to report to your designated launch seat. I suggest taking the next few hours to get some rest, if you can."

Captain Carreras paused momentarily before continuing, gathering his thoughts.

"This is the end of our six month journey, and the beginning of our greatest challenge. You've all performed incredibly so far, and I'm constantly amazed at the professionality and positive spirit of this crew. Let me be the first to say - Welcome Home!"

Each of the department heads rushed away to finish their prep in. Jake, Travis and Natalie didn't have much to do, they were already prepped. Jake went to his bunk room and laid down to sleep, but it didn't come easily. He was far too nervous and excited. He nodded off a few times, and finally fell asleep by 10, as his body felt lighter and lighter in the sheets. His alarm woke him up at 1:45am. He stirred in the bed, and just the slight nudge of his shoulder against the inflated mattress sent him floating upwards. He'd forgotten to use the bed straps.

Getting changed and ready in zero gravity was a challenge, and he was glad that he had left extra time. Once dressed, he secured his belongings once more, opened the hatch to his bunk, and began floating his way down the hallway. His takeoff and landing seat was in section 8, and he had to traverse a few sections to get there. Hundreds of people were in the hallways. They struggled to find the installed handholds on the walls, and the ship was noisy with laughter as they bumped into each other. Jake loved the feeling of zero gravity, and he hadn't let himself enjoy it properly at the River Jump six months prior. He sailed effortlessly through the halls, weaving through the other colonists. When he realized he still had a half hour before the final seating, he slowed down and played in an empty corridor, bouncing off the walls and closing his eyes to revel in the sensation.

When the ten-minute warning sounded, he opened his eyes again and sailed to section 8. Each of the 2 landing sections had a thousand seats spread over two levels. Most people had already taken their places, but a few stragglers like Jake were still sailing in. He awkwardly held on to people's shoulders, and his neighbors helped guide him down to his seat to get strapped in.

They waited there, talking in excitement for a half hour, until an alarm sounded again. The alignment burn was about to begin. A low roar started, and the walls of the module shuddered. Jake felt the motion this time, his body started pushing up against the belts. It increased, and after thirty seconds, his head was swelling with blood, as if he was hanging upside down off monkey bars. A few people screamed, but most were silent. He managed to turn his neck against the crushing force, and saw his neighbors all had their eyes closed. After a minute or so, the G force slowed, and things calmed down. Nervous giggling filled the cabin.

The wait for the time-jump felt like days. Jake talked with his neighbors a bit, as they all nervously gripped their armrests. Some people fell back asleep, which amazed him to no end. He couldn't even sleep on an airplane, never mind while waiting to time-jump through the atmosphere of a planet.

Finally, the alarm sounded again. A countdown started. Jake walked through the landing sequence in his mind - several short jumps backward in time, each slowing the ship in different stages of the atmosphere. They would only travel backwards in time by a fraction of a second each time, but by the last jump the ship would be just above the landing zone. That was the section that Jon had warned him about most. *"If you're gonna hurl at all on this trip, that's when it will be."*

The countdown neared the end *"three, two, one..."* The cabin was whisper quiet, the thrusters had stopped, and the passengers were all too scared to talk. It was so silent that Jake could hear the soft hum of the hulk guns firing into the outer hull. He heard it once, then a delay of ten seconds, then again, then again. Suddenly, a louder roar than anything before it boomed through the cabin. He felt the whole cabin swing downwards, violently realigning itself with the gravity of Mayloz 2.

Screams erupted from the crowd, and a woman near him was crying loudly. Although Jake was holding the armrest firmly, he wasn't terrified like the rest. He wasn't the same man anymore - the one who clung for dear life underneath his ski drone, the one who was always afraid of saying the wrong thing. So much had happened. So much excitement, ambition, disappointment and pain. All of it had hardened him - he had no time for fear anymore.

The cabin swung back and forth while it rotated down to the new force of gravity, as the landing rockets roared. He felt the blood drain from his head, and his butt pressed into the chair with the force of 400 pounds. Another scream erupted from the crowd as the downward force snapped into a final push. The parachutes had deployed.

The G force steadily slowed and Jake felt his body start to rise out of the seat once more. He took a couple of deep breaths, ignoring the sore muscles in his neck.

"Is that it?" a woman on his right asked, panting.

"Not yet..." he replied. "One more big one."

They continued bracing. Another minute went by, and they felt the landing thrusters fire again. The alarm went off once more, and the computer loudly announced *"impact in three, two, one..."*

But they barely felt the ship finally touching down into the water. Jon's rockets had worked perfectly. A wave of relief and nervous laughter rippled through the room. They were on the surface! They had survived a trip of 94 light years, and had landed the largest ship in history in a brand-new ocean. They had done the impossible.

Captain Carreras addressed the ship, getting thunderous applause and cheers. He explained how the thrusters would burn low for a bit to move the ship towards the shore, but how they would barely feel it.

Jake unbuckled, stood up and stretched. The woman beside him gave him a hug, laughing with joy. He hugged her back, laughing as well. People were still cheering loudly and slowly filtering out of the landing module. Dozens of people stopped him to say hi and shake his hand in congratulations. It was a great moment, and it reminded him a bit of being swarmed by the media after their meeting at the UN.

Once he broke free, Jake walked down to the command module. It felt like a different ship now, the hallways were turning left instead of uphill. Travis and Natalie were already there, along with a few other department heads. Jon was still at his station with the engineering team. They excitedly chatted about their experiences in the landing. The man beside Natalie had vomited during the gravity swivel and she'd gotten a splash of it on her. Travis had been hooting the whole time, apparently, as if he was on a roller coaster. More of the command team came through the door, and one of the engineers loaded up an exterior camera feed onto the large holo-display.

Captain Carreras eventually walked in, shook everyone's hand in congratulations, and popped a bottle of champagne. "I can't believe we're actually here" he said. "This is incredible!" They each had a small glass and watched the feed from outside. The mountains of the mainland were getting closer, and closer. The Seed ship wasn't very hydrodynamic, but it could still move. They were doing a steady three knots in the direction of a wide, calm bay. "Well," Victor said, "I think you should all get to the airlock. We'll need to lock the ship down by sunfall, but I believe there's just enough time to take a quick look outside."

They walked as a group to section 12, which had the airlock and landing bridge. Putting on the airtight suits and helmets reminded Jake of the early experiment days, when Travis and he would take turns setting up the emitter room. He knew the suit well, and had his on quickly while some of the others struggled. They waited in the clean, cold room for the final go ahead.

The engineering team eventually radioed them that the anchor was down, and that the landing bridge would reach the shore. At that, Jon checked with the team, and closed the ship side of the airlock to let the room pressure adjust to the outside. It took a few minutes to equalize, and a large green light turned on once it was done. Natalie hit a switch, and the other side of the airlock opened to the landing deck.

There was a slight breeze. Their suits were made of lightweight material, and they could feel the air pressing down on the fabric. It felt good. Jake looked out at the beach while the landing bridge extended from the ship. It was composed of a light gray sand in front of dark volcanic, jagged rocks. Behind those, he could see the strange pink fern trees and the green undergrowth of the forest. The sky was blue, but it was a much different blue than Earth - almost as if a touch of yellow got spilled in the paint. Wispy clouds stretched high up into the atmosphere. It was all somewhat familiar, and yet alarmingly alien at the same time.

The bridge motor whirred as it rotated out from the module and extended itself onto the beach. It clunked down, and they could hear a loud, satisfying lock of the gearing mechanisms. The landing party of twelve walked out on the bridge slowly and carefully. Jake knew that everyone back inside was watching on camera, excitedly waiting for the first step. He breathed heavily in his helmet, still looking around in wonder at his surroundings. They were all walking slowly, trying to comprehend where they were.

Travis stopped at the end of the bridge. Jake joined him, as the rest of the party stayed back a few meters. "So, who goes first?" Jake asked, looking over at him. "You want it?"

"I think we gotta do this together, bud. At the same time."

Jake smiled. "Yeah man, I can do that."

"Been a hell of a ride. But I'm sure glad I'm here with you, bro." Travis grabbed Jake and pulled him in for a hug. Jake hugged him back firmly. Through everything, all that they had gone through, all that he had done and said -

Travis had been a true and loyal friend. They were an odd couple, no doubt. But it worked. Somehow, through all the twists and turns, trials and heartbreaks, they had arrived here, at the last frontier - together.

Travis hugged Jake with that same cowboy strength he'd always had. He looked over Jake's shoulder and saw Natalie, who was crying tears of joy for the two of them. He knew just how lucky he was to be on that platform with her as well. Although he'd always survived on his own, he couldn't imagine being here at the end of this trip without her. He nodded at Natalie and winked, then pulled back from the hug. The two friends turned to look out at the beach in front of them.

"Okay, one…" Jake said.

Before he could keep counting, Jake felt Travis push him hard from behind. He lost his balance, and his right foot fell forward, landing on the warm gray sand.

Behind him, he heard Travis say "Neil Armstrong, Yasmina Caskun…Jacob Fuckin' Crawford."

36.

Captain Carreras sat at a common use desk in the command module, staring at an empty screen. It was time to write a letter home. He wanted to tell his loved ones back on Earth all about the last six months, the feeling of jumping through time, of floating through hallways, the new world - all of it, every second and sensation. He wanted to convey how much he loved and missed them even though he was 6000 years in the future. He didn't enjoy writing at the best of times, and now he only had a thousand words to convey what he couldn't express in a million. He didn't know where to start. He wondered how many people on board were going through the same process.

There were many moments when he felt happy to have his wife and daughter with him, but none so much as this. At least he wasn't writing to them, thank god. His letter would be read by his siblings, by his widower father and his close friends. He missed all of them, but at least he wasn't writing to Bridget. Having his wife on board was such a blessing. He could spend his evenings with her and Zoey, although they still all slept in separate bunkrooms. The ship had been designed with only one class of passenger, no matter their rank. Victor missed having a captain's quarters, but he understood that this was a very different situation than a Navy ship.

There was only four hours left until the submission deadline for the messages. All the crew were to turn in their letters to be loaded on a probe. In an age where video calling, holographic displays and VR meetings were commonplace, writing a letter felt ancient. But they had so much data to transmit back to the Earth, they needed to keep the personal bandwidth as low as possible. Text files would be easy to send. Perhaps, somewhere in the future, they could figure out a way for the crew to send videos home, but not yet.

He hadn't had much time for letter writing in the last few days. It was now day 3 with the 'doors open'. They had gone through 20 additional days on board the Seed ship, waiting as the interior and exterior atmosphere slowly mixed together. He'd had only one day of lightheadedness, but other crew members reported nausea, headaches, and insomnia. Near the end, most people had adapted, but a few remained in the clinic for observation.

There were so many other factors, besides the atmosphere, that went into the decision to open the doors and let people out. His team checked the exterior for radiation levels. The medical team checked the air, water, and soil for dangerous microbes.

The results all came back positive. Obviously, drinking water would need to be filtered and sterilized, but the air was safe to breathe, and suits wouldn't be necessary any longer. They identified strains of DNA that resembled viruses, but none would react to a human host - Earth genetics were too different. As Dr. Pachenko had pointed out to him, viruses can't exist without a host, so it wouldn't make sense to have a deadly virus for *humans* on a foreign planet. Human immune systems seemed strong enough for the different microbes they had found as well. There were a host of single celled organisms in the water and soil, but none seemed to be able to reproduce in human tissue or bypass normal immune functions.

The other life on the planet was - complicated. They'd found life, but the lines between plant and animal were not as strong as they were on Earth. The large, pink leafed plants that Jake and Travis had seen were just some of the photosynthetic life on the surface. As they explored further from the Hawking Ocean, the trees got stranger. The leaves on another species were rigid and followed the planet's star as it moved across the sky. The valley before the mountains was impassable, blocked by a network of vines of multiple textures and colors. Most plants on Mayloz 2 used photosynthesis for energy, as they do on earth, but large plants here could also consume small organic matter for energy, such as microbes and microscopic life forms.

There were animals as well. Again, though, the lines were blurred, as these moving creatures seemed to be able to turn light into simple sugars as plants do. Everything they had seen so far was exo-skeletoned, with dazzling jewel-like colors. They had yet to see anything larger than a housecat, or anything that could be a threat to the colony. On land, that is.

If Earth's evolutionary history was taken as a guideline, the creatures could be far larger and far more advanced in the ocean that the Seed Ship was floating on. Captain Carreras had given an order that no one should enter the water at any time, and the water's edge should be avoided at all costs - at least until a formal survey could be safely performed.

Everything seemed idyllic on the surface, but there were so many possible dangers in this new, bizarre world. Giving the OK to open the doors had been a very loaded choice. Now, with the Captain's blessing, the cargo could finally be offloaded, the agriculture team could begin their work, the exo-biologists could continue their studies, the geologists could begin assessing mineral deposits, and so on. Now that they could breathe, the hard work could start. The turnaround deadline was approaching fast, and they needed to know everything they could about their new home. There was no time to spare.

All of this, and more, was in the reports he had prepared to load onto the message probe. Deep within the storage of the ship they had packed three specialized berlinite devices. One would be loaded with all of his reports, data on the new planet and the letters of the colonists. It was set to River Jump back to their relative time, where it would transmit their info on to Earth from its drift location.

Victor had often wondered why they couldn't just send the info to an earlier point in time. It would be extremely helpful for the team back home to get all this data on the day they had left Earth, for example. They could plan their next steps back in Costa Rica and be ready with the next ship much earlier. Jake had informed him of the policies of Planet 9's time travel program - about avoiding a 'time paradox' by never, ever sending a message to their relative past. Victor admitted that he didn't quite understand how a slightly early message 94 light years away could destroy the universe, but Jake had been very adamant about it. Honestly, it was the only time he'd seen Jake Crawford show any emotion on the whole trip. Jake may have been brilliant, but he seemed cold to Victor, not at all what he was expecting. Regardless, one thing he'd learned from his decades of military command was that precautionary rules save lives.

"Morning Victor!" Travis walked in the command module behind him. "Sorry...Captain."

Victor laughed. Nobody could accuse Travis of being cold. He would have never been called by his first name on the USS Miller. "Good morning, Mr. Strickland. How are you?"

"Good, for sure. Feels so friggn' good seeing everyone outside and feeling the breeze on my face again. VR just doesn't cut it, you know?"

"Have you finished your letter home?"

"Yup." Travis walked over to his locker on the side of the room, taking out a small satchel with his holo-tab and notes. "I don't know if I've written a letter since elementary school, it was weird. I've always just done video calls. Gotta say, though, knowing that my mom won't worry about me - that means a lot. You finished yours?"

"I still haven't started. I've just been working on, well - everything."

"Better get on it, bud," Travis replied. He sat down at the table and brought up a large screen, and was soon lost working an incomprehensible grid pattern that Victor did not understand.

Victor turned back to his screen. He was tired, but he needed to get the letter done. 'He cracked his knuckles and began typing. "Hello everyone, it seems so long since we were all together..." he managed to write before his watch buzzed. It was a message from Chantal Lemieux, the inventory manager.

"Captain, we've got a problem down here. I think you should come and see, I don't know what to do."

The storage compartments of the ship were being unloaded into a staging area on the shore. It was a mammoth task. Equipment, materials and supplies had been neatly secured through every one of the ship's 'spokes', as well as the central dome. Although a large crew had been working for at it for a few days already, unloading fully would take months.

"I'm on my way," Victor spoke into his watch.

"Thanks. Bring the time-jumping crew if you can, it's a problem with their equipment."

The letter, once again, would have to wait. "Travis, I need you to come to the warehouse with me. I just received a message from the inventory manager - I believe there may be an issue."

Travis looked up, surprised. "For sure, I'll walk down with you." He sent a message to Jake and Natalie on the way.

Victor and Travis walked to the landing module, then weaved their way through countless crates and vehicles in the first spoke of the ship. They found Chantal a little way into the central dome storage. She was looking into a large insulated container, about the size of a hot tub.

"Ms. Lemieux." Victor spoke, startling her.

"Captain." She stepped down from a box she was standing on. "Thanks for coming. I don't know what to make of this."

Travis knew the crate well. It stored one of the three time traveling probes. "What's the problem?" he asked.

"Take a look for yourself."

Travis got up on the box, borrowing her flashlight. The crate was empty. When he shone the light down inside, all he could see was the packing insulation and a few forms inside a Ziploc bag. "What the?" he exclaimed. "Where's the probe? Did you already take it out?"

"That's all there is, the container was empty. The insulating foam was all there, but the probe itself wasn't inside it."

"Shit, that can't be right, man. Where's the other ones?"

"We're still getting them out. I just thought you should know that this one was missing. Weren't we meant to be sending one of these out tomorrow?"

Travis was nervously tight lipped. "Let's get a fork lift in here and locate those other two probes quickly" was all he said. He was inspecting the empty box for clues when Jake and Natalie arrived.

"What's going on?" asked Natalie.

"The friggn' probe is gone! The crate was still sealed from when we packed it, nobody's messed with it, but the damn thing is empty!"

All three were shaken by the news. Victor stayed back while they inspected the crate, and helped Chantal clear a path to the others.

The three scientists finished examining the crate, getting no more answers for their effort. "We've got the next one here!" yelled Victor from a short distance away. They rushed over to him. The next crate was still sealed, just as it had been in their Costa Rican laboratory. Natalie opened it hopefully, but collapsed back on her heels after looking inside.

"Sabotage?" asked Travis.

"It can't be..." replied Jake. "The seal was still there, we all saw it."

"I don't get it," said Natalie, wide eyed and frustrated. "We tested these over and over at the lab. They were flawless. This exact same design has time-jumped a hundred times before. They can't just power themselves on. How could this happen?"

The three of them stared at the empty insulation, terrified - and deeply embarrassed. Once the Seed ship had arrived in the Mayloz system, there wasn't all that much for them to do. They were the experts on River Jumping - the team who could put the ship exactly where it needed to be. The team that could precisely calculate how to send a probe thousands of years into the past, across trillions of kilometers to relay their messages home. Once the ship had landed, their only responsibility had been to get info to, and from, the Earth. And, somehow, they had fucked it up. Royally.

Chantal found the third crate, but it was the same. An empty box that they had brought along to Mayloz 2. Victor gave orders to clear the area, it was best to try and keep this news as quiet as possible while they figured it out.

Jake looked at the crate and lost himself in thought. Travis was still searching the area for any clues that could help. The group was quiet for a moment, until Jake exclaimed "Shit!!!"

"What?" asked Natalie.

"It's a Russian doll thing! How could we not have tested for this?"

"Russian.... ohhh, you mean like a nesting doll?"

"Yeah, sorry - a nesting doll, that's what I meant. It's the only solution. We tested these probes with everything. We put them in containers and shook the hell out of 'em. We time-jumped them dozens of times. They were perfect. The only thing we didn't try was the situation they were in on board the Seed ship."

"Ohhh...fuuuuuck...I get it," replied Travis. "It was a berlinite shell within a berlinite shell. The reaction river-jumped them a different amount of time than the rest of the ship." He looked at the others in horror. "How the hell did we not think to test this?"

Natalie looked at the other two with the same embarrassed clench. They had no solution. They had missed a crucial element, and now the new settlement's only connection with the Earth was severed.

"It doesn't look like you three have any good news to tell me" the Captain said, walking over to join them.

Jake explained the situation, apologizing profusely. Victor's face was grave.

"So, we have no way of communicating with the Earth. Is that what you're telling me?"

The three nodded grimly.

"Is it possible for you to build another probe with what we have on board?"

"In theory...yes, I think so" Jake replied. "But it would be years away. Besides building the electronic components from scratch, we'd have to make a metalworking shop that could work with berlinite. It will be a long time before we're set up to do that."

"SHIT!" shouted Captain Carreras. It echoed around the hold. It was the first time anyone had heard him swear. It felt terrible and out of place. "So we have no other way of contacting home, not at all?"

"I'm afraid not" said Travis.

The four of them continued looking at the empty crate, as if some magical solution would present itself if they stared long enough.

Victor looked around at them and talked quietly. "Before I bring this up with the command team..." he trailed off, searching for the words. Deep concern was written on his face. "When we left Costa Rica, we said that if anything went wrong on this new planet - anything at all - we'd push that button and river-jump back to Earth. I am asking you three now, is *this* enough to justify that?"

Travis looked at Jake, then Natalie. Neither of them spoke. He cautiously thought, then muttered "I...I don't think so. It's not good, for sure. But we still have time to make this planet work. We can't give up just because the phone lines are down."

"We'll have to get some kind of dish set up eventually. Jess Bishop will send a probe to find us if we don't get word back within a year or two. We need to be ready to receive a signal. Hopefully we can adapt our existing dish to work for that circumstance."

Victor took a very long exhale. "So, besides not having support from Planet 9, I have to tell everyone on board that their messages aren't going to reach their families."

"I'm so sorry," whispered Natalie.

"Well, on the bright side, I don't have to write that damn letter anymore." Victor tried his best to lighten the mood, but it didn't work. They didn't smile, or laugh. Even being on this alien world, 94 light years from everyone they had ever known, there was a comfort in writing those letters. There was solace in knowing that they'd hear back from their families on the probe's return jump. It was a warm blanket in the cold depth of deep space.

But now, with all the communication lines cut, the true nature of their reality presented itself. They were thousands of years in the future, and trillions of miles from home. And now, more than ever, that unfathomable distance felt real.

37.

Sunsets on Mayloz 2 were spectacular. The different composition of the atmosphere produced wildly vivid colors as the host star settled beneath the horizon. It was unlike anything on Earth - the color spectrum in the clouds would range from purple to orange to green, like a toddler had fingerpainted the sky.

"There's a sky-rhino over there," Travis said. He was pointing out over the Hawking ocean. Sky rhinos were flying creatures that populated Mayloz 2. No one had gotten close to a live one yet, but the biology team had managed to study a deceased one. The animal had a large air bladder, and their bodies had a chemical process that could filter hydrogen from their surroundings. Once enough hydrogen had filled their ballast, they would slowly soar over the shorelines and oceans, looking for food. They were large, nearly four meters long, fat, and had a defensive horn above their mouths. They had been given a long complicated scientific name, but the nickname 'sky rhinos' had stuck.

They were by far the largest creatures that they had so far discovered. Most other animals were quite small and timid. No humans had yet been harmed by any life form on the planet. In fact, the eleven months since they had landed had progressed, largely, without incident. They practiced an abundance of caution, but sometimes it just didn't feel necessary. Mayloz 2 was a gentle world. They had yet to see a large predator, and most of the life sustained itself from a combination of the star's energy and eating small photosynthetic organisms. It 'felt' like a world that was early on in its evolutionary process, but they couldn't confirm that. The star they were circling was at least 7 billion years old, and life on this planet could very well be older than life on Earth.

Jake and Travis were sitting on a rocky ridge above the colony site, looking out over the vast Hawking Ocean. "So, what did you want to bring me up here for?" Jake asked.

"Well, the date's passed, bud - we're past the point of no return. Now that we're *officially* staying here forever, I thought we should have a little celebration," Travis replied. He pulled two steel thermoses out of his bag. "Cheers!"

Jake opened one, expecting the sweetened electrolyte mix that they'd been drinking from the rations. But it wasn't that. It was bubbly, bitter, and familiar. "Holy shit, where'd you get beer?"

"First batch, baby! The barley crop grew super fast, so I convinced one of the ladies in agriculture to help me out. Turned a storage barrel into a makeshift fermenter."

Jake took a sip. It was cold and bubbly, but it had a sour and yeasty aftertaste. "Not gonna lie, Trav. This is fucking terrible," he laughed.

"Yeah, cut me some slack! Those Belgian monks had hundreds of years to work out their shit. I'll need some time to get it right. You...might want to stay close to the toilets later, by the way."

Jake laughed again. "Still awesome, man. Thanks."

"One more thing." Travis reached into his bag and pulled out another small container with a flourish. "These might be the last cigars this whole solar system will ever see. I've had them hidden in my luggage the whole year. The agro team brought a crazy amount of plant seeds, but they didn't bring tobacco." He took out a small acetylene torch and lit one, passing it to Jake "Can't blame them really, but I'll still miss the odd stogie."

Jake accepted it gratefully, looking at the cigar in wonder. "Whoa. That's a crazy thought." Travis passed him a lighter. "I guess, if you had to leave one plant behind, it makes sense. If we could leave that whole lung cancer thing back on Earth it'd probably make the med team happy." He puffed his cigar, getting the end burning bright red. He had never been a huge fan of them, but he couldn't turn down the *last* cigar ever. They were far enough above the colony that no one would walk by accidentally. They could enjoy their contraband in the still peace of the evening air.

Only a few hundred people had moved off the ship so far. Shelters were being built, slowly. Housing had not been the number one priority, however - agriculture was. It was critically important that they learned to grow food in the alien soil.

The agriculture team had been developing genetically modified crops at the Planet 9 compound for years. The plants would only reproduce seeds from a mother unit aboard the ship. Each harvest would be planted with fresh seeds, and no introduced plants on the planet's surface would ever reproduce. It was done so that no crop was ever in danger of becoming an invasive species across Mayloz 2. It was a heavy consideration. In reality, humans themselves were the invasive species here. But they could control their own spread, they could maintain a minimal level of reproduction. Non-intelligent animals and plants were different, and would spread unchecked if they weren't careful. Planet 9 had tried to learn from Earth's history, and were trying to avoid the same mistakes on the new world.

They had success with almost everything they planted. Grain, rice, quinoa, fruits and vegetables all took well to the foreign soil. Their landing area got a healthy amount of rain, which helped, and a small river flowed into the ocean nearby, which kept groundwater at optimal levels. Careful consideration had been taken on which plants would sustain people's health. Tobacco didn't make the cut, although marijuana was grown for the med lab. Besides the occasional bit of lab grown 'meat', the whole colony was on a vegan diet as well, which took Travis a while to get used to.

Once they knew that they could feed the colony, and that there were no obvious threats to the inhabitants, the final decision to stay was made. It was a tough day for everyone when they passed the 'point of no return.' Jake had found it especially hard. It was ironic that his whole life had been spent dreaming of space travel, but now all he could dream of was home. And Mia.

"You know..." Travis said through his cigar. "Sonya, the girl from agriculture who helped me out - she's here alone."

"Jesus, dude. Not this again. You and Natalie are relentless."

"Just saying, man. You seem a lot happier now than you were on the spaceflight." Travis took a long puff on his cigar, and let the smoke slowly rise out his mouth. "We just want you to be ok, is all."

"I'm fine, really. I'm getting better. But, I don't think I'm ready for...that...yet, though. You know?"

"There's only a couple single chicks here, dude. I just don't want 'em all to get scooped up. You'll just end up having sad wanks in your tent for the rest of your life."

Jake laughed. "Screw you." He took a few more puffs of his cigar. "Is Sonya the tall Russian one?"

Travis nodded, grinning perversely.

"She's a little out of my league, don't you think? She's super hot."

"Dude!! You're Jacob fuckin' Crawford! You're a household name back on Earth. You were the first person to walk on an exoplanet! You don't think that's enough?"

Jake rolled his eyes. "I guess. But everybody on this planet is pretty much a genius."

"Well, I also happen to think you're a good-looking man, besides your horribly disfigured penis. But just don't tell her about that."

Jake looked out over the ocean, ignoring the insult. "I just...."

Travis knew what he wanted to say, but wasn't. "I know. I know. But it's been a year and a half now. We have no way of contacting Earth. It's very likely that no one else is coming."

"But..."

"Look, man, Mia was great. She was amazing, we loved her too. But - she chose to stay behind. It's not like she's going to change her mind and magically appear here tomorrow. I know you loved her, but - she's gone man. And I think it's time you accepted that and moved on. Your future is here."

Jake didn't say anything. He took another sip of Travis' terrible beer. Back in university, he had started playing with a cheap home brewing kit and making beer in his laundry room. It was dreadful, awful stuff that rotted your guts and exploded in its bottles. And, from memory, it was still far, far better than what Travis had just given him. Still, he was sitting on a cliff on an alien world, watching a sunset and having a cold beer while sky rhinos drifted across the horizon, and that was worth the meaty aftertaste.

Travis was only voicing what he already knew. He knew from the minute that Mia drove away that he'd never see her again. Being lovelorn over someone who lived 94 light years away was idiotic. He was here on this planet now. These people were his family, his community.

He did miss being in a relationship. He missed having someone in his bed, having someone to go on adventures with. Someone who he could just be himself with, and let go of his constant overthinking, his social anxiety. He missed Mia so damn much. And he often wondered if he'd ever find that again. Jake knew how awkward he was on the inside, and how, in his 40 years, he'd only ever met one person who truly connected with that side of him. He was unsure if he would ever find that again, and he wasn't sure it was even worth trying to find.

In that moment, puffing that cigar and watching the last light off the sun fade away over the water, he finally let go of Earth. He had always known in his head that he'd never return home, but his heart had held on to an unrealistic hope. A hope that the colonies would connect together one day. Hope that he'd see Mia again. And he felt like a dog waiting on the front porch for its deceased owner. It was a pointless endeavor, a fool's errand. He had to get up, stretch his legs, and get on with his life.

The last thread of emotion holding him to his old planet drifted away on the evening breeze with the smoke of the cigar. Jake felt truly at peace in that moment for the first time since he'd boarded the Seed ship.

He took a long puff on his cigar, inhaled it by accident, and coughed awkwardly, ruining the moment.

"You ok?" Travis slapped him on the back.

"Yeah, I'm ok." Jake took a sip, and the coughing stopped. "I guess... I could meet her."

Travis smiled and nodded.

"How much more of this did you make? Could you invite her out for a beer with Natalie and me? I don't think I'm ready for, like - a one on one date yet."

"We've still got bout 40 liters, bud." Jake winced, knowing that, no matter how awful this stuff tasted, they'd definitely end up drinking all that. "I can do that for sure. She's cool, man, I think you'd get along with her. She's crazy smart."

"It'd be fun to have beers with Natalie again, too."

"Wellllll... She ain't drinking right now."

"Why? I know it's bad beer, but I've seen her drink worse..." He trailed off.

Travis stared at him and stupidly smiled, waiting to see how long it would take for Jake to figure it out.

Suddenly, Jake understood. "Holy shit, man! Congratulations, that's amazing!" He clinked his thermos with Travis's. "Are you guys gonna have the first kid here?"

"Nah, there's one couple ahead of us, probably. Shoulda given 'er harder." Travis laughed. "But I'm pretty stoked anyways, man."

Jake realized that his friend had saved those cigars to share this exact moment with him, and he was deeply flattered.

They stayed until well after dark. Mayloz 2 had only one small moon which didn't shine as bright as the Earth's. The clear sky and lack of moonlight gave them brilliant stars to stare at, all clustered in different shapes and constellations than they had ever seen before. Once the cigars finally got too short to smoke any more, Travis extinguished them, put them in a steel container, and they walked back to camp with the assistance of their flashlights.

Jake was still living on the ship, as were Travis and Natalie. Only certain teams had moved onto the shore so far. The geologists, bio research, and agriculture each had small communes of hard walled tents set up. As they were walking back towards the ship, Travis stopped Jake with his arm.

"Dude, why don't we go meet Sonya right now?"

"It's late, man. Let's save it for another day."

"Just go say hi at the agriculture village. Thank her for the beer."

"Man, just..." Jake was feeling pressured, and he didn't want to meet Sonya under such weird pretenses. "Just give me a few days to think about it, will you?"

"Like I've always said, Jake. You think too much. Just jump in, bud." There was no convincing Travis. He was heart-set on introducing them, and Jake had learned that his own nervousness or anxiety did nothing to slow down a strong-willed Travis Strickland.

"Okay, we'll say hi real quick then head back home, deal?" Jake reluctantly walked into the agriculture village with him. A dozen or so people were sitting around a fire. A few of the large pink trees had blown over in a storm a month prior, and their hard trunks burned carbon just like wood on Earth.

"Hey Travis!"

"Hey Cory" Travis responded. Cory was sitting in a chair he'd made of old containers. He was a large man, even larger than Travis, and was one of the few clean-shaven men in the settlement. "She's a beautiful night out tonight, ain't it? I don't think I've seen the stars this good since we got here."

"It's awesome. I took a walk twenty minutes ago. Even the Milky Way looks different, it's so cool."

"Hey, is Sonya still up?"

Cory's tone changed, and his smile disappeared. "Oh - we had to take her to the infirmary yesterday. She collapsed as she was walking, I think she's still in there for observation."

Travis looked at Jake, mouthing *"the beer?"* He looked terrified.

"She had that same purple skin problem."

"Purple skin?"

"Oh yeah - where have you guys been?" Cory looked shocked that they hadn't heard the rumors. "A couple people have been getting it these last few weeks, no one knows what it is. Like, these big blotches of purple bruising that just randomly appear."

"I haven't heard anything about this - there was that guy who had the aneurysm a few days ago, but that's the only illness I was aware of," replied Jake.

"I don't know what to tell you guys, just make sure you're washing your hands and being careful."

Travis was relieved that it wasn't his beer, but he was obviously worried for her. Jake had hardly been aware of Sonya or a lot of people really, but Travis had formed attachments to many of the crew. He thanked Cory, and walked with Jake back on to the Seed ship. They began walking the corridors toward their sleeping modules. They walked past module 14, which had the medical center in it.

"I should go say hi to her. I should at least check to make sure she's ok?"

"If you think you should, yep."

"Like I said, dude, she's on this planet alone. I hope people are checking on her, she's probably crazy scared."

"You should. I'll wait here, though. I don't want to meet her while she's on a hospital bed, that's a little creepy."

"Fair enough, man. I'll be back in a sec."

Travis went into the infirmary. Jake took a seat in the hallway, watching random people walk by. He took extra notice of the families. Travis and Natalie were having a baby! His last two connections to his old life were moving on. They would start their family, and he'd be relegated from a third wheel to an occasional visitor. He was happy for Travis, he'd be a good father. But, still, he couldn't hear the news without feeling a sense of loss.

It felt terrifying to finally let go of Earth, but it had to happen. Maybe it was time to see if he could find happiness again. He wouldn't find a Mia. But maybe, just maybe, he could make someone else happy on this remote planet.

Travis came back out of the infirmary door.

"Shit, that was a short visit. Was she asleep?"

Travis stuck his tongue into his cheek, looking down the hall in confusion. "She's... dead."

38.

Colonizing a new planet was never supposed to be easy. No one who got on that ship expected that they would smoothly build a new home. Years of effort from thousands of people had gone into making the experience as safe as possible. But it was still a ridiculous goal, it always had been. It would be naive to think that every single colonist would survive the first year on Mayloz 2.

Yet, the honeymoon phase had felt so great! They were successfully growing food, more shelters were being built all the time, and there was time for recreation. Survey crews had been exploring further out from the bay each week and discovering more about their new home. The colony had been looking more towards the future than the past. It was starting to feel like they could *actually* achieve this, like they would all be okay on this alien world.

And then - the deaths began. It was more than just an end of blissful innocence. It was a slap in the face, a wake-up call - as if they all suddenly remembered where they actually were and what they had done.

Sonya wasn't the first death in the colony. She was the third of seven in that week. The colony had gone from one death (which occurred just two months into the space flight) to eight, all within a matter of days. There had been two fatal aneurysms, two heart attacks, and three deaths from internal bleeding. Every crew member had been thoroughly checked for health issues before their departure, so these vascular issues were, so far, unexplained.

Four other crew members had also shown the mysterious 'purple bruising' before passing away. The odd coloration of their skin had been an indication of widespread internal bleeding. None of the four had suffered any trauma or had any other medical conditions that would explain it. The infirmary was now filling fast with 'purple-skinned' patients, and the medical team was struggling to keep up with the surge.

News had spread, and people were visibly anxious on the ship. Paranoia was rampant. Everyone checked their skin constantly, and any slight discoloration sent them into raging panics. In the common areas, it was a common sight to see people lift their shirts up, getting friends to check their backs. Most discolorations were just sunburns or impact bruises. But, even still, a few more people would end up with the mysterious disease each day.

The killer was ambiguous. Was it a virus? Was it radiation from their host star? Whatever it was, it was invisible, and that was the most terrifying part. Many people refused to leave the ship until the medical team determined the cause. The lounges and hallways buzzed with activity and terrified faces. Some stayed in their tiny sleeping quarters all day, nervously waiting for answers and quarantining themselves from the invisible killer.

Jake had become nauseous with stress. He didn't remain in his quarters, but he was too scared to do much else. Mayloz 2 had seemed so beautiful and peaceful a few days before, a place full of promise for the future. But, now it was a foreboding prison. He would give anything to be back in Vancouver or Costa Rica. Anywhere that wasn't here.

Being alone in his bunk wasn't working for him. Jake's mind was racing in circles again. He needed to be with his friends. He knew what would happen to him if he stayed alone for too long. He didn't want his mind going through a repeat of what happened in that Venezuelan hotel. Travis and Natalie were in the section 16 lounge having coffee when he found them.

Travis took Sonya's death hard. "I just saw her the day before she died, she was perfectly fine. I don't get it." He was angry about it, even though there was no one to blame or be angry with. "Make sure you don't go where she was, we don't know if she caught something," he told Natalie. "I don't know what's going on."

"It's so sad. She was so young. And we can't even tell her family," Natalie replied. She wasn't crying now, but her puffy eyes were evidence that she had been.

"I really wish we hadn't lost the damn probes. Man, we fucked up" Jake said. It had been 11 months since they'd discovered the missing probes, but Jake still hadn't forgiven himself for it.

"It doesn't matter now" Travis said bluntly. "We're here for good, we're past the point of no return. We have to figure out what killed Sonya. And soon."

The three sat in silence around a table. Everything had been said that could be said. The medical team, the agriculture team and the radiologists were all desperately searching for answers. They felt useless as the river-jumping experts - there was absolutely nothing they could do to help. They had successfully gotten the ship here, but now, without probes, the three of them were kind of just…in the way.

Jake's watch buzzed, and a small holo-message popped up. Travis and Natalie's watches did the same.

"*Urgent Meeting. Command Module 13:00*"

"Sweet, maybe the doc has some answers, finally." said Travis, coldly.

"Okay, that's in forty minutes. I'm going to take a shower and meet you guys there." Natalie got up and left them at the table. She wasn't showing the pregnancy bump quite yet, but she had been getting bouts of morning sickness. The stress of the situation wasn't helping her.

Jake and Travis stayed and had another coffee, then made their way to the command module. Travis' joyful demeanor from a few nights earlier was completely gone. He wasn't trying to set up Jake with girls anymore. He wasn't trying to brew beer or throw parties. He was singularly focused on protecting Natalie and his unborn child. It was the most serious that Jake had ever seen his friend.

They reached the command module ten minutes early but nearly everyone was there already, including the Captain. Jake went up to him to say hi, but Victor had a stern, uneasy look on his face.

"I'll let the doctor tell you everything," Victor replied to Jake's inquiries. Jake sat down, acknowledging the abrupt end of the conversation.

The last few trickled into the meeting, including Natalie. Finally, a few minutes after the hour, Dr. Pachenko walked in. He looked exhausted. His shirt was untucked, his hair was a mess, and he had a surgical mask hanging out of his coat pocket.

"Okay, let's get started," spoke Captain Carreras. "Look, everyone - it's been a really tough week. It's never easy to lose some of your own. We're a small community, and Dale, Virginia, Sonya, Miho, Nugai, Lucy and Pierre will all be sorely missed." They had a moment of silence, bowing their heads. "It's tragic, but unfortunately - we don't have time to mourn. We're all in danger now, and they will not be the last casualties we suffer from this."

The table looked around at each other, each member of the team trying to contain their own fear and put on a strong face. It wasn't working. Jake could see that everyone was just as scared as he was.

"Dr. Pachenko has found what we *believe* caused the deaths. I'll let him explain."

Dr. Lorenzo Pachenko was a competitive marathon runner back on Earth. He was in his early forties, with dark hair, a neatly trimmed beard, and a slim build. He was another veteran of the military, just like Victor. He had taken the appointment as Chief Medical Officer on the Seed project for the challenge of it. A long, varied career had left him with a wealth of experiences, but he was rarely pushed or fulfilled by his military roles. This colony, and developing the medical practice of a new world, this would be his greatest achievement.

He stood in front of the group and said nothing, at first. He looked tired. No greeting, no introduction. He just took out his holo-tab and brought an image up on the room's main display. It was some sort of ten-legged insect with a long tail and pincers. The image was from a microscope's lens. The scale of the creature was unclear, but its body was almost transparent.

"When we arrived on Mayloz 2, we did a full scan of the environment. Hundreds of samples of the water, the air, the soil. We searched for microbes, viruses, and parasites, and we didn't find anything that was reacting negatively to our biology. And, unfortunately..." Lorenzo paused in thought. He looked deeply remorseful. "I gave the go ahead to open up the ship. We saw no credible threats in this area, nothing worthwhile of an extended quarantine. But these creatures...." he pointed at the display, "have always been in the water, air, and soil. They're incredibly small, not much larger than a few bacterial cells. We didn't see any reason to fear them, they don't show any signs of normal parasitic behavior. I've never seen a complex life form this small on Earth. The actual cells of the creatures here are smaller, which allows the life forms themselves to evolve at microscopic scales."

The picture on the display changed. Now, it was a woman on a hospital bed. Her torso was purple and bruised from her upper rib cage down past her hip bones.

"This is Lucy Mcadams 6 days ago. She died two days after this was taken. Lucy was the first fatality from the 'purple skin' disease. We couldn't do much for her except keep her comfortable. In fact, we couldn't find the cause of the internal bleeding until we did an autopsy. Lucy was... being eaten from the inside out."

A hushed gasp came from Liz, the head botanist. "Was it that bug you showed us?"

"Yes. There's not many of them in this environment, but they're everywhere. They get inside our bodies in different ways. Drinking water, contaminated surfaces, they're even capable of floating in a light breeze and can enter us through our lungs. Our immune system appears to be completely useless against them. We didn't consider them a threat upon arrival because they showed such an incredibly slow reproductive rate, which is odd for a small parasitic organism. As well, like I said, the numbers of them in the environment here are exceptionally low."

The screen switched to a graph, showing an exponential growth curve. Weeks were labeled along the x axis, and a small picture of the organism, named "Mayloz 2 - H4153" labeled the Y axis. The line showed minimal growth for months, until, finally, it shot up to higher numbers.

"They seem to be able to control their a-sexual reproductive rate. It stays very slow until they determine the quality of their surrounding environment, and whether there's a viable food source. This 'decision' can take months, even years. They stay mainly dormant in the bloodstream, eating just enough to survive and to test their environment. Once they send the 'go-ahead' chemical signal to the others in the body, however, they begin reproducing at a highly accelerated rate, eating our soft tissues and blood vessel linings as they go. Their numbers will increase from dozens to tens of millions within days, and they'll begin eating their way out of the host. Once the host dies, their numbers get released back into the environment, and they stay at a dormant energy level until the perfect conditions occur again." Dr. Pachenko looked down at his holo-tab, flicking through his screens to find the next bit of info he wanted to show. "It's a brutally effective strategy, and I wish we'd caught it earlier. I really do."

"So, do we have a way to test for them? To see who's infected?" asked Natalie.

Lorenzo looked up. "Sorry, I may not have been clear on how they operate. We don't *need* to test for them." He looked sternly around the table. "We're all infected. They've been inside us in limited numbers since the day we opened those doors. They're simply waiting for the conditions to be right to start mass reproduction. There's no indication that good health or a strong immune system will slow them down. These people were just...unlucky."

"And the aneurysms? That doesn't sound like the same problem."

"It is. They eat the blood vessel linings first. That's what caused the two heart attacks as well, from what we can tell."

"Fucking hell..." Travis caught himself swearing in the meeting, which he tried very hard not to do in a professional setting. No one flinched, everyone was thinking the same. "So, we all just have a ticking time bomb inside us, and no one knows when it'll go off."

Victor Carreras spoke up and took control. "Dr. Pachenko has told me of a potential cure. But it's a rough one."

"They don't respond to any traditional medicine that we've tried" continued the doctor. "Our immune system can't stop them. Therefore, there's no vaccine, no medication that will help us fight them off." replied the doctor. "If we knew that this was possible, if we knew what these things were capable of - I would have recommended the jump back to Earth, whole heartedly."

"We didn't know, though. It's not your fault, Lorenzo."

Dr. Pachenko took a deep sigh. "There is a way to kill them, but it nearly kills us as well. They don't respond to radiation or chemotherapy. Damn things are like microscopic cockroaches, they survive everything. The only thing that kills them off for good is mercury. I've begun treatment with several patients using very high dosage mercury pills."

"Mercury pills?! What is this, the middle ages? Those haven't been used in medicine for hundreds of years!" asked Liz.

"Only in rare cases, yes, you're right. But they haven't reacted to anything else. The mercury in our blood streams will kill them off completely. But, at these doses, the mercury will come very close to killing us as well. It is *not* going to be a fun ride. It'll be a very rough few weeks while it runs through your system."

"So, whoever shows the first signs of the purple skin, the bruising - they'll need to take the mercury treatment?" asked Jake.

"No, Jake - everyone needs to. Travis phrased it right - it's a ticking time bomb. They could start their swarm reproduction cycle inside any of us, at any time. We may be able to kill them off if we see the signs of bruising early enough, but chances are that they'll do enough damage to your internals that you won't recover from the mercury treatment itself."

Jake looked around the table. It was an unbelievably hard blow. Traveling across the galaxy, settling an alien world, exploring new environments - danger had always been part of the agreement, maybe even part of its draw. The fact that they had made it this long without losing a few people was incredible in its own right. He hated himself for thinking like that, but it was true. The road ahead would be rough, yes, but at least most of them would survive.

"I'm afraid we're stuck between a rock and a hard place" began the Captain. "There's...no way ahead that ends well, folks. We have some truly terrible, awful decisions to make."

"I don't understand, sorry. Lorenzo just said we have a cure, so...we take it?" replied Travis.

"These...creatures... From what Dr. Pachenko has told me, they're in absolutely everything here. So, even if we all take the mercury treatments, it's only a temporary fix. We *will* get infected again."

"You can survive the treatment once, maybe twice" added the doctor. "But no more than that. And dying of mercury poisoning is a horrific way to go. I really wish I had another solution. We'll keep looking for another treatment, but I'm not very hopeful that we'll find one."

And, finally, the true, horrible extent of their situation became clear. The faces in the room changed one by one, as they all realized the inevitability of their situation.

"And so, we come to this," said the Captain, slowly and deliberately. "If we stay on this planet, every one of us will be dead within a few years. I hate to put it so bluntly, but it's true. We either die of the infection, or the cure. That's it, that's all."

The realization hit like a sledgehammer.

"And we're past our point of no return. But, only *just* past it, right?" asked Gerrard, one of the environmental engineers. "Surely we can still make it back to Earth?"

"Sorry bud," Travis said pointedly. "That date has passed, it was a clear line in the sand. Even if we had left two months ago, it would have taken the ship four and a half years to catch the Earth. Now, the Earth is drifting away from our jump point at a rate that's *just* too fast. We'd never catch it - we'd spend the rest of our lives in space watching it get further away."

"Well, that's better than dying here, isn't it?" asked Liz heatedly. "We got used to life on board, we can do it again."

Natalie shook her head sadly. "But it was never designed for that. We designed the food and water systems of this ship to sustain 2000 people for a maximum of five years. It was set up that way because we calculated the maximum transit time back to Earth from the cutoff date. So, in the worst-case scenario, if we had left 6 weeks ago, just before the cutoff date, we could ration food and water and arrive home alive."

"Wait, if they're in the air and water, wouldn't we just bring them into space with us as well?" asked Gerrard.

"We could plan for that" replied Lorenzo. "We'd purge the ship, quarantine everyone during their mercury treatments, and use suits for any remaining ground work. It would be tricky, but we could eliminate them. Not that being up there is much better anyway."

"So, if I have this right," started Travis. He counted their options on his fingers as he spoke. "We have three choices. We either get eaten alive from the inside out, die a horrible death from mercury poisoning, or starve to death in deep space. These options aren't getting much better, eh?"

"If only we'd known this two months ago," said Natalie.

"Isn't that just the way the world friggn' works? Things always break the day after the warranty expires."

No one laughed. The table went silent, as they all looked for other options that weren't there. No deal with the devil could be made, and each method of their demise sounded worse than the one before.

"Wait," said Liz. "Isn't Planet 9 coming here anyway? Once they get that fast ship built, and they were only a few years away launch, right?"

"We can't send them a message for help, unfortunately," replied the Captain. "And look how long the ships to Mars got delayed. They may get here next month, or next decade, but it doesn't really matter."

"The Stingray will only hold 200 people, at the most" Jake added. "And it will still be a relatively long journey between the planets. If they got here with that ship, they might be able to bring back a few of us, but they definitely wouldn't have the time to rescue us all before we poisoned ourselves."

"I've only known about this problem for a few hours now, folks," said Victor Carreras. "And I... simply don't know what to do. I've never faced odds like this. I've never faced an unwinnable battle. This decision, the way our colony ends - it can't be made by me. It will have to go to all of us."

'What the hell is going on!?' thought Jake. Four days earlier, he and Travis were peacefully smoking cigars, watching the sunset. That night, on that ridgetop, he had felt happy and content for the first time on Mayloz 2. And now, not only him, but his entire colony, was facing certain

death. Had he brought this on them by feeling the slightest bit of joy? Was he cursed?

Jake had become wary of feeling happy. Each time he felt like his life was back on track, the world seemed to pull the rug out from under him. He'd become a millionaire, only to lose Mia and Travis shortly afterwards. He'd started incredible research at Planet 9 and rekindled his friendship with Travis, only to be exiled from Costa Rica the next day. He'd gotten his pardon, moved back to Costa Rica, and bought a home with the love of his life. And then, when he was the happiest and most excited in his life, waiting to board a ship that would whisk him away to a different planet - Mia had left him. Each and every time that warm, happy feeling of success creeped into his life, fate ripped it back again.

More than anything, Jake was so utterly sick of tough decisions. This 'river' of choices had carried him through success, criminality, love, loss, friendship - and across the galaxy. He'd made the turns that had carried him here, just like Travis said. He had tried to go with the flow, to follow the current. He'd tried to make the proper turns.

Jake knew, *now*, that he'd overthought too many decisions in his life. Small, insignificant choices occupied far too much of his everyday thoughts, and left him exhausted when a crucial event happened. He'd tried to live his life like Travis, but he just couldn't. Travis effortlessly navigated the swells and rapids of his life, blindly accepting whatever happened next. And it always worked out for him. It always *magically* worked out for him. Except this time.

Now they were both at the end, there was no way out. Three channels in front of them, and none of them were navigable. The river was going to consume them, and no matter how hard they paddled, there was nothing they could do about it. It was a cruel, ironic fate that Jake, a man so utterly sick of making impossible choices, now had to choose the way he would die. One way to end it all. One way for the Seed project - his life's work - to fade away and die.

"*Fuck this!*" he thought, as he felt his eyes welling. "*This can't be it, not after everything.*" Yes, they had missed their window to Earth. But there had to be something else they could do. They could go back in time, before these decisions were made, but it wouldn't help. If they went back far enough, they could warn their past selves not to come to Mayloz 2. But, if they had done that, they wouldn't be here - it was a classic paradox. If they jumped back to Jess and Dylan's time, they could send a message to them to stay away, but the Seed ship and the colony would be adrift in space forever. There was no way out, or at least he couldn't see one. There had to be another option, something he wasn't seeing. But, as many angles as he furiously thought of, no solution presented itself.

Jake started to slowly consider which of the three ways that he would prefer to die, making a pros and cons list for each method of demise. He started to imagine which of the pains would be worse. He wondered which of them would be more heart-wrenching to watch Travis and Natalie go through. His mind raced through dozens of scenarios, each worse than the last. "*Fuck that! There has to be another way!*"

Suddenly, it struck him. Jake's eyes shot wide open with a realization. While the room stayed mournfully quiet, he took out his notepad and a sharpie. He scribbled calculations down furiously, making sure he was right before he brought it up with anyone. Did it work? Could this be the way out? Was it right to even bring it up?

Jake elbowed Travis, and gave him a raise of the eyebrows. He slid his notepad over to him to show the idea.

"Whoa…" Travis looked at him in shock. "You sure, Jake? That's, I guess we could…we're not supposed to even…Fuck me, dude…" Travis whispered back, stuttering on his words in shock.

Jake wasn't going to let it end this way. He wasn't going to just sit there and decide which way his friend's unborn child would die. He had to bring another option, no matter how controversial it was.

He raised his hand slowly. "Captain, I believe that there's one more place that we can go."

39.

Victor Carreras had the bridge of his nose resting on his thumb and index finger. He was pretending to be deep in thought like the rest of his command team, but he'd already been thinking about the problem for hours. He had no more ideas, there was no way out. He'd always been worried about the 'point of no return' date on this mission. He had carefully analyzed every possible danger, every notable hazard, right up until that date. The last three weeks had been decidedly more peaceful for him in contrast. The tough decision was gone, and they could start looking to the future.

But now, he'd give anything to go back in time before that cutoff date. Now, he had to decide between three unspeakable fates. If up to Victor, he would jump the ship off of the planet into space, and at least live a few more quiet years without the threat of infections. Still, watching 2000 people slowly starve didn't sound like a great time. Watching his daughter struggle - that was unbearable to think about.

Jake's comment brought him back from his introspection. He opened his eyes. "Yes, Mr. Crawford. Where would that be?" he asked calmly.

Jake was about to speak when he felt Travis elbow him in the ribs. He turned to Travis, who whispered "*we have to double check first.*" He was right. They needed to check the math, especially before bringing such a controversial idea to the group. All the faces at the table were looking at him expectantly. Hopefully. He had to be sure.

"Sorry - I need to use one of our workstations first. Could we have ten minutes?"

The captain sighed defeatedly. "Okay, let's reconvene in twenty minutes. I want every team to brainstorm solutions until then. This may be unnecessary to say to you all, but until we have a plan, this information absolutely does *not* leave this room. The last thing that we need is widespread panic."

Everyone stood up. They started filtering out of the room, moving slowly. They were all clearly still in shock from the news, and a few were hiding tears. Jake moved quickly, passing the slow-moving crowd and making his way to the stellar navigation office. Travis and Natalie followed.

Without saying anything, Jake sat down at his workstation, beginning to input the complex equations he'd need to prove his theory.

"Sooo, you *do* know what you're proposing, right?" Travis sat in a chair next to the workstation and watched him work.

"I don't think we have another choice. I know it's not right, but if the timing works out - that has to mean something, right?" replied Jake. He felt a hand on his shoulder. It was Natalie. Her hand was on her mouth in astonishment as she watched the time-jump computation line up.

"This is either the best idea you've ever had, Jake, or we're going into something even worse." Her hand tightened its grip on his shoulder as he finished inputting the last variables.

The simulation returned its result. Jake's idea had worked. "Ho...lee...shit," muttered Travis. "Should we do this? *Can* we do this? Friggn' hell, guys, where do we even begin?"

"We tell the truth. No more lies." said Jake.

They loaded a few files onto his holotab and made their way back to the command module. They were late, it had taken more time than Jake thought. Captain Carreras motioned for them to take their seats.

"So, Mr. Crawford, what's your idea? Where else can we go?"

Jake cleared his throat nervously. There was no stopping now. "By now, you're all aware of the basic concept of river jumping. We stay still at a specific location in space, and either travel forward or backwards in time to wait for another star system to be in this exact same spot."

The group nodded. Or course, they all knew this, everyone on board knew the basics of berlinite time travel.

"So, the closest alignment of the Earth and Mayloz 2 was 16 months ago. The day we left Earth was the closest that those two planets would ever come to occupying the same point in space. Those 2 days were separated by 6,251 years, and that's why we jumped forward in time by that exact amount. Ever since that day, we've been drifting further away from the alignment, which means that, even if we go back to the same day we left Earth, we'd now be too far away in space to reach it again."

The table all nodded. They knew the details, and were impatient, but Jake felt like he needed to explain from the beginning. Mainly for his sake.

"As you know, we rushed the construction of this ship and the training of this crew to get it ready for that alignment. We knew that it was coming. And we knew that if we had a slow-moving ship like this, we had only one chance to river-jump it within range of this planet. We rushed because we didn't know how many other habitable worlds we'd ever find. Mayloz 2 was the best that we saw. Breathable air, temperate environment, it looked perfect. Mayloz 2 was the only viable option of the thousands of planets we surveyed. Or, at least...that's what the Bishops told everyone. Originally, there were two other options."

Victor looked at him strangely. "Yes, I remember studying all about that. Planet B was too far, and was in an asteroid shooting gallery. Planet C had fatal levels of radiation, did it not?"

Jake looked at Travis, still somehow nervous to let the secret out. Travis took over. "There were no radiation problems. Jess, sorry - *we* all lied about that." He cleared his throat. "Okay, so, where to start? 'Planet C' has a couple different names. It orbits a star called Cepheus HD314. We named it 'Planet C' because it was the third viable option that the river jumping probes found almost a decade ago. But, in quieter circles on Earth, Planet C is known as 'Reyes 3'"

The group was visibly confused, still not knowing why they needed such a lengthy explanation.

"It has a perfect climate for us. In fact, the original probes of Reyes 3 showed a better atmosphere and higher water content than Mayloz 2. It had the chemical signatures of life, a stable star, suitable gravity, a very strong magnetic field - it was, literally, perfect."

"Okay," replied the Captain. "So why did they change the report and say it was unviable?"

"There's an astronomer on Earth - Marcela Reyes, from Chile. She found radio signals coming from that planet. Millions of radio signals - from a highly intelligent civilization."

"What?!" exclaimed Liz. "For real?"

"I've read about this on the internet. It's not real! It's just conspiracy nonsense," said Lorenzo.

"I can assure you, it's very real," added Jake. "The first signals were detected twelve years ago. Travis and I were only made aware five years after that, and that was only so that we could stop Planet 9 from studying it any further. Very, very few people know about it. A small group from SETI, MI6, the CIA and NASA. No one else."

"Why...why would they keep something like that secret?" asked Liz. "Why the hell wouldn't they let people know that? Proof that we're not alone in the universe, and they hid it!?"

"They wanted time to study the signals, to decode them. They wanted to know who the aliens were before they let the information go public." Jake looked around the table at the shocked faces.

"It seems pretty selfish of them," replied Lorenzo.

"If the information was too ambiguous, it would have just thrown another wrench into an already divided world. Especially the way the world is now - no one can decide on anything! For god's sake, there's still millions of people who think the Earth is flat, even though we're out here colonizing different planets. Knowing, definitively, that alien life is out there, but not knowing anything about it - it leaves the door open for conflict, war, propaganda. I didn't agree with them then - I'm not sure if I do know. But we haven't told anyone, anywhere about this until now."

"Well, I told Natalie, but that's cause, ya know," Travis said, raising his eyebrows while he looked at her.

"What have they found? Do you know anything more about them?" asked the Captain.

"Not too much. Decoding signals from an alien race, turns out, is pretty damn hard. Their signals are nothing like ours, and they obviously use different languages and computing formats. All we know is that they're nothing like us, and from what we can tell, they're far, far more advanced. Planet 9 was instructed to make up a false excuse about Reyes 3, and focus on Mayloz 2. We were also instructed, well - threatened, really - not to send any additional probes to the planet, in case they were intercepted. For right now, the inhabitants of that planet probably don't know that humans exist at all."

"And MI6 really, really wants it to stay that way. For everyone's sake," added Travis.

The conversation reached a pause. Everyone was trying to wrap their heads around the new information. Jake remembered how he had felt when he first heard. It was almost a certainty that other intelligent life was out there, he'd always known that. But confirming it was still mind blowing.

"Look, learning about the existence of intelligent alien life is a huge thing to wrap your head around, I get it. You might agree that it should have been kept secret, you might not. But here's the thing; there is a habitable planet out there that's perfect for us, and we can reach it!" Jake projected an image from his holo-tab onto the main display. It showed his calculations from the other room. "All these stars and planets are moving in the same broad direction, right? But they also rotate the galactic core, which means that they don't follow the exact same path. That's the concept of river jumping, we can only get to them if they cross our exact point in the river. Our alignment with Earth passed 16 months ago, and we're now drifting further away from that point every day. But we're actually drifting *closer* to an alignment with Reyes 3.

"We jumped over 6000 years into the future to get here. So, if we jumped 6000 years back, we'd get near Earth, but not quite close enough. We'd cross the 94 light years, but would have drifted too far to reach. However, if we keep going back, another 132 light years *past* the Earth, the location that we're currently in will be occupied by the Reyes system. In short, in 46 days, the alignment of Mayloz and Reyes will be at its closest point. We'll be almost on top of it, only a few weeks' flight away from orbit."

Lorenzo shook his head in disbelief. "Jake, you're a magician. That's incredible. I'll start developing a quarantine and treatment plan for launch."

"Wait a second" interrupted Natalie. "This isn't cut and dry, guys. I don't know if we should do this! There's much bigger things at stake here besides our health."

Travis nodded in agreement. "Yup. I agree. For sure, between dying of mercury poisoning, being eaten alive, or starving to death in deep space, meeting E.T. sounds like the right choice. But, Jesus, if it goes wrong..."

"We promised the secret committee that we'd stop studying that planet. The reason being, that - if they don't know that Earth exists, we could put the whole human race in danger by accidentally revealing our presence. They were worried about a tiny probe surveying the planet, and whether or not that would give us away."

"How much worse would it be if a couple thousand tasty humans show up at their doorstep?" Travis looked around the table sternly. "What if they find out that Earth has all the resources they need? We wouldn't be able to stop them. Never mind the fact that we showed up in a shiny new ship with the technology to river-jump them right there. We could screw over not just ourselves, but all of humanity if this goes wrong. That's not something we can decide on a whim."

"Wait, how do we know that this would be bad for Earth?" asked Liz.

"We don't. But it's a possibility," replied Jake. "And if it's true, we'd be pitting two thousand lives against ten billion."

Victor's head had returned back to his hand. His fingers were holding the bridge of his nose once more, and his eyes were closed. Only this time, he wasn't just pretending to be deep in thought.

It was another impossible choice. He was the leader of the ship, yes, and he could, in theory, make the call. But how could he possibly do that? Keep the Earth secret, and doom 2000 people to their deaths? Or save his crew with a miraculous jump through space to a new home, and risk everyone back on Earth? "This is too big a decision for us. We can't decide, here and now, whether or not humanity should make first contact."

"I hate to be the person who says it, guys, but we're not a part of humanity anymore," said Liz. "We're orphans of it. We can't involve the Earth in this decision. We have no option of contacting our world, or getting back home to them. We are on our own, and we represent ourselves now."

"Maybe this could go right," Doctor Pachenko added. "Maybe they're not inherently evil, and we could work together? Maybe they could even help us get home."

"It's well known through history that when two civilizations meet, it never goes well for the less advanced one." Natalie spoke softly. "I'm not necessarily saying I'm against the idea, but I just think we should all know the risk."

The table all looked at each other once more, afraid to form an opinion. Then, after sitting in their own thoughts for a while, they all turned to Victor for guidance. He put his head back, stared at the ceiling, and exhaled.

"We can't decide this in this room. Everyone needs to be involved. The crew needs to know all of our options. We'll have a vote. They need to make an informed choice on their future."

"It has to be quick, Victor," added Dr. Pachenko. "This illness will only get worse with each passing day. I'll continue to look for cures, but it's my recommendation that we begin the mercury treatments as soon as possible."

They sat and deliberated for another hour, carefully working through the logistics of each option. As the command team finally left the module, Victor put out a ship wide PA announcement.

"Attention, everyone. In ninety minutes, I will be giving you a full update on our situation. As you know, there is a terrible illness spreading among our crew. We have a tough choice to make, together. Please ensure that you are ready and listening, as we will be having a referendum on our options tomorrow afternoon."

He started compiling his notes. The week's events had been so damaging, the revelations so profound - he wasn't sure if even *he* had a full grasp of the situation yet.

He tried to sum it up in his head. So, they were being eaten alive from the inside out by an invisible creature. They had no way of stopping them except for a brutal treatment of mercury poisoning, which everyone would have to go through, regardless of their choices, just to survive. If they stayed on the planet, they would either die of the infection, or the cure. It was possible that Dr. Pachenko could find another cure in time, but not likely.

It was too late to get back to Earth, and if they tried, they would starve to death in deep space. However, they could at least communicate with loved ones back home again before the end. And inform them of the dangers of Mayloz 2.

Or, they could river jump thousands of years further back in time to a different planet. A planet that just happened to be inhabited by a super advanced alien race. It looked perfectly habitable, but by arriving and making contact, they would risk revealing the Earth's existence to a potential hostile species.

Victor chuckled to himself at the ridiculousness of the situation. He still didn't know which one *he* would choose. He'd taken this command as a final challenge, but he'd had no idea that he'd be up against odds like this.

Before making the fateful announcement, Victor walked to his bunkroom. From his pack, he retrieved a bottle of barrel-aged Mezcal - a treat he'd been hiding since they left Earth. He returned to the command module and poured two fingers of it over a single cube of ice. The aroma of it instantly brought him back home. It smelled like relaxing by a campfire in his backyard. It smelled like comfort.

He sat in silence, reading through his notes and sipping his drink slowly. He'd addressed many crews over various commands, but he'd never had to do anything remotely like this before. The ice rattled in his steel cup as he emptied the last sip. The alarm on his watch went off. He took a deep breath, reached for the microphone, and cleared his throat.

40.

Mia had never gotten used to the speed of the Planet 9 shuttle cars, no matter how many times she had ridden in them. And now, having been away from Costa Rica for two years, the fear was worse than ever. She knew they were safe, but it still seemed unnecessary for them to drive at 260. She gripped the armrest tightly, put in her wireless earbuds, and closed her eyes. Only fifteen more minutes until the car would exit the highway, she could try to ignore it for that long.

She was missing a beautiful view. A small line of clouds lay over the sea to the east, but the rest of the sky was a sparkling blue. It was mid-February, and her home back in Vancouver hadn't seen the sun since Christmas. Mia was happy to return to the sunny skies of Central America - only briefly, however. Remaining here would bring back too many memories. Memories of a life she'd tried to move on from. It wasn't necessarily a life she wanted to forget, but it was one that she wanted to leave firmly in her past.

She still technically owned the house south of the compound. After the Seed ship left, however, she'd never once been back to see it. She knew that she should probably sell, but a part of her still clung to it. She wanted to go back to that house, to be with Jake again. To live the happiest years of her life over again once more.

But he was gone. The ship was gone, and it wasn't coming back. No matter how many wishful fantasies she'd had, or how many dreams there'd been of him magically returning to her, she knew that it was all folly. He was a hundred light years away, the return deadline had passed, and there was no possible way for Jake to get back to Earth. And - she'd told him to go.

No decision in her life had been as hard as that night at the Bishops' house. No single choice had left her with more regret. Jake had to go; he would have been miserable if he stayed behind. Before the jump there had seemed to be so much that she loved on Earth, so much worth living her life for. And yet, as soon as the Seed ship river-jumped away, the Earth felt lonely and empty. The things she loved most had left with the ship.

Mia quit her job at Planet 9, moved back to Vancouver, and tried to start her life over again. Her parents were initially overjoyed that she had stayed, as was her sister. But over the months that followed, they began to realize what Mia knew all along. She would never be the same person again. The spark that she'd had, the spontaneity, the impulsiveness - the pure, authentic joy of life - it had all disappeared with the ship. She gave an honest effort to be herself again, but they knew her too well to be fooled by it. It was as if she was an actress playing a previous version of herself.

For two years she replayed the decision of that night, over and over. It wasn't regret that plagued her, but a longing to go back. Back to Costa Rica and her life with Jake. Back to when things were simpler.

The car began to slow, and Mia opened her eyes. It turned into the offramp and drove east towards the Planet 9 security gates. Mia had no company ID anymore, or key fob. She picked up her holo-tab and began searching through her emails for her confirmation. It wasn't there, she'd been so distracted by the emotions of this trip that she had deleted the file. "Shit." Mia took out her passport and began thinking of how to explain her way through the gate. Security at Planet 9 had been extreme ever since river-jumping went public. They'd been the subject of protestors, thieves, and even terrorist plots.

The car rolled up to the gate, and the security guard walked up to the car window. "I'm really sorry, I don't have my..." Mia began.

"Ms. Yang?" he interrupted.

"Yes, that's me," she said, showing her Canadian passport to him.

"Go right ahead. Your car has clearance to park at the Bishop residence." He gave her passport back to her and waved her through the gate.

Mia was surprised at how easy it was, but accepted it. She rolled her window up and took control of the car. It was still a decent drive from the gate to Jess and Dylan's house, and she'd always enjoyed driving the small roads through the forest.

She went straight through the first intersection. The staff housing was on the coast to her right. She'd often eaten at the restaurant there with Jake and his team, staying out far too late on the pool terrace. *"Oh God"* she thought. *"Travis, Jon, Natalie...they're dead too."*

The final deadline had passed three months prior. It had always been hard knowing that Jake would never come back. But the fact that Planet 9 had heard nothing from the settlement - that was so much worse. Jake and Travis would have found a way to send a probe or a message back, no matter what. There was simply no way that they would have failed to get news to Planet 9, which made the continued radio silence deeply disturbing. Jake would have figured out the problem, she knew that. But no message had come, which meant he was most likely dead.

The news had been openly speculating on the fate of the Seed project for the past year. Some journalists still held out hope that the colony was alive and well. Most were far more pessimistic, however. They believed, as Mia did, that they had all perished. Political pundits had jumped on the message probe's absence, calling the project "the most expensive blunder in the history of humanity." Critics called for the international community to boycott Planet 9, labeling Dylan Bishop an "absurd danger to his own followers." In the absence of the probe, or any news from the colony, Dylan had become even more reclusive, never leaving the compound, and never giving interviews.

Grief had consumed Mia at first, but now she was starting to come through to the other side. The three months since the deadline date had been a steady healing process, a time to let Jake go. But now, driving through the compound, she was reminded of all the other friends she had lost on that ship. She'd been so close to boarding, so close to losing her own life along with them. Left behind in anguish at their loss, she wondered which planet would have been worse for her. There were occasional days back in Vancouver that she could forget about the missing ship and try to live a normal life. But here at the compound, the memories were unavoidable.

'Why the fuck did I come back?' she thought, as she pulled the car over to wipe her cheeks. Her breathing increased in cadence, and she felt the tears welling up once more. Soon, she was sobbing into the dashboard. *'Why am I here!?'*

She had enough money to live comfortably for the rest of her life. She didn't need to work again. She especially didn't need to come back and work for Jess, no matter how good the offer was. And yet, a cryptic email from her old friend and boss had brought her all the way back to Costa Rica for a simple lunch meeting. She was drawn back; something was still pulling her here.

Mia regained her composure and engaged the car to drive towards the mansion. She pulled up to the front reception area and got out. Roldan came outside to greet her.

"Ms. Yang, so good to see you again."

"Hi Roldan, you too."

Roldan held out his hand to shake, but Mia pushed it aside and gave him a hug. He was still uncomfortable with the non-professional nature of Planet 9, even after all these years. "Would you like somewhere to freshen up after your flight?" Roldan began walking her to the house. "I'll let them know you've arrived."

"That'd be great, yes."

He showed Mia to a guest suite. His watch buzzed as he was opening the door. "Dylan and Jess will be on the main patio in thirty minutes or so. Can I let them know you'll meet them up there?"

"Sure. Thanks again, Roldan."

Mia put her bag down and walked to the vanity sink. Her reflection showed clear evidence of her tears. Puffy eyes, messy mascara, lightly stained cheeks. It had been a long time, but she instantly thought back to the last time she was in the Bishops' house, where her reflection had looked sadly similar. She washed her face, dried it with one of the elegantly rolled personal towels, and began fixing her hair. She appreciated Roldan's sensitivity in delaying the meeting.

Jess was certainly being cryptic, and unnecessarily distant. Why hadn't she just been sent up to the office if it was a straightforward job offer? Mia thought about every option, every possibility and, for a moment, the sadness left her. Instead of despair, she felt stressed. She felt anxious, she felt confused, and - *she felt like Jake*. Mia smiled, remembering how Jake would obsessively analyze every detail before a meeting. He would work himself into a frenzy predicting every possible outcome, every angle of conversation. Maybe she had picked up his bad habits over their years together.

By the time she put herself together again and changed her blouse, Mia had only a few minutes to walk up to the patio. She hadn't seen Dylan or Jess since the night she left Jake. She had been embarrassed and ashamed, and she was sure she had lost their good opinion. She had chickened out at the last possible moment, after all, and had broken their friend's heart.

She tensed up as she walked out to the deck, fearing judgment or a lecture, or worse - disappointment.

Jess saw her right away and bounded over, smiling and laughing. She hugged Mia strongly. "Welcome back, stranger!"

"It's good to be back," Mia lied.

"Oh, it's so good to see you. I didn't know if I'd ever see you again, after...."

Mia nodded in recognition. It didn't need to be said.

Dylan walked over as well and gave her a hug. It wasn't quite as vibrant as Jess's, but he looked happy nonetheless. "Good to see you, Mia. Gin and tonic, right? With cucumber?"

"O yes! I can't believe you remembered."

Dylan smiled and raised his eyebrows, waving to a server to bring Mia's beverage.

"How have you been?" Jess asked compassionately.

"Fine," she replied automatically, before realizing that these may be some of the very few people on earth who would truly understand how she felt. "Well, actually, not great. It's been a tough couple of years. I was starting to do okay until the deadline passed. That just stirred everything up again, it was hard."

Jess hugged her again. Mia struggled to keep the tears in once more.

"It's a little weird being back here."

"Well, it's great to have you, regardless. Come have a seat!" Dylan beckoned.

Mia walked over to their table. It was right on the edge of the patio, which towered over the ocean view. A thatch roofed gazebo structure stood over it to keep the sun off them. Another woman was sitting with them. She looked about Mia's age. She was very pretty, with long black hair, brown eyes and smooth bronzed skin. She wore a simple shorts and tank top combination.

Mia reached out her hand to shake hello. "Hi, I'm Mia Yang."

The woman smiled. "Nice to meet you, Mia. Marcela Reyes."

The name sounded familiar to Mia, but she couldn't place it. She had heard it somewhere over her years at Planet 9, but exactly where was escaping her. She had met so many people in those years, it had been a whirlwind. She sat down. Jess and Dylan followed.

Jess looked like a 10-year-old at her own birthday party. She was obviously holding something in, something she really wanted to say - and whatever it was made her smile difficult to hide.

Neither of the Bishops was saying anything, so Mia started off the conversation. "So, what's going on, guys? You wrote to me about a job, but... is there something else?" She skipped right over the small talk. Too much of this situation was confusing her, there was no time for social niceties.

"I'm sorry we asked you to fly down all this way, Mia" Dylan said. "We just didn't want to tell you this over a video call."

Mia's interest piqued. "It wasn't a problem flying down Dylan. What's up?"

"Well... we've gotten some information that leads us to..."

"Jake's alive!!!!!" Jess blurted out. The sentence released itself from her like an orgasm.

A wave of emotion washed over Mia. "Holy shit!" she exclaimed. "Are you sure? How do you know? Did one of the probes come back!?" Questions poured out of her in excitement.

Dylan and Jess shared a look, as if they were non-verbally deciding who got to explain it. "Well..." started Jess.

"There was no probe. It's - a bit more complicated than that," continued Dylan. "But we do know that the colony is alive and well."

"How? I don't understand. Wouldn't they have to send the probe back in time to get the message to us?"

"Mia, this is Marcela," said Jess, gesturing to the table's fourth. "For twelve years, Marcela has been studying the signals from an alien planet. The whole project has been kept very secret, but I know Jake probably told you about it?"

Mia turned to look at the other woman again. "Marcela Reyes? Ohhh, you're that Reyes...Shit." Mia caught herself swearing in new company. "Sorry. I just knew I had heard your name before, but I couldn't place it. Reyes 3 - that's how I know it!"

"We got Marcela on our payroll a few years after we heard about her work" replied Dylan. "Planet 9's research division has been funding her research of Reyes 3 ever since. And a few days ago..." Dylan paused. "You know what, I'll let Marcela explain this part."

Mia was thoroughly confused and getting a little frustrated. Nobody seemed to be doing much explaining yet. "Did you start pointing your telescopes at Mayloz 2, Marcela?"

"No, I'm still studying *my* planet," Marcela began. "You see, there are millions upon millions of signals coming from Reyes 3. They vary in amplitude and reach, but they're all broadly similar. As you probably know, all the signals have been impossible to decode. They're far more advanced than anything we've ever used. I've still been recording and cataloging them for a decade, though, hoping that we'd be able to crack their encryption and find out something - anything about the advanced civilization that lives there. But I've never gotten anywhere with it, not with MI6 or with Planet 9."

Mia nodded, still thoroughly confused as to what any of this had to do with Jake and Travis.

"That was all until last week. A new signal showed up on the recordings. It was far, far more powerful than anything before it, as if a focused beam was being projected directly at our solar system. It was a repeating signal - intended for the Earth. It wasn't an alien signal, either. It was a standard text file... a letter from the Seed ship colony."

"What!?" Mia's mind raced. "How the hell are they there? Why is it coming from Reyes 3 and not Mayloz?"

Jess put her hand on Mia's. "They must have river-jumped there. They ran into a problem on Mayloz 2. Some... sort of incurable parasite. Many of them died, others got very sick. They couldn't return to Earth, as they didn't recognize the problem until they were past the turnaround date. They had to choose - either to die on Mayloz or starve to death floating away in space."

"Oh my god…"

"They remembered that the alignment with Reyes 3 was still coming, though, and they made a Hail-Mary decision to river-jump there instead. The Seed ship jumped back in time, far past our current time, and it hit an alignment with Reyes."

"So, they're there now?"

"Sort of" replied Dylan. "If you remember, to get to Mayloz, the ship had to jump into the future. So, the only way to get a message back through time was to relay it back in time using a probe. But, for the alignment with Reyes 3, the ship had to river jump backwards through time. They would have arrived there 8,610 years ago. So - they *were* there, technically…"

Mia had too many questions to ask. She wanted to yell them all at once. "Wait, so - why are we only getting the message now? Wouldn't it be repeating with rest of the alien signals? Marcela, why wouldn't you have picked it up 12 years ago?"

Jess looked at her with caring eyes. "Because of Jake. Because Jake knew the rules of time travel, and he stuck with them, no matter what."

Now Mia was completely lost. Her emotions were overwhelming her. She tried to understand what Jess meant, but she couldn't.

"Years ago, when Jake and I discovered that berlinite could move backwards through time, we put in a lot of effort thinking about paradoxes. Jake, especially, was very paranoid about them. We created a set of rules to River-Jump by. Rules that would govern how communication worked between timelines. If a message came from the past that could affect the series of events that lead to how it was sent..."

"I see," said Mia. "Like a chicken and egg problem."

"Exactly. And that's why we came up with a rule that we would never stray from. And that is - You must never send a message to your *relative* past. Which means that the Seed ship composed that message exactly 24 months and 6 days after they left the Earth, which would be the same time that the Earth received it."

"It's a mind-blowing mathematical achievement," interrupted Marcela. "This signal has been lying in wait for over 8,000 years. And then, 132 years ago, it turned on and beamed its message to the Earth. So that, eventually, I would receive it on the exact same 'relative' day that they composed it. I still can't get over the engineering prowess that came up with that. It's incredible."

"So, 8600 odd years ago, they arrived on Reyes 3" Mia asked. "And, to send us a message, they must have left a device that would turn on... thousands of years after they had all died?"

Jess nodded.

Mia took a second to absorb it. It was a lot to take in, but she was just happy that Jake was alive, no matter which planet he was on. She thought again about the new planet, however. It all came back, the reason they were avoiding it, the conspiracies and secrets. "Wait a second - what about the aliens, though!? Did the message say anything about them?? What do they look like? Weren't we all worried about them being a hostile race or something?"

Dylan and Jess both looked at Marcela. She smiled and nodded, letting them explain once more. Jess was about to burst with excitement.

"That's the craziest part! There is no intelligent alien race there, Mia. There never was!"

"What? That doesn't make any sense. But the alien signals you've been studying - where did they come from?" Mia looked at Marcela.

"I can't believe we never thought of this before" replied Dylan. "They're...us, Mia. They're human."

"Jake and the ship arrived on Reyes 8,600 years ago" continued Jess. "But the 'alien' signals are only from 132 years ago. Those communications that Marcela has been studying - they're like looking forward thousands of years in human evolution."

"But you said the languages, the formats, everyone has been saying this whole time that they're not human. What the hell?"

"If you think about it, it makes perfect sense, doesn't it" replied Jess. "8,000 years ago on Earth, we would have just started basic agriculture. In all the time since, we've invented writing, musical notation, mathematics. We've powered our cities with electricity, sent rockets to the moon, and, eventually, ships to other planets. How far do you think the humans on Reyes 3 have come in the next 8,000 years? Of course we can't understand them! We're seeing an image of humanity in the far, far future. We're looking at the distant descendants of *us*."

Mia took a long sip of her gin and tonic, trying to comprehend what they were telling her. *'The signals were always us'* she thought, amazed. Talking about River Jumping had always made her head hurt, but this was something else entirely. The table stayed quiet for a few moments, as she started to comprehend what was truly happening.

"I'm very happy to know that the ship made it safely, but how do you know that Jake himself is alive? Did they send a list of who died on the previous planet, and who made it?"

"They didn't," said Jess. "But this plan has his fingerprints all over it, Mia. And we figured the letter had to have been written by Jake and Travis."

"Why is that?"

"There was one line describing how beautiful Reyes 3 was. I believe it said that it 'made Costa Rica look like Fort McMurray?' We had to look it up, we'd never heard of the place. Apparently, it's in Alberta?" Dylan laughed. "That had to have been written by a Canadian."

Mia laughed out loud, and then felt a tear of joy stream out of her left eye, followed by many more. Just knowing that they had made it, that they had survived - and that they were still themselves, it was all so perfect. It was an incredible feeling, as if two years of guilt had instantly washed itself away.

"So..." started Jess when Mia had recovered. "We didn't *just* invite you here to tell you, Mia. There is a job offer for you. But it's not in Costa Rica."

"When we said that the signals were the descendants of *us*, we meant it quite literally. The first Stingray ship is ready to launch." said Dylan.

Mia nodded as the realization hit her. "So, you two are going on this one, then?"

"We stayed back here to make sure the fast ships worked. We wanted to leave Planet 9 in a good position," said Jess. "But we never intended on missing the trip entirely. We've always wanted to retire out there, somewhere..."

"The Stingray has been fully ready for over a year now" replied Dylan. "We were planning on river-jumping forward in time to meet them on Mayloz 2. That was, until we didn't hear anything back from the colony. We've been waiting for word, stuck in a holding pattern for so long. Jess was building a new probe to river jump forward and look for the lost ship, until Marcela found the signal.

"We've changed plans. And we're putting together a crew to go join the settlement on Reyes 3. Jess and I.... we wanted to give you another chance. We know how hard the decision was on you last time. There're 192 spots on board, and one of them is yours if you want. No pressure, you don't *have* to. But we wanted to give you the option, Mia. Boarding will be just under two months from now."

Mia was stunned. It was a lot to take in, especially all at once. "And you?" she asked Marcela.

"The planet's named after me. I've spent half my adult life looking at it. Of course I'm going!" replied Marcela, smiling.

'I wish it was that easy' thought Mia. Once again, she was faced with leaving everything behind. She thought of her parents, her sister, of everyone she knew on Earth.

Then again, she'd also be leaving *this* Mia behind. The Mia that walked around in a cloud of regret, the Mia that had lost her spark. Maybe she would find it again - out there on a new planet with Jake by her side. The thought was definitely alluring.

When she thought of Jake a new dread hit her. Maybe he had moved on? She'd be re-entering his life for a third time, and maybe he wouldn't want her back. Perhaps he had found someone else. It *had* been two years, and just because she was stuck in the past didn't mean that he was as well. The thought made her feel slightly queasy.

She weighed the pros and cons in her head. It was an even match; each side could trade punches forever. She felt the pressure in her chest, the ball of stress in her stomach.

It was too big of a choice to dwell on for long. She was in the river now, and there was no time to overthink it. Her gut would point her one direction or another, and she had to trust it, or she would drown in this indecision. She thought of her life on Earth. She thought about who she had been, and who she wanted to be.

She let herself go. Her gut made the choice. It pointed her in a direction, and she followed it.

Mia took a deep breath, reached for her drink, and held it up to toast. "Let's do it!!" The other three cheered in excitement and clinked glasses together on the sunny patio.

Mia flew back to Canada to tie up her loose ends. She finally sold the Costa Rican villa and split the remainder of her money between her family members. She said her final goodbyes (for a second time) back at her parents' home in Vancouver. Her mother cried as she left but made no effort to stop her. Her father kissed her on the cheek and smiled, knowing that she was following true happiness. He no longer worried about her traveling into space. He worried about her staying home.

On a cloudy afternoon in late April, Mia brought her carefully packed belongings to the port at Planet 9. The giant, purple Stingray ship was docked and loading supplies. The quarantine check would begin that evening. It was her last chance to board, the final chance to turn around. And yet, the trepidation that she had felt last time was gone. It was a clear choice now. She felt a new confidence as she walked onto the boarding deck.

Mia took a deep breath and closed her eyes. The salt of the ocean, the distant scent of the jungle, the sound of the birds - it would all be foreign soon. Only the unknown lay ahead. She was scared, but in a good way. And she knew that every challenge that she faced would be easier with her friends by her side.

Her bag went into the loading doors. Mia turned away from the only planet she'd ever known. As she passed through the airlock, she excitedly dreamed about the future, the past, and everything that the current still had in store.

About The Author

Matt Luttrell lives in Alberta, Canada. He's been fascinated by outer space since he was a young child, spending hours in the backyard on his telescope and reading astronomy magazines before bed. 'River Jumping' is his first full length novel. He's spent time as a guide in Banff, a live sound engineer, and a projectionist before studying Information Technology and Geographic Information Systems. These days, he works at a Calgary University when he's not playing up in the Rocky Mountains.

If you enjoyed 'River Jumping', please consider leaving a short review for it on my Amazon page or on Goodreads.com. I'm an independent, self-published author, and it really helps to get my novel out there and seen by readers like you.

◆◆◆

Thank you so much for reading my work, I hope you enjoyed Jake's journey as much as I did.

Printed in Great Britain
by Amazon